JADE EMPIRE

Tales of the Empire, book 6

by S.J.A. Turney

1st Edition

FOR KARYL

Continuing the Tales of the Empire

Interregnum (2009)
Ironroot (2010)
Dark Empress (2011)
Emperor's Bane (novella – 2016)
Insurgency (2016)
Invasion (2017)

The Marius' Mules Series

Marius' Mules I: The Invasion of Gaul (2009)
Marius' Mules II: The Belgae (2010)
Marius' Mules III: Gallia Invicta (2011)
Marius' Mules IV: Conspiracy of Eagles (2012)
Marius' Mules V: Hades Gate (2013)
Marius' Mules VI: Caesar's Vow (2014)
Marius' Mules VII: The Great Revolt (2014)
Marius' Mules VIII: Sons of Taranis (2015)
Marius' Mules IX: Pax Gallica (2016)
Marius' Mules X: Fields of Mars (coming 2017)

The Ottoman Cycle

The Thief's Tale (2013)
The Priest's Tale (2013)
The Assassin's Tale (2014)
The Pasha's Tale (2015)

The Praetorian Series

Praetorian – The Great Game (2015)
Praetorian – The Price of Treason (2015)
Praetorian – Eagles of Dacia (coming 2017)

The Damned Emperors

Caligula (Coming March 2018)

The Legion Series (Childrens' books)

Crocodile Legion (2016)
Pirate Legion (2017)

Short story compilations & contributions:

Tales of Ancient Rome vol. 1 - S.J.A. Turney (2011)
Tortured Hearts Vol 2 - Various (2012)
Tortured Hearts Vol 3 - Various (2012)
Temporal Tales - Various (2013)
Historical Tales - Various (2013)
A Year of Ravens (2015)
A Song of War (2016)

For more information visit http://www.sjaturney.co.uk/
or http://www.facebook.com/SJATurney
or follow Simon on Twitter @SJATurney

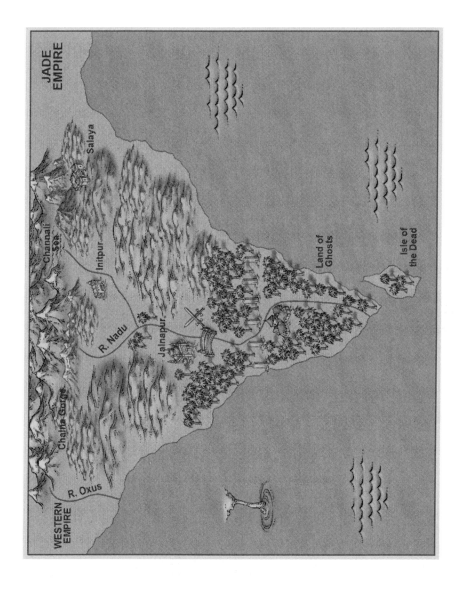

PART ONE

A CONTESTED LAND

CHAPTER 1

I have always loved the dusk. It is my favourite time of day, yet it is also the most saddening. At dusk, the blistering heat of the day is done and we sit, eased and grateful for the cool breeze the sunset brings. We are no longer in peril from the heat. The time of back-breaking labour is done. The time to rest is come.

But the sun has gone, and though the heat has gone with it, so has the light that blesses the day. And though we are no longer labouring, we now miss the camaraderie the day's work brings. And sometimes the simple cool breeze is not enough to make the passing of the golden glow satisfactory.

So it is with days.

So it is with empires.

The world of Aram, rajah of Initpur, crumbled and decayed like the great world of the Inda around him. His grandfather had predicted the great decay many years before. The Inda had been a light shining bright like a constellation across the diamond-shaped land, but they had always been too fractured, too scattered, too diverse. His grandfather had looked both east and west and seen the eventual doom of the people.

To the west the great empire was ruled from Velutio, where one man held sway over a populace of many millions of people, each with a place in the system, each willing to fight and die for their realm. To the east lay the Jade Empire – strict and brittle, but efficient and focused. Two great powers, each the match for the other, but each ever hungry for more land and power, more resources and glory. Aram's grandfather had looked at the old map painted on the wall of the throne room, where his beautiful, small land of Initpur shone like a facet near the top of that diamond, pressed upon from both sides by those empires. And he had predicted the great decay.

'There cannot be two masters of the world, Aram,' he had said. 'And both of these emperors are determined to be just that. One day they will go to war, and if anyone survives, they will inherit the world. But no matter who dies and who survives, the Inda will not live to see it. We will be the first true casualty of their war.'

'But why, Grandfather?' Aram has asked earnestly – he had always been an earnest boy.

'Because we lie between them, Aram. So do the horse lords across the northern mountains, but traversing the great steppe with an army would be a formidable undertaking, with little to no support or forage, and blood-maddened nomads picking at the army. No. Because the lands of the Inda are rich in food and spice and minerals, it will begin with us. If only we were as focused as they, that we might hope to defend ourselves against such a fate.'

Aram had not realised his grandfather had had the gift of prophecy, but it seemed he did. It had begun to happen during the reign of the next rajah of Initpur, Aram's father. It had come not from the western empire, which seemed to look inwards and was content with its river border and watching the Inda world curiously. It had come from the Jade Empire.

It began as raids. Officially, in that officious eastern realm, it was called 'righteous forage', as if simple banditry could ever be righteous. The first Inda ruler to experience the 'foragers' took offence. He was only a minor rajah of one of the remote border lands, with a royal guard of less than a hundred warriors at his command, but the Jade Empire's forage party was half that. He sent out his men and expelled the enemy from his land. His world lasted twelve more days. His people were still celebrating their victory when the forces of the Jade Emperor came for him. They poured across the border in their thousands. And in three days an entire Inda kingdom was gone. Utterly gone. The people were killed and burned and buried in pits, be they high-born or low, worker or scribe, woman or child. The animals were corralled, the crops gathered and the stores emptied, all of it loaded into carts and taken back east. Then the buildings of the kingdom, even the palace, were systematically ground into dust. Nothing remained to mark the passing of that poor, deluded, defiant rajah except the temple. They left just the temple and its blind priest. No one, even the Jade Empire, was willing to risk angering a god.

4

'Why can we not create a grand army and fight them?' Aram had asked his father when the news came in.

'The Jade Emperor's forces are like the sea, Aram,' his father said sadly. 'Vast and unchainable, while the rajahs of the Inda are like beautiful, colourful fish. How can fish hold back the sea?'

'I do not understand, Father.'

'Do you know what "Inda" means, Aram?'

Aram shook his head in confusion.

'In the old language of our people, in the days when the gods led the way, "Inda" was the word for "people". We are not an empire, you see. We are just "the people". And the lands of the Inda are just the lands of the people. There are many rajahs, major and minor, but we are no more capable of becoming one great force than a field of peacocks can become one giant peacock. No man can bring the Inda together, and that is an essential part of who we are. It is also the cause of our doom, as your grandfather understood.'

Aram nodded. He understood too. It saddened him, but he understood.

The years passed and things changed, but only for the worse. Rajahs across the north began to draw their people into their fortresses when Jade Empire forage parties were spotted in the area. The invaders were left free to ravage the land. Then, in a fatally short-sighted move, one minor rajah offered to pay the forage party to spare his realm. They accepted the bribe with relish, and the Inda lord smiled with relief. Until they came back the next year and the price rose.

The same offer was made to other rajahs. It was called tribute, though that was just a hollow word that masked the truth: extortion. Rajahs began to pay whatever they could, and often *more* than they could, to save themselves, their lands and their people, from the Jade Empire. And so began the tribute system that gradually weakened and destroyed what strength the Inda could claim.

Aram's father died in the autumn one year with a satisfied smile on his face. Aram couldn't help but resent that, as though his father had deliberately died while still relatively young, so that he no longer had to shoulder the burden and could pass it to Aram. And pass on that burden he did.

Aram began to deal with the Jade Empire just as his father had. When they came, in the autumn, he had gathered together the anticipated value of foodstuffs, coin, metals and livestock. They came, they examined his offerings, and they left with them. Not always with all of them. Aram was careful to overproduce, because the Jade Empire was nothing if not precise and rule-bound. If they had stipulated nine sacks of grain, and Aram had produced eleven, they would take the nine and leave the rest. But woe betide those rajahs who fell short of their quota. There were such stories as made the blood run cold; the Jade Empire was inventive in its punishments.

The seasons turned, and Aram watched his grandfather's predicted 'great decay' becoming a reality. Initpur had never been a great kingdom, and was relatively poor, and the gradual rapine of the land was driving the people into utter poverty.

Aram became a greybeard early, his sons growing into men young. They watched with dismay as their father had the palace stripped of its gold ornamentation and had it melted down and recast as ingots for the tribute. Anything of value was sold or repurposed. Initpur became Init-poor.

Thus it was that the day Aram's heart began to die, he was standing in a room devoid of wealth and grandeur. A world of faded opulence. Much of the room's paint had flaked away and had not been replaced. There were threadbare patches in the rich carpets. The tables showed signs of wear, were chipped and scratched and poor. The statues of the gods had been the last to go, melted down in a moment of dreadful impiety because, as the poor rajah had said to his sons, he needed to protect his people more than to honour the gods.

The forage party entered the hall, straight-backed and gleaming in shining black and steel. Their leader wore an ornate helmet and had gauntlets with articulated fingers, a cloak of shimmering grey flicking behind him as he moved. He had twenty men with him, and a gang of slaves with the carts who had remained in the courtyard outside, loading the various goods. In the hall was the chest of coins and ingots and the manifest. Aram nodded at his vizier, who passed the list across to the imperial commander.

The officer peered at the paper, his eyes burning like white phosphor through the small holes in his face mask. He made an unimpressed sound, thrust the records back at the vizier and ripped off his helmet, passing it to one of his men. He was a tall and elegant man with sharp cheekbones and a pointed chin that reminded Aram of one of the many devils he had seen in old books.

'You are short.'

Aram had been prepared. He'd known what was coming.

'It has been a poor harvest, and the copper in the Ushan valley is exhausted. There is nothing we can gather. But I have two offers for you. Either a promissory document for your records to provide the shortfall during the next tribute, or the three elephants we have used in the copper valley. They are still young and strong and can be put to work. They would make a more than adequate replacement for the shortfall, I'm sure.'

The officer shook his head. 'That is not in my orders. I am required to return with the requisite supplies or their value in certain other goods. There is no mention of promises or elephants. My men will search your palace and villages and remove anything that fits our list.'

Aram stood for a long moment, clenching and unclenching his fists. The old anger over the decline of his world was settling into him, but he caught sight of his three sons, standing at the side of the hall, along with his wife, and the realisation that he was helpless pervaded him. He nodded.

For more than an hour, the forage party ransacked Aram's world, seeking out anything they could use to fill the shortfall. Aram watched as even items of purely sentimental value were ransacked, their monetary value irrelevant when placed against the ledger of the Jade Empire. His wife's wedding gifts. His own childhood mementoes. Everything of value. Everything of no value. Everything. It brought tears to Aram's eyes, but he would not cry. He would *not* cry, for the boys were watching. There was no helping any of this, and resistance would mean nought but disaster, so the boys must not be driven to intervene. But his wife's wedding gifts, for the love of the six sacred wonders? Aram stood silent, proud, as his world was torn apart.

Finally, under the steady gaze of the rajah and his council and family, the imperial officer and his men reconvened, carrying in a collection of goods. Aram saw with dismay the last few valuables he owned in the world being hoarded by the enemy. His grandfather's ring. The silver statue of the god of healing that had saved his ancestor from the plague that had slighted half the world at that time. A sword that had belonged to Jirish, the slayer of demons. His son's birth gift, a peacock made of jade and gold. Four things only. They had been well hidden.

'This is still not enough,' the officer announced. 'What else have you hidden away?'

'Nothing,' Aram said in a broken voice. What could he possibly have hidden that they had not ripped from him?

'Then there is only one resource left we can take. The value will be made up in slaves. Fourteen slaves will be required, though if they are of inherent value, the figures are negotiable.'

'Slaves?' spat the eldest boy, Jai. Aram flashed him a warning look, but was shocked at the fire in his son's eyes. Gods, no! Had he not tried to set an example of passive resistance to stop this very possibility?

'A resource is a resource,' the imperial officer remarked to the eleven-year-old in an offhand tone. He turned back to Aram. 'In the interest of a continued beneficial relationship, I will allow you to select said slaves yourself and deliver them to the courtyard for transport.'

Jai had made his move before anyone realised.

The imperial troops were scattered, some outside with the carts, some with the box of impounded goods, others standing in watchful positions around the room. Aram was too far away to intervene as Jai leapt forward, ripping a short, curved knife from his belt. He lunged with it, aimed at the spine of the officer.

Always fast, Jai, always active, curse it.

But he was eleven, and not as quick as he thought. And an officer in the Jade Empire does not reach his position through political manoeuvres, but through war. By the time Jai was a pace away from sinking the blade into armoured flesh the officer had spun, an arm lancing out. He grasped Jai's knife arm by the wrist and squeezed, those articulated plated fingers clenching.

There was a crack. By some miracle of fortitude, Jai did not drop the knife, but as the officer let go, his arm dropped to his side, trembling.

'Your boy has the stink of defiance.'

'He is young, with the impetuousness of his years. He will cause you no further trouble. Jai – back to your brothers.'

But Jai was not moving. He was staring balefully at the imperial officer, his gaze carrying two generations of hate. *Gods, no, Jai…*

'I think you are mistaken,' the officer said, meeting that gaze with impassive superiority. 'The boy knows exactly what he is doing. And he has fire in his heart, this one. He knows what the likely consequences will be and yet he continues to defy us, and to ignore the commands of his father. He will always cause trouble until he learns discipline. I think he would not last a day in the Jade Empire.'

Aram's gaze lifted to the rest of his family. His wife, Alesha, wore a horrified mask, remaining still as a statue. Beside her, the youngest boy, Ravi, stood with a strangely blank face, but his stance was protective. The middle boy, Dev, looked as angry as Jai, and was shaking gently. Aram worried that his second son was about to join the one-man insurrection.

'Jai! *Stand down.*'

But still Jai did not move. And Dev looked as though he might leap forward at any moment to join him. Aram's boys. So proud. So devoted. So… foolish.

There was a tense silence. Jai struck again, but this time much differently. He waited for the officer to turn his face away, tossed the knife from his broken hand to his good one and leapt. Still the officer was far too swift. An armoured gauntlet knocked the blade aside and then reached out, grasping Jai by the neck. For just a moment, he squeezed, compressing the major veins and the windpipe, enough to cause Jai's eyes to bulge and his blood to thunder as his lungs burned hot for desperate breath. Then he relaxed his grip, allowing both blood and air to flow, though he did not let go of the boy's neck.

Dev stepped a pace forward and their father's hand rose sharply. 'Stay where you are, boy.' Then, to the officer: 'Please, let my son go. I will discipline him.' *Please. Please let him go. He is just a boy.*

The officer shook his head slowly. 'I think not. There is use for him. He has strength and cunning, despite his youth. But he is defiant and wild. Time in the imperial academies will either knock out the insolence and turn him into an impressive specimen, or it will simply kill him. The choice will be his. Your son will be one of the slaves.'

'No!'

The shriek came from his mother, who collapsed to her knees, Ravi hugging her tight. The fire in Dev's eyes burned a little brighter, and Aram realised two things: he had lost a son today, and if he did not restrain Dev, he would lose two. Half a heart torn from his chest. He could not lose the other...

'Dev. Look to your mother.'

That did it. The sudden realisation that she was on the floor, weeping, shook the urge to act from the middle son, and he joined his younger brother in comforting her. Satisfied that the rest of his family were safe, Aram could concentrate on his eldest son and heir. He looked intently at the officer.

'What can I offer you to leave my son here?' *Desperation now. A coin? A prayer? An arm?*

'Nothing,' the man replied in his unadorned, offhand manner. 'I will take this boy and he will be made or broken in the academy. But I am not an unmerciful man. He is of value to both you and your kingdom, and counts for more than a common slave. I will class him to the value of four slaves. You may choose the other ten and assemble them in the courtyard.'

'Jai,' Aram said, hoarse, his breaking heart audible in his voice.

His pride and joy straightened. 'I have been given the opportunity to save four of our people, Father, and that is a noble thing.'

Aram cried, then, in front of his court and the enemy. He could not have held it back. The officer returned to the courtyard with his men. The vizier went to arrange the requisite slaves, and Aram managed a brief and hollow farewell to his eldest boy before Jai was marched from the room with his head high. He then consoled the rest of his family.

The forage party left that afternoon, moving on to another rajah before eventually returning to the Jade Empire. Once the carts had rolled out through the palace gate, Aram standing in the doorway and watching them take his son, Dev appeared silently next to him.

'You could stop them, Father.'

'How?'

'We have eighty men. They have twenty. One word to your captain and they will not leave our borders.'

Aram nodded. Clever, calculating Dev, yet with so much still to learn... 'There are twenty of them *here*. There are *millions* beyond the border. Before you were born, a rajah like me tried to stand up to the foragers. You have been to the site of his palace. It is a place of annual pilgrimage. You have seen what they did.' *A hollow land, ruined. Obliterated.*

'I would rather fight and be obliterated than simply collapse, Father.'

Aram turned to his second son, ten summers old. 'Unfortunately, Dev, that is not a decision we can make. As rulers of Initpur, we are bound to look to our people. And with Jai gone, one day you will succeed me. This will be your burden to bear. We cannot stand against them, and a grand sacrifice is pointless. It is our duty to protect the people in our care as long as we can. Always remember that.'

But Dev did not. He did not agree. Shunning his father's advice, the next day he took a horse and two of the palace guards and rode away without permission. He visited three other rajahs in the area over many days as Aram fretted in his palace. When Dev finally returned, his father threw his arms around him and gripped him tight. *Never do that again, Dev. I have lost one son...*

'You must not make you mother worry so, boy. Where did you go?'

'I went to find who will fight,' Dev said defiantly. But the strength leached out of his stance instantly. 'No one. No one will stand against the Jade Emperor. One rajah I visited was still wealthy and powerful, but even he would not consider, even anonymously, sending men to a coalition against the Jade Empire. Another rajah would not see me, but his lands appeared to be in a similar state to our own. The third of the rajahs was poorer even than us. His people are starving and they have little more than a roof over their heads. But they are grateful! They are grateful for destitution and starvation because they have nothing left to give, so the Jade Empire now leaves them alone. No one seems to be willing to stand against this evil.'

Aram nodded. 'I tried to tell you. The Inda will never be an army. We are not made like that. Your great-grandfather told me once that this would happen. And this is not the end. This is but the beginning of the end. Soon there will be nothing left to take from the Inda, and our only value will be as territory. The empires both east and west will come to blows and we will be trodden down in the midst of the war. It is, sadly, our destiny. Your grandfather was a great believer in fate. In destiny.'

'I do not believe in destiny,' Dev replied, defiantly. 'The future is what we make it. And I will make it a future for the Inda.'

A small thrill of pride ran through Aram then, but he quickly tempered it. Whatever Dev did, it could not save the Inda. And it would surely damn him.

'What of the southern lands?' a small voice suddenly put in. They turned to see Ravi standing in a doorway. The youngest, just seven years old, had an intensity to his gaze.

'The south?'

'The sacred lands,' Ravi said. 'Men will not go there, I understand. Not even the foreigners. Is that not a place the Inda could be safe?'

Aram shook his head. 'The peril faced in the south is very different from the peril faced here, but it is no less real. The Island of Ghosts is no place for living men.'

In fact, it was more than just the island. For a thousand years, the island that sat off the southern tip of the Inda Diamond had been deserted and shunned by the people, for the spirits that protected the place drove men into a mad frenzy of self-destruction, and they would be added to the ghostly ranks of the place's protectors. But the last hundred miles in the south of the diamond-shaped peninsula was equally shunned and protected. A line of ancient markers marched across the jungle, and no weapon was permitted past that line. No man in his right mind crossed it and, if he did, he was not in his right mind for long. The only humans to be found beyond that line were in a few isolated monasteries close to the border, where devoted monks maintained the markers and the sanctity of the land, their faith protecting them from the madness and the spirits who wrought it.

'No, the lands of the dead are not for us,' Aram said again with a shiver.

12

'Then there has to be another way,' Dev announced.

They hardly spoke the rest of the evening, sitting through a sullen and frugal meal.

The next day, Dev was gone.

Aram's heart broke once more as the boy's room was searched. Wrenching. Torn. He had somehow known it was coming. The signs had been plainly visible had he but accepted they were there. No. He'd not believed it. That Dev could go too. That he would lose another son. Dev had taken a horse once again, but no guard this time. At first, Aram presumed he had ridden off again to test the water with other rajahs. But the note he had left in his room made clear what had happened.

Dev had discounted the south because of his father's tales of the spirit protectors. He had discounted the Inda as unwilling to save themselves, from the bitter experiences of his previous attempt. He discounted, as did everyone, the horse clans to the north, who would never help, only raid. That left only one avenue. Dev had gone to petition the western empire, in the hope that they would be willing to do something about the Jade Empire. An old land of legions and discipline, swords and muscle, to put an end to the Jade Emperor's masses with their infamous war machines. Two worlds, similar in so many ways and yet poles apart, who had been separated throughout history only by the Inda Diamond.

Aram had sent out his men then, desperately, through his own lands and even beyond, trying to find Dev, but the boy was long gone.

Gone.

Aram's heart ruined.

The diminished family of the rajah of Initpur lived out the winter and the spring in misery. Aram was a broken man. His wife had stopped speaking the day Jai was taken, though it became clear within the next month that she was pregnant. She gave birth to a baby girl in the late spring, and young Ravi looked after mother and child, protective and wary.

Summer came with an unseasonably long drought. The crops were a poor yield. It was a dreadful year, everyone agreed, and as autumn came around, Ravi felt a steadily growing fear of what would happen when the Jade Empire came again.

They did not come. Autumn bled into winter, and the reality hit Aram hard. They were no longer worth looking to for tribute. Had Jai and Dev restrained themselves for one year, they would all still be here and safe – albeit safe, hungry and poor.

Five more years passed. Aram's hair turned from grey to balding, sparse white, though his beard remained long. Ravi grew into a precocious and thoughtful thirteen-year-old. His closeness to his mother and sister never changed, and Aram watched the boy's heart shatter when his mother contracted a wasting disease in the winter and passed from the world of the living. Ravi found the statues of the old gods that had been gathered around her bedside and swept them away, declaring them meaningless. His sister lasted only one year longer before the same illness claimed her.

As the body of the six-year-old girl rendered down to ash on the pyre, Ravi turned to his father.

'This is a wicked world, Father.'

Aram could do little but nod. In less than a decade it had stolen from him two sons, a wife and a daughter, as well as a kingdom, a future and hope.

'I am leaving tomorrow,' his youngest son said.

No.

How.

Why?

'Ravi...'

'Please do not try to stop me, Father. I must go. I cannot be part of this world anymore. I will shave my head and take on the golden robe of a monk. I will seek peace in holy solitude.'

All Aram could do was nod his understanding. It would be a blow to lose his last son, but how could he deny Ravi this? He knew, deep in his heart, that the only reason Ravi had stayed all this time was for his mother and his sister, and the boy might be right that the only place left to find peace was in a monastery. Certainly even the Jade Emperor's men were wary of offending gods. They never destroyed temples or executed monks, even when an example needed to be made for the people. It would be the safest place for Ravi. And there was no true kingdom of Initpur left for him to inherit, anyway. Just some fields and some huts and a half-ruined palace full of sad memories.

'Go with my blessing, Ravi, and I pray that you find peace in your new world.'

A family riven and scattered, a world oppressed, and a heart broken.

His last boy left the next day, and the seasons turned once more. Around Aram, over the next decade, the Inda culture was systematically extinguished. Even the greatest rajahs were reduced to poverty and squalor. No word came of Jai, away in the east, or Dev, off to the west. No word even from his son the monk. Aram lived a life now dedicated only to the survival of the folk in his care.

The Inda lived as best they could. Many continued to survive quietly as peasants. Some took to crime. In the northern mountains, not far from Initpur, a new bandit leader arose, and men of the sword flocked to him. Even most of Aram's guards went to join the growing force in the hills. After all, what soldier wanted to continue in service to a lord who could reward him with nothing more than bread and a roof for his head?

The time of the Inda was drawing to a close. If all was proceeding as Aram's grandfather had predicted, soon the empires would come. Aram listened to the villagers in his hall prattle on about petty grievances, as though their arguments were not worth spit compared with what had already happened and what was yet to come. When they had finished and he had promised to think on the matter, he made the vizier hold the next visitor back and leave him for a few moments.

Once he was alone in the room, Aram crossed to the map of the diamond-shaped Inda world on the wall. The paint was faded and flaking. With a sad and resigned air, he reached down and picked up an earthenware cup from a chipped table. Smashing it, he gripped a shard so tightly that blood dripped from his tight fist as he reached up to the map. With a single swipe, he carved off the small painted palace that had been the first victim of the Jade Empire, when they had come in their thousands and demolished that rajah's realm. He then moved swiftly through the land, obliterating all those rajahs he knew to have gone, their estates swallowed up by neighbours who could afford still to pay tribute, others who had thrown themselves from towers in despair. One by one, he scratched them out of the painting. As he worked, he moved south, as had the empire. Finally, he stepped back. The only untouched part of the map was more or less blank – that southern land of ghosts, with the island hanging like a teardrop from the point of the diamond.

More than three quarters of the rajahs had been erased. Only the richest rajahs remained, or those tenacious enough to live in squalor and poverty, like Aram. The world had already changed terribly. How long now before even the greatest rajahs were at his level? Not long. Especially now that many of their men were fleeing to bandit chiefs like the one in the north.

He turned from the map and wandered across to the balconied window, peering out. His lands contained twelve villages and small towns. The last time any record had been taken, before the tributes began, the population had been around eight thousand. He would estimate it at probably half that now. And though they were no longer starving to death or being taken as slaves, the next stage of his grandfather's great prediction was conquest.

'I have to save them.'

There was no reply. He was alone in the room. But he could feel the approval of Jai and Dev at the sentiment. The way the breeze ruffled the curtain beside him made it seem plausible that somehow they were here in spirit.

'I must prepare. I will have to be adaptable. I cannot see the future the way my grandfather could, so I cannot plan too precisely. But I need to be ready, and so do they. The time is nigh.'

He strode back across the room and opened the door. His vizier stood outside, looking surprised at this sudden display of energy by his rajah. It was understandable. Aram had done little but wallow and mope for years now.

'Audiences are ended for the day.'

A groan of dismay rippled through the gathered plaintiffs, but Aram waved it aside. 'I want a full record made of every living soul and everything of value in this land that can be moved. I want it done fast. We must be prepared if we are to endure. The clouds are beginning to gather, my people, and they herald a storm the like of which the world has never seen.'

And with that he turned and entered his palace once more, with the spirits of Jai and Dev nodding their approval as they walked invisibly at his side.

CHAPTER 2

The traveller in foreign lands sighs
The moonlight shines upon his tears
His home is behind him now
And he must move ever forward

The Traveller, by Gueng Ji

Jai stood silent and still, concentrating on the blade before his eyes: his own chisel-tipped, razor-edged straight sword with the silver dragon hilt and the red silk streamer trailing from it. The weapon of a master swordsman, which he was. But so was the man he faced. The blade was unwavering, vertical, held in both hands like some sacred icon. The courtyard was soundless bar the faint whispering breeze that caressed the blossom on the trees at each corner, four trees of four colours to reflect the seasons and the four branches of swordsmanship that contained the forms.

The man in the demon mask opposite him, with the archaic decorative armour of an Ishi master, maintained precisely the same pose – a stance that was as much ritual as it was educational – for the forms of steel had been taught thus in the Zu Academy since time immemorial.

'Jai!'

The voice, high-pitched and sharp as their blades, cut through the silence like a knife through satin. Jai had been studying his opponent throughout the long moments, waiting for the call. Many of the opening moves he favoured would not be of use against this one, either because of that demon armour or because of how he would react to them. Jai could identify two moves that might give him the opening he needed. One required Jai to act first. The other, his opponent. Either would be a gamble, but even as he sorted once more through all the information he had gathered and stored, he decided on the former. The heavy, bulky lower leg and footwear of the armoured man should hamper his ability to react, which he would only do correctly if he were inventive and widely read. Few of the Jade Empire could be said to be innovative. Change was frowned upon.

Jai launched forward, sword aloft, now held only in the right hand, the left reaching out like a mournful lover, caressing the air as though this were naught but an elegant dance with a blade. Which, of course, was exactly what it was, for that was what the Zu Academy excelled in. He loped forward in high, arcing strides that were more akin to gymnastic leaps than steps.

The armoured demon moved ritualistically to the right, one foot stepping purposefully, the other sliding in its wake, the sword spinning in an arc and dancing out to the left, still held in two hands.

The attack of the mountain gazelle met with the defence of the bending reed.

But in the books of forms, of which there were hundreds in the academy library, there were many minute variations of the standard forms, devised by masters over the centuries. The demon was rigid with his adherence to the traditional defence of the bending reed. There were nine variants, but a man who took such care and attention over the gear of his rank was not a man given to experimentation. And there were so many variants of so many forms that no graduate of the academy could know them all.

Jai did not know them all either. But he knew more than anyone he'd met. *If there is something to know*, his grandfather had once told him, *then it is worth knowing it*. And so he knew the nine variants of the enemy's defence as well as the form itself. And he knew the twelve variations of the attack of the mountain gazelle.

The demon was unprepared. In every common variant, Jai's left foot would be the first to plant and brace as his sword came down in a diagonal arc right to left, designed to cut at waist height and allow the attacker to pivot past and prepare again. This variant was little understood, drawn from a dusty tome found in the dim recesses of the library's darkest corner. Its author was a master who had been taken from the clans of the horse lords many centuries ago, and was not popular because of his racial origin. But he had been innovative. He might be shunned as unworthy by many, but Jai recognised value in the unpopular.

His left foot skipped where it should have planted. His right came down and he spun on it, the sword coming round and suddenly descending from left to right. The demon's defence was on the wrong side. He was beaten in a blow and he knew it. To his credit, he did not try a desperate change of defence. He did not have time, and it would have looked like poor showmanship for an Ishi master.

Jai's sword swept down and met the demon armour at the join of the laminated wood plates, where it would have cut the leather ties and scythed into flesh beneath had he not stopped the blade a hair's breadth from landing.

Carefully, he withdrew the blade and stepped back, lowering it to the side and bowing formally. The demon did the same, and once the ritual of it was concluded, he straightened, sheathed his sword and began to remove the helmet.

'You are... unusual,' the man said. A compliment or not, Jai couldn't decide. An acknowledgement of skill, most certainly. Jai bowed again, and the Ishi master left the courtyard.

'That was interesting,' said the teacher, stepping down from the arcade at the courtyard's edge. 'I do not think Master Huang approved.'

'In battle, Master Huang would now be dead and his approval meaningless.'

The teacher frowned at Jai. 'Survival and victory are paramount, Jai, but it is always better to win with finesse and an acknowledgement of tradition than otherwise.'

Jai shook his head. 'I do not agree, master. Respectfully, if tradition gets a man killed, then it is at fault. Victory is what matters.'

Oh, how he and Dev used to argue over things like that. Dependable Dev, who attached such importance to information and order and yet lost to a well-placed poke with a stick from Jai every time they sparred. What would Dev say if he could see Jai now?

The teacher sighed. 'You are not the defiant Inda boy who came to our academy all those years ago. Your captor believed you would be dead within days and yet you found odd reserves of strength and willpower that have seen you not only survive but rise to be among the best. Yet there are aspects of you that have not changed. You are still wilful and insolent. You are lucky to have had me for a teacher,

I think. Many of the others in this place would not have put up with you so easily. Why did you come back?'

It was a good question. Jai had left the academy four years ago, with one of the highest grades ever awarded. He had been given his pick of assignments and could have entered the cavalry or infantry, or even the imperial guard, with his qualification. But he had eschewed the grand and the renowned. He had no wish to blaze a path through the ranks of the empire. Instead, he had joined the Jade Empire's scout service and been with them ever since, rising through rank and reputation with impressive rapidity, but refusing transfers to more prestigious careers. His had been a successful, but peripheral, career, patrolling the edge of the lands from which he had come over a decade ago. Once or twice he had considered returning home, but he was no longer truly Inda and, while he recognised that fact and accepted it, he was not at all sure how his father would receive it. If his father was still alive, that was.

A week ago he had received a summons from the regional governor, and had ridden to the fortress town of Yuen in answer. He had spent much of his training time in Yuen, at this very academy, and the coincidence of his being summoned here was interesting. He was needed at the Palace of Arms, but he had ridden fast and felt certain he could bend the rules long enough to visit his old academy. Why he felt the need he could not say, but it was good to see his teacher again, and the chance to practise against an Ishi master was not something one encountered every day.

He smiled at the teacher.

'I think I needed to know I was still good. Many of my skills are tested with the scouts, but my mastery of the forms of steel are not, and I feared they might have atrophied.'

'Clearly they have not.'

Jai smiled and then glanced up as the clong of a bell rang out across the academy.

'I have tarried longer than I intended, Master. I must leave. My compliments once more on your teachings and patience.' He bowed respectfully with clasped hands.

The teacher bowed in return and smiled as Jai hurried from the courtyard, through the halls and corridors and out into the main square of the fortress town. The Square of Four Winds was typical of

Jade Empire architecture. It was, like the people of this land, both hard and delicate, martial and beautiful. Its smooth stone lines and gentle curves surrounded a flagged square that showed the wear of a million booted feet at parade. The plants and trees and small gardens surrounding it were magnificent and well-kept, and only from above could a man realise that they spelled out the four names of the war gods. The Jade Empire was a place that had fascinated Jai ever since he came here. He had quickly realised that there was more to these people than the simple bandits who crossed the border and took Inda goods. They were an enigma and Jai was not yet close to unpicking the knot of their world.

The heavy tramp of many feet caught his ear, and his interest was piqued at the sight of a spear unit crossing the other corner of the square and descending the Stone Lion Stairs towards the Gate of the Painted Stars. Like all Jade Empire units, they were impressive in their uniformity. Each man dressed and armed identically, moving identically. When one man looked left, all men looked left. Training was harsh and rigid in the empire's schools, but it produced soldiers that worked well as a unit.

All morning, military divisions had been moving through the town, and he had passed numerous units on his journey south to Yuen. Something big was happening, clearly. His pulse quickened at the notion that he would be involved in whatever it was. It was too much of a coincidence for him to be summoned to this place where so many armies were massing without the two being connected.

He hurried across the square to the Palace of Arms, showed his documentation to the guard and was admitted. The building was grand and constructed of dark-grey granite, every corbel and antefix decorated with lions and dragons, the twin symbols of the Jade Empire's westernmost forces. Each office in the building was well signed but it still took him precious moments to find the room to which he had been ordered. The door lay wide open as he arrived and he stood in the doorway, feet planted firmly apart, back straight, waiting.

'You are late,' said the man in the red and black uniform standing by the window opposite.

'My apologies, General. I was visiting the academy and a practice bout with an Ishi master overran. It is my error.'

22

'Ishi masters are always slow.'

The man turned, arms clasped behind his back, and stepped into the room. 'You are the master scout Jai of the Inda. You come very highly recommended by some, while others tell me you are too troublesome. An interesting quandary. Come in and close the door.'

Jai did so, falling back into the same stance as before.

'Why should I choose you above your peers, Master Scout Jai?'

'To answer such a question, General, I would need to know for what I am to be chosen?'

The General smiled. 'A good answer. Excellent. We have made a promising start.'

Jai studied the man before him. General Xeng Shu Jiang was a man approaching fifty summers, his black hair now silver at the temples. He was tall. Jai was tall himself, but the true-blooded sons of the Jade Empire were not lofty men in general, so the man's stature was striking. And there was about him an energy one did not often see in high-level command, like that of an acrobat tensing, ready to spring. Jai liked him already. Most importantly, though, the man had questioned him and had approved of his inquisitive reply. Another attribute unusual among the general's peers.

A quick glance around the room intrigued him. He had met two types of senior officer in his time among the empire's scouts. Some decorated their office with paintings and poetry. They were old-style officers of ancient blood, who considered it important to proclaim the culture of their ancestors even on their walls. Others had maps spread everywhere and lists and records in piles. Not disorganised men, as such, but officers who were as interested in maintaining their army as in commanding it – 'hands-on' men. Both types of officer had their advantages and their disadvantages. General Xeng Shu Jiang's office was plain and unadorned, the surfaces clear, all records locked away. It gave away nothing about the man's personality, and that intrigued Jai.

'You have a reputation,' the general said. 'Can you surmise what that reputation is?'

Jai nodded. He was well aware of his reputation. 'I do not know, General, who you have spoken to, but they will have called me insolent, probably undisciplined, argumentative, possibly even untrustworthy, and proud. But they will have grudgingly acknowledged that I am also the best at what I do. It is a reputation with which I have lived throughout my time in the empire.'

The General nodded. 'You missed arrogant. Although perhaps what you think of as proud, others see as arrogant.' Jai acknowledged as much with a nod. 'Are you aware of *my* reputation, Scout Jai?'

Jai frowned. 'Little beyond the fact that you are reckoned the hero of the Shanshan peninsula, where you suppressed the bandit kings in two months, something no general has been able to do so for centuries.'

The general waved aside the campaign and the compliment as if they were meaningless. 'I am also highly regarded and considered troublesome. I have never embarked upon a campaign without succeeding. But I am unorthodox at times in my approach. I do not like to conform to the rigid rules of our ancestors if there is a more sensible way available, and you will know, I'm sure, how popular that can make a man in the empire. I fear you and I are somewhat alike.'

Jai smiled then.

'I have a problem, Jai,' the general said suddenly, straightening and flexing his fingers. 'And I fear I need help with that problem. Help, I think, that you can provide.'

'General?'

'I need to speak plainly with you, Jai. Not with the formality of office. I suspect that of all the souls in Yuen, you are probably the only one who can accept that notion without it sending shivers through you. To circumvent the strictures of social and military formality is not in the nature of the Jade Empire. But then you are not *of* the empire, are you?'

Jai nodded his head. 'I am Inda-born, General, and Jade Empire-trained. I am a child of two worlds, and I would like to think I have taken the best of both.'

'Good. I have been given a commission, Jai. A task. I received the orders from the hand of the Jade Emperor himself one month ago at the capital. A commission from the emperor is not something that can be refused. Not more than once, anyway, as a headless body talks little. I am to lead a grand campaign. One of the biggest in many years.'

Jai felt a chill run through him. A suspicion.

'Yes. You can see it, can't you, Jai? You are perceptive. I have been ordered to conquer the lands of the Inda.'

He huffed and leaned on the table. 'Suddenly you are conflicted,' the general said quietly. 'And if you were not, then you would not be half the man I believe you to be.'

Jai swallowed. In truth he had seen this day coming since the moment he had been taken by the foragers. Possibly even before that. He had put off thinking about it, but it crept into his mind in the dark of occasional sleepless nights and lodged there. He had never yet reckoned fully what he would do if called upon to wage war upon his homeland. He twitched just a little.

'I swore to serve the empire, but to conquer the lands of my fathers is not a pleasing prospect.'

The general nodded. 'And simply because of this potential conflict within you, I am not binding you to my service, but offering you a place by my side. I will understand if you do not have it within you to campaign in your homeland, but there is a role for you and I dearly hope you will take it, for I need you, and I think that *you* need to be there. But I will not force it upon you. I am not the emperor. My commissions can be refused without the rolling of heads.'

'*Why* do I need to be there?' Jai asked, more curious than nervous.

'Because there are men who conquer with gusto, Jai, carving their reputation in the bodies they trample. I am not one of them, but if I cannot surround myself with good men then I will inevitably end up with their sort, and this conquest could turn into a bloodbath despite my best intentions. I hope to enclose and add the Inda to the empire, rather than crushing and occupying them. And I will find that easier with men like you by my side – men who are clever and innovative, and who have a vested interest in the survival of the Inda.'

Jai was nodding now. 'I understand. But you said you had a problem. The nature of your officers is not the problem of which you speak, I think, General.'

'You *are* perceptive, Jai. Good. Yes, there is a huge problem here. As a scout who has served on the western borders for the past two years, you will be as aware as anyone that the Inda have never been more readily conquerable. They are poor and weak and divided. We have made them so over the decades. This is imperial policy. It is how we weakened and then annexed the lands to the south-east of the empire, and it is a very effective method.'

Jai tried not to feel the old bitterness rising – the memory of his jade and gold peacock that had been a birth gift taken away by that forage officer. He kept his face carefully blank.

'My, how you struggle with that,' the general said, not unsympathetically. 'It is a hard thing, and I am sorry for your troubles. But we all have roles to play in this great theatre of life. Yours, I think, was defined when you were taken. Now you can use that to help minimise the troubles for your people.'

The general waved his arms, taking in the elegant room in which they stood. 'There is yet hope to be found in all of this. The Inda have been all but ruined over the decades. If they can be enclosed within the arms of the Jade Empire, there need no longer be poverty and starvation. Instead there will be order and comfort. There will no longer be lords – the rajahs of old – but imperial governors instead. The lot of the people will be better. That, though, is in the future. More immediately, we have the tiresome task of attempting to conquer with care. No matter how much I try to instil control, soldiers are soldiers and armies are armies, and men will attempt to rob, rape and kill, whatever the orders from their general. This will not be pretty, but we need to keep control as best we can.'

'Yet this is not the problem of which you speak either, General.'

General Jiang chuckled. 'Perhaps too perceptive for your own good. Correct, Jai. I really do hope you will accept a place with me. No, the big problem is what lies across the world, beyond the Inda.'

Jai pursed his lips. 'You mean the western empire, General?'

'I do. If their mad emperor – what's his name?'

'Bassianus, sir.'

'If Bassianus is advised that we are conquering the Inda, there is a very good chance that he will not let us do so with impunity. Despite the readiness of the Inda for conquest, I fear our own Jade Emperor has made a mistake with this policy. We will move across the Inda and take control, but the western empire will not simply sit back and watch us annexe lands right up to their river border. The Inda have always been the buffer between our two great empires. Remove that barrier and the two biggest powers in the world are facing one another.'

'You think there will be war with the western empire?'

'It is inevitable, one day,' General Jiang replied. 'I had hoped it would not happen in my lifetime, but now I suspect we are about to begin that very process. And the Jade Emperor is no fool, so I can only assume that this policy and the conquest of the Inda is a deliberate beginning to the process of taking on the great opponent across the world. There is no other good reason for wanting the Inda lands.'

'They say the western emperor is mad,' Jai noted. 'That he is but a shadow of his predecessors and is as dangerous to his own people as to others. The mad cannot be predicted. Perhaps he will not react to our invasion?'

Our invasion? Why had he said that? When had he made the decision that he would be part of it?

'Perhaps,' conceded the general. 'But the problem is that even mad emperors have sensible officers and advisers. Generations ago there was another mad emperor in the west, and their empire collapsed and all but vanished under his careless brutality. Yet the soldiers of that land rebuilt it from the ruins and began a new dynasty that has grown and flourished. You cannot write off an empire because of one man, no matter how powerful or how mad.'

'The Jade Empire's army is much larger than the western empire's, as I understand?'

The general straightened from the table at last. 'So we believe, but we cannot be certain of that. The western empire is not as rigidly organised as we are. And though at times we have had spies in their court, they do not last long, for our people are simply too cultured and disciplined to pass well as westerners. What we know of their military and capabilities is gleaned as much from rumour and educated guesswork as it is from espionage and factual report. What we do know is that they have no knowledge of the black powder and how to use it in rockets and cannon.'

'Do *they* have spies in *our* court?'

'More than likely they have had, though in much the same way I am sure they would be uncovered and removed quickly. The westerners could no more masquerade as one of us than we as them.

Such things are not to be known by men such as us, though. We are soldiers. Matters of imperial security are kept within the capital and the palaces.'

There was a long pause once more.

'I fear we are about to make a grand, world-changing mistake, Jai, and I very much hope it is not the final one. We must go west. We must take the Inda lands or die trying. We cannot refuse the emperor. But the stakes are high. If we succeed in doing this without provoking the west and we can secure the Inda lands, then we ensure safety and power for many years. If we make just one mistake, we might see a conflagration that ends the world. And as much of this rests upon our western foe as it does upon us.'

The general turned and strode back to the window. 'Come.'

Jai fell in beside General Jiang, slightly behind as was fitting for a subordinate in the military. His breath caught in his throat. He had known that units had been gathering, but nothing could have prepared him for what he was seeing in the valley below Yuen.

The entire valley floor was a sea of gleaming armour. Rank upon rank of infantry in their columns and squares, their banners hanging limp for lack of wind. Archers in their hundreds, cavalry gathered in huge blocks. Even rocket units and cannon – twenty cannon or more – sat at the periphery. There had to be twenty thousand men down there. It was the largest single gathering of soldiers Jai had ever seen.

'That must be the entire army of the western province, General?'

General Jiang laughed. 'You have served in the scouts on the periphery, Jai. You have not experienced much of the true imperial military. This is just one muster. This and two places like it are gathering to form the core of the First Army. That will number sixty thousand. Two other armies of like number are being mustered in the northern and southern areas of these provinces. And other ancillary units will be attached in due course. We will have just short of two hundred thousand men when we cross the border. And that is less than a quarter of the forces upon which the emperor can draw. This is the number the imperial court believes to be sufficient for the conquest of the Inda.'

Jai's eyes were still wide. 'And is it?'

'For the conquest of the Inda, yes. If the western empire decides to intervene, then no. Jai, I have officers in place in my force, and

they are all men selected by me and by those I trust. As far as possible, this army of conquest is my own. There is just one place I have not filled, and that is the position of my adjutant.'

Jai's brow furrowed as he turned to the general. 'Adjutant?'

'Yes. It is a position usually filled by a senior officer with a distinguished career behind him, a reputation for strategy and a bloodline that stretches back to the first emperor. That is the tradition. I told you I am not an adherent to tradition. I do not need a strategist. I am a good strategist myself. I do not need a senior officer. I have plenty of them. And I most certainly do not need an ancient bloodline. What I need is a man who knows the Inda and their thinking and terrain, a man who can think on his feet and who will aid me in the most painless, pacific conquest we can achieve. You understand?'

'I do,' Jai said, turning back to that huge array of soldiers in the valley. They did not *look* like an army of painless, pacific conquest.

'Will you accept the position?'

There was a long silence, and the general finally turned to look at the young Inda scout by his side. Jai nodded. 'I will.'

'Good. I do not know whether you still pray to whatever the Inda believe, or whether you pray to the gods of the Jade Empire, but I urge you to start beseeching whoever it is for their favour in the coming days.'

In the valley, someone began one of the great martial chants of the empire, and in moments the rhythmic chorus rolled across the valley, back and forth.

The music of conquest.

CHAPTER 3

From: Gaius Ancius Veridius, governor of Lappa and imperial praetor of the eastern provinces
To: Orosius Devinius, senior overseer of fortifications and military emplacements

Devinius, thank you for your recent reports. They have been most enlightening, and will be acted upon at my earliest convenience. My predecessor seems to have let matters along the River Oxus run to ruin. I shall impose my authority upon the border commanders and have all matters set straight forthwith. Please convey my respects to your superiors.

Dev stood patiently in the dim antechamber, watched over by the serene and rather disapproving busts of emperors, generals and heroes from a dozen centuries of imperial achievement. He was tired, and not just because of the long journey from Germalla. He was tired *and* dispirited. It had taken him years, after his brief stint in the imperial military, to achieve a post of frontier importance, and that post had immediately wrenched him from the capital and sent him to the Pelasian border for a year, and then to the barbarous northern periphery where tribal lords seemed to look down on his Inda colouring just as much as many of his peers in the empire. Finally, a month and a half ago, he had received his orders to document the eastern border and the installations facing his Inda homeland, the region for which he had been aiming all this time, and barely had he reached the Oxus River and begun his tour there before he received the letter by imperial courier. A summons to Velutio. A thing to dread, but Dev was too tired to be worried and too irritated at being dragged from his beloved east to care why.

His gaze danced around the antechamber once more. The walls were painted so perfectly, providing a trompe-l'œil which suggested he was actually in an open colonnade with wide gardens and lakes

stretching away to either side beyond those implacable marble ancestors who so clearly disapproved of him, looking down their aquiline marble noses above sneering marble lips.

Bastards.

But they were *strong* bastards, and *clever* bastards. The sort of bastards he'd hoped to find when he came west all those years ago. He tried not to think on the fact that one of those faces had been a most notorious slave beater. Every time the subject of slaves came up, his mind would draw him an image of Jai in chains, defiant. Dev had long since lost hope that his brother had lived. Jai would never have accepted being a slave, and his martial soul would almost certainly have led him to do something foolish early on.

Dev did not like the way that slave-beating, frowning old hard bastard looked at him. If he had had an ounce of art in his soul he would have loved nothing more than to come to this room with a chisel and make one of the old bastards lining each side smile for once. He was chuckling at his own thought as the door opened and one of the imperial guard, a wolf-pelt cloak on his shoulder, gestured for him to enter. As he passed through the door from the dim antechamber into the brightly lit palace hall, a serious-looking functionary in a rich but plain tunic cornered him.

'Have you been in the imperial presence before?'

Dev shook his head.

'You will not look at the emperor directly unless he addresses you by name, rank or function. You will not speak unless requested, which I presume will happen since you were summoned. You will keep your language civil, your speech short and to the point. Be respectful, address everyone by their rank or position, and if you do not know it, use "Lord". Remain standing unless told to sit. Do not cough, sneeze, fart or yawn. Be unobtrusive and useful. Do you understand?'

'I do.'

'Go in and stand on the green circle of the first carpet.'

Dev stepped into the presence of the emperor, gripping the reason he was here so tightly in his hand he was crushing the vellum.

An imperial summons. No one wanted an imperial summons. It was said that in the days of this emperor's grandfather such a command was often a sign of great things and imperial favour.

31

Quintillian had been a great man. His son Camillus had started well, but some sickness that laid him low in midlife left him slightly deranged. His own son died in an accident, and the boy he adopted by his second wife now sat on the throne. No one seemed to be under any illusion as to how appropriate Bassianus was for the role. And now no one saw a summons to court as a sign of great things. At best you were used and discarded. At *best*...

As Dev came to a halt on the green circle indicated, he took in the court around him, being careful to catch the ruler of the western world only from the corner of his eye in passing, remembering his instructions. Other men had clearly been directed to similar positions around the room by functionaries and waited on coloured carpet circles in the periphery while the emperor and his court held centre stage. Bassianus the Just – *the just what?* was the common whispered joke – sat on a perfectly serviceable wooden chair as would anyone else, not some great gilded throne as Dev had expected. His court reclined on couches that reached out in an arc to either side of him. The courtiers wore white robes of state, while the emperor sported a rich purple mantle with gold edging.

He did not look mad to Dev. Rich and indolent perhaps, but not mad.

He was a young man, perhaps twenty-five summers old, unblemished and undeniably handsome, with a shock of white-gold hair and olive skin. He had a lazy smile as he listened to the droning voice of some official from the treasury who was concerned with coin devaluation.

The treasury fellow finally finished his tedious report and was dismissed with a bored wave of the hand. The man shuffled out of the room, a slave dumping an armful of papers on him as he left.

As the room temporarily emptied of supplicants, the glorious son of gods who ruled the west with a capricious hand glanced at the seats to his left.

'I have had one of you poisoned,' he said, and stifled a giggle. There was a brief moment of silence and then this new imperial joke had been aired long enough and everyone smiled indulgently.

'No,' the emperor grinned, 'I am not fooling. One of you will die. This month there was simply not enough adulation at my officiation of the festival of Solus. I am not pleased. It is a function of my court

to guide the people and make sure all public events are appropriately attended, and you failed. One of you will die for that. And when Solus is celebrated next year you will be sure to spark a more appropriate fervour among your clients and their people.'

There was an odd silence which was finally broken by a strangled gasp. Dev stared in disbelief as one of the courtiers looked down in horror at the jewelled beaker of wine in his hand. His eyes widened as he made desperate gagging noises.

'Ah, Audens. It was you, then. Good. Your northern barbarian fat nose always offended me anyway.'

He grinned as the poisoned courtier cast the wine cup to the floor, rich red liquid splashing across the carpets as he clawed in futile panic at his throat. The emperor chuckled once more as Audens' legs began to spasm and jerk, lashing out randomly. Bassianus gestured at the flautist in the corner. 'Play something jaunty, in time with his dance,' he laughed.

And so the ruined courtier thrashed slowly to a stop, froth on his lips, his distended and swollen, discoloured tongue protruding, in a pool of his own shit and filth as a poor, nervous musician tried to keep his melody light for a man to die by.

To Dev's further horror, the stinking mess was not removed but left there, his peers shuffling slightly away from the corpse.

Another speaker was announced by the monotone court organiser as though nothing untoward had happened, and the new plaintiff was admitted from another door, allowing Dev little time to reflect on the dreadful nature of what he'd just seen. This was Utis, a minor aristocrat from the Gota borders who claimed imperial citizenship but clearly had little in the way of imperial blood. The borderline barbarian stepped before the emperor, and Dev's shrewd eye caught three things in quick succession that struck him as impolitic. The man was not standing in one of those circles clearly positioned for all non-court attendees; he approached the emperor, looking at him levelly; and when he came to a halt in the wrong place, he spoke first. Of course, Dev had not been to the imperial court before, and perhaps the same rules did not apply to all visitors, but from the slightly uncomfortable shiftings in the posture of the courtiers, he'd be willing to bet they did.

'Majesty,' the Gota lord said in the thick, jagged accent Dev remembered from his time on the northern border. 'I come to beseech you for military aid. My Gota neighbours are pressing upon my lands, rustling animals and committing acts of banditry. Mere months ago I had sufficient soldiery to protect my lands, but the northern marshal saw fit to reduce my garrison to strengthen his own. I cannot—'

He stopped mid-sentence, sprouting an arrow from his left eye socket, the shaft so deeply embedded the point broke the back of his skull and only the fletching projected from his face.

Dev stared in shock as the Gota lord crumpled without a whimper, dead before he hit the floor.

Now the emperor's madness became apparent.

Bassianus, lord of men, descendant of gods and master of the world, rose from his chair, stepped over to the corpse and nudged the head with a sandalled foot. The dead man's cranium rolled back until the arrow point hit the floor and then stopped, the blank face staring up at his killer around the fletching. The emperor Bassianus extended an index finger and wagged it.

'Please, Lord Utis, permit me to speak.'

A ripple of nervous laughter sounded dutifully from the court.

'You had those men stripped from you by my order, Utis, as you were using them to increase your personal holdings at the expense of imperial neighbours of more long-standing loyalty than you. It is something of an affront to use your soldiers against my people and then ask me to replace them to protect you from your own. You suffer from a lack of vision,' he announced to the world at large, then chuckled at his own joke. He stepped away and the head rolled back down. 'Put him in a box or a bag or something and send him back to his relatives. And use the courier system so he goes relatively fast and doesn't smell too bad when he gets there.'

Guardsmen dragged the unfortunate northern aristocrat away, leaving just a small spray of crimson on the floor as sign of his passing. So neat. So quick. So barbaric. Not for the first time, Dev wondered whether he had been wise in running west when he left home. The western empire was not the glorious hope for the future he had expected. From the tales he heard and some of the subalterns he met, he suspected it once had been, in generations past, but now

34

he no longer held out much hope for this emperor saving the Inda's world.

The doors at one side opened to dispose of the corpse, and then closed again.

'General Flavius Cinna,' announced the court functionary once again, and another door opened.

The man who entered filled the room immediately. Rarely had Dev seen a man exude such presence without even having to open his mouth. He strode in, took a position in a yellow circle directly opposite the emperor, dropped to one knee and bowed, then rose once more, noting the blood stain with interest as he did so.

Flavius Cinna was a stocky man in his forties, with iron-grey hair cut in a very archaic, severe style. He wore his uniform like armour and a scar ran down the length of his left arm from the tunic sleeve all the way to his middle finger. His very stance spoke of dependability and strength. Here, Dev felt certain, was the empire of older days in which he'd placed his future. Here was what he had been searching for, not that figure in the purple robe.

'General, you are well?' the emperor said conversationally.

'Hale and hearty, Majesty. And your august self?'

'Tolerable,' the emperor sniffed dismissively.

There was a strange silence and Dev realised that the soldier could speak no further as he had no idea why he was here. Finally, as though he'd won a battle of wits, the emperor chuckled and wagged a beringed finger at the general.

'Cinna, you will be aware, I presume, of the reports from the east? Of the Jade Empire?'

Dev's eyes shot wide, darting from the general and risking a brief sidelong glance at the emperor. Reports from the east, of the Jade Empire? He'd heard nothing of this, and he had been on the damned eastern border a matter of days ago. Was this common knowledge, or simply something within the court that had not reached the civil and military administration yet?

General Cinna simply straightened a little.

'From what I understand the Jade Empire is massing forces on the Inda border, Majesty.'

'Indeed,' the emperor replied, a strange gleam in his eye. Dev realised with a start that he'd seen that same gleam just before the northern lord grew an arrow from his eye. He tensed, half-expecting this general to die in moments. But beneath that tension, his mind was whirling. The Jade Empire was massing troops? Was this it? He had come to the empire so many years ago after Jai had been taken in the hope that the Jade Empire could be made to pay for their actions. Was this the time? He found himself almost stepping forward, but General Cinna broke the strange, tense silence.

'Majesty, if I might be so bold as to express an opinion as a long-term military strategist, I would heartily recommend sending a deputation to the Jade Emperor and coming to an agreement over the Inda territories.'

No, thought Dev, trying not to move, his fists clenched.

'Oh?' The emperor's tone had a sudden dangerous edge. Dev waited for the arrow. 'Go on.'

The general scratched his chin in thought. 'The Inda lands are largely worthless in terms of goods and minerals. We can get everything we need from lands within our boundaries, and those few luxuries the Inda produce that we cannot are a cheap trade resource, certainly not worth losing men over. The Jade Empire has been systematically stripping the Inda of assets for years. Now it seems likely they intend to annexe their lands. If they are allowed to abut our own territory there will inevitably be friction, but an agreement could be made in advance. Our border on the Oxus River is a good one. Defensible and patrollable. A treaty with the Jade Empire could grant them the lands they have already ruined to within, say, fifty miles of the Oxus, where there is another smaller river. There would then be a safe demilitarised zone between our peoples.'

'You do not advocate a military solution?' the emperor asked, apparently genuinely puzzled. 'And you a soldier and a hero. Even the fat peaceful aristocrats in my court are advocating the mustering of troops.'

'Majesty, it takes a soldier to know when not to fight. The Jade Empire is strong. Perhaps as strong as us, perhaps even stronger. We have no idea just how sizeable their army is. But I do know that the only land borders they need to protect are with the horse lords, who have been no real threat since the days of the Khan, and with the Inda. They can afford to commit almost their entire military to Inda lands without leaving a land border open to another enemy. We do not have that luxury. The north is held only by military might, else the Gota and other northern tribes would simply eat away at our territory and perhaps even retake Alba. Pelasia has been our ally for generations, but that alliance has been constructed on increasingly shaky ground and has never been closer to collapsing than now. We cannot afford to pull much of our force from the other borders. And rest assured, Majesty, that if we committed to war against the Jade Empire, it would be one that would shake the world to its core. No, Majesty, I would not advocate a military solution.'

The emperor Bassianus tapped his lip as though pondering his choices, then sat back languidly.

'Sadly, General Cinna, the decision has already been made. The moment we hear that the Jade Empire has crossed their border and moved into the role of conqueror, we will react. We will not allow that collection of eastern degenerates to annexe those Inda states. They must be made to see the error of their ways and be driven back behind their border once more. This, Cinna, is your commission.'

The general shifted slightly. His keen, steely eyes roved around the courtiers, none of whom held his gaze. They came to rest once more upon the emperor.

'I will, of course, carry out the commands of my emperor without complaint or question, Majesty, but it would be remiss of me to not make one plea for diplomacy.'

There was a collective intake of breath, and Dev winced. That was the sort of insolence that made men sprout arrows. Perhaps it was Cinna's reputation, or perhaps that bearing and presence that had automatically made him the centre of the room, but the emperor nodded and waved an accepting hand at him.

'Majesty, the Jade Emperor is a man who does not back down or submit. None of them ever has. A man who would do so would never manage to become Jade Emperor in the first place. When he commits to something, the Jade Emperor sees it through to the end. It is part of what and who he is. If war is declared, it will only end one way, but a diplomatic solution is always possible until the first blow or the first insult. We have that opportunity right now. We will never have it again.'

'Your opinion is noted,' the emperor replied in that same bored tone.

'Majesty, if we go to war against the Jade Empire it will not be a simple undecided border dispute.' The court were holding their breath now. Cinna was on very dangerous ground, and Dev could see again out of the corner of his eye the emperor's increasingly irritated face. Still the general went on. 'A war against the Jade Empire will be a war of extinction. Whether the vanquished would be us or them I cannot say with any certainty, but even the winner will be left weak and vulnerable. If they won such a conflict, they would likely fall to the horse lords or one of their subjugated peoples within the year. If we won with such losses as we would suffer, the Gota and the Pelasians would divide up our territories like beasts sharing a kill. I cannot advise such a course of action that leads to such a war.'

'How lucky you are, then,' snapped the emperor angrily, 'that I am not seeking your advice. Your opinions are noted, but the order stands. You will make ready. The moment that slippery eastern dog sends his men across the border, you will retaliate. I give you the freedom and authority to commandeer whatever you need. You will gather what force you deem necessary and cross the Oxus in response. You will not stop until they are defeated and driven back across their border.'

The general, beaten, straightened and saluted.

'I obey, Majesty.'

'Good, because you come recommended to me as the very best strategist in the imperial military, and I would hate to have to scoop out that brain for insolence and rely on the *second* best. And to complement your strategic brilliance, I have had a search made of our military and administrative personnel. We have found more than a dozen soldiers and servants of Inda birth, but I have selected one to serve as your adviser.' His hand gestured to Dev. 'Orosius Devinius here, I am given to understand, was the son of one of their kings before he came to the empire voluntarily to serve. He has a good military record here and is clearly of a strategic mind himself, since he has been serving as an overseer of eastern border fortifications. Devinius will, I am sure, be invaluable as your second.'

Dev bowed. Clearly he was not required to speak.

'Very well, Majesty,' the general said quietly. 'I beg your leave to withdraw and begin my work.'

'You have my permission,' Emperor Bassianus replied loftily.

38

'You, Devinius,' the general said, gesturing to Dev. 'Walk with me.'

With a nervous look to the emperor, who nodded his assent, Dev left his green circle and walked quickly over to Flavius Cinna, who saluted his master, turned smartly on his heel and left the room the way he had entered. Dev hurried after him, and the door to the great room closed with a click, leaving them alone in a long, wide corridor lined with statues of very martial-looking gods.

'Are you a sycophant?' Cinna said, stopping so suddenly that Dev almost walked into him.

'What, General?'

'You are Inda-born, you willingly serve the government of that emperor in there and made no comment at the possibility that you might be required to invade your own lands to face off against a foe who is almost certainly more powerful than us. That makes you either stupid or a sycophant, to my mind. Which is it? Are you daft enough to want a world-ending war amid the ruins of your homeland or are you so far up the emperor's backside that only your feet stick out and you are willing to do the worst things imaginable to please him?'

Dev stopped and stepped back. The general looked genuinely angry, and Dev was suddenly quite aware that his easy acquiescence in the hall did not look strong when placed against the general's outspoken attempts to change the emperor's mind.

'I have my reasons, General,' he said, somewhat weakly.

'Yes. I am sure you have. And I want to know what they are. If I am about to initiate the end of the world and the only way I can prevent it is to win, I will not have a man I cannot trust at my side. You tell me everything right now or you can spend the entire campaign in the baggage train commanding sacks of grain. I am a forthright man and a sane one, despite the general tendency to morons and dangerous lunatics in imperial command, and I will have the truth from you or I will have nothing to do with you, hang the emperor's command.'

Dev nodded. There was sense in what the general said, and there had to be respect if they were to serve together.

'I am neither,' he replied to General Cinna. 'Neither idiot nor sycophant. I am Inda before imperial, always. To men such as those in that room I am Orosius Devinius, but in truth I am Dev, and that is who I have always been. Dev, son of Aram, the rajah of Initpur. I remained silent over the matter of war with the Jade Empire because war with the Jade Empire is what I seek. It is the reason I came to the empire many years ago, for the Inda are far from strong enough to fight the eastern menace, but you are not. I would burn out my eyes and tear out my heart if it would help you beat the Jade Empire. Fervour it is. Not sycophancy or idiocy. Just fervour. And I will serve you to the end if you will be straight with me.'

'Why?'

Dev frowned. 'Why what?'

'Why do you hate the Jade Empire that much? I trust zealots almost as little as I trust idiots and sycophants.'

'The Jade Empire took everything from me.'

Cinna shook his head. 'Not good enough. You're holding back. They took everything from *all* the Inda, yet surprisingly few of you came to us with a burning urge for revenge. Why you?'

Damn you, Dev rumbled silently. He fixed the general with a steady gaze.

'Because they took my brother. As a slave, simply because we did not have enough gold.'

He was shaking. Cinna's eyebrow rose a little, and he nodded. 'Good. That at least was the truth. I can see it in your eyes. And quite understandable. I approve of your motivations, though I do not trust them. Revenge is a dangerous thing. It leads men to do unpredictable things and to make mistakes. If you are to serve with me, I do not wish to find myself armpit-deep in shit because of your personal need for justice. I don't care what gods you believe in, but I want you to swear on whoever they are right now that you will not put your personal vengeance above our task.'

Dev nodded. Their task *was* his personal vengeance. What did he have to lose? 'On the life of my father and my brothers and upon the seven sacred gods of the mountain, I give you my word.'

Cinna stood for a long moment and then nodded, turning and walking on so that Dev had to hurry and fall in step next to him. 'Very well,' the general said. 'I have no intention of making this worse than it is, but it is my personal belief that we cannot win a war against the Jade Empire without committing our entire military. And if we do that we will essentially hand the empire to the Gota while we are busy trying to win in the east. Had we better relations with the Pelasians we might have sought help in that quarter, but the previous emperor's eschewing of his Pelasian first wife in favour of a 'racially pure' imperial one did us no favours there, and the Pelasians are as likely to send help to the Jade Empire as to us these days, so we are better off not involving them at all. We will withdraw one cohort in four from the other provinces and add them to the eastern army. That should give us somewhere in the region of one hundred and fifty thousand men. If we draw more, we threaten the rest of the empire. I will give orders for them all to muster on the Oxus one month from today. You recently came from the eastern border, I heard?'

Dev nodded. 'I was running a report on the upkeep and faults of the fortifications there.'

'You found plenty, I presume?'

'It was not a pleasing list to write.'

Cinna nodded. 'Governors who are given the responsibility of border fortifications tend to leave the military side to their officers, but they siphon off funds for their own use and leave the soldiers scrabbling around trying to meet the shortfall. Happens all the time. I tend to haul people over the coals when I spot it, but it doesn't stop it happening. Ancius Veridius is governor out there now, if I remember rightly. He's no better than the rest, but if you've recently reported to him, he'll be careful to put things right for a while, in case the palace sends for a full audit. I think by the time we get there things will be moving back to rights. And you know the Inda lands beyond the border, I presume?'

'Relatively well, General. It has been a number of years, and I was young when I left, but we used to visit other rajahs regularly, so I know plenty of places in the northern Inda lands, all the way from there to the Jade border.'

'Good. Because while the Jade Emperor's men are on a mission of conquest, we are on a mission of prevention. They will have to fight for every mile they push, while I want to deal with the Inda through negotiation and pass through their lands without fighting. It is the only way we can hope to outmanoeuvre and surprise the Jade Empire. What do you know of the forces of the northern rajahs?'

'I can tell you who had small or large forces over a decade ago, but that will have changed, General. With the tribute paid to the Jade Empire, my own father found it increasingly difficult to pay the men under his command. Thus it will have been with all the rajahs. My assumption will be that only the most powerful of the rajahs will now have men at all, and they will be forces of no real consequence.'

'Makes sense,' Cinna mused. 'And unemployed soldiers only ever go a limited number of ways. They become mercenaries, selling their services to greater powers, which in this case I suspect will be the Jade Empire yet again, since we've not see it happening. Or they change career and become innkeepers, or private guards, or drunks. Or they take to the hills and live by banditry and violence. So we can expect to meet a number of bandit groups, no doubt. Still, they should not bother a full army in the field. If the Inda rajahs are used to paying this tribute to the Jade Empire, while they might baulk at the idea of providing us with safe passage and fodder while in their lands, it will be nothing new to them, and we can offer them one thing the enemy cannot.'

'What is that?'

'A future. The Jade Empire is coming to conquer them. We are not. Once we have passed through they are free again. If I were a gambling man, I would put money on the emperor following up any workable victory with a new command to settle the lands we fought in, but at this time, I made very careful note of my orders. We are to push back the Jade Empire to their border. At no time was I given the task of conquest, and so I will not begin it.'

Dev nodded as they strode on. He liked General Cinna, and it seemed the man held the future of the Inda in his hands. He would have to be nurtured and supported.

'I have no fears about engagements with cavalry and infantry,' the general said, suddenly. 'They will be hard-fought, but I know what I am about with such matters, and with your local knowledge our strategy should be sound. What I fear is coming up against the enemy's cannon. They only deploy such dread weapons in full campaigns, but there are still tales of the one used against Velutio last century. The remnants of the beast are kept in the palace, but no man has ever been able to fully figure out how it works. If their cannon can do what I hear to the walls of a city, it pains me to think what it might do to a cohort of men. Still, I have engineers and scientists who can ponder that as we work. Now, we must look to preparations. Do I call you Devinius or Dev?'

'Dev, General.'

'Good. Very well, then, Dev. Return to your lodgings and gather your goods. Meet with my staff at the Hall of Warriors by third watch. We, my young Inda friend, are going to chastise the Jade Emperor.'

CHAPTER 4

The fast warrior hurries into danger
The strong warrior walks into danger
The agile warrior dances into danger
The clever warrior walks around danger

From The Path of War, by Hu Xin

Jai watched the army moving into position with breathless anticipation. He was new to battle. Yes, he had served in the Jade Empire's military for many years and trained as a swordsman, but he had been a scout, often working alone in bandit-infested territory, or with small groups of like men, testing the border regions. He had never until recently witnessed the true horrific majesty of an imperial army at war and, though he had now seen it numerous times in quick succession, still the tense expectancy remained.

The army had moved from Yuen with impressive speed and efficiency. It said a great deal about General Jiang that Jai had barely had time to gather his gear and draw what equipment he felt he needed from the Palace of Arms before couriers were urging him to join the staff as the general was preparing to move out.

The First Army had made Jai's breath catch in his throat. He had been impressed to see them gathered in that wide valley, but to witness them on the move was a different thing entirely. The army slithered along the valley from Yuen like a great centipede of silver, black and red, uniform and perfect, like a grand piece of the silversmith's art, like a flexible blade, aiming west. It was magnificent. And Jai pushed every ounce of his soul into the belief that they were a force of inclusion and civilisation, who would repair the long-term damage to the Inda. Because if he even for a moment allowed himself to be that son of Aram who had defied the Jade Empire's foragers, he could not be the man he now needed to be.

44

And if he had thought that the gathered forces from Yuen were impressive, he had felt his conception of the scale of the world change when they reached the garrison town of Chengdi and the force doubled in size with the mustered units there. This massive army had moved west then, towards the border, where his preconceptions were once more destroyed as they met an even larger muster that joined them to form the full First Army. Jai had never seen so many humans in one place, let alone soldiers. An ocean of silvered figures filling the world. Here and there cavalry wings rose like reefs from the silver, and great dark cannon moved on carts like ships on the surface. It was an incredible thing to behold, and Jai felt a little of his trepidation over the possibility that the western empire might face them fade. How could any other people in the world match this?

And this was but a third of the Jade Empire's force. The Second and Third Armies were elsewhere, moving into position as per General Jiang's orders. While the First Army marched into the Inda heartland, where the strongest of the rajahs ruled and there would still be noticeable resistance, the Second Army was moving through the mountain passes in the north, securing the hardy but small northern kingdoms close to the horse clans. And the Third Army had moved south, into the jungle proper, to secure the southern rajahs. A trident. A three-pronged attack.

Jai had frowned as he listened to the plan, carefully wording a response to the effect that their campaign might have been more effective if Jai had been included in the early planning. A force this size would have trouble manoeuvring in the northern mountains and would be too unwieldy to deal with the rajahs there, and the south was hardly worth consideration, since much of it was empty, ruled only by ghosts. General Jiang had nodded his understanding. He had been forced to move precipitously by imperial command and had erred on the side of caution. But he had taken terrain into account. The northern army was largely infantry and the southern heavily weighted with cavalry. Only this central force was an equal mix. The three armies would converge, having secured their territory, on the largest of the Inda kingdoms – Jalnapur on the Nadu River.

Jai had understood. The Nadu River was the furthest the Jade Empire could hope to move without challenging their opposite number in the west. Crossing that river would bring them close to enemy borders and almost certainly be considered an act of aggression. And the Nadu ran from north to south along much of the Inda Diamond. The northern reaches wound through narrow valleys and rocky precipices, unsuitable for an army to cross. The southern reaches were too wide for an easy crossing, and largely within the forbidden lands of the spirits anyway. Only the central section was viable, and the only good bridge was at Jalnapur. It was the reason for the kingdom's wealth and power, this ability to tax those who crossed. It was a natural bottleneck, but was also that line which, when crossed, would increase the chance of western opposition exponentially.

And so the three armies had passed into Inda lands on their grand campaign of annexation. Jai was impressed with the ease with which Jiang and his second and third generals kept in touch. Every day riders reached the army with the latest reports of the movements to north and south, and then returned with news to go the other way.

Jai's focus became the First Army pure and simple. Those in the south would encounter precious little true opposition, though he had sent warnings to stay out of the spirit lands and not cross the line of markers bearing their weapons. General Jiang had wholeheartedly supported these words, and the soldiers of the Third Army would obey the command. They were Jade Empire; obedience was in their blood. Beyond simple obedience, soldiers faced enough horror in their lives without deliberately offending gods and spirits, and so that line of markers would remain uncrossed. To the north the Second Army would be slow going through the mountains, but should encounter little resistance. Jai was more than grateful not to be with them, for somewhere on that campaign, the Jade Empire would encounter the rajah of Initpur, and Jai was not at all sure he could have done that. Without his needing to ask, General Jiang had sent strict instructions that the rajah of Initpur and his people were to be treated leniently and with respect.

And so the First Army thundered into the west. Initially they encountered only minor border kingdoms, most of whom capitulated upon their arrival. For the first twenty days of moving through those lands, it became a simple diplomatic mission. Rajahs would leave their palaces, accompanied by their courts and priests, and welcome the Jade Empire to their lands. It was all praise and acceptance with wide smiles and open arms, though Jai knew his people well enough to see the utter dejection and defeat that sat behind their gleaming eyes. Each kingdom was subsequently allotted an imperial commander and left with a garrison of two hundred men to begin the process of assimilation. The rajahs were required to officially renounce their titles and take an oath of obedience to the Jade Emperor, upon which they became a private citizen like the rest of their people. In due course, if they showed talent in administration, they could rise to rule after a fashion, in the name of the Jade Emperor, but they would never again be rajahs of the Inda.

The first battle had taken place four days ago, though perhaps 'battle' was too grand a term. Engagement, perhaps. Or slaughter? The two hundred thousand men of the First Army had poured from one of the valleys of a low range of hills and out onto the grassy plains of Pala to find the local rajah's forces waiting for them. The native ruler had done well. Remarkably well, given the restrictions of manpower and resources. He had mustered almost a thousand men and eight elephants. They had stood, defiant, at the entrance to Pala village, the rajah's palace rising on a low hill beside the river at the far side. They had formed into a square as if expecting cavalry, the elephants to one side, kept in check by their mahouts, four archers in each of the fortified howdahs on the beasts' backs. More archers waited in the centre of the square.

'How likely is it we can talk them down from this?' General Jiang had asked Jai.

Jai had replied with an air of sadness. 'Not at all. The rajah knew we were coming, as he has had time to gather forces. And he must have known the size of our army, for word will have carried ahead of us. If he is willing to stand now, he has no interest in negotiation.'

The general agreed. 'Then we need to make a statement. One example here could prevent similar stupidity further along.'

Jai had swallowed hard but nodded. He forced himself to watch as the army of which he was a leader brought death to his own people. The general was right. If ten thousand could be persuaded to simple surrender in future because of a few hundred deaths now, it was worthwhile. Jai had shuddered at the thought that war was not the skill of the forms of steel that he had so painstakingly learned in the academy, but a soulless, callous matter of numbers and logic. A man with a pen could be a better general than a man with a sword, and yet while a sword blow could kill a man, one stroke from that pen could kill thousands.

It had been brief. So brief. General Jiang had taken his time and let the army move into battle positions, giving the defiant rajah a last small chance to surrender. Still he did not, and so as the last of the First Army's units fell into position, the general's orders were carried out. While the army had been manoeuvring, a triad of destruction had been settled onto a low terrace on the nearest hill behind them, loaded and sighted.

Despite being in use for a thousand years, cannon were still dangerous to handle. It was not for nothing that rocketeers and artillerists were the highest paid of all the imperial military. There was, by common reckoning, a one in four chance of something going wrong. It was not always fatal, but could be extremely nasty even when not.

The three cannon fired. The first had been badly settled into its cradle and the detonation simply threw it from its bed. The great stone ball was hurled harmlessly off into the grassy plain, way beyond any soldier of either side, but two of the artillerists died horribly, crushed under the great iron beast as it fell from position. The second cannon had been sighted too high, and the ball struck a building in the village behind the rajah and his men, demolishing it in an explosion of bricks, plaster, timber and tile shards. But the locals had neither time nor the luxury to turn in dismay and examine the damage, for the third cannon had been perfectly positioned and sighted. The stone ball, perfectly spherical and a foot across, hit the square of men in the centre. Such was the power behind the missile that the three men in the front rank died instantly, one near vaporised by the direct blow, the other two mangled by its passing. The second rank fared no better, nor the third. The stone ball had lost very little momentum even by the time its gore-coated, glistening bulk passed through the centre of the square, pulverising archers and obliterating men.

The shot almost made it through the block, finally coming to ground at the far side and tearing the legs from men, smashing bones and crushing torsos in its passage.

Jai watched in horror. A line just over a man wide had been carved through the enemy, killing and injuring perhaps a tenth of the gathered force. To stack terror upon terror, the triple detonation had panicked the elephants, and their mahouts stood no chance of controlling them. Two of the great beasts turned and ran through the village, screaming archers desperately trying to stay in the shaking howdahs. Three more ran for the open grass. One hurtled towards the serried ranks of the Jade Empire, though it sprouted a thousand arrows before it could reach them and fell, a sliding mass of grey flesh, coming to rest some fifty paces from the front lines, where the two Inda archers who had survived threw up their hands in surrender. The other two elephants once more reinforced the reason so many great generals would not field the beasts among their force. A panicked elephant is deadly and uncontrollable. The two great animals thundered through the square of men with almost as much grisly destruction as the cannon ball. Men died in their hundreds.

Jai estimated that if he'd been counting he would have reached less than fifty from the first cannon shot before the whole thing was over. The pitiful remnants of the defiant rajah's force surrendered and were disarmed. The lord himself was executed. Jai might have tried to argue against that, but did not trust himself to speak. He was still sickened by what he had witnessed. Later, he came to understand the general's decision. The rajah had been a symbol of defiance. They had utterly flattened such defiance but could not complete the task without tearing down that symbol. At least the death had been clean and quick, unlike the mangled half-dead from the cannon and elephants, who were then given peace at knifepoint by their comrades.

Four hundred or so Inda dead. Many more wounded. A rajah beheaded and a garrison installed. And the losses to the First Army? Two unfortunate artillerists. This, then, thought Jai, was war.

But despite the horror of what he had witnessed, the general had been astute. In the subsequent three days they entered the lands of some of the stronger rajahs and found that men who might have considered standing against them were capitulating easily. Defending forces of several thousand men were simply disbanded and turned over to the invader. In one notable case, a rajah gathered a force of men to stand against them and the soldiers themselves revolted, fleeing into the countryside before the Jade Empire arrived, leaving a distressed rajah with no army and no option other than surrender.

And so it had gone.

Until this morning. Jai had warned the general that here he would be tested, and it seemed that would be the case. The Rajah of Salaya had been reckoned one of the most powerful of all the Inda lords a generation or more ago and, despite the continual draining of power and wealth from the land, such was Salaya's prominence that he remained stronger even now than many others had been in their prime. And what strength the rajah could rely on from money and men was as nothing compared to that gifted him by the gods.

Salaya occupied a high, rocky ridge in the shape of a spoon. The long extent of the handle contained the civilian town and a grand temple, and the bowl of the spoon was a fortress. Even General Jiang had drawn an impressed breath at the sight of it. Jai had been here once as a youth, when his grandfather had sought aid in methods of extracting copper from his local valley – the town of Salaya had become rich on copper mining, and its engineers were reckoned the best. As a boy Jai had marvelled at the place.

The town was not walled, but the sheer cliffs upon which it rested were as defensible as any rampart in the world. The fort that occupied the bowl shape at the other end *was* walled, and what defences they were. Already resting upon two hundred feet of sheer cliff, they were a double circuit of walls, the outer low and squat, the inner high and delicate, with painted turrets at equal spaces along the rampart. Only across the top of the ridge facing the town was it a single wall, and any attacking army would have to ascend the heights just to get that far. All around the ridge, the cliff had been carved into the shapes of gods, adding a certain eeriness to the entire ensemble. The only access to the ridge top was a ramp carved into the rock that wove back and forth like a gently folded scarf. Each turn in the ramp was guarded by a gate with towers.

'Manpower?'

Jai shrugged. 'As many as eight or nine thousand, at least. In its days of glory, Salaya housed a garrison of twenty thousand, but those days are gone.'

'Still,' the general said, 'eight or nine thousand men could hold that place for some time.'

'I doubt negotiation will work,' Jai added. 'The rajah is one of the proudest in the land. To him not being the lord of Salaya is tantamount to being dead anyway.'

'Then we must take it. The cannon will be of little use from here. We cannot sight them high enough to damage those walls. We could take a lower gatehouse or two out with them, but then we run the risk of damaging the ramp in the process, and destroying the only point of access is poor strategy. I think the cannon should be left out of the initial stages. I do, however, have a plan to make things a little easier. My Inda is not strong. Will you be my voice?'

Jai nodded.

'Ride with a hundred men to the base of the ramp and shout to the effect that the ordinary people of Salaya have one hour to descend the ramp and leave the town before the attack commences.'

'You know the rajah's men will not open the gates to let them out?'

The general nodded. 'Sadly, that seems likely. But I will then have adhered to the etiquette of war, and when the first phase begins, the citizens will, I believe, perform half the task of conquest for us.'

Jai frowned his incomprehension, but took an honour guard and rode to the ramp. He would have liked to stay out of arrow range just in case, but needed to be close enough to be heard and understood, and he couldn't have said what range arrows had from such a height anyway. Under the stern gaze of the defenders, Jai delivered the ultimatum – an offer of survival for the people, unspokenly extended to the garrison, of course. The rajah's men at the various ramp gates jeered. Straining his ears, Jai could hear no such similar taunting from the civilians far above. They would be watching in terror as the largest army ever seen in Inda lands assembled before them, preparing to capture their town. Soldiers could jeer, the people would not.

Moments later, message delivered, Jai rode back to join the general where they watched with interest from a good viewpoint on a rocky hill. It took less than a quarter of an hour for the panic to begin – people starting to leave the built-up jumble of the clifftop town. They massed in two directions. Some moved towards the great high gate of the fortress, seeking safety within the rajah's strong walls. Others pressed at the top gate of the ramp, seeking to flee Salaya as ordered, carrying their most valuable goods on their back, children in tow. Neither path was fruitful, just as Jai and the general had anticipated. The rajah was not about to weaken his defensive position by doling out precious space and supplies to the common people, and those men guarding the gate were not about to open the only access to the mountain top for a few locals.

'It begins,' the general said, quietly.

'But they still cannot leave.'

'That is because they are not yet desperate enough. Another half an hour and things will change. Watch.'

Down below, the First Army was reorganising. Jai was not surprised to see the heavy infantry in their armour of black and silver moving to a position at the fore, facing the ramp. His heart jumped a little as he spotted the rocket teams moving into position. As dangerous as the cannon, if not more so, those dreadful weapons were rarely fielded without good reason.

'Rockets?'

The general nodded. 'I try not to use them unless I have to, but they have their place. And if they must be used, we are experiencing the very best conditions for it. Dry weather and no wind of which to speak.'

Time passed in an odd semblance of peace. The ridge top of Salaya was just too far away for the commotion up there to reach Jai's ears, and the Jade Empire military stood silent and confident, awaiting the order to move. Finally, General Jiang turned to Jai. 'It has been an hour, I think?'

'Agreed, General.'

Jiang waved one hand and behind him a great red flag was thrust into the air and hauled back and forth. Within moments the rocket teams burst into frenzied activity. Jai watched, tense, as the first missile launched. The great tube whispered up into the morning air, the long launching stick falling away. It missed the ridge by some fifty paces, coming down harmlessly into a field nearby with a nerve-chilling bang. There was a new round of jeering from the mountain, but it did not last long, for another dozen rockets launched in the wake of the first, and only two of those went astray. Ten blazing tubes arced up high into the air and dropped neatly over the clifftop into the town. The muffled bangs made Jai wince. He had watched a rocket demonstration at Yuen some years ago. It was not the tube that did the damage. The tube just contained the black powder that propelled the rocket. It was when that tube reached the end and the rocket dropped that the real damage occurred. At the lower end of each missile was an iron container holding yet more black powder. As the rocket's fuel disappeared, it lit the taper of the iron ball. The main detonation varied. Sometimes it would happen somewhere in the air before landing. Sometimes it would happen on impact. Sometimes the ball would land and there would be a long pause before the bang. Jai listened to the muffled *crumps* amid the combustible buildings of the town and could picture those ten iron containers detonating, sending deadly shards of hot metal in every direction, followed by a boiling cloud of fire that dissipated instantly, but not before igniting anything close enough.

Gods, let the people of Salaya have fled their houses already, prayed Jai. It would be a horrible way to go.

Even as the rocketeers reloaded for a second salvo, already the tightly packed buildings of Salaya were burning. The second wave of missiles simply added to the horrid conflagration, and it was not long before the civilian town was a roaring inferno. The desperate, panicked townsfolk flooded now against the ramp's top gate. The general had known. He had understood. There was no way the rajah was going to admit the common folk, and it had not taken long for them to realise that too, so they pressed hard for the ramp and perceived freedom.

Jai and the staff could not see the action up there, so high and so distant was it, but the results quickly became evident. The guards must have been overthrown and outnumbered by the panicked townsfolk, for the gates were suddenly thrown open and a veritable flood of humanity issued forth down the slope towards the first turn in the hairpin ramp and the next gate that guarded it.

'Concentrate on the interior near the top gate,' the general commanded, and flags were waved in response. The rocketeers sent up a third grouping, this time aiming for the area where the town petered out near the fortress entrance and the upper ramp gate. A new conflagration began there, right behind the tailing figures of the refugees. It was well-timed and well-placed. The great timber doors of the fortress had just opened and men issued forth under orders to secure that top gate, but the moment they emerged the whole area exploded in flame and shrapnel, and those unwounded quickly hurried back inside the fortress, leaving burning, dying comrades and slamming shut the fortress gates once more.

Jai watched, as impressed as he was sickened, as the ordinary people of Salaya opened the mountaintop to their enemies. Bend after bend, gate after gate, the poor Inda overcame the guards and threw open the portals, fleeing their burning town to throw themselves upon the mercy of the Jade Empire.

'Pass the word to all the captains,' General Jiang announced. 'The people of Salaya are not to be harmed. They may leave freely and with all their goods and family.'

Jai watched as the last few gates at the bottom of the ramp were overcome and the people of that burning town ran for safety to the countryside. To be certain, another rocket volley was aimed at the space near the top gate, and then new flags were being waved.

'Come, Jai.'

In the wake of the General, Jai crossed the battlefield, walking his horse between the ranks of infantry and cavalry, archers and sappers. As he reached the base of the cliffs at the fore of the army, the towering walls of Salaya high above, Jai was impressed. The civilians had gone. The ramp was open, and already teams of oxen were dragging three cannon into view. At an order, the heavy infantry began to march. Jai watched as the ranks stomped forward with rhythmic thuds of feet and clonks of armour and weapons. They moved through the open first gate six abreast and began to climb without slackening the pace. Twelve hundred men, or thereabouts, snaked up that ramp. As they reached the halfway point, further orders rang out and shields were raised above heads, forming a mobile roof. Just in time, for at that moment arrows and stones started to drop from the fortress walls. Fortunately, the attacking force gained regular respite as they wound this way and that, for only one side of that switchback ramp ran beneath the castle walls.

There were casualties, but not enough to weaken the force. At each corner, they passed through deserted gates and continued to climb. And behind them the cannon were slowly rising, each pulled by a team of eight huge oxen and tended by a group of artillerists.

At the general's beckoning, Jai joined him and a group of cavalry who rode onto the ramp after the cannon. They rose slowly, and Jai was as nervous of the great iron menaces on the carts in front as he was of the missiles dropping from the walls. He remembered all too well the two men being crushed by the weapon that fell off its cradle in the first engagement, and had no wish to go to the afterlife in that manner.

It took an hour, and it was probably the most nerve-shredding hour of Jai's life. Every time the ramp wound back towards the fortress end, he winced and braced against the arrows and rocks. Unnecessarily so, of course. General Jiang had no intention of leaving the world in such an ignominious manner. Bodyguards rode on either side of the officers, holding up posts that supported a timber roof which covered them as they moved. But there was still the ever-present threat of falling cannon, and Jai watched them intently throughout, drawing a sharp breath every time one even faintly rocked in its housing at a corner.

Eventually the cannon were drawn into the square before the top gate and the officers emerged onto the ridge of Salaya behind them. Jai watched as the ranks of infantry, still largely intact, spread out to face the wall of the fortress. In some places the flames of the blaze here had not yet died out, but the town of Salaya was largely burned now, and the open spaces just a charred mess. It was amazing how an entire town could disappear within an hour in the dry season.

The cannon were moved into position and prepared as the cavalry who had followed the general up the ramp now settled into neat units at the rear.

'Rajah of Salaya, hear me,' the general said to Jai, gesturing to the walls. Jai repeated the words loudly in the Inda tongue.

'Your town has fallen and your fortress will not last the hour. If you yield now, you alone will forfeit your life. If you force me to break down your walls, there will be no quarter given for soldier or citizen, or even your family. Do you understand?'

There was a pause and finally a tall figure in rich red and gold appeared at the battlements above the gate.

'This is sovereign land, not part of your empire. Leave Salaya at once, or the gods will not be able to identify your corpse.'

Big words, nervously spoken. Jai could imagine how the rajah's wife and children were now reacting to his response. Did he not realise this was a new type of war? Had he not seen what the Jade Empire had wrought? Cannon and black powder, fire and death inflicted from a great distance. He could not have been prepared for what Jiang and his army had brought west, but surely he was gaining an inkling now as the town burned? Could he not see the cannon? Even the glorious, ancient western empire had no such weapon in its arsenal.

The general turned and nodded. A yellow flag was waved.

The three cannon discharged in quick succession.

The first struck the gates of the fortress, turning them into a thousand pieces of kindling that hurtled through the air, killing and maiming more of the men behind the gate than the great stone ball itself. The second shot punched through the stone frame of that gate, taking the remnants of a wooden door with it and adding shards of dark red stone to the debris that scythed through the air. The third blow had been aimed by an expert. Like all red sandstone structures, the fortress of Salaya had been carved by the winds over the centuries, and the projecting tower to the left of the gate had clearly been one of the most exposed. The stones had hollowed out, such that the mortar between them projected further than the stones themselves. It was this very spot that the great stone ball struck. The wind-weakened sandstone gave way like a child's pile of wooden blocks at a petulant kick.

There was a tremendous crash and a cloud of red dust. As it cleared, Jai watched, wide-eyed. A hole perhaps two feet across had been punched through the wall at the bottom of the tower. Cracks were already spidering up between the blocks, and the wall of the tower began to shift perceptibly. Horrible groaning noises and the sound of cracking stone echoed across the watching army. The defenders atop the gate were as yet oblivious, still reeling from the ease with which the gates themselves had been obliterated. They only became aware of their fresh peril as the tower collapsed beneath them. The cracks interconnected and reached up to the parapet, spreading out to the section of wall alongside and across the arch above the ruined gate. A man up there gave a cry of alarm and, before another could respond, the entire left-hand tower and the section above the gate collapsed into a pile of rubble, a massive cloud of red dust billowing out across both forces.

Slowly, the haze subsided. Inda warriors were staggering and limping from the rubble, clutching broken arms, weapons discarded. They were beaten and they knew it instantly. The impregnable Salaya had fallen in two hours.

'Your orders, sir?' asked a captain as his men kept their weapons out and pointed at the surrendering men.

'No quarter, you said,' Jai reminded the general.

'Agreed, but there will be civilians in there too, and this should be an example, not a slaughter.' The general turned to the captain. 'Put the warriors to the sword. Swift and sharp – a soldier's death. Search the rubble and find the body of the rajah. If he is still alive, remedy that. His family are not to be harmed and nor are any other civilians you find. They may join the refugees on the plain below.'

Jai heaved a sigh of relief. Though he felt for the warriors who would die, they had chosen their lot, but he had not been relishing the sight of a population slain. His initial opinion of General Xeng Shu Jiang seemed to have been well founded. If there had to be a conqueror of the Inda, Jai was grateful it would be him.

And now, when they had finished here and installed a garrison, the way was open to the heart of the Inda Diamond. Few places that stood in their way would be as troublesome as Salaya. And then the armies would combine at Jalnapur, and they would stare across the western hills towards Velutio and the western empire.

Gods, but let them stay behind their river, Jai wished fervently.

CHAPTER 5

Duty is a curious thing. It often leads us to act in a manner that is directly contradictory to our desire. And only a man without conscience is also without duty. The soldier has a duty to his commander. The citizen has a duty to his lord. The priest has a duty to his god. But duty is reciprocal. It is the duty of gods to watch over their believers. It is the duty of a commander to support his soldiers. And it is the duty of a lord to protect and serve his people. Thus it is that a man can do the unthinkable when there is no other way for him to discharge his duty.

I pray that I choose correctly. There is no small future riding on my decision.

The sound of horns in the middle distance drew worried looks from the gathered, suddenly shocked people. Aram glanced sharply at the leader of his guards, and the man – one constant of Initpur since the days of Aram's father – nodded and gestured for the soldiers to follow him. Fifteen hardened, ageing soldiers in laminated lacquered wood-and-chain armour scurried off through the dust.

The village of Nalla was the westernmost settlement in Aram's kingdom and the last to be mobilised as part of the scheme. Many weeks after its creation, Aram's plan was still a fragile and mutable thing, for it relied upon numerous factors outside his control. When word had come that a giant force of the Jade Empire's military had moved into the neighbouring kingdom, Aram had put his plan into action and assumed all would follow his design. He had been wrong.

All goods and population had already been catalogued, the people informed and routes laid out in discussion with each village's headman. As soon as the word of impending invasion went out, the people began to move and gather, travelling west all the time, across Initpur, away from the Jade Empire. What Aram had *not* counted on, though, was the tremendous slowness and disorganisation of his people. He found it baffling. They knew what was coming, knew what had happened to the kingdoms east of here. If it had been Aram in one of these villages, he could have gathered what mattered to him, slung them on a donkey and left the village in the time it took to draw a dozen breaths. Yet some of these villages had taken half a day to empty, such was the tardiness and fussiness of their occupants.

Aram had left the palace, sending on four of his precious few remaining men with his own baggage to the meeting place, while he took the other fifteen to round up any stragglers. The first few villages had been clear, though his men had found a few of the precious resources the villagers had been instructed to bring still *in situ*, and had been forced to act as porters as well as soldiers, drawing the important supplies with them. Slowly, throughout the day, Aram and his men had moved through the villages of Initpur methodically, gathering what was supposed to have left with the population, urging the occasional reluctant ageing villager out of their house and seating them on the pack horses to carry them to safety.

It had not worked as smoothly as Aram had anticipated, but finally, as the sun began to descend towards the Kalagund Hills that marked the heart of the next kingdom in the west, Aram and his men had cleared all but Nalla, which marked the last stage of the plan. When the Jade Empire rolled over Initpur there would be no rajah to kill, no people to enslave or control, and no goods to take. The kingdom would be empty.

But Nalla had been no better than any of the others. In fact, Nalla had been altogether lazy and slow in its preparations. As the golden orb touched the treetops and the seething, crackling summer air still steamed the parched ground, Aram and his men had entered the village to find a wedding feast in progress. A wedding feast, for the love of the seven sacred gods of the mountains!

The forces of the Jade Empire were rolling across the northern lands of the Inda, crushing, controlling and enslaving, yet the people of Nalla were dancing and throwing flowers. It had almost been enough to make Aram weep. He and the soldiers had interrupted the wedding feast mid-dance, striding into the dusty square. The soldiers had silenced the three musicians, and the dancers had spun to a halt in baffled dismay. The bride in her bright and colourful traditional dress had risen from the table in confusion, shock and anger on her new husband's face.

The father – apparently Nalla's headman, which only served to make the whole farce more stupid still – had demanded of his rajah why such a joyous and sacred occasion should be halted like this. Aram had rounded angrily on the man and reminded him of the plans set in place so many days ago. The forces of the Jade Empire were close, and Nalla had been instructed to move out like every other village.

The husband had scoffed then, noting that they were far in the west of Initpur and that it would take long enough for the enemy to move across the kingdom that the feast would easily be finished and the village evacuated before the Jade Empire came.

Aram had opened his mouth to give an angry retort, but that had been when they first heard the horn. He had thrown a pointed look at the father, who paled in an instant.

'Isha. Bilau. Gather everything that matters and do it now,' the old man had said, sharply.

Aram had shaken his head as the horn blew again and received an answer from another somewhere in the hills. 'There is no time now. That is why the call came to you when it did. You are out of time. You have to move. Now. All of you. Go to the meeting place. Run or ride, but move.'

There had been baffled looks of consternation, and now the horns blew again. The people were more than worried now. Panic was beginning to set in.

'Go.'

Another blast. Aram glanced sharply at the leader of his guards, and the man nodded and gestured for the soldiers to follow him. The square exploded into activity as the fifteen soldiers drew their swords and hefted their spears, hurrying to the eastern edge of the small community. Men and women were running now, shouting for their children. Musical instruments lay discarded on the ground and the bride's dress tore as someone trod on the colourful, delicate hem in the commotion. She did not notice.

Aram looked around at the chaos and cleared his throat.

'Calm down!' he bellowed, and the whole exodus stopped suddenly, like a child caught doing something he shouldn't. 'Panic kills people as readily as combat. Gather your loved ones. Leave everything else. Run or get your beast, but do it sensibly, aware of the others around you. Get to the meeting point and wait there.'

Idiocy. This should have happened hours ago.

Leaving the villagers, who were now at least moving with purpose, Aram drew his own blade and followed his soldiers. The horn honked again, this time worryingly close. The old man peered at the sword in his hand. It had been his father's and his grandfather's before him. Unlike the precious blade that had been taken by the foragers all those years ago, this was worth little and had thus been ignored by the interlopers. It was not precious, delicate or artistic. It was a warrior's blade, steel and brass, with a curve that displayed a few small notches that had been too deep to fully polish out. A blade that had seen war. His great-grandfather had used it in anger, defending Initpur against the territorial ambitions of a neighbour, but it had not been drawn from its scabbard in anger for three generations. Aram had never used it. He had never used *any* sword, or even struck a man in anger.

But there was a first time for everything. And his duty was to his people.

He found his own men at the same time he found the enemy.

The soldiers of Initpur – once a small army his great-grandfather had led in combat and now fifteen hungry old men just like Aram – were bracing themselves with their spears held out as men did when facing a tiger or suchlike on a jungle hunt. But this was no tiger.

There were only a dozen of them, for which Aram felt he should be grateful. The bulk of the Jade Empire's army were still some distance away, moving through the deserted villages, but scouts had ridden on ahead. These men were lightly armed and armoured – ten with spears and belted swords, two with bows and daggers, all wearing light vests of leather that flexed well in the saddle. Aram felt a sudden panic flow through him. What should he do? Realistically he would not add a great deal to the force arrayed here and might perhaps be more use herding the people, but he had a duty, and how hard could it be? Leather grip goes in the hand, pointy end goes in the enemy.

He moved into one of the gaps between the men, where they filled a roadway between two old brittle fences at the edge of the village. His roving eyes caught the other men with swords and he took in their stance and the way they held their blade. Imitating them, he braced, his left foot forward and his right at an angle behind. He gripped the sword in both hands and drew it back, held out at an angle in the same way as his men.

'None can escape,' Aram said to his men. Several of them nodded. It was the right decision. If no scout reported back to the army, then there would be enough time for the people of Initpur to disappear into the woods and move into deeper jungle. It would not be worth the effort of the enemy general to follow a ragged band of natives into such terrain. But they had to buy time, and that meant killing the scouts.

He glanced over his shoulder at the vanishing figures of the last few villagers and then wiped the sweat from his brow with his sleeve before settling the sword back into position. It was hot for this early in the year. How did soldiers fight well in this heat?

The plan was good. The village of Nalla lay at the edge of the mountains. To the north and east of here lay the true valleys and heights. To the south lay a low range of hills, and then open farmland. But to the west... well, there were more hills and mountains, but in between there was a wide vale of woodland that became steadily more tropical as one travelled south. And within that vale lay the great River Nadu. Here, in the north, there were crossing points if you knew where to look, but it would save them from imperial pursuit, for it would be far too difficult for a full army to cross. Once on the far side of the river, they could travel south and seek refuge in the lands near the border of the western empire, where they might hope to be safe from the Jade Emperor's men.

All that relied on them getting out of Initpur alive, of course.

The scouts charged. Aram concentrated not on his stance or the weaknesses of his enemy or his own strength, or any of those things he understood warriors considered at this point. He concentrated quite simply on staying where he was and not turning and fleeing, which was what his heart, his brain and his legs were all telling him to do.

The scouts advanced, urging their horses across the open ground at the edge of the village, and Aram realised at that moment that the enemy had fully expected the paltry collection of poorly armed old warriors here to break and run. To the credit of each man of Initpur, not one man turned away. Not even Aram.

In a moment that gave him heart, the first kill went to the commander of his guards. A scout tried to ride him down, but the man held tight to his spear and at the last moment brought the tip up slightly, slamming the butt back into the sandy soil. The horse hit the spear and the point punched through its chest. The startled scout made an attempt to stab down with his own lance, but the horse reared and fell. Aram just had time to watch the rider disappear beneath the massive bulk of the dying horse before his attention was drawn back by the man riding directly at him. He had no spear. How did you attack a horseman with a sword? Possibly he could sever a leg from the horse and bring the man down, but he didn't like the thought of that, since the horse had never done him any harm, and he would almost certainly be crushed by the beast as it either ran or fell.

It was in that split second of confusion that Aram learned his first lesson of war. Reaction is sometimes more important than planning. The scout's spear lanced out at Aram even as he dithered and panicked, unsure what to do. Without conscious decision, his sword came up and slashed this way and that in a very inexpert manner, attempting to keep the spear from his face. He had also automatically sidestepped in his confusion, so as not to be in direct line of trampling. Somehow, the flailing blade managed to cut through the ash shaft of the enemy spear.

The rider's momentum carried him past Aram. The rajah looked around for the next enemy, but it seemed they were all engaged with his men. With a terrified leap of the heart, Aram realised that his erstwhile assailant was now behind him. The scout was already wheeling his horse for another charge. He had cast aside his broken spear – still a good six feet of shaft there – and was drawing his sword now. Aram took two steps towards the man and dropped, scooping up the discarded shaft.

What was he doing? The thing had no point, just some splintered shards at one end. It was not long enough to brace against the ground as his men had done. Panic filled him, and he started to back away as the horseman charged.

It was only as he stumbled into something that he realised he had been backing away at an angle and not straight. His spine was against one of the fences. The horseman was coming. Panic filled Aram now and he dropped, trying to climb between the rails of the fence. The horseman was still charging, picking up speed.

Aram felt death swooping down from the sky, ready to gather him up in its arms. He was stuck. Somehow the scabbard at his side had caught on two pieces of timber. He had one leg through the fence and was at a truly uncomfortable angle, jammed and unable to extricate himself. The horseman seemed set on killing him. He realised that the weight of horse and rider might just be enough to smash through the old fence and the man trapped in it both, crushing them all.

As death stooped ever lower from the clouds, opening its cloaked embrace, the grey horse of the scout closed in, the Jade warrior on its back snarling imprecations in his curious tongue.

The sword was useless.

Aram found that he had his hand on the butt of the broken spear, and in desperation he stopped struggling with the fence and gripped the length of ash with both hands, fighting the dreadful weight as he held the long pole at one end and pulled it back against the timber of the fence. The tip dropped and wavered, danced and circled. The horse was on him.

The splintered shaft missed the horse as it flicked and wobbled. The horse hit the fence hard. Somehow, and Aram could not have explained it other than as blind luck or the favour of the gods, the horse smashed through the fence and continued on into the field beyond. Aram was not only whole and unharmed, but the shattered rails of the fence where the horse had passed seemingly through – over? – him made it possible to free himself.

He staggered in confusion and realised oddly that he was unarmed. His roving eyes found his sword lying in the dust next to the fence, unbloodied still. Where had the broken spear shaft gone?

His eyes took in the horse, now racing in mad circles around the large paddock, the rider still on its back swaying with every turn, the shattered ash pole jutting from his chest.

Dead.

How had that happened? Aram was perplexed. Had that wavering point not missed? No. It had missed the horse, hadn't it? His brain reassembled the flashing jagged memories of the past few moments, and he realised what had happened. The wavering point of the spear had frightened the horse enough that it had turned slightly, smashing through the open fence next to him, rather than riding him down. And somehow as the horse had passed, the roving point of the shaft had hit the rider. Even without a steel point, braced against the fence timbers, the shaft had punched through the leather vest and the man's ribs, driving deep.

Aram looked up. Death had gone on to hunt new prey.

He was alive. He had won.

He let out a wild, crazed laugh.

Death turned back to look at him for a moment as an arrow whispered through the air close to his ear and thudded into the broken fence. Aram's head snapped around, but he was in no further danger from that source as two of his men were now busy pulling the archer from his horse and stabbing him repeatedly.

His gaze took in the scene. Could it really be over already? He'd always thought battles lasted much longer than that. They did in books and songs and paintings. Seven of his men remained standing, including their commander, though he was cradling an arm and blood was pouring from it. The enemy were down. Had he gifts to give, he would have made these men wealthy for what they had just done. But he was poor, and few men were willing to work for the tiny sums he could pay.

Something occurred to him, and he spun round, examining the fallen. Eight of his men lay dead, but that was a small figure given what they had achieved. That was not what nagged at him, though. Eleven. There were the bodies of eleven of the scouts and nine horses. The absence of horses was no worry. Horses would undoubtedly flee as soon as their riders were dead. But one of the enemy was missing.

'One got away,' Aram said in a worried whisper.

The leader of his guards nodded. 'He was wounded. He may well die.'

'Or he may find his army and tell them about us. We have to go, and we have to move fast.'

He waited impatiently, dancing from foot to foot as one of the guards bound a strip of linen around the officer's arm to staunch the blood flow. Then, gathering up what weapons they felt might be useful, they each sought one of the enemy horses, caught hold of the reins and climbed into the saddle. Mounted, they gathered together and raced through the village and out into the woodland trail beyond.

It was a terrifying ride. The meeting place was only a mile from the village, a huge clearing – more of a moor, really – where once upon a time trade fairs had been held, when the land was still rich in resources. Even as they raced along the track through the woods, continually ducking to avoid being swept from the saddle by stray branches, Aram could hear a frenzy of horn-blowing carried from some distance on the gentle breeze. Was that the sound of the Jade Empire advancing, or did it signal that a wounded scout had returned to his column with news of a group of defiant fugitives? Either way it was an ill portent.

Aram and his men burst out into the clearing and his heart leapt into his throat at what he saw there.

In his grandfather's time he had witnessed the fairs held on this sward. Many thousands of people would gather here along with tents, trade stalls and pens of animals for sale. There were just over three and a half thousand people in all of Initpur these days, and that number should fit neatly in less than a third of this space.

Why, then, was the clearing almost full?

A path opened up through the crowd as they emerged, and the riders slowed as they moved through the mass of bodies and pack animals. At the centre was the gathering of supplies that had been pulled together from the various villages and the palace. And standing in front of them were two dozen armed men in two different but unfamiliar uniforms. Aram rode towards them and reined in.

The men bowed.

'Who are you?'

'I am Mani, and this is Bajaan,' one of the soldiers replied, indicating another, dressed differently. 'We are of the men of the rajahs of Kahali and Magur, seeking new lands to settle.'

Aram frowned. The two kingdoms they had named were far to the west.

'You are travelling in the wrong direction, then,' Aram said. 'I am the rajah of this land, and the forces of the Jade Empire are mere miles from here.'

The soldier's face turned grave.

'Then we are to be crushed between hammer and anvil. The army of the emperor Bassianus has crossed the western river and moved into our lands. They have not made war upon us yet as such, but their mere passage strips the land of all food and goods, and our rajahs hand it all over in the name of peace. But we all know this Bassianus by reputation from tales from his own people. He is not a man of his word and his embassies cannot be trusted. Their generals smile now and hold out a hand in greeting, but there is death behind their smile and a dagger behind their back.'

Aram shook his head in dismay. He had been counting on being able to move into land close enough to the western empire to hold off the Jade Emperor's armies. But it seemed his grandfather's predictions were coming true. The two great powers were marching on each other and the Inda lay in between.

He mused for long, silent moments.

'It is forbidden,' he said.

'Majesty?' prompted one of the foreign soldiers.

'Mmmm?' Aram looked up. 'Oh. Thinking. We were moving west. East is not possible. And to the north are the mountain bandits and then the lords of the horse clans. There is only south.'

'But the empire will be moving all across the western lands, even stretching to the south,' the soldier called Mani said.

'None of them will go far enough south, because it is forbidden.'

The soldiers' faces paled. 'The land of ghosts?'

Aram nodded. 'It is forbidden. And sacred. And haunted. And because of that it is the one place none of our enemies will go.'

'With good reason, Majesty,' Bajaan replied. 'Men go mad and die there.'

'But there are monks just beyond the border. If they can survive there, so can we.'

There was no answer to that, though each man and woman within earshot would now be looking inward, wondering if their own soul was pure enough, their heart pious enough, to protect them as it did the monks.

'Our enemies have left us with no choice,' Aram said loudly, turning to his own people. 'One way lies the Jade Empire on its merciless war of annexation, another the western empire, with its efficient killers and mad ruler. To the north are the bandits and the horse clans who would kill us all and use our flesh for saddles. Only the spirit lands of the south remain. If the monks can survive beyond the sacred markers, then so can we. We shall cross the Nadu River and travel south along its western side until we enter the lands of the south. It is a very long journey, through dangerous lands, but we shall prevail.'

There was an air of nervous uncertainty among his people. He straightened. 'If the gathered people of Kahali and Magur wish to travel with us, then they are welcome. All the Inda need to be safe now. There is no call for rajahs in this new world, just survivors. I was a rajah, but I will be a survivor, and I pledge to make you all survivors too if you will come with me.'

It was a good speech, he thought. Good enough to rouse the spirits of most men. But there was still uncertainty here. In centuries the only men who had crossed into the ghost lands of the south were the monks who maintained the shrines and the occasional criminal on the run who was never heard from again.

'The south is frightening,' he said. 'I know. It is the unknown. But the unknown is preferable sometimes to the known. And we know what is coming through the woods right now. Listen.'

He stopped and there was an eerie silence.

There, distant, but clearly audible, were the war horns of the Jade Empire. A murmur of worry filtered through the crowd.

'If you stay here you will hear those horns becoming swiftly louder. And then you will start to hear the drums of their infantry. And then the rumble of their cavalry. And then it will be too late and you will be bowing to the Jade Emperor, at sword point if necessary.'

He turned to his own guards. 'Get the wagons moving. We make for the river at speed.'

And with that, he turned his horse to the west and started to walk it towards the great Nadu River. The very thought of passing into those dead lands in the south chilled him to the bone, but it was the only choice left, and his duty was to brave the dangers and lead these people to safety.

Safety… in the land of ghosts.

CHAPTER 6

From: Orosius Devinius
To: Petilius Iuro, Garrison commander, Lappa

Sir, please find attached the seal of Flavius Cinna, general in command, Inda Expeditionary Force. The general requires a levy of all available recruits from the Lappa region. Funds will be made available in due course from the imperial treasury. All free populace between the ages of sixteen and fifty and not engaged in a reserved occupation are required to appear before military medical boards. Training is to begin immediately for each cohort of one thousand raised at Lappa. Officers have six weeks to assemble and instruct the units before dispatch to the forward post at the Oxus bridge. Please consider this your highest priority, as any shortfall in manpower on this campaign could endanger the empire's eastern border in general, and Lappa directly.

Six weeks was all it had taken to gather the forces and bring them east. Dev had expected it to be quicker, but Cinna had assured him that from the planning to the execution of a campaign, six weeks was almost unbelievably swift, especially with some of the forces having been drawn from the western provinces and marched across half an empire to join in.

Dev watched the imperial army campaign in his homeland with a strangely detached feeling. These western rajahs were not men and lands he had known well as a boy, and did not quite feel like his people in some odd way. And they certainly seemed not to have their own good in mind, for far from joining in a grand alliance with the empire as Dev had hoped, they had mostly held out defiantly. And yet there was something familiar and heart-wrenching about that proud defiance. It reminded him of his own people when the Jade Empire's foragers had come.

General Cinna's wary optimism at the possibility of gaining allies among the Inda as they moved had gradually waned as they moved east and met ever less enthusiasm among the natives. Moreover, he had included Dev less in his council over the last week or so, perhaps seeing little value in a native who could not help deliver his people.

In fairness there had been no fighting over more than half the small kingdoms they had passed into, and where there had it had never been a truly troublesome engagement. Most rajahs had few warriors to show and little power, and the empire passed through their lands without trouble, but also without gaining the manpower or alliances they had hoped. A few of the rajahs had seen the empire coming and had sent their people east, away from the great gleaming legions, under the guard of their soldiers, sacrificing their own power and safety for the good of their citizens in a manner horribly reminiscent of a value Dev's father had always espoused. But some of the more powerful rajahs had manned their walls, steadfastly refusing to open their gates and granaries to this vast force.

Vast.

That was a laugh. Oh, it *was* a vast force, certainly in comparison to any Inda army, yet from the few sketchy reports they'd had of the Jade Empire's military moving in its three-pronged attack in the east, that monstrous oriental army dwarfed General Cinna's. And Dev knew well the tales of cannon and explosives that had won the Jade Emperor a great realm, for none could stand against such monsters. The easterners' numbers were superior, for they had such a great swathe of land from which to draw them, but the numbers were not what worried Dev and his general – it was the technology. For all the vaunted engineering prowess of the west, their world had somewhat stagnated. There had been no true breakthrough, in military terms, for centuries. What hope had they against an army of equal discipline, but with more men and better weapons?

They needed these rajahs on side, not defiant and troublesome, if they were to maintain any hope of matching the enemy.

This latest one had clearly known he was beaten from the very first parley when he realised he was facing odds of more than a hundred to one, and yet there he now stood on the walls of his fortified palace, watching his world end as his flag snapped in the breeze above him.

Dev sighed.

'When this place falls, we turn north, I think,' the general said next to him. 'Intelligence places the all-important crossing of the Nadu some fifty miles north of here and another fifty to the east. We are moving quickly through the land, but not as swiftly as I had hoped and anticipated. I had intended to be at the river by now and moving north, clearing any resistance to the rear. Instead we slog east. Your countrymen are not as submissive as you had suggested.'

Almost an accusation. Dev fought the urge to point out that he had made no such suggestion. It had been Cinna's supposition, though Dev had done nothing to disabuse him of the notion. He had *hoped* that the local lords would see sense and join them, but he had always known that any attempt to create links between Inda rajahs would be troublesome at best.

He shook his head, biting down on all his retorts and plumping for straight fact. 'It is in the nature of the Inda, General. We are all different. No two rajahs think or rule alike. It is our greatest strength, in our diversity, but it might also be our greatest weakness. There is no uniformity of thought or purpose as there is in the empire, and so no one can predict the mind of any rajah with any certainty. I believe those here in the west have had little to fear from the Jade Empire over the years and therefore do not see us as a welcome sight in opposition to an enemy they have not met. Those rajahs who have been ever under pressure would be more accepting, I think. Hopefully as we move closer to the enemy, we will find more lands willing to join with us.'

The general harrumphed, clearly unconvinced, and watched his men take another kingdom.

Four cohorts pressed on the main gate while the bulk of the army waited on the hillside. Even four cohorts gave the imperial force near ten-to-one odds, and there seemed little point in manoeuvring the many thousands of others for such a small engagement. Those units approaching the fortress gate held their shields over their heads to protect themselves from the falling rocks, tiles and occasional arrows plunging down from the crenulated walls of the palace – each shield resting upon the one in front to create a stable and protective roof of leather and wood.

This rajah *was* proud. Stupid and wasteful, but proud nonetheless. Four hundred men in position on his walls facing an army of one hundred and twenty thousand – a smaller number than the general had originally hoped, but it seemed that few units they seconded were up to the strength noted in records. Still, four hundred against over a hundred thousand made for idiotic odds. Even four hundred against the four thousand committed to the gates was breathtaking. Admittedly, the rajah and his men held a strong little place, but still it would fall easily enough. What was the point in resisting in the face of such odds?

One of the imperial captains had advocated simply levelling the place along with its master and defenders. It would have been remarkably easy with the siege engines that had trundled into camp in the wake of the army the previous night. Catapults, bolt throwers, jars of pitch and the like. Had Cinna let his artillery captain loose on the palace at dawn it would now be little more than a pile of shattered rubble with the occasional arm or leg sticking out of it. The battle would have been over almost before it began.

But the killing would have been total and indiscriminate. The whole place would have gone.

It had been the first moment in some days that Dev and General Cinna had spoken their mind at the same time and been in complete concord. Both had flatly refused to allow the artillery to crush the place. There were considerations to take into account, and not simply the humanitarian desire not to see innocent civilians killed in their thousands just to take the walls. There was still a message to be sent here to other rajahs. Admittedly they'd been sending that message over and over since they crossed the Oxus and it had seemed to have little effect on the Inda royalty thus far, but that was no good reason to change to a violent, destructive strategy.

Both Dev and the general still hoped to bring some of the natives to their banner, despite everything negative they had encountered thus far, and to do that they needed to appear to be the Inda's saviours and not their conquerors. Thus, while they could not leave a potential enemy in control of a fort behind their lines, they still sought to remove defiant commanders and their men while leaving the populace unharmed. Better still, following each of the few similar engagements they had dealt with on their journey from the

Oxus, the general had distributed money among the people for reparations once the rajahs and their warriors had been cowed. Until there was no longer any hope of alliances, this was still a battle for Inda hearts, not their lands.

There was a flurry of horn calls at the fortress gate, and Dev squinted to see what was happening now. The cohorts had finally reached the gates and were smashing at them. Their prime weapon – a great bole of ash with a cast bronze ram's head affixed to the tip – had been brought forward under the shelter of the shields and was now being swung rhythmically back and forth. Here and there a man fell to enemy missiles, and Dev and his commander watched those wounded who survived their blows staggering from the rear of the lines seeking a medic. Not for the first time Dev was grateful that his organisational skills made him valuable to command and saved him from standing in the press with sword drawn. He could fight – *had* fought, in his early days in the western army – but that was not where his talent lay. He would never be a natural swordsman, and even the most martial of armies needed men who could plan.

Bang.

The gates shook at the impact, dust billowing up around the action, and the desperate men atop the wall cast down their tiles, rocks and arrows with whatever strength they still had after the hour-long barrage. The missiles largely bounced and careened off the roof of shields harmlessly. Those men were doomed.

Bang.

Dev twitched. Why could these people not see sense? He'd explained to the general about the individuality and unpredictability of the rajahs, of course, but despite all that it was clear that *this* rajah was going to lose. Why did he not capitulate and save his people?

Bang.

Dev tried not to superimpose memories of his home on the scene before him – the gates of the palace of Initpur resounding to the blows of the ram, his father Aram atop the battlements proud and defiant. He failed. The mental image made him shiver.

Bang.

'A new tactic is required when those walls fall,' the general said to his second, quietly.

'Sir?' Dev turned to him, wincing involuntarily at the next blow from the ram.

Bang.

'I have attempted to bring peace, as we move, with the authority of the emperor, and I think we are both painfully aware that our tactic is failing.' The general glanced around, noting that his staff were all busy, then leaned a little closer and lowered his voice. 'I believe that the name of the Emperor Bassianus does not improve our case. A man who has killed more of his own citizens than any outside enemy in the past decade. It seems his poor reputation stands strong even this far from the border.'

Bang.

Dev's mind whisked him momentarily from the siege of an Inda fortress and dropped him into the imperial court. The look he'd seen in the eyes of the emperor as the northern lord's face was pierced by an arrow. The nervousness of the courtiers. The level of palpable fear in the room. The line of danger General Cinna had walked in merely by speaking his mind. He remembered his father many years ago speaking of the mad western emperor. And the stories had only got worse. The general was quite right. What kind of figurehead were they fighting under?

Bang.

The general's voice drew him back away from the sound of a bronze ram on weakening timber. 'If we are to play the part of a relief force sent to free Inda lands from the clutches of the Jade Empire – which I might say is very much the part I *wish* to play – we may need to play down imperial authority a great deal and seem to be more sympathetic to the Inda and less reliant upon our emperor. When those gates fall, I want you to take the lead in negotiations. You know what we seek. I will act as your second in the matter.'

Bang.

Dev nodded, a shiver of nervous energy running through him. He was an administrator. He'd served in the army, of course, but he was no officer or ambassador. He was a strategist and administrator, quite simply. Yet as a man Inda-born, his words might carry enough weight to change matters, as the general seemed to believe. It was certainly worth a try.

Bang.

Crack!

The gates of the fortress palace finally gave under the constant assault, the left-hand gate crashing back at a twisted angle, one great hinge torn from the stonework in which it was embedded. Another blow easily smashed the other gate aside, and the cohorts roared as they surged into the place like floodwater through a broken dam, easily overwhelming the small force behind the gates and thundering through.

Dev watched with a touch of nervousness – not for their own men, but for the Inda. The imperial army had been lucky so far, in each attack they'd been forced to launch since the Oxus, that the officers of the victorious troops had managed to keep their men under control and there had been no indiscriminate slaughter, rape or looting. Oh, there had been a couple of minor incidents, of course, but they had been dealt with swiftly and brutally under military law, and the message seemed to have sunk into the army as they watched the flesh flayed from the culprits' backs with barbed whips.

Thus there was a good level of control as the men rushed into the fortress and seized yet another kingdom. Would the rajah and his men fight to the last? In the five fights they had so far waded through, twice every last man had fought and died for his land, including the rajahs; twice the rajahs had taken their own life before the imperial troops could grab them; and once the rajah and a few choice men had somehow escaped, slipping the net and vanishing when the fortress fell.

They needed a clean win this time.

The imperial soldiers flooded the square behind the gate and were momentarily lost to view from the officers' platform a quarter of a mile from the walls. Dev watched intently, squinting into the sunlight and, after a few tense heartbeats, their men emerged onto the wall tops and the towers. There were a few small bouts of resistance and swordplay in attempts to retain control of the towers and gate top, but as the invaders' numbers grew continually on the ramparts, the fight went out of the defenders. Men across the defences cast down their swords and bows and raised their hands to the victors. The imperial officers, back on their observation mound, remained silent and motionless, watching and listening carefully. The moment of uncertainty passed. The rajah, visible as a colourful figure in gleaming gold armour on the wall top, surrendered to the imperial officers, and the kingdom was theirs. Dev cupped a hand to his ear, but they could hear only the sounds of men securing the walls. There was none of the tell-tale screaming that signified men running amok in the city.

A clean win. Hope for the future. Perhaps an opportunity.

'Come,' General Cinna said quietly, calling for his groom and swinging up expertly into the saddle. Dev did the same. Since leaving home, he had spent little time in the empire on horseback until crossing the Oxus with the general, but he had occupied much of his youth riding at Initpur, and controlled a horse with the confidence of a natural cavalryman.

In the wake of the general, he trotted towards the ruined gate, the imperial units moving aside to create a path for them. As always happened as soon as the general moved, his flag-bearer, three standards, two musicians, several senior officers and a whole unit of bodyguards seemed to appear from nowhere and fall in behind, turning it into more of a procession than an embassy.

They approached the fallen walls, the shattered gates in the damaged archway standing open like a mouth of broken fangs, and Dev felt the tension build within as they entered the fortress. A spokesman for the empire? To the Inda. Against the Jade Empire.

Their horses were taken by soldiers in the square beyond the shattered gate, and the two senior men, closely followed by their entourage, climbed the stairs to the wall walk, sweating in the burning sun. Dev was unused to such armour, and suspected he would never be comfortable wearing so much iron in the summer. The Inda defenders were now disarmed and kneeling along the parapet with their hands behind their heads, imperial soldiers covering them with spears against any sudden move.

The rajah and his vizier stood atop the gate, disarmed, but upright and proud still, despite everything. Dev felt his heart jump once more as the general slowed and let his second take the lead. The son of Aram stepped onto the gatehouse and faced the beaten Inda lord. The rajah wore a vest of bronze scales that shone like gold in the sunlight. Beneath, he was clad in tunic and trousers of blue and crimson. His head was covered with a turban of pale yellow bearing an impressive jewel at the front. His beard was neatly clipped. Dev looked him up and down, wondering at the same time how the rajah saw him. True, Dev was Inda, and he certainly had the colouring, but he had been in the empire so long he wondered whether he even looked Inda any longer. He decided in that moment that he needed to grow a beard, despite the prevailing imperial trend towards being neat-shorn and clean shaven. If he were going to attempt to appeal to the Inda, he needed to look less like an imperial lackey. He would also need to dress slightly less like a captain. Whatever he had to do to elicit a more sympathetic reaction, and shove thoughts of the mad emperor Bassianus from their mind.

'Highness,' Dev addressed the man with a bow of the head. There was a momentary glint of danger in the rajah's eye. *Highness* was an honorific applied to a member of a rajah's family – a noble who did not rule. *Majesty* would be the form of address the man was expecting, but the fact was simple: he might be noble, but he no longer ruled in this land. He was a *Highness*. No more than that.

'You are… Inda?' the man replied suspiciously.

Dev nodded. 'My father is the rajah of Initpur in the north. I have the honour to serve as a senior commander of this imperial force as well as carrying the blood of Inda kings.'

'Curse you, then,' spat the rajah.

'This doom was levelled at *your* command, Highness, not ours,' Dev said coldly, earning a warning look from the general. This was delicate. Dev counted to five and started again, calmly. 'We sought only an alliance against a mutual enemy who is rampaging through Inda lands from the east. We offered you every chance to join us and avoid conflict. Instead you chose to pit your small but noble force against those very men who would aid you against a foreign aggressor.'

The rajah's lip curled. 'In the name of your lunatic emperor, whose word is as constant as the surface of the Oxus, flowing and changing with every heartbeat. I would sooner trust a cobra than your master.'

'Still, the Jade Empire—' Dev began urgently.

'Pah!' snapped the rajah. 'The Jade Empire's reach grows ever stronger. It is said that the army moving through the north is the largest ever fielded in the history or our world, and that the emperor has countless reserves to throw after it. You seem strong enough, you believe you are strong enough, to ruin my home and my lands, but by comparison you are weak. We accept your offer and we simply die with you. But if we defy you, when the Jade Empire consumes our lands we will be vaunted and favoured as men who stood against you. If faced with two evils, young son of Initpur, it is always sensible to support the stronger.'

Dev sighed. 'Then you will not join us, even now?'

'To march with you is to make the rod with which the Jade Empire will beat us later. No. I will not march with you, even if it means my head. And nor will any strong and sensible rajah of the west. You are destined to lose, children of a mad emperor.'

Dev felt his heart sink. This was not what he'd hoped for at all. He knew the Jade Empire were strong, worried even that they were *too* strong, but was it such common belief that even western rajahs clung to it and shunned and pitied the west? How, then, could Cinna hope to hold them back? He turned to the lines of soldiers kneeling along the walls, trying not to note the look of disgruntlement on the general's face as he did so.

'The offer remains open to any man who wishes to join us in defending the Inda world against the Jade Emperor.'

There was not a sound from the soldiers. No capitulation. No acceptance. Just silent defiance still. Dev bit his cheek. 'This is insane.'

'Dev,' said the general, a warning tone in his voice once more, but Dev was incensed now and went on, sweeping his arms wide to take in the rajah, his vizier and many of his men in one gesture.

'You would *seriously* rather fight those who would aid you for fear of those who, gods willing, will never set foot upon your land?'

The rajah straightened a little. 'Once, many years ago, when my father ruled here, we had a thousand men. Now we have less than half that. Our world crumbles, son of Initpur, but as rajahs we must always put our people first. I look to the future to divine the path my people are destined to walk, and it seems clear that it is the path to the Jade Emperor. And so I place my head beneath your blade now to buy us the favour of the Jade Empire when that time comes. It is a small price to pay for a future, and no lord of the Inda would do less. You will find no ally among the rajahs, servant of a madman.'

Dev shook his head. 'There will be men of clearer vision who can see the threat posed by the Jade Empire. They will join us.'

'Only idiots and the desperate and lost will join you, and of what value are they in war? Or those as mad as your emperor, of course. Seek the Sizhad if you want an ally, but remember that when you handle fire, burned fingers are inevitable.'

'What is the Sizhad?' General Cinna put in, stepping forward now.

'Not what. Who,' the rajah replied with an odd hint of menace.

'Who, then?' Dev asked, a sudden surge of hope thrilling him.

'You have been away from Initpur many years if you do not know the answer to that, young warrior. The Sizhad is the only one who might join with you, for it is said he is as mad as your emperor. He is a bandit chief in the northern mountains.'

The general huffed his dismissal. 'Bandits. Hardly what we seek.'

'I'm not so sure,' Dev said, his brow creasing as he studied the rajah's face. 'Even when I was a boy the bandit chiefs in the north were already becoming stronger than many rajahs. Every kingdom became weaker over the decades as the Jade Empire stripped them of their assets. It did not take long for the rajahs to reach a level of insolvency in which they could not afford to maintain the glorious armies they once commanded. And where does a soldier turn when he is no longer paid? Many moved into the mountains and became bandits.'

The defeated rajah nodded. 'At one time it was said that every valley in the north had its own bandit king. We were never plagued with them here in the west, of course, but one hears all manner of tales. Slowly the more powerful bandit chiefs crushed their opposition and incorporated their warriors. The stories coming from the north now speak of this Sizhad as a madman and a zealot. A lunatic, but with an army of impressive size, and gathering more to his banner with every day the Jade Empire wages war. You want a man to help you throw back the eastern invader? The Sizhad is the only man who might answer your call. But you invite a wolf into your midst at your peril.'

General Cinna beckoned and led Dev along the wall walk, away from the rajah and his men. Once they were in relative seclusion on a tower top and the soldiers had been dismissed from it, the general stopped. 'You know these people better than I. Our strategy seems to be failing badly. Are the words of this rajah true? Will we meet the same resistance everywhere we go?'

Dev sighed. He wished he had answers to give.

'As I said before, General, it is hard to tell the mind of a rajah. But it does seem that the Jade Empire casts a longer shadow than us, and we will meet that all the more as we travel east. And the rajahs will look to the future of their people. My great-grandfather would have done precisely what this man did today. The old man looked to the future even half a century ago and saw what was coming.'

Cinna peered back at the defiant rajah and then along the line of kneeling Inda warriors.

'Captain? Execute the Rajah and his commanders.' He caught sight of Dev's crestfallen expression and sighed. 'Give his men the choice between service with the legions and following their master into the next world.'

Dev nodded. The rajah had to die. There was no denying that. At least this way the rest stood a chance...

'And is there any truth in what this man says about the bandit chief in the mountains?' Cinna said.

Dev chewed his lip. 'The bandit chiefs have always been untrustworthy and dangerous. And a zealot, the man said too. How far can a zealot *ever* be trusted? But he is certainly right about one thing: this Sizhad will be strong. The bandit chiefs have defied the strongest rajahs over the centuries and have also kept the horse clans out of their mountains. And if one of their number has become powerful enough to crush his rivals, then it is possible that he represents the edge we seek. The question is whether we can afford to rely upon him.'

The general scratched his neck thoughtfully. 'Then we need to find out more, and if he can be of value we need to bring him in. With our policy thus far failing as badly as it is, there is no point in continuing as we have been. I shall take the army and drive directly north-east for the vital crossing of the Nadu River. They believe the enemy are too powerful? Then let us meet them at a bottleneck, where their numbers and their technology become limited in value. They may have discipline, vast ranks and terrifying weapons, but they lack what has always driven the west: initiative. Even facing horrendous odds, we might be able to hold the Jade Empire there until we find support elsewhere.'

Dev felt his blood chill. He knew what was coming.

'You will take half a cohort of cavalry and Captain Tyrus, who is an excellent judge of men and forces, and find this Sizhad. Test him. Examine him between you. If you and Tyrus judge him to be what we need, negotiate and bring him to our banner. I will send two chests of gold with you as a taster for him, but I give you full authority to act on behalf of both myself and the imperial government in negotiations. Find him, Dev. And if he can help us, bring him.'

The young Inda officer shivered and hurried to hide the moment of visible weakness beneath a salute. The general either failed to notice, or ignored it, dismissing Dev with a nod.

The northern mountains.

A bandit chief.

A zealot.

Two hundred miles or more of riding. Anywhere up to five hundred miles, in fact, depending upon where in the mountains the Sizhad could be found. With the constant threat of other bandits, local rajahs and the very real possibility of bumping into the forces of the Jade Empire somewhere in a valley. The Sizhad clearly had a strong army. And Dev would ride into his lair with five hundred men and two chests of gold.

When he thought about it like that, it suggested that the emperor Bassianus was not the only madman involved in this war.

SUMMER, THE NORTHERN MOUNTAINS

The Sizhad stared down at the parched soil. The mud had cracked and receded, leaving crevasses of darkness. If one looked closely at it, it could be a distant view of a massive landscape, rather than just the patch of ground before his crossed legs. And in some way, it *was* like a microcosm of his world. Parched and brown, dusty and formed of plateaus and heights, valleys and dark ravines.

He felt his eyes drift out of focus for a moment as the drug took effect.

Leaning back slightly, he looked up into the glaring, fiery orb of the sun for as long as he could manage without his eyes burning clean and robbing him of vision. Persevere. The sun was the way. Devotion was all. Blinking, half-blinded and with odd yellow-purple blotches obscuring everything, he leaned over the bowl once more, inhaling the burning root.

The smoke filled his being, reaching out into every extremity and making his flesh tingle. The root had caught light easily this morning. A good omen. The glaring rays of the sun, focused with a single lens into a beam of light that burned through the coarse fibres. Ritual. Devotion *and ritual* were all.

Slowly, the ground coalesced into detail before him once more. He knew he was half-dreaming now, as was the way and the path.

The valleys were flooding.

No. Not the valleys. This was not his world. Just a patch of earth. The cracks in the dry dusty ground were flooding though. Was it blood? It *looked* like blood. It could be water tinted by the dusty red earth, of course. It was hard to tell with the root smoke filling him, but then that was the point of devotion and divination and prophecy. It was ever vague, the sun-granted images melding seamlessly with the real and mundane before his eyes.

The red torrents surged and crashed through the crevasses, occasionally meeting and forming stronger currents that then flooded on into new cracks. So much blood.

So much blood.

But now the blood was changing. It was still surging, but no longer along the cracks, for the ground was full, and now it was rising. Not how liquid should. It was bulging at the centre and bursting upwards into the air, leaving the cracked ground and growing like a slender column of blood in the sunlit air. The Sizhad watched in fascination as the red liquid put forth leaves and formed into smooth shapes, crafting a rose of crimson before his very eyes.

A rose from the parched earth, reaching for the sun.

Prophecy was a wondrous thing. He felt sure he knew what it meant. And it had been born from valleys flooded with blood.

Blood. It was all about blood.

Devotion and ritual *and blood* were all…

He rose, unsteadily. Two of his close companions hurried over to help him, but he waved them away and steadied himself.

'Brothers, the time is nigh. Sharpen your blades.'

PART TWO

THE EDGE OF DESTRUCTION

CHAPTER 7

The wind blows but never dies
The reed bends but never breaks
This is the way of things
Wind and reed go on
The contest is endless

War, by Gueng Ji

The urgent calls of the scouts echoed back across the wide valley. Jai glanced sidelong at General Jiang, who nodded in response. Both urged their mounts forward to intercept the agitated riders, leaving behind the bulk of the men. The column stretched on for almost three miles, despite being well spread out to the sides, given the ease of the shallow and bare terrain. An immense force that shook the world with their passage. The earth sizzled in the sun, baked dry, the grass brown and unhealthy. Dust rose in endless clouds about the booted feet of the infantry, and only the cavalry astride their mounts and the officers at the front escaped the choking miasma.

These were two of the Jade Emperor's armies now, that of the southern prong having met up and joined forces with General Jiang's column a few days earlier. The numbers were quite awe-inspiring to see, and Jai had watched the force move like a silver centipede across the dusty brown world with awe, certain that no army on earth could stand against them now. And what would it be like when the northern army joined them, he wondered? That being said, they had heard nothing from the north in over a week. While that was quite explicable and reasonable given the difficulty of the mountainous terrain there and the distances involved, Jai had found himself in darker moments wondering whether the vicious bandit chiefs in the north might be strong enough to face an army of the Jade Empire. He had kept his worries to himself, though, not wishing to concern the general, who was dealing with the lack of communication stoically.

Still, even without the northern army, the sheer size of the force was mind-boggling. Jai glanced over his shoulder as he started to move, casting an impressed gaze over the dust cloud and the great colonizing force within it. The only troops to ride at the front of the column with the commanders were General Jiang's Crimson Guard, resplendent in gleaming silver cuirass and all-red uniform beneath, right down to the wicked painted wooden face masks of the helmets, cunningly formed into the shape of legendary demons.

As Jai and the general kicked forward, the Crimson Guard split into three wings, accompanying their master on both flanks and to the rear.

The scouts – men serving in the same role as Jai had occupied just months ago – reined in on a narrow roadway between two fishing pools and bowed their heads respectfully.

'What is it?' the general asked in a businesslike manner as he hauled on the reins and stopped before them.

'Enemy sighted, General.'

'Inda?'

'Imperial, General.'

Jai felt the world lurch beneath him. They had heard that the western armies had crossed their border, of course. News of such magnitude travelled fast, after all. And it was not even as though he and the general had not been expecting something like this, but he'd never thought it would happen so *soon*. He was not sure he'd ever be prepared to hear such tidings, mind, and suddenly the unpleasant truth of the situation impressed itself upon him. While they had been conquering, annexing and negotiating with Inda lords, it had felt surprisingly glorious and simple. It had been something of an adventure. It had not truly felt like a war. This changed things entirely. The empire would not capitulate or be so easily overwhelmed.

'So soon?' General Jiang replied, mirroring Jai's feelings perfectly.

The scout simply nodded.

'They have moved with impressive speed, then,' the general mused. 'I had expected to come within perhaps fifty or a hundred miles of their border before a major reaction. They cannot have moved thoroughly through Inda territories as we did, securing each land. They have not had time. Jai, what is your assessment of their motives and methods?'

Jai pursed his lips as he thought on the matter. 'If they are not consolidating as they go it means they have focused on a goal, and that goal is almost certainly us. They have ignored all else in a rush to confront us. They are not intending to control the Inda, they are just coming to oppose the forces of the Jade Emperor.'

The general nodded. 'Quite so. This imperial general is focused, as you say, and it is on us that he is focused, which concerns me. He has come fast and direct for one reason, Jai: Jalnapur.' Jai nodded, realising what that meant. In the excitement of the news, he had forgotten quite where they were. Less than a mile away, at the end of the valley, lay Jalnapur, the fortress palace on the Nadu River. The only feasible crossing for an entire army throughout its great north-south length. It was the key to the west of the Inda Diamond. Or conversely, the lock, if you were an imperial general intent on preventing Jade Empire expansion.

'I had assumed we would be across the Nadu before we met them,' Jai said quietly.

'I too,' the general replied, 'but the wily enemy general has sacrificed security to his rear in order to reach this place before us and secure it. It is, I fear, a failing in our culture that we are sometimes unable to think in such fluid terms. The empire has bred intuition out of its sons in return for total obedience. It is our strength, but I sometimes fear it is also our curse, as seems to now be the case. Our latest reports suggest that we outnumber the enemy two to one – though that cannot be confirmed until I see them with my own eyes – which would give us a tremendous advantage in the open field. But at a bridge? A determined man with a hardened force could hold a bridge against superior numbers for a very long time indeed. The only sure ways to dislodge an enemy from such a position are either by trickery and subterfuge or by simply throwing men and resources at it in swathes and hoping that a gap opens up in the midst of the killing.'

'I do not like the sound of the latter,' Jai replied.

'Quite. That would reduce our forces, even if we win, to unmanageable levels. But sadly the former is not likely. This general is clearly sharp. I doubt he would fall for trickery. Which leaves us with two equally unpleasant possibilities. Either we settle in for a long fight and a war of attrition, or we accept that this is the furthest we go and seek another path somewhere north or south. Again, the former is not to be wished for, but the latter is the sort of decision that makes heads fall off back at the imperial court.'

Jai sighed. 'So what do we do, General?'

'We try everything we can short of direct assault. To begin with, we have two advantages: numbers and artillery. Numbers only come into play when attrition becomes the killer or in open field warfare. But artillery? In my understanding, the westerners rely upon torsion projectile weapons, launching bolts and rocks like backward barbarians. We, however, have cannon. Before we commit men to an endless war, we try everything, and first we see if we can pulverise them into submission.'

He wagged a finger in the air. 'But before we attempt any kind of action, we need to meet with them. However strange these western men might be, they are said to be civilised, and civilised men talk before they draw a blade. If there is even a hope that we can resolve this without vast bloodshed, it is our duty to do just that.'

Jai nodded, and without further pause the two men rode for Jalnapur, the scouts accompanying them and the Crimson Guard retaining their protective formation. The valley was wide, the seasonal stream at the centre long since dried for the year, and the collection of horsemen rode easily around the long, gentle curve until the vale opened out into the wide floodplain of the Nadu River. The vast swathes of bright green crops here were an odd sight after so many days of parched brown vegetation, and the general held up a hand to stop them at the edge of the great plain.

The enemy were visible a mile away as a huge mass of shapes scattered over the flat land on the far bank, though it was near impossible to pick out much detail at this range. Jai wondered why the general had stopped, and waited as Jiang rubbed his chin, deep in thought.

'Such wide fertile plains are not simply fed by one river, no matter how large. The Nadu floods, Jai.'

89

'Yes, sir.'

'Is it a simple matter of meltwater in the spring, or the effect of the monsoons of which I hear?'

Jai frowned. They had never suffered seasonal flooding in Initpur, at least not on the scale it was witnessed in Jalnapur. The area was too dry and hilly. They had seen occasional burst river banks and the like at home, but nothing that did more than surprise a few farmers and cattle. He tried to think back on what he knew of the Nadu and the central Inda lands from his father and grandfather.

'There *is* meltwater flooding – we see it in Initpur – but that is not responsible for this fertile land. This is certainly because of the monsoons.'

He'd heard of such weather, of course, even if it did not affect life in the northern hills. Dreadful, incessant rain so hard it tore through leaves and sent animals running for cover, flooding the low-lying ground and making it dangerous for months, then incredibly fertile for half a year. Fragile structures were washed away within monsoon months, the unwary drowned, plains flooded...

He caught the look in the general's eye.

'Monsoon season is already upon us,' he said nervously. 'It is unusual, I think, that it has been dry this long.'

'So we can expect to be subject to deluges in the coming days, and these flat lands separating us from the western empire's army will become a quagmire, or possibly one great lake.'

Jai peered out across the plain. The imperial troops beyond the river had deployed on the flat ground near the bridge. Were they unaware of the possibility of monsoon, or were they not concerned about it? Was their general even half as clever as Jiang seemed to expect?

'This terrain and the season could effectively nullify our artillery advantage,' the general sighed.

'Sir?'

'We can field men down there facing the enemy, much as they have, but we cannot place the cannon there. Their weight and the pressure they exert upon discharge make them unstable on soft ground, and they are too unmanageable to move swiftly if the rains come. It takes half an hour to remove them from their cradles and load them onto carts, and the oxen draw them away slowly too. We could find ourselves fleeing for high ground in a growing inundation and not being able to bring the cannon with us. It is an unpleasant choice to make. The artillery are either effective and at extreme risk, or they are safe and largely ineffective. I do not mean to lose my cannon and the advantage they grant, which means that we must deploy the cannon on the valley sides, here. They might still be able to touch the enemy, but it will be at maximum range. I shall be interested to see what the enemy have done with the disposition of their forces, given the terrain and potential flooding.'

He turned and called to one of the Crimson Guard officers.

'Wait here with your men. As the army arrives, have the cavalry move to the north and position themselves for my return. The bulk of the infantry should deploy at the edge of the plain before us here. Have the cannon masters site their weapons on the ridges facing Jalnapur and the bridge. No weapon is to be within twenty feet of the flood plain's level. I shall return shortly.'

The officer saluted and, accompanied by the remaining two thirds of the guard, Jai and the general rode down to the flat, fertile fields, selecting a low, wide causeway that carried a road to the bridge. By necessity the horsemen pulled in, moving four abreast at most. Despite the potential danger of riding directly into the enemy's sight, the general insisted upon leading the way, the Crimson Guard at their back, and Jai took in every detail of the field of battle as they approached.

The Nadu River was almost half a mile across, a vast force of water cutting through the land like the wavy blade of a sacrificial knife. The bridge – a grand, decorative, white stone edifice – was one of the greatest structures ever built by the Inda. A feat of art and engineering both, linked to a causeway on both sides that rose above the common flood level, it was famous even in Initpur. The fortress palace, and the connected walled city of Jalnapur, rose on the far bank beside the river, again on ground high enough that the rising waters during monsoon season could not flood the streets. The palace itself, walled only low on the river side, was one of the most breathtakingly beautiful buildings Jai had ever seen, all ornate windows and arches and graceful balconies in white and gold with delicate turrets twisting up into the blue. Interestingly, there was no sign of imperial military on its walls.

The enemy forces were scattered. Though they had appeared one great mass from the far bank, the truth was clearer from close up. The enemy general had deployed his forces carefully, using every facet of the landscape, some close to the bridge and the river bank, others further back. Missile troops were clearly stationed close to infantry in small groups to support one another. Each area of manpower had been fortified with low earth banks, wicker fences and shields of timber lathes. An impressive feat. And another example of how different these westerners were. That they split their force up into such small units of a thousand, even a hundred men, and yet trusted them to follow a plan. The force of the Jade Empire simply could not function like that. The chain of command had to be in place. Without senior commanders passing the orders down, disseminating like ripples along a cobweb, the ranks of men would be uncertain and unable to act appropriately. Did the westerners have command capability even at such low levels? But in a way, Jai could understand how. In the east there was one branch of the military that functioned in such a way, and he was intimately familiar with them: the scouts.

Here and there, Jai could see earth mounds with wooden structures and machines atop them, and it took him moments to realise what they were. The imperial general had solved his artillery issues by having his men raise artificial hills upon which the machines were placed. Unless floodwaters rose high enough to submerge the bridge, his machines would be safe on islands amid the lake. Jai was impressed, and so, judging by his expression, was General Jiang. Perhaps this man *was* as astute as the general had thought after all. Jiang was right: these westerners took chances, thought outside rigid lines.

They rode onto the bridge slowly, Jai's heart beginning to pound nervously. There was a myriad of odd noises from the forces spread across the far bank, and any number of them could signify those great bolt throwers preparing to loose deadly missiles, as far as Jai knew. He could picture himself or the general being plucked from their horses and hurled back into the guardsmen's ranks, dead on impact.

Even as an academy-trained master swordsman, with a passing knowledge of the art of cutting arrows from the air, there was no form invented by man that could save a man from artillery fire. He shuddered, but no great arrow came.

The two men, backed by an army of demon-faced, red-clad riders, came to a halt halfway across the bridge and waited. It took some time, but finally a man on horseback emerged from the imperial forces, six gleaming riders in white tunics and silvered scale shirts behind him. The man was dressed in a similar white tunic, but with a cuirass of bronze decorated with two embossed stallions, a ribbon of red tied around his chest and a cloak of crimson hanging from his shoulders. He was a serious-looking, heavily built man.

The enemy commander rode onto the bridge confidently and reined in a dozen paces from the Jade Empire's officers.

'A grand day for such an auspicious meeting,' the man said in the imperial tongue. Jai quickly translated it in his head. Their language was well-known to many of the Inda, for imperial traders had journeyed well beyond their border for centuries. Jai opened his mouth to translate for the general and was surprised when Jiang replied in perfect western imperial, with just a slightly odd oriental accent.

'We must make the most of such clement weather,' his commander said, conversationally. 'I understand the monsoon season is overdue.'

Small talk. Jai frowned. It seemed odd to hear in the circumstances.

'The monsoons will make warfare difficult,' the imperial general replied. 'Perhaps even impossible. They last for up to three months yet, or so I am told. This could be a very slow, dull, wet season.'

'But with remarkably little blood,' Jiang noted. 'Perhaps we should pray to our respective gods to send us monsoons at their earliest convenience.'

The imperial general laughed.

'Now would that not be something? For us to inform our emperors that war was cancelled on account of rain.'

Now General Jiang chuckled too. 'I am not convinced that such an excuse would satisfy the Jade Emperor. Nor, from what I hear, your emperor Bassianus.'

The man nodded. 'I am Flavius Cinna, commander of the imperial expeditionary force.'

'How grand,' smiled his opposite. 'An *expedition* sounds so much more pleasant than an invasion. I am Xeng Shu Jiang, general of the Jade Empire's Inda occupation force.'

'And there, in a nutshell,' replied Cinna, 'is where the problem lies. My master is not content to sit back and allow the Jade Emperor to occupy the lands of the Inda.'

Jiang nodded. 'I understand, though I am at a loss to understand his reasoning, beyond the simple desire for war. Your empire constantly invades and annexes lands, and the Inda owe you no fealty. As such, any move against us is a simple act of aggression and cannot be considered an attempt to preserve the Inda's sovereignty.'

Flavius Cinna nodded. 'Let us not descend into accusation. I would like to think we are above such things.'

Jiang smiled. 'Good. Let us put forth our positions succinctly so that we can move on to the unpleasant business of crushing one another's forces. I am here with my army at the behest of the Jade Emperor with a remit to annexe all lands of the Inda from the northern boundary with the horse clans to the forbidden lands in the south, and as far as the Oxus River, granting us a solid border with your empire, across which we can trade and coexist peacefully. If you will remove your forces beyond the Oxus and leave the Inda to us, there need be no further conflict.'

Cinna straightened in his saddle. 'Similarly, the emperor Bassianus, Light of the West, Child of the Divine, First Citizen and Father of His People commands that the illegal invasion force of the Jade Empire remove themselves beyond their former border and abandon all land conquered from the Inda. If you comply with this simple request, I shall withdraw imperial forces, the Inda shall once more be free and there shall be no war.'

The two men sat silent for a moment.

'Of course, neither of us can accept the other's terms,' Cinna said eventually, 'because we are both bound by duty to our emperors and neither of them is a man given to bending to the will of another. You will understand that I cannot defy my master's orders, and I am aware that the same applies to you. And so we are at an impasse. An impasse that can only end in victory for one of us.'

'Or mutual destruction,' Jiang said wearily.

'Indeed. You have an advantage of numbers, but I fear that the terrain nullifies that. I am an expert at not sacrificing men unnecessarily, and there are a large number of reinforcements being gathered from several sources. The outcome here is far from certain.'

'Then we should most definitely pray for the monsoons,' Jiang said with an odd smile.

'I have no wish to open a conflict. We are here in order to help prevent conquest, not to bring death unduly. Thus we shall withhold action until the first of your men sets foot within fifty paces of the bridge,' Cinna announced, 'excepting, of course, yourself, your adjutant and your fearsome guard. You may return to your army unmolested.'

Jiang inclined his head. 'I am afraid I can make no such promise, given that your force is already close to the bridge. Parley is complete, I believe. Now the war begins. It is a sad and rather shameful war, and I deplore my part in it, but duty is duty, and I must commit. It has been a pleasure, General Cinna, and a shame we could not meet under more peaceable circumstances.'

The imperial general saluted casually. 'Would that the emperors sought out *our* ears rather than we theirs, eh? War it is, then. Good luck, General Jiang.'

'And you, General Cinna.'

The Jade Empire's commanders turned and began to ride back across the bridge. Once they were out of earshot, the general pulled in beside Jai.

'What did you learn?'

Jai frowned. 'Their commander is clever and noble. Perhaps even a match for you,' he added hesitantly.

'Indeed. I thought as much myself. And he is as unhappy about this meeting as I. This conflict will be long and difficult, I think. He has no more wish to throw away lives than I. What else?'

'His army is curiously spread out across the plains, with reserves at least as far as the slopes a mile beyond the river.'

'Yes. He has positioned his army carefully to make it almost impossible for us to accurately estimate his numbers or strengths in terms of any particular class of troop. And they are highly mobile like this. He can have large numbers of men at the bridge, the riverbank or the town at short notice, and equally can have them retreat to high ground speedily. The man has dug in with remarkable speed. Did you see his supply wagons?'

'No,' frowned Jai.

'They were on the hill in the distance – just visible, but clearly still arriving. That suggests that Cinna's army has been here for little more than a day. Two at the most.'

Jai whistled through his teeth. 'And in that time he has raised artillery mounds and dug in and fortified. He *is* quick. And shrewd.'

'But despite the fact that he claims to oppose us and have no interest in the Inda, I note that there were no Inda allies visible among his forces, and he has seemingly not occupied Jalnapur. I do not think the Inda are any more supportive of him than they are of us, for all his words. However, we cannot consider the town a weak point. They will be no more inclined to welcome us than the western empire. And you can be sure that Cinna has artillery in positions to cover any approach across the water to the town.'

'What do we do, then, General?'

'We start to test them. We keep our forces well back from the river and use the cannon, even at full range. And we need to determine the strength and range of their artillery. I loathe the very idea of sacrificing men, but we must know their capabilities if we are to plan a strategy. Come on.'

They rode back across the causeway and the flat land to the slopes half a mile from the river, where the army was currently falling into formation. There would be no hiding *their* numbers from General Cinna, though that seemed less important in the grand scheme of things. Unless something unexpected had happened, both Jiang and Jai knew they outnumbered the enemy by a good margin, and Cinna knowing that could only help.

The two officers waited, tense and silent, at the best viewpoint – a sandy ridge two thirds of the way up the slope – while the army deployed. It would take half the day for the vast force just to move out into the valley, but Jiang had defied usual military convention and had the cannon positioned just a third of the way along the column rather than at the rear, so the great artillery pieces were already finding positions and being unloaded and assembled within the hour. Once six cannon were positioned in a line along the hillside, and others still being brought forward, Jiang rode across to them, gesturing to the officer in command of those artillery pieces.

'I want two shots from each gun,' he commanded. 'A full barrage of six at a time. Have each artillerist pick a position among the nearest of the enemy, and coordinate with each gun crew so that no two select the same target. I understand that there will be some need to find range with the first shot and I am content that many of them will disappear into the river, but I must make one thing clear: no shot is to touch the bridge. We cannot afford to damage the crossing, or the west is lost to us.'

The officer saluted and General Jiang rode back down to Jai. 'Now we see whether our cannon can reach the enemy. It is a stretch at such a range.'

There was a long pause, during which the sounds of thousands upon thousands of infantry and cavalry settling into position echoed across the valley side. Finally, a runner approached the two officers, bowing deep and delivering the compliments of the artillery commander. He was ready. General Jiang had the flag waved, and the two men watched, breathing slowly and expectantly.

The cannon fired almost simultaneously, one gun slightly behind the others. Jai concentrated on the results, but in his mind's eye he could imagine that gunner being upbraided by the officer for his tiny delay.

The whole valley fell silent as the boom echoed across the hills and up and down the Nadu River.

It was hard to keep track of all the shots, and Jai saw the results of only four of them. Two disappeared with an eruption of water somewhere in the middle of the river. One struck the side of the causeway leading up to the bridge and bounced off at a tangent, carving a path through crops and coming to rest some way short of the river. The fourth shot actually came down on the far side of the river, ploughing into the ground some ten feet or so from a position of enemy troops behind their earth bank and wicker shields.

'Pray the second volley improves,' muttered the general to Jai, 'or we can consider our advantage a waste.' The two men waited, tense. Across the valley nothing moved. The shock of the barrage had stopped everyone. Just visible half a mile away, citizens of Jalnapur had gathered at the low river wall to watch with horrified fascination. None of these people would have seen cannon in action before.

The second volley was in perfect time, six shots resounding with one retort. Jai held his breath as the great stone missiles arced out into the sizzling air. Once more he lost track of some of them. Two more vanished into the depths of the Nadu. One scored a long trough through the ground on the far bank. The fourth he saw strike the turf mound protecting a small imperial unit. The bank exploded in a shower of brown dirt that was thrown into the air to a height of three men. A similar cloud off to the left told Jai that one of the ones he'd lost track of had also hit. Both targets were within perhaps twenty paces of the river. No shot had yet gone beyond that, but still, it had to have the imperial soldiers shitting themselves that the Jade Empire had weapons that could reach across the valley and the river from the very periphery and still kill.

When the clouds of earth settled, Jai was disappointed to note that the missiles had simply dislodged earth and thrown it into the air as they embedded themselves, and had not torn through the banks and into the units behind. The cannon had clearly thus far brought them no closer to success. General Jiang's face was bleak as he turned to an officer standing nearby.

'Order a unit of scouts to cross the causeway and approach the bridge. They will be placed in grave danger for some time, but that cannot be helped. Their bravery will be noted in dispatches and reflected in rewards. They need to get close enough to the bridge to draw enemy missiles. The imperial general said that he would not loose artillery until we were within fifty paces of the bridge, so the riders need to get close enough to open hostilities. As soon as the enemy shoot at them, they need to plant a red spear in the ground. They will then trot their horses back to us ten paces at a time, planting a spear in the ground each time until the enemy missiles stop coming. That will give us some indication of their effective ranges. Jai, keep a careful watch. I imagine their catapults will have the longest range, and their bolts will stop loosing first.'

Jai sat astride his horse on the bluff and watched as a unit of one hundred scouts on horseback, drawn from the Jade Empire's northern badlands, trotted out onto the causeway, closing on the bridge. He peered tensely into the distance as the riders neared the great white crossing. His breath was shallow, nervous.

He'd been waiting for it, of course. They all had. And yet the response almost unhorsed him, so much did it make him jump. The western empire did not have black powder. Nor cannon nor rockets. Nothing that made a loud, impressive bang. And yet here and now the artillery of General Cinna brought a lump to Jai's throat.

They made no noise. Not at this distance, anyway. Probably closer to the bridge they could be heard, but from up on the ridge they were more or less silent, especially compared to the noisy cannon. The enemy artillery were so well spread out across the far bank that Jai had not thought there to be many. Cinna's response to the riders disabused him of that notion immediately.

Unexpectedly, given the lack of accompanying noise, Jai watched in horror as around a hundred imperial missiles converged on the scouts. The result was utter carnage. Great iron bolts as long as a man's arm transfixed horse and rider alike. Balls of stone as large as the ones the cannon released pulverised men and beasts. And as if that were not enough, two great pottery jars smashed into the ground amid the unit and exploded, sending out burning pitch in flying, scorching droplets.

Jai's eyes were wide. The hundred horsemen were gone. In five heartbeats two hundred living, proud creatures had become a mass of mangled, burning limbs, thrashing and screaming. There was no way artillery of any sort could be that accurate without some practice. Clearly the imperial artillery had been on site long enough for every artillerist to find and mark his range.

Jai's horrified gaze turned to the general, whose face was stony.

'Lesson learned,' Jiang said in hoarse tones. 'Do not underestimate General Flavius Cinna.'

CHAPTER 8

The gods love and protect, hate and destroy. The gods nurture and encourage, demand and punish. It is the way of gods. But they also teach. In the early days of the Inda, the gods would select promising men and send them visions and understanding. Those men would become gurus, often living ascetic lives in high and forbidding places that are nearer to the cloud-homes of the gods. Those gurus would in turn disseminate wisdom to the people.

The last guru among the Inda was already dead by the time of my great-grandfather's grandfather, which should perhaps have been seen as a sign of what was to come.

One of the most revered of Inda teachings is respect for the dead. When the Inda die, their body, which is simply the shell for a good person to inhabit, is burned and the ashes scattered on water. As the body is consumed, the spirit leaves the mortal shell, is cleansed and refreshed, purified and made ready to be born into a new shell. Thus the people will always go on. But sometimes the body cannot be cremated, and this is a dreadful thing. Because if the shell remains, the spirit is tied to it and cannot move on.

These are what we call ghosts or spirits. They can be good, it is said, but most are not, because whether a man is good or not while living, the sheer torture of being tied to an unpurified corpse and the mortal world drives him mad with rage. No one knows when the southern lands of the Inda became the province of such tortured souls, or what happened there to cause such a state of affairs, but the spirits have ruled that land since time immemorial.

It is said that the last guru was the man who taught the way to contain the south, who set the monks to its protection and maintenance. It was he who had the line of markers created and the guardian monasteries and their orders instituted. He was the last guru, and without him there would be no control there. *In my lifetime I have never heard of a living soul – with the exception of the guardian monks – willingly passing into the land of ghosts.*

Until now.

Aram glanced back over his shoulder. He could not see the valley where the refugees waited, but then, with the endless downpour, he was lucky to be able to see his own hand before his face. The monsoon had begun days ago. The mass of travellers, now numbering many thousands with the occasional hopeless wanderers collected along the journey south, had watched nervously as the great wind had come up suddenly, sweeping in from the south-east. The clouds gathered like hungry raptors over the central Inda hills, great boiling blue-grey waves in the air. Then the rains came.

Aram and his people were largely unprepared. The monsoon season barely touched the northern hills, and few of those in the huge throng of humanity travelling south had ever encountered such precipitation.

Within hours the small seasonal streams they had been lightly crossing had become torrents of churning water carrying pieces of vegetation along with them. Slowly, wearily and carefully, the army of humanity moved on, keeping parallel with the great River Nadu.

They had come upon the war zone rather suddenly after the sixth day of torrential rain. The mass of bodies had been slogging through the jungle along one of the trade paths, feet sinking into churned mud, when the western empire's pickets found them. There had only been fifty or so imperial troops in the group, compared with the vast number of travellers, though few of those among the Inda refugees were armed or trained for war and so Aram had held his hands up and approached in peace. The soldiers had demanded to speak to the leader of this great column. Aram, along with the officers Mani and Bajaan and a few warriors, had bowed to the pickets, and had been escorted to the imperial commander in his headquarters not far from the walls of the city.

Aram's heart had gone out to each and every human at Jalnapur, be they Inda, western or eastern. The locals were suffering in that they were trapped within their city with war raging outside the walls, likely starting to feel the privations and hunger as well as the danger. And the two great armies were to be equally pitied as they slowly and systematically pounded each other into ruin across the great

101

river. If Aram had still maintained any hope for the future, the sight of Jalnapur stripped it away.

The monsoon had not put an end to the fighting, but it had clearly changed its nature. The vast majority of the imperial manpower rested in sullen, sodden camps on ridges and high bluffs around the Jalnapur basin, the flat lands near the river little more than an uninhabitable quagmire. The same had happened on the far side of the river among the Jade Emperor's men. And yet there were small pockets of soldiers on the causeways and the raised platforms watching the bridge and manning artillery. Despite the conditions, imperial catapults threw their great rocks through the downpour in a futile attempt to dislodge the small parties of eastern soldiers. And occasionally a noise like the splitting of a mountain would ring out across the river as the Jade Emperor's cannon discharged and pounded naught but sodden earth on this bank.

Aram had been escorted to the general, one Flavius Cinna. The man had been courteous and polite, if a little formal. He had expressed a desire to address the refugees in an attempt to persuade some of them into joining the war on his side. Aram had refused. These, he said, were the poor victims of war seeking refuge and peace, not a place to die for a foreign power. To his credit, the imperial general had been quite accepting and understanding. He had been contrite that he could offer no help to the refugees. His provisions were barely adequate for the men under his command, since the monsoon had disrupted his supply lines back to the west. In the end, Flavius Cinna had sent Aram on his way with good wishes and the somewhat unnecessary advice to move swiftly out of the war zone and find somewhere safe.

An argumentative fellow in Aram's small party had voiced the possibility of staying in the west, waiting out the war to see if perhaps the westerners might be victorious and grant them some kind of a future. Aram had, with a heavy heart, discounted that possibility. Even if the westerners did triumph at Jalnapur, it would bode ill for the Inda. General Cinna might offer concessions, but he was just a soldier in the army of a madman who would then rule the Inda world. Besides, with the depredations the war had wrought in the region, how would they survive so many months' wait? Many would starve. No. Moving on was the only option.

And so Aram had returned to his weary people and they had moved on, skirting the great miasma with its downhearted armies and their pointless attempts at mutual destruction. So vast was the war zone that it took three days to pass before they reached an area that was not filled with camps and pickets and foragers.

The copious food stocks the refugees had brought from their homelands had swiftly dwindled on the journey and, while the jungles, forests and lakes of the Inda Diamond were replete with sources of nourishment and the column packed with farmers, fishermen and hunters, the days spent journeying through the lands of Jalnapur were hungry ones, for the soldiers had already farmed, fished and hunted the region almost bare.

It came as a relief when the column once more moved into relatively untouched lands, and meat, fish and foraged fruit and vegetables became sufficient once more to support the refugees. It had quickly become apparent that they were not the only occupants of the south. Throughout their journey they repeatedly came across small scout units from both empires. While it was not feasible for a huge force like the Jade Emperor's army to cross the Nadu here where it ran to almost a mile wide, small units had crossed in boats in order to rove, scout, spy and forage. Here and there as they moved south, Aram and his people would come across the evidence of engagements between the enemy forces. A clearing full of bodies, skin white as marble, agonised expressions locked onto their faces in death. Blades lying around, discarded and coated with mud and blood, slowly rusting in the corrosive atmosphere of monsoon season. Elsewhere a collection of bloated grey-blue uniformed bodies had jammed up against a log, forming a dam in a small river, washed down there from some unknown conflict upstream.

It filled Aram with dismay to see so many untended dead. He was no guru or deep philosopher, and couldn't have said whether because the foreigners did not adhere to the Inda's beliefs their afterlives worked in a different manner. But in his experience, no matter what a man believed happened after the moment of death, almost all cultures advocated a respectful and ceremonious disposal of the body. Would this endless slew of violent deaths and the abandoned, unattended corpses it created eventually turn the entire Inda

Diamond into an extension of the land of ghosts? It was a horrifying concept. An empire of the dead.

Nine more days they journeyed, keeping back from the river and moving warily, waiting and moving around patrols when they encountered them. Finally Aram had spoken to a local fisherman, who had told him that the line of markers which heralded the edge of the dead lands was less than an hour's good walk away. Aram had suspected as much. For the last day or more of travelling, they had gradually passed fewer and fewer settlements, not because they had been cleared due to the war as further north, but because they had never been founded in the first place. Few people were comfortable living so near the land of ghosts.

Knowing how close they were, and still close to choking on fear at the very prospect of moving into the dreaded southern lands, Aram had left the column resting in a wide valley nearby while he and a small party of his trusted men moved south to examine the way ahead.

The rain, which had been incessant now for many days and had turned the world into a quagmire, battered down upon his head, and the constantly drumming thunder of heavy drops on waxy leaves made even loud conversation difficult. Thus they almost walked into the midst of disaster completely unwittingly. In fact, Aram had stepped out of the undergrowth onto the bank of the tiny racing stream before Mani grabbed him and hauled him back. The small party ducked into the lush greenery and peered out at the scene before them.

A party of twenty or so Jade Empire scouts had stumbled upon a group of western soldiers of smaller number. The Inda watched in sickened dismay as the fight unfolded. Half a dozen men were already dead, most of them western, though two Jade soldiers in their grey uniforms lay gurgling and crying among them. As they watched, a Jade Empire officer hefted a long spear with a crimson streamer trailing just below the gleaming head and rammed it down, punching through the leather protection of his opponent's armour, grunting and heaving as the point found a soft spot between ribs, and pushing down until the weapon stood proud of the screaming victim. The easterner simply let go of the shaft and ripped his sword from its sheath – a delicate blade with a slight curve, the hilt of carved ivory.

The transfixed, dying western soldier clutched at the weapon rising from his chest, howling and crying as his killer leapt into the fray to butcher another.

The rain washed away the vast torrents of blood, but the death and carnage was still there to see. An arm severed below the elbow. A leg transfixed with a spear, the wounded man yelling his pain as he toppled to the ground to flounder in agony in the mud. Swords punched through leather, linen, flesh, muscle, organs.

Men screamed and swords clashed, all oddly muted and barely audible over the thunder of water on foliage. Aram was uncertain what to do. He and the half dozen men with him remained still and silent, watching as the last few western soldiers were done away with. Nine eastern scouts remained as they began to move round the clearing, administering swift and precise killing blows to any wounded man. Aram risked a whispered question to the Inda warrior by his side.

'Why are they killing even those with *light* wounds?'

It was horrifying, but Aram watched as an eastern scout with a flesh wound on his leg that would leave him with little more than a limp was quickly and efficiently dispatched. Bajaan, his face creased in disgust, gestured towards the great river, just visible through the trees. 'They are in unfamiliar lands and cut off from their people. They cannot afford to be slow and careful for the sake of one wounded man, so they kill him and continue to move swiftly and subtly. It is barbaric, but in their eyes it is sensible.'

'And there is also the possibility in these conditions of infections in the wound,' Mani added. 'Many of those who survive the injury will die from disease unless they are treated by a man of medicine, and these scouts will have no such luxury.'

Aram nodded his own sadness at such a thing, trying not to feel angry at these foreigners who would now leave the bodies of their dead in the dell to become yet more restless spirits roaming the world of the Inda. But what did he care now how many new ghosts there would be, when he was bound for a land already filled with them?

His heart lurched as he took in the brutality and suddenly found his eyes locked in a mutual gaze with one of the Jade Empire scouts. Even as the soldier shouted and started waving a warning to his companions, Aram felt Mani and Bajaan grabbing him and hauling him backwards into the jungle.

Then they were running as behind them the scout tried to make himself understood in the torrential and deafening rain.

'Where are we going?' Aram managed between breaths as they pounded across a narrow churning torrent of water and onto a muddy trail between heavy-hanging boughs.

'South.'

'South?'

'You'd prefer we went north and led them to the civilians?' Bajaan asked harshly, and Aram nodded and ran on, the sounds of pursuit just audible through the roar of the monsoon rains as the half dozen Inda thundered along the wet track.

'Wait,' hissed Mani, coming to a sudden stop. The others slithered to a halt behind him and looked at the ground ahead to which their companion was pointing. The muddy track was covered in boot prints. A group of people had already been along here at some point.

'You think there are more ahead?' Aram whispered.

'I don't care. Whoever they are, they've helpfully laid us a false trail. Come on.'

Mani jumped sideways into the thick grass and then hurried into the deeper foliage. Bajaan did the same, gesturing for Aram to follow. The old man did so, with little grace and some difficulty, and the other warriors followed suit until the whole group were off the path. They shuffled ten paces from the trail and huddled behind the splayed bole of a tree, creepers and shrubs growing up around it and helping hide them.

They saw the enemy scouts before they heard them. Aram and his men hunched down and tried to make themselves small and invisible as the grey-clad eastern soldiers pounded along the trail, following the footprints south. They shouted to one another in their strange, sing-song language as they ran, disappearing from sight after a few moments. Mani and Bajaan shared a look, counting under their breath. When they reached a sufficiently high number, they gestured back to the trail.

'That was all of them. Now we go.'

And that was that. In a matter of heartbeats the small Inda party was back on the muddy trail and moving north towards the valley a couple of miles away where the refugees waited. Half an hour later the great flood of humanity began to flow south once more and, despite his own words of reassurance and the comments from Mani and Bajaan, Aram felt increasingly tense and nervous with every footstep. He half-expected a spear to lance out of the undergrowth and rip into him, or screaming easterners to leap onto the path.

Nothing happened.

Slowly, they moved south, the path widening to allow as many as three or four people to walk abreast. Gradually the column shortened as the walkers gathered as close as they could for safety. Even moving three or four abreast the column was over a mile long, such was the number of souls travelling south, and the pack beasts at the end dragged it out even further, though only the fittest of the beasts remained. The carts had long since gone, and the slower beasts had become casualties of hunger as they passed the depleted war zone.

The vegetation was gradually changing now, more exotic and unusual plants proliferating as they moved ever further from Aram's home in the northern hills. Aram, as nervous about their destination as he was about those they might meet on the way, almost turned round as they reached the markers. Some things were less palatable even than dreadful war.

Placed here before any living memory, the markers drew a stark line between the living and the dead. They said, with their bleak, stone faces, that no man could live beyond them, that the dead ruled here. Oh, there were the monks, of course, who looked after the markers, but they were holy men, protected by the gods. No common man ever passed these markers. The old stories were terrifying.

This particular marker was ancient, even by Inda standards. It was a pillar of stone standing four times the height of a man. The main column was carved into narrow pilasters, each filled with grotesque faces and grasping, stony hands. The base was covered in the script of the ancients who had first learned the ways of the Inda gods, a language only monks and holy men learned these days. But the top...

Aram shivered. The top of the column had been carved into two figures, one facing south and the other north. The one he could see, glaring in his direction, was a human figure, with a handsome, if rather stylised face. But the carver had done something odd. The eyes were not simply shaped stone orbs like the rest. They were matt black. It was like looking into nothingness. Even the light sank into them without a hint of reflection. It was quite simply the eeriest thing Aram had ever seen. Questions assailed him, though the loudest and most insistent was why in the name of everything sane had he agreed to come here?

Of course he knew the answer to that well enough, and it still held true. To the east, the Inda were now under the dominion of the Jade Empire, little more than slaves to a strict and harsh regime. To the north the bandits held sway with little care for human life, and beyond them the horse lords with even less. And to the west? For all the civility displayed by the general at Jalnapur, they had seen how the lands near the war zone had been plundered of all resources. The same would be true all the way back to the imperial border at the Oxus River. And whatever the general personally intended, all men knew that the emperor Bassianus was not to be trusted. Even if the west won against such terrible odds, there was no doubt in anyone's mind that the mad emperor's troops were here to stay.

South was the only way.

He looked at that statue again and shuddered uncontrollably. Monks lived there. Only in the northern peripheral area, of course, but they managed to live there and not go mad. If monks could do it, Aram assured himself, then surely the gods would look favourably upon their beleaguered people and protect them in the same manner. Had not the last guru taught that men could live there when he set the guardian monks to their task?

'I don't like this,' Bajaan said quietly.

'No one does,' Aram replied, 'but we have little choice, and if the monks can survive here, then so can we.'

'*Have* the monks survived?' Bajaan asked.

'What?'

'Look around you.'

Aram did so, more intently this time, and what he saw sent fresh waves of panic through him. The stone of the statue was slightly green with algae and moss and was dirty and stained. The undergrowth had been allowed to grow close to it, and saplings and shrubs grew off to either side.

'The monks are supposed to maintain the markers,' Bajaan noted. 'And the way between each marker is supposed to be kept clear and empty so that every marker can be seen from its neighbours. This is not a good sign.'

No, thought Aram, it most certainly wasn't. Images of sharp-fanged ghosts stripping the flesh from his bones flooded his mind and threatened to send terror rushing through him. He could not cross the boundary. No man could. Yet they had to. *He* had to. His legs shook, yet seemed rooted to the spot, unwilling to take that single, dreadful step.

'We have no choice,' he said with far more confidence than he felt. 'We must go. Do not mention this to the rest.' Though that would make little difference. Plenty of them would pick up on the facts as they passed. Aram wondered silently how many of those thousands following him would turn away at the marker, even having travelled half the length of the land to get here. Many, he suspected. He had almost been one of them himself, after all. And those people would settle somewhere in those sparsely populated southern lands. And if they survived the numerous roving patrols of both empires, they might turn into a village one day. Then eventually the war would be won by one power or another and their village would become naught but a statistic in the ledgers of an emperor, whether he be an eastern autocrat or a western madman.

Aram steeled himself. There was only one choice if they were to remain free Inda, and that choice was staring at him with those bottomless black eyes, as if waiting for his decision. 'Remember that no weapons must pass the markers,' he said, unbuckling his belt and removing the sword, still sheathed, dropping it carelessly to the ground beside the path. Mani and Bajaan followed suit. Now was the time, Aram thought, taking a deep breath. 'The gods will protect the Faithful,' he announced, and strode past the marker.

Two things almost made him turn around immediately and run north for his very life.

Firstly, as though even nature could not survive in the south, the rain stopped the very moment his foot passed the great carved monolith. The wind simply stopped blowing and the air dried out in a heartbeat.

Secondly, as his head spun around in surprise, he caught sight of the back of the marker. The carved figure at the top of the southern side was a smooth, slightly stylised figure just like its counterpart. It might have been considered a blessing that its eyes were closed. But instead, the figure was gripping the stony surface of its chest and hauling the 'flesh' apart as though opening a coat. And in the depth of the hole he had opened in his chest, where a heart should be, was that same black substance into which light just fell forever. Aram was grateful the figure was too high to reach, for he had the horrible urge to touch the black and see what if felt like. Logic said it was just some type of weird stone, but he couldn't shake the impression it would feel clammy and slippery.

He shivered again, uncontrollably. He was in the land of the dead. He had crossed the line. He was not dead yet, though something had clearly changed, and the hair stood proud on his neck as he felt the weight of a world of ghosts pressing down upon him. Every step might bring that ghastly vengeance upon him, but he would take the steps. It was his duty.

Slowly, he recovered himself as best he could, though the prayers he chanted repeatedly with silent breaths through pursed lips were fervent and desperate. He turned to the others. Every face he could see was staring goggle-eyed and terrified at him. Not one had followed him across the line.

'See how the gods favour us? Even the rain stops,' he said, trying to sound positive.

Mani – good, dependable Mani, whom Aram was beginning to see as true leader material – cleared his throat to address the crowd.

'Ahead lies uncertainty and fear. But it is *dry* uncertainty and fear with only unseen incorporeal danger. Behind you lie the armies of two emperors who want nothing other than to strip you of your freedom and your value, and to turn you into their subjects. That is a very real, corporeal danger. And that enslavement will only happen if you *survive* the war, for there could be years of conflict yet, raping and ruining the lands of the Inda. These southern reaches have been largely spared thus far, but that will not last for long. Uncertainty and fear is to be sought and treasured when the alternatives are certain pain, hunger and subjugation. Walk sheltered beneath the hands of the gods, and follow good Aram, who leads the way.'

Aram tried not to let his legs shake the way they wanted to and plastered a horribly fake smile of confidence across his face. Beckoning the others, he turned and walked into the land of ghosts. Behind him, he heard Mani and Bajaan following, and then other tentative footsteps too. He desperately hoped he had made the right decision.

He walked, each step inviting horrible death, yet miraculously not bringing it, and the others quickly caught up with him, a steady stream of civilians scurrying after them, desperate not to find themselves separated and alone in this place. The trail they followed turned slowly east, and after a short while met another such path, becoming a wider trail. Aram strode on, trying to exude authority and confidence.

Both fled him in a trice as they turned another corner in the dense, tropical forest.

There, across the path before him, lay the bodies of nine Jade Empire scouts. Aram stumbled to a halt and stared at them. Bajaan and Mani hurried round him and peered closely at the corpses, turning them over. There were no wounds! Aram shivered, a frisson of supernatural fear creeping across his flesh. The scouts had all died together, weapons in hand, but none of them were marked or wounded. In fact, the only sign of anything unusual was the look of utter horror on each face. Aram tore away his gaze.

'Did they die of fright?' Bajaan asked quietly.

'That's how it looks,' Mani replied, then gestured at his leader. 'Do we burn them?'

Aram shook his head. 'Tradition does not apply here. These men broke the sacred taboo and brought weapons, so the spirits dealt with them. We don't interfere. Clear them off the road so the others don't see their faces, but that is all.'

It was too late for that, of course. Many of those following were close behind and had already seen the eerie, grisly obstacle, and the rumour would spread from them quickly throughout the crowd. How many, Aram wondered, who had crossed the border would now turn and flee out of this strange land altogether once more? *Too* many, he suspected. But they would only exchange an unknown fate for a certain and unpleasant one.

He waited as the bodies were moved aside into the undergrowth and hidden from view, and then gestured forward and began to walk again.

'What now?' Mani asked, falling in beside him.

'Now we see if we can find the monks. They alone know how to survive in these lands, and their presence will comfort the civilians with us.'

And me, Aram thought to himself as he walked ever deeper into the forbidden land, shaking with every step.

CHAPTER 9

From: Orosius Devinius, commander, 6th Cohort, Germalla Cavalry
To: Prefect in command, forward scout station, Chara Gorge

Sir, my unit and I are engaged upon a special mission in the mountains. Being aware of the broad dangers posed by the region and the specific peril of my task, I request that you keep this message for a period of twenty-four days, and if my unit and I have not returned to your station by that time, please forward it to General Flavius Cinna at Jalnapur.

D ev hauled on the reins, nerves beginning to twitch.
'That must be it.'
The cohort's captain nodded his agreement silently. Ahead, the valley they had been following narrowed between two rocky spurs that stood tall and powerful, twin sentinels set by the gods to guard an important place. Atop each spur they could see a ruin – a small tower, stone tumbled from the top, crenellations gone, holes in the walls. Testament to the once powerful rulers of this land in days long gone, when the mountains had still been the territory of rajahs, before the horse lord raids began and the bandits claimed the region.

Behind those twin peaks the valley disappeared east into the brown dusty mountains, deep enough that the bottom of the gorge was hidden in shadow even in the early afternoon. It was, Dev had to admit, the perfect hiding place for a bandit.

Everything he had heard of the Sizhad had increased Dev's concerns over this mission.

They had travelled north and east for many days, entering the mountainous region carefully and keeping to the more populated areas to begin with. Dev had approached each Inda settlement pacifically, leaving his cohort out of sight on the road, and taking

113

only the captain and half a dozen men with him. At first the locals had been reluctant to speak to Dev, despite his clear Inda origins, because of the imperial threat he represented. It had taken much cajoling, and occasional threats, to learn anything. As they followed the trail of hints and clues north-east, though, the attitude changed. Not the reluctance, of course, but at least the reason for it. The further into the region they travelled and the closer to their quarry they came, the more fear and respect they encountered for the Sizhad. People became unhappy discussing him not because the questioner was imperial, but because of the potential consequences from the bandits themselves.

But slowly they had found their way to this place, and now Dev felt reluctant to enter, and not just because of the danger that valley posed, though that was very much a concern. Clearly, from what the region's inhabitants had intimated, the Sizhad had a sizeable army of fanatically loyal warriors that seriously outnumbered Dev's.

Fanatics. That worried Dev, and from the look on the man's face, it was of equal concern to the cohort's captain.

'What do you know of these sun worshippers?' the captain said.

Dev sighed. 'Not a great deal. They are an uncommon sect who have shunned the traditional gods of the Inda in favour of the sun itself. They've been around for over a hundred years, but they've always been a mysterious and private bunch. They tend to live in the wilderness and avoid contact with the towns of the Inda, in some sort of self-imposed exile. Why, I couldn't tell you, but they've always been considered a peaceful, if odd, bunch. I've never even heard of a sun worshipper taking up arms, let alone forming an army. It is so strange that I really don't know what to expect from this, but I recommend keeping your religious views to yourself and not mentioning the sun or the gods in this conversation. Same goes for your men. Let's not provoke anything if we can avoid it.

'I think I would rather be in Jalnapur getting the shit kicked out of me by the Jade Empire,' the captain said with feeling.

'I know what you mean. Come on. Let's get it over with.'

As the captain signalled to the cohort and the riders began to move forward, Dev rode at the front with the officer, both sitting high and proud in the saddle as befitted imperial officers. Those twin sentinels with their broken stone fangs closed on either side, reaching to the sky, and in a quarter of an hour they passed from the bright sunshine into the deep shade of the valley. At least the weather was holding here. Word was that the monsoons had begun further south in the lowlands, and the rains would be dreadful for the general and his forces. It would be weeks before the weather changed here in the mountains, and even then it would be a pale shadow of the storms further south.

Dev blinked in the relative gloom, allowing his eyes to adjust to the change. The defile snaked through the peaks. He could see the mountains rising to the east, mapping in his head the shape of the valley. The captain looked at him quizzically.

'You've been here before, sir?'

Dev shook his head. 'I've never been within fifty miles of this place. The villages on the lower slopes I was familiar with, but no sensible rajah or his men came this far north. Too dangerous. There has been no authority but the bandit chiefs in these mountains for a hundred years.'

'I hate bandits.'

Dev threw a warning glance at the officer. 'I would be grateful if you kept sentiments like that well and truly buried for now too.'

The captain nodded, though he looked no happier. The five hundred cavalrymen closed their ranks, moving four men abreast and barely leaving breathing room between themselves and the beast in front. Tension had grown throughout the ranks on their approach to the Sizhad's realm. Moving at a sedate, cautious pace, the cohort travelled along the shadowed base of the valley. Small stands of trees and scrubby grass filling out into shrubs and bushes represented the majority of the area's vegetation and there was no sign of current settlement. A seasonal stream wound along the centre of the defile, though at this time of the year it was little more than brown dust and smooth rocks. There were no fields, farms or bridges, huts or shrines. The place was devoid of civilisation, though here and there on the hillsides and among the trees and bushes they spotted ruins that suggested this place had been a rajah's pride once, many years ago, before the bandit chiefs rose.

Dev shivered and stroked his horse's mane, opening his mouth to speak to the captain and shutting it again in surprise.

The Sizhad's men were suddenly everywhere.

Dev was impressed even through the shock as his horse reared and he fought to control the reins. The captain, beside him, was in similar trouble, and the entire column had halted, panicked, urgent voices ripping through the strangely silent valley.

They must have been secreted among the trees and rocks and within the ruins. At some unheard signal they had risen from their hiding places as one. They were all in white and pale beige with white turbans. Some held spears, others swords, but most had bows with an arrow already nocked and the string drawn back to the chin. And there were so *many* of them.

It took him a moment to realise that the captain was telling his men to stand down, and Dev turned as his horse finally reluctantly settled, to see that a number of the cohort had drawn their swords.

'No,' he bellowed, echoing the captain's own commands. 'Sheathe your blades. We're here to talk. We want them as allies.' Although, in that moment, he was not sure how much he really wanted them at all.

A man stepped out onto the road, his apparel identical to the rest and yet somehow carrying an air of authority. He faced Dev and the captain and folded his arms. Dev looked him up and down. The man showed no fear at the approach of a cohort of imperial cavalry, but then why would he? He had several hundred warriors himself, and many of those would be able to pin two men apiece with arrows before they had to consider a blade.

Dev and his men had walked into the lion's den, and the truth of that suddenly insisted itself upon him as he looked into those eyes and saw not only a lack of fear or concern, but a worrying mix of disdain and unshakable faith.

'Please stand your men down,' Dev said to the man in a good northern Inda dialect, slightly tempered by many years of imperial living. Behind him the cohort were once more sheathing their weapons and settling their horses. 'We have come in peace to discuss matters of great importance with the Sizhad.'

The man in white cocked an eyebrow slightly, though whether it was at those words or the accent in which they were delivered, Dev could not tell. He remained still, arms folded, silent.

'I am an envoy of General Flavius Cinna, carrying the authority of the emperor Bassianus.'

Still the man said nothing, but something about his silence and his stance told Dev everything he needed to know about the man's opinion of his mission.

'Will the Sizhad see us?' he prompted, rapidly coming to the conclusion that this had been a mistake and that it might be better to cut their losses now and turn away. There was a long silence and, just as Dev was about to announce his intention to do just that, the man spoke.

'You and your men will surrender your weapons if you wish to travel any further.'

Dev turned to the captain, who shrugged, though his expression showed his reluctance. Dev sighed. One of the advantages of the empire was that the organisation and discipline kept things running smoothly. A disadvantage was that to keep up such discipline meant complete obedience. Dev could not imagine approaching General Cinna without even trying to complete his mission. But there was no advantage to endangering everyone when he did not have to. He turned to the men and singled out the second officer a few ranks back, speaking to him in the imperial tongue in the hope it would go over the locals' heads.

'Take four files of men back to the nearest imperial station. Wait there for ten days, and then if we do not return, ride for the war zone. The rest of you, unsheathe your swords and daggers and throw them to the ground.'

As some four hundred riders turned and began to trot their horses back west with a tangible air of relief, the other hundred dropped their blades. Dev and the captain reluctantly added their weapons to the collection. Not one of the Sizhad's men lowered sword, spear or bow.

'Come,' the leader said, and turned. His men remained where they were, but the leader began to stride away up the valley with a purposeful gait, his white turban trailing two silk streamers of gold. Dev and the captain shared a look, shrugged, and began to walk their horses on after the man. The remaining cavalry joined the column, and slowly they moved deeper into the valley.

It was a long ride. Three hours they walked their horses in silence as the man strode ahead, never breaking pace. The valley narrowed gradually and twisted this way and that, as Dev had anticipated from the view of the peaks ahead. The pickets who had ambushed them had not followed along but, though they had appeared to be alone with the white-clad man as they moved along the valley, the ever-present threat hovered in the air, prickling Dev's skin, and he felt certain that if he made one hostile move, the valley sides would suddenly erupt with white figures intent on bloodshed. And so they walked their horses steadily in the company of the white-clad leader, peacefully, unarmed and in silence.

Finally, as the light began to change, suggesting that the sun they had not seen for hours in the deep valley was now descending towards the western peaks, they turned a corner, and Dev's breath caught in his throat.

Arrayed before him was an army on a massive scale.

He had not been sure what to expect of the Sizhad and his force. The bandit chiefs were portrayed as uncultured rabble in the tales of the rajahs of old, and though this one had become the greatest of all of them, Dev had still expected roughness. He knew that the man had managed to gather a sizeable force – that, after all, was why they were here – but he'd had simply no idea *how* sizeable.

This place had once been a sacred site. The valley opened out into a huge wide bowl, with a flattened hill at the centre, wide enough that the centre and the eastern end were still bathed in bright sunlight. A lake sat gleaming at that side, fed by a glittering cascade from the mountains and granting fresh water to the entire place. The huge circular depression was one giant military camp full of tents and small cabins, camp fires and supply stores, and everywhere were white pennants bearing a golden sun design. Dev had never commanded an army, but he had served in one and had made a short career out of evaluating the value of military installations on the empire's fringe. What he saw made him break into a cold sweat.

There were over a hundred thousand men here if there were a dozen. Corrals of horses suggested cavalry. He could see several archery ranges. There were small areas given over to the construction of machines of war. This was no bandit king. Such a title could clearly not be applied to the Sizhad. This was an army, ready for war.

At the centre of the huge bowl, that flattened hill bore a structure that had been a temple to the Inda gods. Dev could see the four towers that had stood at each corner. They had once borne the likenesses of the war gods. Now each bore yet another white and gold sun flag. The great, monumental and decorative temple of red stone and white marble in the centre had a huge ornate portal over which hung that same banner.

'I hate zealots,' the captain said under his breath, and Dev shot him yet another warning look. The party was escorted down to the camp at that same sedate pace, allowing plenty of time to drink in the impressive strength and unity of the force around them. They passed beneath the scrutiny of the Sizhad's men and Dev felt once again not an iota of worry or respect from even the lowliest spear man, just disdain and conviction. The very idea of that sort of faith instilled in this kind of army made Dev shiver.

Some of the men hawked and spat as they passed, not quite hitting the visitors, but coming close enough to display how little fear and esteem there was in this place for the empire. Dev tried to steady his nerves as they rode through the seemingly endless ranks of the Sizhad's army. Finally, they ascended that low hill, passed through a gate in an outer boundary wall, and approached the great doors of the former temple.

'You two,' the white-clad officer said, pointing at Dev and the captain and beckoning.

Dev nodded and turned to the nervous-looking horsemen behind him. 'Stay here and do nothing. I am about to attempt negotiations and I want no unpleasant incidents out here impacting on that.'

The four file officers saluted, and the fifth of a cohort of men settled in as Dev and the captain dismounted, paced around for a moment to exercise sore muscles, stretched, and then followed the white-garbed man into the doorway.

The building had once been a glittering, wondrous homage to the Inda gods, but now the intricate wall designs had gone, whitewashed so that the entire building was gleaming monochrome. The temple was of a familiar design, for all its grand scale and recent changes. Square, it contained a wide internal courtyard, each side housing several chapels and shrines, now all stripped bare, whitewashed and repurposed as storage places. The two men were led through the building and into the courtyard.

The great square was flagged with white marble, and due to the size of this wide valley, the height of the mound upon which the temple sat, and the design of the building itself, the sun still reached almost half the courtyard. The two visitors blinked again, having to let their eyesight adjust once more.

The Sizhad was also not what Dev had expected. Despite the strange uniformity of the army he had seen in the great valley stronghold, somehow Dev had still expected a grand prince or hulking warrior. Either dripping with jewels and gold like the powerful rajahs of old, or armoured and dressed in leathers and furs like a mountain man. The Sizhad was neither. He was dressed in the same simple white clothes as every man in his army. Unlike the others, though, the Sizhad's turban was not white, but yellow, as he sat cross-legged on a small mat at the centre of the courtyard with his head down. He looked humble. Young. Peaceful.

'Why have you come?' the man asked quietly. His face was lowered. In prayer? Dev wondered.

'I have come as the representative of Bassianus, Emperor of the West, and his esteemed general, Flavius Cinna, who currently fights a war to drive the Jade Empire from the Inda Diamond.'

'Sit,' replied the Sizhad, gesturing to the white marble flags before him, gleaming in the sun. Dev did so, uncomfortably. The stone was sizzling hot to the touch and he could immediately feel his trousers and boots warming. The captain remained standing off to the side. Good. This might go better Inda to Inda.

Then the Sizhad looked up and Dev's world broke asunder.

'Ravi?'

The great bandit chief and fanatic, master of countless thousands and ruler of the mountains, gave Dev a sad smile. 'Ravi is gone. Ravi died long ago.'

Dev stared at his youngest brother. It had been too many years, and Ravi had been so young when Dev had left, but he would know him anywhere. He still had the three marks by which Dev would always recognise him. The slightly cleft lip where he had fallen and ripped his mouth on a table corner as an infant. The scar above his brow, between the eyes, where Dev had hit him with a sharp stick when they had been playing a game of warriors and heroes as boys.

And most telling of all, the mismatched eyes, one green, one brown. It was Ravi and there was no denying it.

A thrill of possibility ran through Dev. There was a chance. A *real* chance.

'Ravi, we need your help. We can save the Inda. Drive out the Jade Empire. But we cannot do it without your aid. Join us. Bring your men to war and we can save the Inda, Ravi.'

His brother's face remained impassive, and in one glance at his eyes, Dev knew he would fail. This was his brother, all right, but it was not the same Ravi he had left in Initpur all those years ago.

'The Inda cannot be saved, Dev.'

'They can,' Dev replied urgently, hopefully.

'No, they cannot. The Inda are dying. Their time has passed. The world of old gods is fading.'

'Is this your new sun worship talking, Ravi? Don't you understand? This is more important than a simple *cult*.'

Something terrifying flashed through the Sizhad's eyes, and Dev recoiled at the sight.

'Do not insult what you do not understand, Dev. Any other man who sat there and said such a thing to me would be burning by sunset for his impiety. I spare you for the sake of our father and what we have shared, but do not push me.'

'Ravi, what happened to you?'

'I told you. Ravi is dead. Ravi, son of Aram, died years ago. He survived Jai being taken. And he survived you leaving, though you broke his heart. But when his mother died and took his sister with her, he knew then that the Inda were doomed. Those false gods we trusted smiled at us as they took our loved ones, our heritage, our world. For a time, I was lost. I said farewell to our father, who would decline along with the Inda, and went to join a monastery.'

'Our father—' began Dev, but the Sizhad was still speaking.

'I thought to understand the gods and why they seemed to hate those who worshipped them. The great teachers among the monks sought to enlighten me, and they succeeded. I realised, despite their own beliefs, that what we worshipped were not gods, but demons. We had been tricked at the dawn of our civilisation and had been paying tribute to demons, who kept us safe as long as we were useful to them. But then the empires rose to either side of the Inda and we became diminished. So those demons stopped preserving us and instead began to nurture those two great empires.'

'Ravi, you cannot believe—'

'Do not tell me what to believe, Dev. I have seen the truth. I left the monastery and wandered. I found peace and understanding in the hills with a holy man who opened my eyes to the sun. Where the old gods atrophy and decay like the demons they are, the sun remains strong and powerful. He gives light and life and dispels the darkness in our lives. He is constant and pure. And he can take the life of the wicked as easily as he gives life to the worthy.'

'Horseshit,' huffed the captain standing nearby, and Dev shot a glance up at the man. He was too late. The Sizhad barely nodded and an arrow arched out from somewhere in the shadows and slammed into the captain's calf, sending him hurtling to the floor with a squawk.

'I owe you no such considerations as I owe my brother,' the Sizhad said in a cold voice. Dev made to move, but realised immediately that he could do nothing here, given the sheer power exuded by the master of this place. The captain had been insulting, despite Ravi's earlier warning, and he would be punished. A small group of white-clad men scurried over to the writhing captain. Dev frowned. None of them were armed, and he couldn't imagine what they planned to do. The men turned the captain so that he was lying on his back, crying out in pain as the arrow in his leg was knocked this way and that against the marble, blood pouring out with each jolt.

Dev's blood ran cold as he watched the pained, struggling captain pinned to the sizzling marble with men holding down each limb in a tight grip. Another pair huddled around the captain's face, and when they moved back, Dev was chilled further to see that they had used some kind of glue and dressing combination to pull open his eyelids and hold them there. The captain stared in panic, unable to do anything else. Then the two held his head tight.

The sun burned down on the captain, who tried desperately to look away. He could not. His eyes rolled around, but with his eyelids held open and his head pinned in place, no matter where he looked the sun was still there, at least in the periphery, sizzling into his retinas.

'If you surrender to the sun and gaze up directly, this will be over quicker,' the Sizhad said in an oddly comforting voice, but such considerations were beyond the captain now. His desperate shouts were becoming extremely distressing, and one of the men finally gagged him.

'He will not die,' the Sizhad said, addressing Dev now. 'He will either come to understand the truth, or he will leave here a blind man, unable to stand against us.'

'Torture, Ravi?' Dev said, disgust inflecting his voice, still watching the panicked captain.

'*Enlightenment*, Dev. And I keep telling you: Ravi, son of Aram, is dead.'

Dev turned to his brother. 'Yes. I see now that you are not the Ravi I knew. He was a gentle boy. A good boy. Respectful and loving and part of a good family. Not a cold, zealous killer. Very well. Let me repeat my reason for coming here, not as an old friend and sibling, but simply as a representative of the empire.'

The Sizhad nodded and Dev forged ahead.

'You have an army here that could turn the tide of the war. Not using it helps no one. You could support the Jade Empire, but you would only hand the world to them. Or you could ally with General Cinna, drive out the Jade Empire from Inda lands and free us all. Whether you worship the sun or the old gods, you must still see the value of saving the Inda?'

'As I told you,' the Sizhad replied, 'the Inda cannot be saved. Nor can the lands of the mad western emperor, nor those of the rigid, short-sighted Jade Emperor. They all worship those same demons who ruined the Inda. And now they are doing the same to the empires. But it is all part of the plan, Dev.'

'Plan?'

'For the unification of the world. As the old peoples and the demons they worship battle one another and create worldwide ruin, we grow only stronger. The empires will destroy the Inda. Then they will destroy each other. And when they are too weak to protect themselves, then my army will move. We will take back the world from the demons that have destroyed it. We will remove the mad emperor and his brood and give back hope and truth to the people of his empire. And we shall rip the Jade Emperor from his throne and open the eyes of his people.'

Dev couldn't help but glance back over to the captain at those words. He had fallen still and was issuing strangled sobs.

'And the Inda will be no more, but only as the empires will be no more. We will all just be children of the sun, in peace and harmony forever. Do you not understand, Dev?'

'I understand that you have gone quite mad, brother, and that you would willingly see the world burn for the love of your cult. You have the resources to save your people, yet you will not.'

A few paces away, the white-clad men were now removing the arrow from the weeping captain's leg and binding it.

'There is another way, Dev.'

'Oh?' Dev turned back to his brother. 'And what would that be?'

'Join us. I can teach you. Bring you understanding. You could be my brother in a new way. A powerful, sacred way.'

'My duty is to my commander, my empire, and also to the Inda and their preservation.'

The Sizhad's expression hardened. 'I cannot let you go.'

A chill ran through Dev then. He hadn't, throughout this encounter, considered that possibility.

'What?'

'As well as being a commander of the enemy, you have seen all there is here to see and I have described the future to you. Whether you join me or not, you must understand that you can never go back.'

'Ravi—'

'Ravi is dead. There is only the Sizhad. You will be detained and given time to consider my offer. The same offer will be made to each of your men. I hope they choose enlightenment and understanding and decide to join us and change the world. But if they do not I cannot allow them to return to your false general and his demons.'

Dev could think of nothing further to say, his expression blank as he rose. Three white-clad men were crossing to him now as the others helped the wounded and blinded captain to his feet, where he limped and hobbled around staring sightlessly in every direction.

'Take them to the chamber of night. Let them consider the value of the sun.'

124

Dev felt the hands on his shoulders and went quietly, rather than struggling. It would avail him nothing and he would need to preserve his strength. He had to get out of here and bring word of this new and awful threat to his general.

For all this talk of the sun, the world seemed to have taken several steps into darkness.

CHAPTER 10

War wears many faces,
Death wears but one.

Ancient proverb

Jai stood beneath the awning and squinted into the rain. All was quiet, but that would never fool a student of war. The sea can appear becalmed, but currents beneath the surface would still drag a man to his death.

Death.

Throughout these months back in his ancestral homeland, Jai had seen enough death to last him a lifetime. Long gone now was the enthusiasm and conviction the army had felt in those early days of capitulations and grand demonstrations. Now the world had settled into a morass of mud, blood and shit. He wondered how many students would have shied away from the Zu Academy and its arts of war if they had been introduced early to the stink of rotted corpses and opened bowels. Because that, apparently, was war. And for Jai, weaned on the elegance of academy swordsmanship, the difference between duels and war had been a brutal lesson to learn.

Jalnapur was a name to be cursed. Jalnapur *was* a curse. For more than two months now they had been fighting here. After several weeks, the northern army had finally arrived from plodding around in the mountains where they had led a strangely successful campaign. Successful in that they had suffered few losses and garrisoned many former rajah's palaces. Strange because they had met few rajahs and few warriors in the process. They had known that bandit chiefs lurked in those mountains with large forces, but had been entirely unable to locate them, and even under torture the locals had revealed nothing.

The addition of that third great Jade Empire force to Jiang's army made not a jot of difference in the reality of Jalnapur. The simple

126

fact was that the entire battle, and because of that the entire war, relied upon that great bridge stretching across the Nadu River. If either side managed to cross the Nadu and secure a bridgehead, they could hope to win, but as long as that bridge remained at the centre, unreachable by either side and limiting the fielding of troops, there was little hope of an end to the hostilities, and numbers made precious little difference.

General Jiang had even considered moving south and constructing a new bridge or finding another way to cross, but had soon dismissed the notion. Now that the two armies were facing off, if either moved, the other could track them along the length of the Nadu and wherever they stopped would simply become the next Jalnapur.

The losses to the army over the past two months had been appalling. Every day saw a small but steady stream of casualties, either men who had been scouting too close to the bank and met with imperial arrows, or those who manned picket points or the like who had become the victim of opportunistic enemy artillery. The hospital, which sat back behind the nearest hill where the heady stench could not drift across the army and sicken the healthy, was permanently in business. Bags of bloody bone went in one end, limping or whimpering men coming out of the other, along with amputated limbs, unspeakable waste and the numerous patients who failed to survive the fly-ridden, eye-watering interior. The smell of blood and foulness and sickly-sweet putrefaction combined with the spicy aromas of the many ancient natural remedies the surgeons employed in addition to the blade and the needle.

And the next hill along was, if anything, worse. It contained the three great catacombs hollowed out by soldiers with grim faces, and the place of burning, where white-robed priests rendered the dead into ash so they could be placed in the catacombs.

It was a mechanical process to reduce the army by degrees, and it was little consolation that much the same would be happening across the river. Indeed, Jai understood that the western empire burned their dead as a matter of course, and the columns of black smoke could be seen daily some distance behind their lines. The Jade Empire traditionally buried their dead in the ground whole, the deceased after a battle being interred beneath a tumulus. But this battle was different, since over many weeks the dead had been stacking up daily. Cremation had been the only sensible choice, unless they were to create the greatest cemetery in history, and no one wanted to be responsible for *that* monument.

Jai's eyes strayed to the storage shelters up on the slope. Great stacks of timber rested there beneath huge canvas roofs. The rains had been almost constant since monsoon season began, and even the place of burning, where the pyres were constructed, was covered by an enormous high roof, else the timber would simply smoulder forever in the wet. Instead, the charnel fire burned and threw smoke up from the pyre, where it gathered at the canvas roof thirty feet above, before billowing out of the sides. That roof had already burned away three times and been replaced swiftly on each occasion.

Dreadful, the things this war made a man do.

The artillery rarely fired these days. The enemy took a few potshots, probably just to keep themselves busy, and the general made sure that the cannon all fired at least once a day, though they were largely ineffective. Occasionally, Jiang would commit a full unit or two to an onslaught at the bridge, in the hope that he would catch Cinna off guard and they might miraculously gain a foothold on the western bank. Every time the hospital was flooded, the pyres burned brighter and longer, the burial details were busier and the general drank until he no longer felt shock at the losses he had caused in his own army. Still, they came no closer to a change in the status quo.

Sickeningly, the vast majority of deaths at Jalnapur were the result of disease or misadventure. Men were swept away by the river surprisingly often. The Nadu's strong current easily carried men to their death, especially when they wore heavy armour and weapons and neared the bank to urinate. Men slipped in the mud on the hillside and broke legs, smashed heads on rocks and suchlike too. But the worst were the diseases. Fevers, parasites, rotten flesh in the damp, unhealthy conditions and the ever-present threat of dysentery carried off more men every day than all the blades, arrows and missiles the westerners could throw at them.

Tellingly, suicide took more than a few too.

Jai had watched General Jiang slowly losing hope. All their grand schemes to occupy the Inda lands and include them in a peaceful, forward-moving manner had failed miserably. Instead, they were locked in a war of attrition with an enemy who, while numerically inferior, was clearly shrewd and bloody-minded. There was no way out. No alternative. Jai and the general had discussed every option numerous times over the weeks, but nothing could be done. Moving north or south along the river would simply change the location of the hell they endured. Moving into the northern mountains was too much of a gamble. There was the faint possibility they might cross the Nadu and move west that way, but they also ran the risk of meeting western forces in the mountains, where it would come down to an unpredictable combination of strategy and luck, for numbers meant considerably less in such terrain and the cannon had to be readied and sited before they were of any use. And General Jiang was certain that his opposite number was every bit the tactician that he was, so strategy could not be relied upon any more than numbers. Plus, in the north there was always the potential danger of horse clan raids, or bumping into this large mysterious force they said inhabited the mountains and yet an entire army had failed to find. No, the north was out.

And far enough south was the land of ghosts. Jiang was sceptical about such a place, but he knew enough of his soldiers would fear it, and Jai was certainly adamant about not going there. That left only retreat – pull back from the bridge and try and entice the imperial general to cross it and face him in open battle somewhere. Neither Jai nor the general believed even for a moment that Cinna was insane enough to do such a thing. No, he would just remain in place, watching the bridge and sending out odd scouts to keep track of their location. There would be no long-term benefit there.

And so they continued to rot and drown and die in the soggy lands of Jalnapur, from which the civilians had long since fled, slipping into starvation and deprivation and watching their town take occasional peripheral damage. Once, thanks to a cannon misfire, the lower town wall had been breached and within four hours the whole place had been flooded under a foot of stinking water.

Every five or six days the rain abated briefly and the army looked to the sky in the south for a reprieve. Then, always within a day, the clouds boiled up on the warm wind once again and the downpour recommenced.

Today was such a day. The rain had stopped an hour before and the entire plain of Jalnapur steamed in the heat, the water burning to vapour and creating a fog that made artillery useless, or at least extremely haphazard.

Jai glanced over his shoulder. The general's headquarters, a solid construction of timber and tile, sat silent and sombre, two guards by the door. The general had been locked away inside for almost an hour now – it had still been raining when he entered. It was extremely unusual for the general to hold any sort of meeting, no matter how small, without Jai being present, and the former scout was intrigued. A rider had thundered into camp earlier from the north – tired, sodden and dirty. He had visited the general, being taken straight into the headquarters, and the pair had not emerged since. It seemed, though, that the time of waiting was over. Even as Jai watched, the building's only door opened and that rider emerged once again, staggering wearily away, presumably in search of dry clothes, food and a bed.

Jai held his breath. Whatever this was, it was clearly important.

His heart sank as the commander appeared in the doorway. The news had clearly not been good. General Jiang, whose face had grown visibly older in just two months, bore a whole new level of bleakness. He scanned the world outside the door, his eyes coming to rest on Jai, and he beckoned him and turned back into his headquarters. Jai, heart in throat, followed his commander and found his way to the general's office, where Jiang sat disconsolate in his campaign chair.

'I made an attempt that no sane man would, and I failed, Jai.'

'General?'

'I tried to change the Jade Emperor's mind almost a month ago. Such a thing is not done lightly. Any attempt to do so is generally seen as criticising the emperor's choices. I was humble yet forthright. I begged him to reconsider his policy and consider terms with the emperor Bassianus. I set out in a stark manner the difficulties we face and the very real danger that we could lose or at least fight to an endless standstill here, creating a permanent state of war that would sap the empire. I tried to find something positive to say, though I floundered. I did everything I could, knowing that more noble men than I have lost their heads for less than this. But I have failed.'

'The messenger was from the emperor, sir?'

Jiang nodded. 'The reply is simple. "There will be no peace," the emperor commands. I am to bring him the lands of the Inda, even if it means conquering the western empire in the process. The way he phrases the matter makes me suspect he yearns for Bassianus's head on a platter more than the Inda kingdoms anyway.'

Jai sighed. 'At least he has not punished you, sir. We are no worse off than we were.'

'Oh we are, Jai. We are. The Jade Emperor is thinning the ranks at home. He will keep a skeleton force in place elsewhere, because he is sending every soldier he can spare to Jalnapur to give us the edge we need.'

'Surely that's good, sir?' Jai frowned.

'No. That is bad. The army we brought west was carefully selected. All the officers in high position were known to me and were men of the western provinces who knew of the Inda at least a little and could be relied upon to take into account the stability of the region in what we have done. And the armies themselves were drawn mostly from areas that deal with delicate subjugated lands – men unusual for the empire in that they think for themselves a little, and allow their environment to factor into their ideas, rather than displaying the blind obedience that is symptomatic of the imperial military. I trust them to do as I command. Now, though, the Jade Emperor will send me martinets and morons, officers who care not a breath for the fate of the Inda. Men who will roll over this land like a titanic boulder, crushing all beneath them in the belief that such cruelty will instil order. And some of those men will be of high enough rank that they will feel confident in challenging me. Our war is about to change, Jai. I had thought this campaign at its lowest ebb, but I have had my eyes cruelly opened.'

'So what do we do, General?'

'We do whatever we can to conclude matters before the relief force arrives. It will be at least a month, I expect. But if we can secure Jalnapur by then, perhaps I can keep the new officers under control. If they find us mired in this debacle, I will spend more time fighting for control of my own army than fighting the enemy.'

'A push for the bridge?'

The prospect hardly thrilled Jai, but after so long suffering this dreadful standoff, could slaughter be any worse? Was a blade in the gut not to be sought before the amputation of a rotten foot?

General Jiang nodded. 'And no time like the present.'

'Sir?'

'On looking out just now, I note that the rain has stopped again. When we have a break in the rain we have several hours of thick mists. The forces of General Cinna cannot be expecting an assault any more than they have during any other day of this dreadful battle. We move fast and see if we can seize the bridge. There is a small chance. It is not a good one, but it is there. If we can get enough men onto the other end of that bridge to hold it while we bring up reserves, we might just create a bridgehead and then start to take the fight to the other bank.'

Jai nodded. Not smiling, though, just like the general – a nod was all. Both of them knew just how small the chance was. Even with the element of surprise and the enveloping mist, it would be nothing short of a miracle if they could get enough men across that bridge to make a difference.

'Summon four regiments of light infantry and two of heavy, also one wing of cavalry. Find out which archer regiment has the best record and have them stand to as well. Have all the regiments muster at the parade ground at the foot of the slope and then take them forward yourself. I have something to take care of, but I will meet you at the approach to the bridge.'

'Me, sir? And you?'

'Indeed,' General Jiang said. 'Soldiers take heart and fight better when they know their commanders share their peril. And with the sullen mood of the army these past two months we need every morsel of spirit we can raise. Go now, and fast. We must take advantage of the mist.'

Jai left the headquarters, his head spinning, blood racing. He barely registered what he was doing as he passed instructions to messengers standing close to the viewpoint before the headquarters. Consulting the records for the archers was simple: a small building close to the headquarters housed all records. The Jade Empire was strict on record keeping, and every month a full set of figures was sent back to the capital for the perusal of the administration. Selecting the unit of archers with the best kill rate and the lowest casualties was the work of but moments, and Jai was still buzzing with anticipation as he delivered orders for those units to assemble.

A quarter of an hour later he was standing on the parade ground as the regiments assembled. Three thousand light infantry, fifteen hundred heavy, two hundred horse and six hundred archers. It was a paltry gathering considering the size of the army, yet when they were gathered together like this, it was hard not to be impressed. Another quarter of an hour and every chosen man was assembled and ready for war, their officers standing at the front of each unit and saluting Jai as though he were the general. A lump rose in his throat. Suddenly this seemed an immense responsibility. What order should he lead the men in? He searched his deep memory, picturing those dusty texts of ancient generals he had studied in the academy. Yes. Sun Lao's approach to the Gorge of Ang seemed appropriate. Taking a deep breath, he looked around at the gathering.

'We move to the bridge, men, where the general will have further instructions, and we march in the Sun Lao formation. Archers first, moving with weapons readied. Then the heavy infantry in support, with the light infantry behind them and on the flanks, the cavalry in the centre at the rear. There will be no talking or music. We must remain silent throughout. With fortune on our side, we will surprise the enemy and manage to secure the far end of the bridge. Fall in and advance.'

As the units began to move in accordance with the desired formation, Jai tried to decide how he should place himself in the column. On horseback with the cavalry would clearly be the natural position, but he would prefer to be at the fore when they encountered General Jiang. Passing the reins of his horse to a groom rather regretfully, he placed his hand on the hilt of his sword and strode across to fall in with the commander of the regiment of archers.

Moments later they were moving towards the causeway that cut through the boggy, wet ground before the bridge and then onto it, marching six men abreast, the only sound the gentle crunch of soft leather boots on the raised bank's compacted surface. Jai counted off the red distance markers as they moved inexorably towards the enemy. The journey was extremely eerie. The thick white fog enveloped the world like a fleecy blanket, hiding the sky and the ground alike beyond a few paces. The mist was oddly warm and saturated one's clothes in a matter of moments. The entire plain of Jalnapur was muted, and Jai could hear very little other than the muffled crunch of thousands of footsteps. Occasionally on the route they passed close to one of the picket positions and could hear low, murmured conversation and the distinctive sound of sheathed weapons or armour clonking. No one, he noted, came to check on the column of men, but then they would be coming from behind the Jade Empire's lines and therefore would not unduly worry the pickets.

His heart skipped at the sudden appearance of the general. The mist muted and hid the world so thoroughly that the column was almost upon him before they knew he was there, but then that was entirely the point of this push, after all. General Jiang emerged from the mist like a ghost slipping its shroud, an image that made Jai shudder and stayed with him even as the Crimson Guard flowed, blood red, from the white blanket behind him.

'Jai,' the general greeted him with an incline of the head.

'General.'

'Archers to the fore. Zhou Chen's stratagem?'

'Sun Lao, sir.'

General Jiang smiled and nodded. 'Also appropriate for the clearance and seizure of narrow approaches. Good. Have the army halt in units at the end of the bridge, which is some seventy paces ahead.' He turned to the archers' commander beside Jai. 'Your bowmen will follow me.'

As Jai, frowning, waited for the infantry to catch up, the general moved off to the left into the mist, the archers following, along with the Crimson Guard who were never far from the general's side and who were, on this occasion, dismounted. In half a hundred heartbeats the archers, the general and his guard were gone, and by the time Jai counted to a further ten, even the sound of their movement had been swallowed up by the mist.

With the heavy infantry now at the front, Jai moved on to the bridge. He had never felt more like a soldier than now, hand on sword hilt, marching towards the enemy with a unit of heavily armoured men in lacquered black and carrying long glaives. The sound of their movement, so close to him, was much louder than the archers had been, their weapons clonking and clattering, their boots crunching, armour knocking and rattling, and Jai began to wonder whether they might even be audible to the enemy. He dismissed his own fears in a trice. The enemy waited across half a mile of bridge and what noise there was, already muffled by the fog, would also be well hidden by the churning river.

They reached the near end of the bridge and Jai signalled the halt.

They waited. The white mist once more folded in upon them, and without the noise of moving soldiers, the world once more became a weird, eerie place. Finally, after what seemed like an age, General Jiang reappeared with his Crimson Guard.

'Speed or power, Jai,' the general said in a businesslike manner.

'Sir?'

'I am inclined towards the light infantry as Zhou Chen would have it: take the bridgehead at speed with the element of surprise and bring up the heavy infantry to hold it against counter-attacks while the cavalry move forward and prepare to make sallies. But you are also a student of the academy, and you have favoured Sun Lao. There is something to be said for punching with a strong fist and then following up with the soft underbelly in support. Present your case, but quickly. We need to move.'

Jai shook his head. 'No, General. You have led successful campaign after successful campaign. I have studied the texts, but I have been just a scout. Your option will be the correct one.'

The general chuckled quietly. 'I wish I shared your belief in me. But it shall be as you say. Bring the light infantry forward. We shall accompany them, you and I.'

Jai felt his pulse quicken again at the thought of such dreadful danger but drew his sword and checked it. Clean, unmarked and well oiled. His academy tutor would have been proud. The general did the same as the light infantry regiments moved to the fore, the heavy foot dropping back efficiently. While it must have been mere moments in the manoeuvring, to Jai it felt like lifetimes he endured, waiting for the order to move.

Finally everyone was in position, and the general gave him a questioning look. Jai nodded. At least they were in no danger of the mist lifting. That would only clear when the rains came again. Jai chewed on his lip, made sure the thong from his sword hilt was around his wrist, and waited.

'Mid-pace. Advance,' called the general, and they were off. Much to Jai's relief, two dozen of the light infantry moved in front of them at an unheard order, and the Crimson Guard closed in for support. Still, as they moved up onto the bridge, Jai was horribly aware how close to the front of the army he was.

The advance was steady, and Jai counted off the paces. Just after he had made it past five hundred steps – a quarter of a mile at the standard military pace – the general called for pace and a half. The army sped up, and Jai gave up counting as they pounded across the bridge. This was it... they were moving in for the fight. As Jai concentrated, expecting the far end of the bridge and potential violent death to come into view at any moment, he suddenly became aware that the general was looking out over the left-hand side of the bridge, and his own gaze followed. Peering into the whiteness, his eyes widened in surprise as a huge grey shape coalesced in the mist. A great raft filled with archers had been anchored in the river, some three quarters of the way across, and tied to the bridge support to hold it in place. A similar shape could just be made out beyond that raft. As the archers saw the army passing on the bridge, they took the prearranged cue, and hundreds of arrows sawed quietly through the air towards the defending positions on the far bank. The dull thud of the bow strings and the hiss of the missiles was hard enough to detect on the bridge and had to be completely inaudible on the far bank.

'Charge!' called the general, and the infantry picked up the pace to a run.

Jai cocked his head slightly as he jogged, half-expecting to hear the shrieks of startled pain as the arrows hit home on an unsuspecting imperial troop. Nothing. That unsettled him. Of course, if could be that they missed, loosing blind in the fog, or that the cries were too muffled at this distance. But still, Jai felt his nerves tingling.

'General...'

'I know. I feel it too. And that smell...'

The end of the bridge came upon them suddenly, and with it came terror.

The lead elements of the attack, the light infantry clad in bronze fish-scale and linen shirts with a small shield and a ji – a wicked combination of spear point and sickle blade atop a five-foot pole – met the wiliness of General Flavius Cinna with screams. The ground all around the end of the bridge was peppered with arrow shafts, standing proud like a field of wheat anticipating the scythe, but there had been no imperial soldiers there to suffer their barbed points. The end of the bridge was deserted...

... but first it had been prepared.

The charging infantry fell from the end of the bridge, their momentum making it almost impossible to stop as they reached the pit that had been dug there, and they plunged into it with cries of alarm. More men behind them, aware of their comrades' fate, were unable to avoid sharing it as the press of men charging behind forced them on into the same hollow. A pit forty feet square, seemingly full of water, since it had filled with the constant rains. A pit that held submerged horror. Jai grabbed the side of the bridge and clung on for dear life as the press of men, unable to stop in time, pushed more and more soldiers into that watery maw. His wide eyes saw the water swiftly turning red and, as a man plunged in and the water sloshed aside, Jai realised the floor of the pit beneath the water was covered with ash stakes, sharpened to needle points. Dozens of men were impaled now, thrashing in the water and screaming.

From the far side of the bridge, where General Jiang had mirrored Jai's action and was even now climbing onto the bridge's decorative parapet, Jai heard his commander bellowing for the column to halt and the archers to cease their barrage.

It took a lot of shouting, and dozens more men went into the pit, but finally the arrows stopped flying and the column slowed and stopped, shaking with horror and agitation.

Then came the western empire's fangs. The thuds of the artillery were so muted by the mist that Jai hadn't noticed them until half a dozen giant iron bolts suddenly ripped into the crowd on the bridge, most of them passing through at least one or two men before burying themselves in a third. Jai heard the general shouting the order to fall back and felt his own spirits plunge. Not only had the surprise attack failed, it had resulted in ignominious disaster.

But even now, as more bolts ripped into the men, Jai realised there was something else coming. The urgency in the general's voice wasn't due to the deadly bolts alone. He caught sight briefly, through the press, of General Jiang up on the parapet of the bridge. The commander was running now – running along the side of the bridge with the grace and skill of an acrobat, passing his own men in his flight, but shouting as he went, urging them to flee.

Without questioning why, Jai was up and clambering atop the parapet moments later.

He realised then what the smell was: *naphtha*! He'd not recognised the odour initially, because the Inda only used it for lamps and the Jade Empire never deployed it, favouring black powder for their weapons.

The fire arrows came just as the bolts stopped. The first half dozen thudded into panicked bodies as the light infantry were trying to flee, but it took only heartbeats for one of the missiles to reach the thin, pungent, flammable coating on the floor and sides of the bridge. The entire fifty-pace span of the bridge at the western end suddenly erupted in a conflagration. Jai almost plummeted into the water below as desperate hands clawed at the white stonework. Then he was running. He could feel himself slipping here and there, but the balance he had learned in his martial classes at the academy had given him excellent judgement and reflexes, and he ran the narrow gauntlet with a seething mass of panicked humanity to one side and a fall into a deadly, swollen, churning river on the other.

He could not have said how long the run was, but as he reached the first, less densely occupied area, he finally breathed deep and slowed, dropping from the parapet. The mood of the army was more sombre than usual as they retreated from the attack, as evidenced by the fact that he was forced to push his way through the withdrawing units rather than them standing respectfully aside for an officer.

He found General Jiang standing by the second red distance marker on the causeway, a servant helping him out of his armour. Jai noted with shock the angry black and red burn marks up the general's left forearm and the singed tatters of the uniform on that side. He approached nervously, half-expecting the general to fly into a rage. Instead, as the commander turned to his second, he looked tired and defeated.

'The archers are gone, Jai. I saw a catapult rock hit the nearest raft. Those who survived the blow went into the river. That means that the second raft was cut adrift and they have likely perished too, further downstream. Utter disaster.'

'We could not have known, sir,' Jai said. It sounded feeble to his own ears, but not only was it a consolation, it was also the truth.

'We *should* have known. I underestimated the man on the day we arrived in this giant graveyard. I knew then he was clever and prepared. I should have anticipated this.'

'How, sir? We are fighting for control of the only crossing of the Nadu for an army of this size. How could we have guessed that he was willing to render that crossing impossible?'

'Because, Jai, he is not here to conquer. He has no real interest in this side of the river. His remit is simply to oppose us, so he is happy to prevent us from crossing and bloody our nose at any opportunity. This is poor, Jai. We are left with just two options: wait for the reinforcements who will turn this whole annexation into a war of murder and enslavement, or throw every man we have at General Cinna at one go in the hope that sheer numbers can dislodge him. I hate both options.'

'I too, general.'

General Jiang sighed. 'Once we are settled in again and all is back to normal, come to the headquarters. We must try and find another way. If this campaign falls into the hands of some of my peers, there will be no place safe in the world for the Inda to seek refuge.'

CHAPTER 11

I was not made, I think, to be a leader of men. I was rajah, yes, of a lesser kingdom in the north, but a rajah is a ruler and it is my belief that a ruler is not the same thing as a leader. To the people of Initpur, I was the ruler, but my vizier was the leader. I made the overall decisions, but it was he who enacted them and turned my decisions into acts. Thus I was a ruler, and not a leader.

All that changed when we left Initpur. My vizier was still with me, but things had changed. I still made the wide-reaching decisions – wider reaching than ever before, in fact – but my vizier was as much a novice in this new situation as I. We were both refugees now, like all those who followed us, and it had become my task not only to make an important decision, but to also enact it.

We had left Initpur to languish under the control of a foreign power, and with it I had left behind the position of ruler. I had become a leader, albeit a reluctant and worried one. And now all I can do it try and lead well, and hope that I am not leading the last of the free Inda to their doom.

During the refugees' desperate journey south, there had been voices of dissent. It was to be expected in any gathering, particularly one the size of the Inda refugees, and especially considering the terrifying direction they were taking. Aram had patiently weathered all discord and shattered their arguments with logic and the stark truth of their situation. A few of the more recalcitrant had abandoned the column, shunning Aram's vision of safety in the one place that all Inda knew to be unsafe. As they had passed the derelict sacred markers, though, they had left behind perhaps half their number. It seemed that the reputation of these lands was horrifying enough that even a definite future of war and conquest seemed preferable to the uncertainty of the south.

Not for Aram. And for the thousands who still accompanied him. The journey through the haunted lands beyond the marker had been quiet and nerve-racking. Those who had chosen to continue did so with tight lips and darting eyes, constantly aware of every rustling leaf and every flicker of movement. The sense of unseen presences and of being shadowed as they travelled was all-pervasive.

There had been a horrible incident only half an hour beyond the markers when a terrified woman discovered that her husband had brought a small utility knife with him. Aram doubted that such a thing counted as a weapon, but it caused a tremendous fuss and polarised the group. The old man who owned the knife had had such opprobrium and bile heaped upon him by the others that his heart had given out and he had expired in the heat of debate.

In the aftermath two things had happened: every blade, be it a utility knife, a dining one or even a razor, had been cast aside in a pile with much prayer and apology. And one man had suddenly become the voice of dissent.

In retrospect, Aram should have seen it coming. Parmesh had been the vizier of some lord now trodden under the western empire's nailed boots. He had been one of the most vocal of the complainers throughout the journey, but his voice had been somewhat lost in the crowd until the incident with the knife. Now, Parmesh was a constant drone of gainsaying. Not direct opposition, mind. Aram would have known how to deal with a clear enemy. But Parmesh was not an enemy and had accepted both Aram's leadership and his objective. He was just the voice of general background disagreement, and as such had become something of a leader in his own right.

The first night in the south lands had been a night of little sleep and persistent tense silence. A young man had started playing a veena, its ponderous wavering metallic notes ringing out through the jungle, delivering a traditional tune – a haunting melody. He was almost mobbed in an effort to stop him. No one wanted haunting melodies right now. All night, some among the four thousand refugees would raise a quiet but panicked alarm, claiming to have spotted the ghosts or seen eerie movement in the trees, to have heard distant footsteps or muffled breathing in the undergrowth. Each search had produced nothing. Anywhere else, Aram would have put it down to nerves or superstition, but here in these forbidden lands he could feel it too. Three times in that one night his flesh prickled at the sensation of being watched by some unseen observer. Of course, it did not help that the rains had stopped the moment they passed into the dead lands, and had not returned since. Uncanny.

The second day had been as troubling as the first, and Aram had noted how Parmesh was now with him at the front at all times, questioning everything, second-guessing every decision he made. Fortunately, dependable Bajaan and Mani were also ever-present, backing him up and helping him keep control. Thus the four of them became an odd tetrarchy, with Aram the senior. Thus it was that when they found the monastery's outer marker, it was the four of them who went ahead.

The monastery's territory was apparently delineated with markers on the approach roads, though the precise meaning of the stones was lost on the travellers. Aram and his people had known about the line of markers that set the boundary of the haunted lands, but no one other than the guardian monks themselves had ever been to their monasteries, and so no one knew anything about them. The sacred images of the gods made it clear the stone by the road was the work of the monks, but the writing on it was in the ancient forgotten tongue and utterly incomprehensible.

The huge mass of shivering, nervous refugees remained in the best area they could find, three large clearings that seemed to be a natural feature of the jungle. Aram and his three companions steeled themselves and began to move forward along the path they had been following for some time.

For the next half mile, Aram was fascinated to see the change in the land around them. The thick jungle receded a little, the verges of the path trimmed back to create a wide grassy swathe. Then the trees and creepers, ferns and bushes disappeared entirely, giving way to cultivated fields. The crops had been planted in season and carefully cultivated patches of wheat and tea were now ready for harvest. A river had been diverted to create heavily irrigated areas where rice was grown in paddies, and that too was now ready for harvest.

Pens of animals were visible from the road – horses, cows and goats, all animals that could live indefinitely on the green pastures they were allotted and the fresh water diverted into their enclosures. A large lake close to the path teemed with fish, several small jetties striding out over the rippling waters and inviting a man to cast a line.

142

It was idyllic, especially after the perilous journey, and a blue sky punctuated with a few small high clouds only added to the beauty. But it was marred by one thing: neglect.

The crops had been lovingly sown and nurtured, but had been left to go somewhat wild, weeds and saplings springing up among them. Aram was no farmer, but Initpur had been rural enough in its economy that he had learned much of what farmers knew as a matter of course, and he estimated from the condition of the fields that they had not been tended for between two and three months. A similar conclusion could be drawn from the lack of upkeep on the lake jetties and the overpopulation of fish, and from the unkempt appearance of the animals, who had reverted to a wilder nature for all their domestication.

Moreover, the eerie feeling of being observed – or at least of not being alone – was gone. Here the land felt actually deserted. It was most odd that the untouched jungle felt alive with presence, while the one place they had found that showed all the signs of civilisation seemed utterly empty.

'Where are the monks?' Parmesh asked quietly, for once his question echoed by Aram's.

Where indeed?

Leaving the question unanswered, Aram led them on. More fields. Barley and mustard. Coops of near-feral chickens. Sheds covered with moss. Farm implements tangled with weeds. Months. The monks had not worked their lands for months.

The monastery was impressive. Far more impressive than Aram had expected. It had been perhaps two centuries since the monks had first come south at the guru's instruction, founding their monasteries and maintaining the marker line. One might expect a certain level of ornateness and ornamentation to develop over that time, but what surprised Aram was not the intricacy of the place, but the scale.

The complex was surrounded by a low wall, perhaps five feet high, buttressed in places, with gates that stood open on the various approach paths, of which several others could be seen even from this road. The gathering of structures inside put the palace complex of Initpur to shame. It would dwarf any palace or monastery in the north. Towers and roofs rose above that boundary wall in a huddled collection that filled an area large enough to muster an army.

Mani whistled through his teeth, impressed.

'I had no idea there were so *many* monks at these places,' Bajaan added.

'There aren't,' Parmesh reminded them in flat tones.

'What now?' Mani pressed, ignoring the ever-present voice of gloom.

'Now,' Aram replied, 'we search the monastery. Perhaps we will find the monks, or at least their remains. Perhaps we will learn where they have gone if they still live. Come on.'

They approached the walls and passed through the iron gates tentatively. As they did so, Mani grasped one of the swinging portals and gave it an experimental nudge. It shrieked with the tortured sound of rusting metal. The gates had not been closed for months either.

'This is making me nervous,' Parmesh muttered.

Aram and the others were nervous too, but they felt no need to add voice to their fears. It was uncanny. It was wrong. The main complex was of ancient construction, begun two centuries ago when the monks first came here and continually updated, embellished and extended over the decades. A huge ornate frontage contained a great doorway, which once again stood open and creepily inviting. A bell hung by the gate and Aram reached up towards it but changed his mind and walked on.

The walled enclosure contained more than the main monastery complex, though. There were orchards with fruit hanging from sagging branches, and vegetable gardens, overgrown but full and thriving amid the weeds, sheds and barns, structures of all sorts. And oddly, in an area that would otherwise have been naught but a wide swathe of open, dusty ground, three enormous wooden barn-like buildings.

'Let's look in there first,' Aram said, pointing at those three great structures.

The four men approached the nearest nervously, slowly. The building was high enough to contain two levels, like a barn with a mezzanine hayloft. It had numerous shuttered windows too high up to peer in without standing on a man's shoulders. Aram considered that, but decided to circle the building first.

The door was shut. That came as something of a surprise, considering the open nature of every other portal they had seen. Aram glanced at Mani and Bajaan, who both nodded. Parmesh was frowning his usual disapproval.

Reaching out, Aram grasped the handle of the plain, utilitarian door and pushed it inwards. He had not been sure what he was expecting, but whatever it was, this was not it. The building was a bunkhouse on a grand scale. Well-lit by those high windows, the great shed contained at an estimate sixty or seventy beds in neat rows. They were bare and plain, and without sheets, but they were clearly beds. At one end a rudimentary washroom had been constructed, the stone sinks empty.

Frowning himself now, Aram climbed the stairs and discovered half as many beds again on the second level.

'Accommodation for a hundred people,' Aram murmured quietly as he descended once more. 'Apparently recently constructed and unused. However many monks there were here, it seems unlikely there were a hundred.'

'*Three* hundred,' corrected Mani. 'Those other two buildings are identical to this from the outside. Let's check them out, but I'll be surprised if they're not exactly the same inside.'

They did so, and proved Mani's guess correct. Three huge bunkhouses, each capable of housing a hundred people, all, they estimated, constructed within this past year.

'Why did they feel the need to house three hundred guests?' Bajaan whispered nervously.

'Perhaps they had visitors from other monasteries. From the length of the marker line, there must be more than a dozen monasteries across the land. Perhaps twice that.'

'Whoever they were expecting never turned up,' Parmesh pointed out.

'Come on.'

Aram led them on a quick tour of the external structures. During almost an hour's exhaustive search, they found tool sheds, storage sheds, barns, granaries, workshops, a bath house, laundry house, structures given over to the production of wool, cheese, milk, honey and much, much more. But most interesting were the thing they were not expecting, and the thing they didn't find.

They did not find a living human, nor any sign of the passing of one, be it a rotting carcass or cremated remains. Unless the monks were to be found in the main complex, then they had not died here, but had left the place. And if that was the case, why had they left their crops unharvested? Even in a rush, the refugees had gathered all the food they could before they left.

And the thing they found that they had not expected: two more sets of three bunk houses in other places around the complex. Housing for a thousand, or near enough.

'This place is setting my nerves truly on edge,' Mani said as they completed a circuit and reached the main entrance once more.

'I think we all feel the same,' Aram replied. 'But for all the oddness of this place, there is one thing I have noted here that is different to everywhere since we passed the marker.'

'What's that?'

'It does not feel threatening.'

The others nodded, even Parmesh. With this strange sense of empty abandonment came a certain security after days of feeling wraiths surrounding them in the jungle. It was with a heightened sense of curiosity and jangling nerves that they entered the main complex.

It struck Aram as odd that here in the land of ghosts, the most forbidden place in the world, and in the house of dedicated monks, he was already witnessing more wealth and comfort than the Inda had known in three generations. The wall paintings were still vivid. The silver and the gold remained in place and had not been melted down two decades ago to pay harsh imperial forage parties. They moved through the monastery slowly and with eyes widening with each new discovery.

Aram had visited small monasteries in Initpur and neighbouring kingdoms during his long life. Their organisation was hardly uniform, but all the elements were there in some form or other. The temple, formed of a decorative square building, giving a side to each element and a face to each of the four gods of every circle of the heavens. The monks' living quarters – ascetic and plain, functional and modest, with the majority of the workshops being kept outside the monastery proper. The sacred pools. The great assembly hall with its inscribed columns and room for the monks to kneel. The stepped symposium, open to the air, where the monks could engage in open and learned discourse.

These components of any Inda monastery were to be found in this place, certainly, and the four men traipsed through them in worried awe. But there were new components here too, features that they had never seen in other such places.

A library.

As they entered the large hall with its rack upon rack of cubbyholes, each designed to hold a precious scroll, Aram's breath caught in his throat. The Inda had their own language, of course, and many could read and write it – those of sufficient rank in the social scale and those who had devoted their lives to religion, at least. And great tales from the past had been written as sagas to be passed on through the generations, as well as laws and important pronouncements. But never in his life would Aram have dreamed there had been so many things written down as to fill this place. A man could spend his life in the pursuit of naught but reading and still not work through this library.

A quick, rather nervous and reverent search revealed three things of note. The scrolls maintained here were an eclectic mixture of folk tales, legal and religious lore and varied teachings. They were written in more than one language, the large majority being in that ancient tongue decipherable only by the monks who learned it as a matter of course. And not all of the writings were present. There were quite some number of empty holes, though they showed signs of use, all of which suggested that specific scrolls had been removed, probably a few months ago when this place was abandoned.

There was also an exercise hall.

At least, that was what it seemed to be to Aram, and the two soldiers, Bajaan and Mani, confirmed his theory in part. Monks exercised, of course. A body needed to stay healthy and fit to serve the gods, after all. But it was the habit of monks to gather in the open air and practise yoga. This hall might be used for a similar practice, but Mani pointed out the various padded mats and posts with cushioned sides. Though he had trained himself in the use of both sword and spear, Mani recognised the accoutrements of a dojo – a school for the teaching of unarmed combat.

'What?' Aram said, his eyes widening.

'Fighting without weapons. Or at least the forging of fist and foot *into* weapons,' Mani replied.

They stared in wonder.

'Monks do not fight,' Parmesh said firmly.

'Evidence suggests that these ones do,' Aram replied. 'An elegant solution, wouldn't you say? It is lethal, supposedly, to bring weapons past the markers. We saw what happened to the Jade Empire patrol who did just that. And yet the monks clearly felt the need to be able to protect themselves, and so they found a way. They became trained with their own body as the weapon.'

'Monks do not fight,' repeated Parmesh. 'It is one of the great laws from time immemorial. It is why no war touches a temple. All the Inda respect priests and monks because they are men of learning, of piety and of *peace*.'

'Yet we do not know what the last guru told his monks,' Aram countered. 'The messages he bore were for their ears only, and no man has passed the markers to study the monks and their world. Perhaps the guru told these men specifically that they could fight in such a manner. Perhaps they were allowed. All I can say is that if I spent my entire life in the land of ghosts, I would want to be able to protect myself too.'

'You *will* be spending your life in the land of ghosts.'

Aram threw a glare at Parmesh. Was he just being deliberately negative? They moved on.

The third surprise came in the form of a map.

Aram was immediately reminded of the faded painting on the wall of his old palace at Initpur. His map had shown all the known lands of the Inda with each kingdom and main city noted, as well as the roads, bridges, passes and chief geographical features. It had been painted by a master generations earlier, and had been one of the best of its kind. But like all the Inda's maps, past a certain line of latitude the one at Initpur had remained blank. A white mist that represented the land of ghosts and the Isle of the Dead hung from the tip like a single teardrop.

Not so the map in the monastery. Aram felt his pulse quicken and his breathing become shallow as he stepped onto the map, which was constructed of twenty or more different coloured stones on the floor. In fact, it *was* the floor. Aram had heard that the western empire built pictures like this. Mosaics, they were called. He'd never seen one. And what a picture to be greeted with.

The lands of the Inda were all marked, just as his own had been, though in a more rudimentary, less artistic fashion. But past that line, where northern maps ended, this one began. Here, the land of ghosts was a true land. What had to be long-gone settlements were marked, though unnamed. Major roads seemed to be included as long paths of grey. The marker line was there, as were the monasteries behind them. That southern isle was the only part that remained empty and devoid of features. Perhaps the most impressive thing about the image, though, was the bridge.

If only the two great armies fighting at Jalnapur could see this map. There they fought over a marvel of engineering: a great bridge spanning the half-mile-wide torrent of the Nadu River. But there, perhaps a hundred miles south of this very monastery, another bridge was marked. And it was not in the nature of rivers to narrow as they neared the sea. Indeed it was rare for a river not to widen considerably. That bridge, then, could be a mile long. Or perhaps a series of bridges and causeways across a delta. Either way, it would represent another great feat of engineering and a viable alternative to that blood-soaked bridge surrounded by corpses at Jalnapur.

It took only moments for Aram to find Initpur and then trace their route with his feet in tiny steps across the map hall, around the great war zone, past the site of their near destruction at the hands of a scout party, across the boundary and to the monastery that had to be this one.

His eyes strayed on as he came to a halt, following another grey trail down to that bridge and to the distant mystery of the white teardrop at the far side of the room. He shook his head. No. This was far enough. The very nature of this map suggested that the monks had roamed all across the land of ghosts unharmed in order to chart its features, but the white teardrop confirmed that even they had not crossed to the Isle of the Dead. And if the monks were safe, then Aram could convince himself – though not without difficulty – that his people could also be safe. But if the monks would not go there, then neither would he.

'The monastery is empty,' Mani said.

Aram nodded. 'And it feels safe. Or at least safer than anywhere we have been.'

'Then what happened to the monks?' demanded Parmesh.

'I do not know. But they were not killed here, for there is no sign of fighting or death, and there are no bodies. It would appear that they made a purposeful decision to quit the monastery. They took some of their writings with them, but left everything else. I cannot say why, nor can I answer why they constructed so many guest quarters, but I do know one thing: this place could be no more fitting for us if the monks had planned it themselves.'

He felt an odd frisson of energy shiver through him at that thought and he frowned and looked at the others. Their expressions suggested that the same thought had occurred to them.

'You don't really believe—?' began Mani.

'I don't know,' Aram interrupted. 'But whether this was meant to be or not, it shows that the gods are with us. We have shelter in a place that feels safe. We have abundant food and supplies, space for all our people, and it is safe from both the empires whose boots stamp upon the lands of the Inda.'

Bajaan nodded. 'If we make better use of the space in the bunk houses, we could probably house almost half the people in them.'

'And two hundred more in the accommodation of the monks,' Mani added.

'And what of the rest?'

They turned irritated looks on Parmesh and Aram waved a hand. 'There is so much space. So many barns and workshops that could be cleared out and remade as housing. And there were stocks of timber, tiles and bricks in three or four storage sheds. We could build more. Fewer than a hundred monks built these bunkhouses with their own hands. We have many hundreds of builders, carpenters and masons, roofers and more. And of manual labour: thousands. In a week we could have trebled the accommodation here. And we have farmers to gather the crops and tend the animals. We have fishermen to work the lake. We have everyone we need to make this place viable, and this place has everything we need to survive and even thrive. I told you all from the start the gods would protect us as they did the monks.'

150

'As long as they don't throw at us whatever they did to drive the monks away,' Parmesh grunted.

Aram refused to rise to the bait this time. 'We will return to the people with this welcome news. The survivors of the Inda have a refuge after all.' He turned to Parmesh. 'And we will be of one accord with our happy news. We can no longer afford to be divided. We must work together or we shall fall apart. If you cannot be part of this, Parmesh, then you should leave.'

The dissenter shrugged. 'I agree with you. I have reservations, yes, but I can see the logic in this, and I can certainly see no better way, so I shall sing the praises of the monastery and hope that no one asks us where the monks went.'

Again Aram glared at the man, but took a deep breath of relief and then smiled. 'And once we are settled, we shall seek out other survivors, including those we left beyond the border, and offer them sanctuary.'

Sanctuary. In the land of ghosts. Who would have guessed?

CHAPTER 12

Ravi,

I am sorry. You may believe that you are no longer the brother I once knew, and there seems precious little echo of him in the man I saw when I came here, but I cling to the hope that Ravi, son of Aram, is inside there somewhere, and that you will yet regain your humanity.

When you find this, I know you will be angry. Do not take it out on those who do not deserve your ire. I pray to see you again one day, but not here, and not like this. Take care, and may all the gods – yours and mine – watch over us both.

Dev

Oddly, it was the Sizhad's army itself that offered Dev his chance. He knew what was required just one day into his captivity, and it was all because of the rigid requirements of the 'Faithful'.

Dev and his cavalry were kept together in a pitch-black room in the temple, where it would have been impossible to tell day from night and one hour from the next had they not been periodically removed from the stygian gloom. The great room was cold, but dry and clean. Dev had been surprised to note when he was thrust inside – the interior illuminated by the doorway for a brief moment – that the room was not equipped with rudimentary latrine facilities, even in the form of a bucket, and yet was clean and smelled only of cold stone.

The reason for that had become clear shortly thereafter. It was seemingly one of the tenets of the Sizhad's faith that cleanliness was paramount. The Faithful had to be clean in all their undertakings. It was one of the few positive attributes Dev could see in their creed, but a useful one for him, nonetheless. Four times each day the door was opened and Dev and the other occupants of the room were brought out, marched from the temple complex and escorted to a latrine block, where they were given just enough time to empty themselves and clean up before being escorted back to captivity. Each time they were made to pause and listen to the chanting and the music of religious ceremony. It seemed the four visits were carefully chosen to coincide with the Faithful's rigid timetable of worship: a song of thanks for the rising of the sun, a song of glory for the sun's apex, a song of mourning for its setting, and finally a dirge at midnight for the sun's absence. At the beginning of each ritual, the sons of the Sizhad were required to be clean, and it seemed the same principle was applied to each of the prisoners, given the timing of the visits.

Latrine time was not the only reprieve from the gloom. Every few hours the door was opened again when a man was taken from the room or brought back. Thus is was that Dev endured his confinement without too much discomfort, though he felt for each of the men taken away, whether they were brought back or not. Each time, he understood, the soldier was taken before the Sizhad and given the chance to recant his faith in the old gods and convert to the worship of the sun. Some did, for men will give up anything, even gods, when faced with certain fates. Those who refused were blinded, as the captain had been, and released back into the dark cell, presumably to remind Dev of the decision he himself would have to make. Or perhaps they were being kept for something else. Somehow, he couldn't imagine the latter purpose being anything good.

It was now, by Dev's reckoning, his third week at the mountain fortress, and most of his men were sightless or had deserted to the enemy. The Sizhad was keeping Dev for last, and he would soon face that dreadful choice, but he was prepared now and planned to avoid such a fate. Three weeks of slow, painstaking planning, but he was finally ready, or at least as far as he was able to plan. Some things would always require luck and adaptability, even for a man with a brain like Dev's.

He could hear the soldiers coming in the distance, and in the pitch darkness of the room he began to strip off his old clothes to the waist and don the new ones.

They had been laboriously collected and made, and he felt sure they were pitiful when seen in the light, but they represented his only chance. It had been slow and dangerous work, but on almost all of those trips to the latrines he had seized the opportunity to tear a strip from the edge of the dirty, wet white towel that hung on a rail by the water trough. Each time he had tucked the strip into his tunic and taken it back to the cell. It had taken him four hours to prise a great splinter from one of the benches in the room, and he had made his fingers bleed over and over again digging a small hole in one end. By the end of the second day he had a rudimentary needle that he spent many further hours narrowing and sharpening, and separating a single thread from his tunic was easy enough. He began to sew in the dark, praying he was doing it right.

Three weeks. He'd almost laughed as he imagined the poor idiot whose task it was to wash the latrine's linens looking at the filthy sodden towels and wondering why they were all smaller than he remembered, yet no one seemed to have pieced together the puzzle of the shrinking towels. And so Dev fashioned himself a rudimentary white tunic and a long strip of similarly white material – laboriously, and with painful bloody fingers, in the dark.

The guards were approaching now, their conversation a muffled hum, their booted feet crunching on the stony ground outside, for the 'chamber of night' was part of the ancillary buildings of the temple complex, within the wall on the hill, but outside the temple itself. The horsemen in the room, mostly silent and blind, began to shuffle towards the door in anticipation of the uncaring zealots who prodded them with spear butts, guiding the sightless to the latrine. Their supervision of their charges had gradually diminished as the blind began to outnumber the rest and the danger they posed decreased. They were now, to the guards, little more than cattle.

Dev kept his trousers and boots on, but discarded the tunic and vest in favour of his rough, stinking white tunic. As he shrugged it on, wrinkling his nose at the scent of a garment made from unwashed latrine towels used by a hundred men at a time, he began to shuffle around the edge of the room. Reaching into his trousers, he removed the strip of white material and wound it around his head in the best impression of a turban he could manage in the dark. It was rough but should pass, for he knew a turban's wrapping well enough.

In Dev's experience, people rarely saw details unless they were searching for them. He prayed that this was true of the guards today as he fell into position against the cold stone wall some four feet from the door.

A jingle of keys and a rattle of locks, and the door swung open. Light poured into the room in a wide beam, and the very few men who still had their eyes blinked in discomfort. The vast majority saw nothing. Dev chewed his lip, lurking in the darkness along the wall. He waited as the guards began to urge the men out, and finally, as the crowd in the room began to clear, his chance arose.

A number of the blind prisoners were milling about, uncertain where they were going until they bumped into something. The guards, irritated by the duty they had been assigned but doing it with the oddly disgruntled stoicism of their faith, entered the room and began to move like a farmer's dogs, herding the blind and confused to the door.

Dev took a steadying breath, his pulse racing, and stepped out of the shadows into the crowd of bumbling sightless men pushing out into the world beyond. As though he were a leaf fallen into a meltwater stream, Dev found himself carried forth in the press of men. He emerged into the world once more, and edged his way to the periphery. Trying to look unobtrusive and haughty, he held his turbaned head high and joined in the irritated comments as the soldiers drove their herd towards the latrines.

Not a single man looked at him. He may have been wrapped in filthy and stinking material, but, at a passing glance, a man in a white tunic and white turban was just another guard. Dev strode along beside the miserable mob of blind captive horsemen as though he had every right in the world to be who and where he was. If there was one major flaw with his disguise it was the lack of a spear, a weapon that was carried by all the others, but there was nothing he could do about that. They crossed the open ground below the temple and passed through a postern in the temple's boundary wall.

Outside, two more alert guards stood either side of the door, and Dev steeled himself as the crowd funnelled through the gap. The guards were paying attention to the men passing between them, and they would almost certainly single out the spear-less guard with the stinking white turban, even if he was clearly Inda like them.

Dev fell into position as the crowd funnelled through the doorway and, as he approached the exit, removed a stone from his pocket. It

JADE EMPIRE

was not a large stone, perhaps two thumbnails in width, but was weighty enough. Raising his hand to his face as though to scratch it, he gave the stone a sharp jerk and cast it through the doorway just above the milling, sightless crowd. His luck held as the projectile cracked one of the blind men on the back of the head. The poor cavalryman gave a cry of pain and alarm and stumbled forward, knocking into other prisoners, who squawked their surprise and fell in a tangled heap.

The Faithful who had gone through first hurried over to deal with the mess, and another white-clad zealot only ten men in front of Dev pushed his way forward to help too. The guards to each side of the door should be distracted, if only briefly.

Dev emerged from the temple amid the flow of men, quickly moving aside so as not to become the focus of the two gate guards. The commotion at the front was quickly resolved and the gathering herded on once more. The gate guards resumed their inspection of the prisoners as they passed, having entirely missed the thing for which they searched.

Dev fell into step with them all once more as they descended the hill towards the latrine block just over halfway down the slope. He held his breath as they approached the mud-brick structure. The prisoners were roughly shoved into the doorway and the guards began to fan out near the entrance to wait for their charges to do their business. They would not go inside. They had no desire to share a latrine with unbeliever prisoners, and no need to keep such close tabs on them, for there was no escape route within. Dev had checked. Even the drains were too small for a man to pass along, and the windows were too narrow, to help contain the smell.

Dev spread out along with the other white-clad men, moving along the wall. Still hardly daring to breathe, he was so tense, the former prince of Initpur took the one chance he could grasp and slipped around the corner. He stopped there for only two heartbeats, half-expecting someone to shout after him. Nothing happened. No noise.

Then he moved. He was aware that he would smell. Despite having had the chance to use latrines and wash each day, none of them had properly bathed for three weeks, and the home-sewn white clothes he wore bore the odour of sewage. There was a faint breeze coming up the valley, as was often the case, and Dev had carefully chosen which side of the latrines to duck around based on that draught. With a quick silent prayer to Vayu of the Winds, he strode purposefully away from the squat mudbrick structure towards the massive campsite. The wind carried the aroma of the latrines this way, and his own smell was lost in the gusts. Better still, because of the prevailing odour of urine that often wafted this way, there were fewer men to be found there even than elsewhere in the camp.

Dev trod boldly down the dusty slope, between the first two unoccupied tents, and then moved among the large white canvas dwellings in a zigzag pattern. As soon as he was out of sight of the latrines he paused, listening. The timing was good. The chanting of the noon celebration was beginning at the temple and at each of the sun shrines strategically positioned around the valley for this purpose. The whole ritual took the best part of an hour, and it seemed from what Dev had observed that every man who was not engaged in important duties was expected to attend the ritual. There would be a diminished population in much of the camp for at least half an hour, and here in the lee of the latrines, it would be less still.

Dev heaved in a breath, trying to conjure up in his head the image he had burned into his memory each time he had emerged from that postern gate: a visual map of the camp. His plan only went so far before it relied upon luck and initiative, but he was not at that point yet. Pausing by one of the tents, he listened carefully. He could hear snoring and murmured conversation nearby, but nothing from this one. Preparing himself to face anything, he ducked inside.

Empty.

Sighing with relief, Dev scoured the tent until he found a clean white tunic and a belt. There was nothing else of use. Emerging back into the hot sun, he looked about quickly and then paused by another tent. The gentle sounds of a man asleep, presumably someone who had been on night duty. He moved swiftly on, pausing and listening again. Silence. Another tent produced trousers and a spare turban, which he purloined, using the stolen tunic as a makeshift bag. Two more tents taught him to move with care, both of them occupied by muttering men. The third was silent, and he entered cautiously. To his delight, he found a spear lying by a seat with a rag beside it, the blade half-coated with polish. He hurriedly rubbed off the polish with the rag and ducked outside again. He now carried the perfect disguise, though he would still smell.

Checking his mental map once more, he hurried on between the white tents. Once, as he moved along the line of temporary homes, he almost came to grief, stumbling to a halt as two chatting soldiers emerged from another gap between tents. Dev ducked into the nearest doorway and held his breath, sending out prayers to a dozen of the more appropriate gods. A figure lay in one of the cots within. His eyes were open and he was muttering. Dev swallowed nervously. The man looked straight at him, then turned away and muttered on. It was then that Dev realised the reclining man was soaked with sweat and had a pale, waxy sheen to his skin.

Fever.

He waited, as far from the sick man as possible and trying not to breathe in too much of the fetid, moist air, until the two chatting soldiers moved away and their voices were lost. A moment later he emerged into the sun once more and took three deep cleansing breaths, hoping his contact with the feverish man was distant enough to save him from potential illness. He was alone outside once more. For a hundred heartbeats he hurried through the tents, passing close to the few men wandering around, but not close enough for them to pay him any real attention.

He found with dismay the place he sought. The large trough of water fed by a channel, buckets standing nearby, he'd spotted on several visits to the latrines, was unreachable. A small gathering of Faithful occupied the open space before it, their faces turned to the sun, chanting their litany. He could wait until they finished their ritual and dispersed, but by then there would be men everywhere again and the whole plan would be in jeopardy.

A thought struck him and he ducked to the side, moving between the tents in a wide arc until he found himself standing beside the raised channel that fed the basin. The water had to come from somewhere. Perhaps there was another place he could bathe and remove the tell-tale stink? He needed to be clean and changed before the devotions ended and men flooded the camp once more.

As swiftly as he could, he followed the water channel – a tube of pottery that rested on a wooden bridge-like structure which gradually rose as it came nearer to the source – and frowned as he came across something unexpected behind a small locked storage shed. A second channel branched from the first. He was torn momentarily, but logic dictated his decision. The source was further away and high up near the waterfall, but the second destination could not be much further from the one he'd just left. Decision made, he turned and followed the second branch. The channel wound its way through the camp and Dev followed it, his nervousness growing with every pace. He could hear the chanting and singing of the Faithful rising in a crescendo. Soon they would be done, and the camp would come to life again.

Three times as he followed the channel he had to duck out of sight and work his way around stray soldiers. He discovered the second pipe's destination quite suddenly as he turned a corner and found himself staring out at open greenery. A fence separated him from a wide meadow of grass and the forty or fifty horses roaming the lush green, grazing contentedly. Two white figures were just visible on the far side of the corral, but they were mostly obscured by the herd of wandering horses.

Dev smiled as he understood the water's destination.

A large trough sat just inside the fence, fresh water pouring into it constantly, four drains emptying the excess and channelling it along irrigation channels through the grass, keeping the paddock green. Swiftly, Dev propped his spear against the fence, climbed over and dropped down the other side. Praying that no one stumbled across him right now, he tore off his clothes and dropped them in the gap between the trough and the fence. Bracing himself, he dropped into the water and began to rub himself all over, vigorously. The trough was freezing despite the hot sun and Dev shivered, teeth clacking together as he swiftly bathed.

Rising, he alighted on the grass once more and straightened, squeezing the water from his hair and shaking to discard the worst of it. Hurriedly, he untied the tunic-bag and began to pull on his new clothes. He paused suddenly as he realised that the singing had stopped at some point while he was in the water. Even as he tried to listen to see if the ambient noise of the camp was increasing in this locale, he heard a bell being chimed frantically in the temple, the ringing picked up by others. His absence had apparently been noticed. Had they already found the small note he'd hastily written on a piece of torn material with the blood from his now-crusted fingers?

He threw on the tunic and began to wind a fresh turban expertly around his skull. Pulling on his boots finally, he momentarily wondered whether he might manage somehow to take a horse from the corral, but quickly dismissed the notion. It would be far too difficult. Leaping the fence, he collected his spear and began to move with a steady, assured pace through the camp. There was no need to run or hide now. He was dressed like them, looked like them even down to the two months' growth of beard, smelled relatively fresh, and could speak their language with a local accent.

Indeed, no one spared him a second glance as the army flooded the camp once more, their devotions complete. Occasionally one of the warriors passing him would incline his head and utter the ritual phrase 'Praise the light.' Each time, Dev bowed his head in return and replied 'The sun is the way.' He had heard the damned exchange enough times in three weeks, after all.

Finally, he stopped at another water container, where thirsty soldiers were filling cups. He did the same, supping down the refreshing clear liquid as his gaze slowly circled the valley. Leaving the way he'd entered would be foolish and fraught with danger. Firstly, if he was being looked for, that would be the first place they would seal off. Secondly, that valley was well garrisoned by hidden men, as they had learned when they arrived.

He could see three possible alternatives. One rose to the north of the valley up a steep ravine to a quarry, which would be close and almost certainly a dead end. To the south-east another path rose, and he could see the glinting white dots of guards on it. They would be difficult to pass, and that route would be the second to be sealed after the main valley as the alarm spread. Dev needed to go south. He knew that, and so would the Sizhad.

The east was the nearest end of the valley. He had been navigating that way ever since the easterly breeze had carried the latrine scent to cover his escape. There lay the lake fed by the glittering cascade, which also fuelled the water channels that ran around the valley. There was no path into the surrounding peaks there, but the cascade fell in at least six falls over a steady decline, which meant that with luck and strength, a man might climb it. No one would look for him there. Of course, he would find himself in the mountains without a road to follow, but there was one possibility. The only great lake in this stretch of the mountains was the Channali Sea, which was the source of the river that eventually ran past the Initpur palace of Dev's youth. The sheer volume of water coming over the cliff here hinted at a vast source that could very well be that same lake. It was a slim hope, but one Dev clung to. If that cascade led him to the Channali Sea, he could follow a second river down into the lowlands.

Moments later he was moving at speed towards the east. Horns were being blown all over the place now. The hunt for the escaped officer was on. Units were being called to attention. Men were hurrying this way and that. It was the perfect cover for Dev to move fast. In their urgency to catch him, they were helping mask his movements. It seemed like an eternity of running, but eventually he emerged from yet another line of tents onto a grassy sward beside the lake. Laundry-washing places were evident around its edge, and he could see the two large pipe bridges arcing up to the top of the first waterfall, the source for all the water distribution around the camp.

The southern fringe of the lake was given over to orchards, helping supply the huge army, and Dev felt a boost to his confidence. Scurrying along the line of the tents, he entered the orchard between two mango trees and disappeared amid the greenery, keeping his bearings by making sure the lake's shore stayed just in sight on his left between the trees. Jackfruit and lemons, mango and pomegranate rushed past as he left the populated part of the camp behind. He reached the rocky slope at the edge of the lake without having encountered another human soul and stood at the bottom, looking up at the jagged rocks down which the cascade tumbled. Somehow it seemed a lot less feasible from this angle. He pondered silently as he watched the great torrent crashing down into the lake some four hundred paces out into the water. Should he dirty his clothes again now? Against the grey rock, the white would stand out. But then, if he could reach the falling water, the white would blend in well.

He almost died while considering the rock, and only comprehended the danger when he spotted the shadow of his assailant on the rocks. He lurched urgently aside, and the man's spear point hit the huge boulder where he had been standing, damaging the steel badly as it scratched the rock and skittered off to the side.

Dev spun, letting his grip slide down his own spear shaft as he did, so that by the time he was coming round to face the man, he held it tightly by only one end. He smashed the seven-foot shaft into the man's back and heard a crack of ribs. The attacker exhaled with a grunt and staggered, his weapon flailing. Dev was on him before he could recover. This was not about a swift kill now, but a silent one. He didn't know how the man had found him and decided he was the missing prisoner, but he couldn't have him shouting for his friends whatever the case.

He knocked the winded soldier to the ground and dropped onto the man's back, his knees digging into his spine. Casting his own spear aside, he grasped the man's head by the temples and pulled it back, slamming it down onto the hard ground. The man gasped in pain, and Dev repeated the attack again, and a third time. The man was thoroughly dazed now, his arms flopping, breath ragged. Dev released the pressure, rising for a moment, then retrieved his spear and brought it down hard in the middle of the man's torso. It grated between ribs and transfixed organs before plunging on through flesh and bone and into the ground. An image from his youth flashed into his mind: he was on his back as yet again Jai's sparring stick found his throat. How impressed Jai would be if he could see Dev now.

The man expired in agony, but with relatively little noise and fuss. Dev cursed his luck. As soon as this body was found, the route the prisoner had taken would be evident, but there was little he could do about that. There was nowhere in the orchard to effectively conceal a body, and he could hardly spare the time to carry it somewhere. He would just have to move quickly and hope to gain distance on any pursuers.

He left his spear where it was, standing proud of the body. He could hardly climb rocks holding it anyway. Moments later he was grasping the first visible handhold and pulling himself up. As swiftly as he dared, but with the dexterity of a mountain goat and the care of a lover, he caressed the rock, finding grip after grip, spidering up the steep slope. At every moment he expected to hear the sound of a man shouting at him, but still there was nothing. Slowly, he moved across the rocks as he climbed, so that he was now above the lake and not the orchard. It was little comfort. The lake might well provide a nicer surface to fall into than the trees, but the angle of the rocks suggested that Dev would have bashed out his brains on them long before he reached the cold, glassy surface.

Swallowing nervously, he reached for the next handhold, his foot slipping frighteningly for a moment before he found better purchase. Slowly but surely, he moved up and north. The going became tougher as he started to encounter wet rock, but with determination and infinite care he continued to climb. At least the falling water would now be blending nicely with his white garments.

He almost cried as he pulled himself over a lip and realised he had reached the top of the first fall. Here he could see the sources of the distribution tubes, cold fresh water slopping into them at a rate of knots. It briefly occurred to him that, had he a source of poison right now, he could probably kill a sizeable part of the Sizhad's army. But he hadn't. And every moment he spent here carried the danger of a gruesome death at the hands of a man who had once been his younger brother.

Dev scrambled across the rock, skirting the small pool and making for the next fall.

He was going to make it.

He was going to survive.

Though how long his world might survive still hung in the balance.

LATE SUMMER, VELUTIO

General Flavius Cinna took a deep breath, preparing to try again.

'Majesty—'

'No, Cinna. There will be no peace. You have shown that even a force of men outnumbered and with less effective artillery can hold the west against the great army and the thunderous cannon of the Jade Emperor. And now you expect me to believe that you cannot win this war for me? That I must agree terms with that cadaverous green-eyed monster in the east? No. A thousand times, no, Cinna. I will give you a simple choice…'

Cinna recoiled from the emperor's spite. The man's eyes were rolling like a mad dog's. The rest of the court had pulled away and were leaning back in their seats as though sitting any closer might make them the next target.

'You will take my commission as it was given and bring me the Jade Emperor's head on a platter, Cinna, or you may take your own life here and now and I will find a more competent officer to take your place.'

Cinna felt his anger settle in the pit of his stomach and form there into a diamond of hatred. In the blink of an eye he measured the number of paces between him and the madman on the throne. He had no sword, but the emperor always had one next to his seat for when he felt the need to cause bloodshed on a whim. Around the hall's shadowed periphery there would be hidden archers with their arrows ready. Fifteen paces. He could cover it in three leaps. A few more heartbeats to snatch the sword and then a single blow would free the empire.

He straightened with a sigh. It was a dream. Nothing more. He felt certain that the moment the emperor lay on the floor bleeding out his life, Cinna would be lauded as a hero by the room's various occupants. But Bassianus had a madman's hold on his people. As long as he was hale, they would do nothing against him. Cinna would sacrifice himself readily for the empire – he had sworn to do just that many times as a soldier – but even at the height of his physical power, he would have been unlikely to cross that distance without taking at least one arrow. By the time he grasped and drew that sword one would become six. He would be a hedgehog before he could land a killing blow, transfixed with dozens of arrows. And all for naught.

Still he would have tried, but for the other consideration: if he were to die with no direct heir in place, which psychopathic sycophant would be promoted in his place to stomp on the Inda? Cinna had been largely unsuccessful in his attempts to bring the natives on side, and Dev had vanished without trace in the northern mountains. Cinna had requisitioned what he needed from the natives and tried to conduct the war with the minimum damage to them and still they suffered. Imagine what would happen under a man who cared *nothing* for them? No. He had to return. He'd had to try to persuade the mad old bastard one last time. But he'd failed and he would have to try again.

'Your face resembles a whore who was short-changed,' snorted the emperor, laughing at his own crude humour. The court chuckled dutifully, and once again Cinna counted how many steps separated them, just in case.

'My apologies, Majesty. I merely fear for our outnumbered forces.'

The emperor nodded sagely. 'Very well. I shall send you the northern army in its entirety to give you the edge you need.'

Cinna felt his heart lurch. *No...*

'Majesty, that would endanger the whole empire. I took what forces we could spare to start with. There are no others.'

'Nonsense,' Bassianus sneered. 'The northern chiefs are our allies now. Have been for generations. The border forts are manned by limitanei troops. The full military is superfluous. The northern army will march for your camp at Jalnapur forthwith, and with them you will win me my war. Then I shall be called "Conqueror of the Jade Empire, and master of the world".'

Cinna fought to stop his eyes rolling in despair. The man was insane. He played with the future of the empire like a child played with a wooden doll.

'Majesty—'

'You have your orders. Go and win my war. Unless you wish to fall on your sword right now?'

Cinna counted the number of paces for a final time, wondering if there was any chance of saving the empire today. No. He would die before he struck the blow. He bowed and retreated from the room, heart hollow, hope gone. He was to win an unwinnable war, and to help him the emperor was about to sacrifice the security of the empire itself.

The gods were cruel sometimes.

PART THREE

AN EMPIRE FALLS

CHAPTER 13

From: Orosius Devinius, adjutant to Flavius Cinna, general commanding
To: Senior officers, all forward positions

Withdraw all extraneous personnel to rear lines. Sappers and engineers will be moving forward to secure the bridge zone against further potential attempts to cross.

Dev looked up from the note wearily and rubbed his sore knee with his free hand, tapping the desk with the pen. He had been back at Jalnapur for only five days and had not had even an hour's peace to catch up on his sleep or recover from his ordeal in the north.

His mind wandered from the mind-numbing administrative work and beyond the room and the plain outside, back over all the days since his captivity.

He had climbed the rocks at the fortified valley's eastern extremity with difficulty, constantly aware of the possibility of pursuit, though encountering none. It would likely have taken them in excess of an hour to come across the body in the orchard. It would not have taken them long to determine what had happened and where the killer had gone, but pursuit would be difficult and Dev had a good head start. Still, he moved at pace and only stopped once he was a number of miles from the camp.

Following the ascent of the six waterfalls, he had followed the river to the great lake. It had taken some mental arithmetic and study of the sun's movement to work out which of the torrents that led down from the Channali Sea was the one that passed through Initpur, but in the end he chose the likely one and began his long descent. In the end he had chosen incorrectly anyway, but only just, and the river he followed down out of the mountains had meandered through a land he knew that neighboured Initpur.

He had found the going in the lower hills little easier for some time. Though he was no longer in danger from the Sizhad's men, he *was* in Jade Empire-controlled lands, and had been appropriately circumspect in his movements. The few encounters he'd had with enemy patrols and garrison troops had come to naught, for he was Inda and dressed as such, and with his mastery of bluff and lie, he twisted out of trouble each time. Finally he crossed the northern tributaries of the Nadu River, careful to avoid conflict, for here some sort of secondary war was being waged between small roving imperial units on the western side and Jade Empire units to the east.

Once safely across and in imperial-patrolled, independent territory, he managed with some heated debate and a great deal of laboured explanation to requisition supplies and an imperial horse and turned south, following the great river to Jalnapur. He arrived at the war zone and the headquarters there to discover with some surprise that the general was absent. Cinna had been gone for a month, back to Velutio to petition the emperor, leaving his senior officers with instructions to hold their ground and not waste men in any crazed endeavour.

Dev had been held at the picket line for some time before his identity could be confirmed with one of the senior officers, but finally he had been permitted entry and was shown to the command post.

He had then been given only enough time to bathe and dress appropriately, and throw down a quick snack of bread and broth, before the officers began to bring him problems and decisions. Dev had panicked, though only inside where the men could not see. *Cinna* was the commander. Dev knew his military and his strategy but had no experience at all of command. Yet thanks to his position as Cinna's adjutant, he was now the ranking officer and things were expected of him.

He had spent the next few days snatching sleep and food when he could and resolving issues and disputes, granting leave to some units, changing the positions of others, dealing with supply problems and supplicants from various Inda kingdoms. It was a trial, keeping him constantly occupied and denying him time to rest, though that was a bittersweet thing in itself. He needed to rest. He needed to recuperate from over two months – was it three? – of journeying, imprisonment and flight. He felt broken and exhausted. But whenever he did get those precious chances to rest and close his eyes, his mind filled with scorching memories of Ravi and his rabid followers. The knowledge that his dear, sweet brother had become this Sizhad tore at his heart, and he was glad that his father was not around to see such a thing. But worse even than that was the knowledge that no matter what happened between the two great empires fighting over the bridge, in the north lurked a new force that was biding its time, waiting for the world to weaken so that they could bring their faith at the tip of a blade to an undefended world.

His brother...

Dev sighed and leaned back in the seat, ribs bruised from weeks of travel and hips sore from riding. The pile of reports and petitions on the left side of the desk was higher than it had been when he'd arrived. How was that possible? He'd not seen anyone come in and add to it. Yet someone must have, because the pile on the right of resolved issues was tiny. Someone had taken them away to deal with. He could barely imagine what someone without his natural administrative talent would have done with it all. Probably best not to ponder too much on that.

He sighed and cast his pen irritably across the table's surface, closing his eyes for a moment and wishing away the pile of documents before him. He was aware of the presence even with face lowered and eyes closed. Captain Gracilis was in the doorway, clearing his throat. Dev did not even look up at him. He knew the sounds the captain made every time he appeared there a million times a day, each time bearing a new problem for Dev to solve.

'Tell them to go away, Gracilis,' he said in a despairing tone. 'I don't care whether it's argumentative officers, brawling troops, irritable medics or discontented locals, they can wait. I've too much to do already right here.'

There was an odd silence, and Dev looked up with a frown to see that Gracilis was grinning.

'What is it?'

'The general is back, sir.'

Dev felt his heart leap and could not stop a smile from sliding across his own face at the news. On top of every other worry and burden he had struggled with these past five days, he had been deeply, if privately, concerned for the general. The bulk of the soldiery, and probably the officers too, would not have considered the danger Cinna was in, but Dev had been there when the general first received his command in the imperial court. He had watched as Cinna pushed his luck as far as it would go and almost fell to the emperor's insane displeasure because of it. And the man had gone back to try again, tempting fate. Dev should have spent those five days counting off the hours until the general's return, but he hadn't, for he'd harboured more than a faint suspicion that Cinna would by now be cold and white, lying in a burial pit somewhere outside Velutio's walls.

The news that he was not only alive but had returned to Jalnapur was a balm to the soul and the most welcome tidings Dev could possibly imagine.

'Where is he?'

Captain Gracilis jerked a thumb over his shoulder. 'Just passed through the gate of the Fifth Cohort, so he should be here any moment. He comes at pace.'

That could be either good or bad...

Gracilis retreated from the doorway, leaving the general's adjutant alone. Dev spent the time as he waited for the general arranging things on the desk to look slightly less disorganised, and tidying up his own appearance, which was somewhat dishevelled even in uniform and had been ever since he got back. Perhaps it was time to shave again too.

He heard the general arrive before he saw him and rose to his feet expectantly.

'Devinius is back?' Cinna said somewhere outside. 'Thank the gods.'

Captain Gracilis's voice came in reply. 'He's done an admirable job of keeping your desk clear, General.'

A snort. 'Perhaps I should go home and leave him to it, then?'

Gracilis chuckled outside as the general appeared, dusty and travel-worn, in the doorway.

'Gods, but you look a mess, Dev.'

'Good to see you too, General.'

Cinna smiled, though it never reached his eyes. There was something there that put Dev on edge, though he couldn't say precisely what it was. The general looked… haunted, somehow.

'At least the damned rain has stopped,' Cinna noted. 'When I left for Velutio it was still coming down like the wrath of the sea god. I gather monsoon season is now officially over. Ground is still sodden though.'

Dev nodded. 'Engineers tell me it will be weeks yet before the ground becomes firm enough for any real action.'

'Good. The last thing we want is to have no reason to avoid a huge fight. Every day we cannot launch a major offensive preserves lives. I expect my opposite number is thinking the same thing and relishing the wet ground too.'

Dev braced himself. 'You have news from Velutio, General?'

Cinna's last trace of a smile vanished and Dev's spirits sank. He leaned back as the general turned and closed the door for privacy. Cinna then removed his gloves and dropped his helmet and cloak onto a cupboard top before sinking into the chair opposite Dev and motioning for him to take the commander's seat behind the desk once more.

'It could have gone better, I'll admit. I had to go, though. I was nearing the end of my tether here. You and your cohort had vanished without trace, the rain was unceasing, there was no hope of movement at the river, and disease and illness were starting to take hold in the camp with the poor conditions. I'd spread out the men and tried to keep them as healthy as possible, but the whole thing was plummeting further and further into the mire. I had to take the chance and try to persuade the emperor again. I failed.'

'You live, General, and that in itself I consider a win.'

Cinna gave a humourless chuckle. 'In my attempt to improve matters, I have inadvertently made things worse, Dev.'

'Sir?'

'I sought to explain to the emperor that we simply do not have the strength to win this fight. Instead of seeking a sensible alternative to this disastrous war, the emperor has promised me enough reinforcements to win it.'

'That's madness,' Dev replied.

172

'Something for which our beloved emperor is noted, I would remind you.'

'But we already stripped the military of all the manpower it could spare and reaped a heavy harvest of able-bodied men from the provinces in the levies we ordered. Where will the emperor find such men for you?'

'He is committing the northern army in its entirety.'

Dev's eyes widened. 'Surely not? I spent years up on the border there cataloguing our strengths and resources. We were stretched even in peacetime. And what peace we *can* claim with the barbarians across those borders is tenuous, all the more so under the current ruler, since they do not trust the emperor. If the army is withdrawn the northern border will crumble within the year. Probably just a few months, in fact.'

Cinna nodded. 'All this I told the emperor. He is of the opinion that the barbarians will cling to their oaths and that the feeble border forces can hold the line. He is utterly mistaken, of course, but that matters not to the man who rules the world.'

'For now,' Dev added darkly.

'Indeed. Even now the northern army is being mobilised and redeployed. The weakening of the border has begun. Even if it gives us the men to win here, which seems far-fetched to me, the empire will be in the gravest danger throughout. We are in an impossible position, Dev. The emperor is wrong, and his judgement cannot be trusted, but we are still hopelessly in his power.'

Dev took a breath to steady his racing pulse and straightened in the chair.

'At the risk of heaping further troubles upon you, General, I also have grave news.'

Cinna slumped in the chair. 'I wish someone had offered me wine on the way in. Go on.'

'No wine here, sir. Not had the opportunity. The news from the north is dire. I sought the Sizhad as you ordered and found him in a mountain stronghold of impressive dimensions. He has become more than just a bandit king, General. The mountain people regard him with a strange mix of abject fear and mindless worship. He is a religious zealot, promoting monotheistic worship of his sun god, and his men seem to see him as some quasi-religious figurehead, like a high priest.'

No need to add that he is my brother. What help might that be?

'And his force? He will not commit to our cause for religious differences, then?'

'It goes beyond that, General. *Way* beyond that. The Sizhad has an army to be reckoned with. It is perhaps not as strong as ours, and certainly not as powerful as that of the Jade Empire, but they are well-provisioned, well-equipped, well-rested, and perhaps most worrying of all, they are absolutely fanatically loyal to their master. With that kind of strength, numbers are less of a factor, as you know.'

'He cannot be bargained with?'

'No, sir. He is a zealot who sees all the gods – western, Inda, even the eastern ones – as demons. He will not deal with any of us.'

'On the other hand, that means that he will not join the Jade Empire against us either,' General Cinna noted, clearly attempting to find a bright side to the problem.

'General, the Sizhad only remains uncommitted as yet because it is part of his grand plan.'

'The zealot has a plan?'

'He is waiting for us and the Jade Empire to complete a war of mutual destruction. He is watching us weaken each other and waiting for the moment where even together we could not stand against him. If you think the people we are fighting now are ardent for their cause, wait until you see the Sizhad's believers. They will burn the world to suit their cause.'

General Cinna twiddled his thumbs as he sat, frowning, deep in thought.

'The world offers a plethora of ways to commit suicide, does it not?' he said, finally. 'The northern barbarians will watch the army pull out and it will be mere weeks before they pour over the border and ravage the empire. The only thing that might stop them is another invader. The Sizhad will crush us, then, to rid himself of the gods. And I still fear that the Pelasians will take advantage of the weakening of the empire and push from the south. The empire faces peril in every direction. And oddly the force against whom we are currently engaged in the most bitter war is the weakest threat of them all.'

Dev nodded. 'What can we do, though, sir? The emperor cannot be persuaded, and unless he catches some dreadful illness and passes on unexpectedly there is unlikely to be a change for the better in imperial policy.'

Cinna suddenly rose purposefully from his seat.

'General?' Dev frowned.

'When the men in power play the fool, Dev, it is the duty of men of action to act. I am about to break my oath to the emperor and defy him. Such a thing is, needless to say, suicidal, but something needs to be done, lest the world go up in flames before our very eyes. I will seek peace myself with the commander of the Jade Empire force across the river, independent of the emperor. I saw wisdom and reason in him when we first met here, so there is a small chance he might be reasoned with, and if so, perhaps we can still end this madness. And if we *can*, then I hope that when news of my rebellion reaches Velutio, other men of action will follow suit. The emperor is insane. He needs to be defied, no matter what oath we all took.'

Dev was nodding even before he stood.

'I cannot ask you to join me, Dev. This is certainly the end of my career, if not my life.'

'Men of action must act, General, you're quite right. I am with you, and I am sure many of the officers—'

Cinna cut him off with a raised hand. 'We are talking mutiny against our emperor, Dev. Such a thing will not sit well with many, no matter what they've been through. This decision goes no further than you and me and my personal guard, and perhaps a couple of officers I've known since the days of my youth.'

'What do we do, then, sir?'

'We seek a parley with the enemy. We need to approach the enemy general carefully, and speak somewhere other than the bridge. This is a delicate matter and, at this stage, a rather secret one, to be discussed well out of earshot of the men.'

'Let me approach the enemy, then, sir. I will try and arrange a meeting between you and their general.'

Cinna thought for a long moment and finally nodded. 'Do it. Take my guardsmen with you, but leave them at the bridgehead and go on alone. We cannot afford for the enemy to view your approach as any kind of provocation or trick, and after so many months of mindless killing, being accompanied by troops will probably just buy you a cannon shot to the face. You know this land. Find us somewhere mutually acceptable to meet and arrange it if you can.'

Dev nodded and hurried to the door.

'And be careful,' the general added. 'While you arrange matters, I will approach the two men in this army that I believe I can trust. Before I left I set something in motion and it's too late to stop it. I do hope it will not impact upon our attempts at negotiation. Still, nothing we can do about that now. We must just try what we can. To work, young man.'

A moment later, Dev was outside. His view took in the great plain of Jalnapur. The soggy land was hardening. Now, in more peaceful years, crops would be planted for rapid growth and quick harvest. Not so this year. The only crop growing over these months in that fertile soil was corpses. Soon the ground would be firm enough to move vehicles on, and then the world of Jalnapur would become a ceaseless barrage of death. The only thing that had effectively nullified the enemy cannon thus far had been their inability to bring them close enough to do any real damage. Soon, though, those great machines of destruction would be brought down onto the plain within range of the major imperial positions and the killing would begin in earnest.

But neither had the general been idle during the monsoon period. Despite the conditions, engineers and workers had been churning out weapons constantly for months, while master artillerists had been training new men in their art. The imperial army had arrived at Jalnapur with around fifty onagers and two hundred bolt throwers. Now, after a summer of construction, they had surpassed four times that number, ammunition being produced in such vast quantities that storage was becoming an issue. And while the forces of General Cinna had effectively quadrupled their artillery, the Jade Empire's army could not have done the same. They simply had not the resources to create new iron cannon.

So the Jade Empire had the powerful weapons, but Cinna's men had the edge in artillery numbers. The Jade Empire's commander would bring his cannon down in the hope that they would win him the bridge, but the moment the ground was dry, the new imperial artillery would be moved into place, and the barrage they could unleash would terrify even the gods. No one on the plains of Jalnapur would be safe, no matter under whose flag they stood.

Dev swallowed. And that was another motivation for what he was about to do. Not just to preserve the empire at home… Home? Was that right for a man Inda-born? Still, it was not just about preserving the empire. It was about halting this madness too.

Overcoming his nerves, Dev set out through a field of corpses and blood to make peace.

VELUTIO, PALACE OF THE EMPEROR BASSIANUS

The courier shook with fear as he stood outside the door. The four men who had ridden south with the tidings had sat, sour-faced, in the antechamber a short while ago and drawn lots for the 'honour' of attending the imperial court. Luca had lost. Cold sweat poured from his hairline.

'The grey circle,' the court functionary repeated. 'Wait there until bidden to do so, and then deliver your report succinctly before handing over the appropriate documentation.'

Luca nodded. He didn't trust himself to speak yet.

The doors opened and, willing his legs to stop trembling, the courier entered, marching straight to the grey circle. He tried not to look at the previous plaintiff, who was being dragged from the room by two of the imperial guard, stumbling and wailing his grief over some unnamed ill. Whatever had caused it clearly tickled the emperor, for the divine Bassianus was chortling his glee and waving beringed hands at his lackeys who were laughing in turn, though not with their eyes.

Gradually the hilarity over the departed plaintiff's woes subsided and the room fell silent. The courier stood with head lowered, eyes on the floor at the emperor's feet, just able to see the lord of the west and son of gods, but respectfully not meeting his eye.

'Speak.'

Luca tried. His voice had gone, his mouth dry, tongue stuck to the roof of his mouth. Slowly, he forced out a squeak, which became a word. He had to repeat it twice before it was intelligible.

'Majesty.'

'Go on...' the emperor huffed impatiently.

'Majesty, I bring word from Lord Divis of Castro Gatara in the north.'

'Never heard of him,' laughed the emperor.

No, thought the courier. Because all of your army is in the east and the only men left in the north are poor, petty lords.

'My lord Divis regrets…' – a nervous clearing of throat – 'regrets to inform the imperial court… that the north is overrun.'

The emperor was suddenly leaning forward in his chair. 'What?'

'Majesty, the Gota came south in force. They left the mountains. There is burning. Raiding. Slaughter.'

'What of my border forces?' the emperor snarled.

'Limitanei, Majesty,' murmured one of the courtiers nearby. 'They are little more than barbarians themselves. They probably joined the incursion.'

Luca nodded. That was very much the case. The few loyal units remaining in the north had been overrun in mere days, leaving the entire region at the mercy of the barbarians.

Bassianus, Lord of the World, shot his courtier an acidic look and rose from the chair, stepping towards the courier, who flinched with each step. He held out the missive from the north in a shaking hand, the wooden scroll case sealed with wax. 'From Lord Divis, Majesty.'

The emperor stopped two paces from the shaking courier and snatched the wooden tube. Luca waited, praying for dismissal. The first blow from the scroll case knocked half the sense from him and sent him staggering to the side. The wood was hard, designed to prevent any damage to imperial documents on long journeys.

'You have stepped outside the circle,' snarled the emperor, and Luca, dazed and panicked, hurriedly stepped back in. The emperor swung again, this time with all his might. Luca felt his eye socket fracture under the blow, and even in the wash of agony and fear, made sure not to step out of the circle. The blows came again and again and Luca took them in silence, other than an occasional whimper, blood flooding his vision. At some point he collapsed, for he was suddenly on the floor, still in the grey circle, wondering how soon he might die. Finally, the rain of agony stopped and the courier realised that the emperor presumed him dead. He made no movement to disabuse his lord of the notion as Bassianus straightened, covered in blood spatter, and turned, gesturing to his court with the tube.

'This is Cinna's doing. He delays and prevaricates, and now he has forced me to strip the last of my defences. Because of his weakness we stand to lose the north. I will *not* have this. I will replace him. We will end this Inda war and quickly, so that we may reclaim the north.'

Luca felt himself being dragged from the room, watched the emperor recede, still ranting.

I did not die, the courier thought. *This was a good day.*

CHAPTER 14

The blossom falls, stirred by the wind
Breath is held
The world turns

Poem in Huazo form, author unknown

Jai reined in on the hillside, his men gathering in a knot behind him. Jalnapur stretched out below him like a festering sore on the flesh of the world – a canker in need of removal. Everywhere he had been these past three weeks he had seen deprivation and misery, but nothing on the scale that Jalnapur offered.

In a last effort to find a solution before time ran out, General Jiang had dispatched Jai – the most adept scout in the army – with a unit of horsemen to try and find another feasible way across the river. It was likely suicide, but it was the only path they could seek that offered even the *possibility* of progress. If they could find a place suitable for cavalry to cross the great river unobserved, even slowly, they could send a contingent round the rear of the imperial force and create a distraction.

If, the general reasoned, they could create enough noise and chaos with cavalry at the rear of the imperial forces, perhaps they could distract the enemy enough to keep them occupied and draw them from the riverside. It would perhaps weaken the bridgehead enough to permit a strong enough force to break it. The cavalry would have to be extremely noisy, of course.

Jiang, though he professed to hate even the thought of it, could then launch a full assault with the slim hope of gaining the far side of the bridge. It was a small chance, and even if it succeeded it would take a horrendous toll in lives – especially those doomed cavalry on the far side – but when weighed against what would happen when the reinforcements arrived from the east under their vicious commanders it was still preferable.

And so Jai and his hundred riders had set off south along the banks of the great Nadu, keeping to the hillsides and avoiding the low ground, which was still treacherous following the monsoon, though it would soon be dry enough for action. He didn't hold out much hope for his mission. He'd never been south of Jalnapur, but by all accounts the river was too wide to bridge any further south, and the western empire patrolled the lands on the far side just as thoroughly as Jai's allies patrolled these reaches. Any ferry crossing would be made under the watchful eyes of the enemy, Jai was sure.

Of course those ferries *were* being used, though. The general had committed numerous scout units to the south the day they'd arrived at Jalnapur. Those men had crossed the river wherever they could and set about causing havoc on the far side, burning crops and trying to make life more difficult for the enemy. But in a way that action, though it meant there were already units active somewhere across the river, had ensured that the imperial forces would now watch any potential crossing far closer than they'd done at first.

Yet it had come as a surprise to Jai when they'd come across the enemy unit sometime in the second week of their mission. While Jiang had sent plenty of men across the river, they'd had no reports of the western military crossing to this bank – something to do with Cinna's policy of halting the Jade Empire's advance rather than pressing home an attack, he suspected.

He and his men had ridden clear of a path that meandered through a stand of mango trees and out onto a grassy common, only to see a dozen riders below, encamped in a hollow, with their horses tethered nearby. They were wearing native clothing, but in an instant Jai knew them for the enemy. There were no Inda cavalry these days, unless they were in service to a foreign emperor or a bandit. And these were so clearly a regimented military group and not civilians, not to mention the foreign, western look of their camping equipment.

Jai had given the order even before the shout of alarm went up from the camp, his own force falling upon the enemy like the wrath of the war gods. A hundred men bore down on twelve, the aggressors already in the saddle and drawing weapons as they thundered down the grassy slope into the gathering, the startled campers rising urgently to their feet and searching for their weapons.

Jai had, of course, joined in. He was no administrative strategist, for all his position with the general. He was a swordsman – a killer trained in the empire's greatest academy. His sword escaped the scabbard with a threatening hiss.

The forms were different for mounted combat, of course, and he was less familiar and practised with them than he was with infantry fighting, yet still probably more so than most, given his years as a scout and all that time in the saddle.

His chosen target had to be an officer, judging by what he saw as he descended the slope at speed with his men. There was a certain stance that identified an officer in a combat situation. The others looked or called to him, and he was the first man armed and directing the others. One of Jai's riders was making for the same target but, as he saw his commander heading straight for the officer, he turned and chose a new victim.

It was slaughter. At odds of perhaps eight to one, with the stronger party armed, mounted, prepared and confident, the result was a foregone conclusion, but Jai had to hand it to the enemy – they did not simply back down. Every man attempted to fight. No quarter was given, but none was asked for either.

The officer held one of those straight, waisted blades of which the westerners were so fond, gripped in both hands and pulled back for a strike. It was no genius move, but then a man facing cavalry was always left with few options. The sword came back for a sweep at elbow height, the perfect position for hacking into a mount's legs and unhorsing a cavalryman. He would then duck as he swung, hoping to avoid the counterstrike from the man in the saddle of the doomed beast.

In the Jade Empire's academies it was called the attack of the sweeping blossom, for some arcane reason that Jai had never found fully explained. It was the first anti-cavalry manoeuver taught to any academy student, and so basic it had only two variants. There were four potential counters to the form, dependent upon position, agility and horsemanship. Jai was confident in all of those, but had the latter in spades. The defence of the leaping tiger, he'd already decided as he closed on the man.

The enemy blade reached its optimum position and began to sweep forward, its keen edge seeking the horse's vulnerable legs. The officer's eyes widened as Jai's horse jumped unexpectedly, and it was the last thing he would ever be surprised by. Jai's horse leapt over the man's arm and its now harmless blade, and as he passed by he leaned heavily to the right in the saddle, his sword coming down low, past his mount's belly.

The blade slammed into the top of the man's skull, and Jai was past him before he folded like a collapsing tent frame under the blow. Jai hauled on his reins, bringing his beast to a difficult and uncomfortable halt immediately after the jump. The horse stumbled a little and then danced to the side, shaking his head in irritation, pulling on the reins in mute defiance of his rider. Jai allowed the beast its anger as he watched his victim.

The imperial officer, his head displaying a wide rent, parting the hair with a line of pulsing red and white, collapsed to his knees, making an odd keening noise. Then he screamed and began to shake wildly.

Jai's brow folded in concern. He wasn't expecting that, though head wounds could do all sorts to a man. The dying officer suddenly fell backwards and onto the turf and began to thrash about, shrieking and wailing. Jai turned to take in the situation and, satisfied that his men had the situation well under control, he dismounted and left his agitated horse to calm down as he stalked over to the thrashing man.

His eyes widened as he approached. The officer gradually stopped flailing and began to lie almost still, twitching just a little, sightless eyes staring at the uncaring sky, blood and worse pouring from the wound in his head. But it had not been that injury that had caused the man such pain, nor was that the worst sight that met Jai. A hole had been eaten through the officer. His torso was steadily dissolving in on itself like... Jai couldn't think of anything unpleasant enough to compare it to as bile rose in his throat at the horrifying sight. His gaze caught a glint and he spotted the broken glass container, opaque and greasy where it had been coated with something. The source of the nightmare. He then spotted the man's sword, where it had been touched by the escaped substance too. It was eating through the steel of the blade like woodworm at an old, rotten cupboard.

Acid!

Powerful acid too. Why would imperial troops carry such a dangerous substance? What could they intend to use it for? The answer was simple, of course.

'What in the name of the gods...?' asked one of his men hauling on his reins and pulling up close to Jai.

'Acid,' Jai replied. 'Strong acid that eats metal. And there is only one reason for enemy soldiers to be here with such a thing. They were after our cannon. General Cinna is a cunning one. He's been dreaming up ways to nullify our artillery advantage and if he'd managed to get that acid to one of our cannon and smash it, it would have rendered the gun unusable. It would be my guess that we will find more such phials in this camp.'

And they did. Fifteen in all, including two that had broken on the people carrying them, with nightmarish results. Seemingly the enemy general was as desperate as they were to put an end to this as soon as possible and was beginning to try any strange, dangerous ploy that came to mind. Clever, though.

Despite the unpleasantness of the task and the need to continue with their mission, Jai detailed half his party to bury the enemy dead and say a few words over the site while the others went through the camp, searching for anything worth taking and then dismantling and disposing of it all. In less than an hour the bodies were gone and the horsemen ready to move on. With the revelation that the enemy might now be on this bank and could turn up at any moment, they had moved on more cautiously from there, continuing to search in vain for any potential crossing of the river.

Sure enough, they had checked every mile of the bank fruitlessly until they reached...

Jai's stomach still churned at the memory.

A stone marker with a face that stared deep into the soul of the observed, eyes black as the darkest soul. He'd felt a strange kind of panic rise within him just at the sight of it. The riders with him had milled about uncertainly outside the boundary. They were not Inda – they didn't *entirely* understand – but they had been told about the land of ghosts and its perils, and they respected the boundary nonetheless. No man, no matter his origin, wished to anger gods or ghosts. His second in command had asked what to do. Jai had been torn.

The Inda had learned long ago not to cross that line, though the monks who maintained the markers – not very well, judging by the poor state of this one – managed to live on the far side. If Jai and his small party obeyed the old rules though, perhaps they would manage for a short foray. He would hate to report back to the general without trying everything he could, and as yet he'd nothing positive to tell Jiang other than that he had foiled a plot against the guns.

Swallowing his fear and wiping the unnatural sweat from his brow, Jai had given the orders. Each man had removed his weapons, grudgingly. Some had been forced to reveal hidden blades, and it was only when Jai was satisfied that no one had been stupid enough to disobey him that he stepped towards the marker.

Death. Death and madness. That was what awaited a man who crossed that ancient line. He shivered uncontrollably. Yet what had he just left at Jalnapur if not death and madness? Shaking, and moving swiftly in an attempt to hide that fact from the men, he crossed the boundary. His body chilled oddly, and he almost turned and ran, *did* turn, but was somehow given the strength not to flee by the sight of the others. He was the second in command of the largest army in the world. *He* knew what the markers meant, but how could he hope to lead these men if they saw weakness in him now?

Forcing himself not to panic, pushing down the terror and burying it beneath sheer will, he took another step south, and still did not die. Plastering what he hoped was confidence across his face, he beckoned to the men and took another five steps, each one making his legs shake a little more. There, as the men began to follow him past the marker, he paused for some time, half-expecting vengeful spirits to descend upon them and tear apart some soldier who had thought to sneak a knife across. Nothing happened, though he continued to shiver uncontrollably at the feeling of some unseen presence around them.

If he had thought he was suffering fear-sweat at the marker, before long he'd experienced a whole new level in the lands beyond. The horses were nervous, clearly, though not as much as their riders. They had spent only a day beyond the marker, and no one had gone mad, vanished or died, but still it was not an experience Jai would wish to repeat in a hurry. Here and there among the overgrown paths that had served the monks, they had found eerie, mute evidence of other interlopers. Twice they had stumbled upon the clothing, armour and weapons of scout parties just like theirs lying by the side of the road. No bodies. No sign of them. Just everything they owned. And no sane scout would have been content to strip naked and leave everything. Jai was certain that they were dead, or possibly driven insane enough to flee naked into the woods. Either way, they had gone. It made him shiver, and had started to put the wind up the other horsemen.

Moreover, each rider clearly shared Jai's sense that they were being observed during their journey. Not once did they see a distinctive shape or hear audible words, but there was movement in the undergrowth that did not seem to be animal in its origin, and noises that sounded like the whispering of a thousand faint voices. One of the men had expressed the concern that enemy scouts were observing them, but Jai had shook his head and brushed off that possibility. Whatever it was observing and following them – ghosts and spirits, presumably – it was certainly not imperial scouts from the enemy force. Oddly, the noises and movement did not seem to alarm their steeds as much as the men, though that was of little comfort to Jai. Horses perhaps had less to worry about from ghosts.

They had found something late that day and Jai had deemed it sufficient to call their foray into the ghost lands a success and go no further. They had turned round and retreated to the marker line with an immense sense of relief and an impressive turn of speed.

They had found *something*. Not something truly useful, and Jai twitched at the thought of reporting it, but still, it was what it was: a crossing.

Some distance south of the markers, one of the paths they had followed, which seemed to lead somewhere significant, judging by the odd, arcane symbols on the stone posts at every junction, had led to the banks of the Nadu. The great river had swept on south through the dead lands wider than ever, but where the path met the water's edge they had found a ferry. It was a simple barge only twenty feet long and ten wide, but it *was* a crossing, and most certainly not one watched over by the enemy. The barge was attached to one of a pair of ropes, which had impressively been slung across the great torrent somehow and fastened to huge trees at each side, and which could be used to propel and guide the craft across the river. A similar vessel sat at the far side, attached to the other line. A two-way crossing.

Jai had been rather concerned about the state of the rope and of the vessel. They seemed to be as poorly maintained and as neglected as the markers had been, the rope slimy and going green. However, when he and half a dozen burly riders had hauled on it to test its efficacy, it had proved to still be sturdy and safe. Attaching it to a saddle and putting a horse's weight to it had proved a safe test too.

The crossing fitted the requirements of the general to the letter, for all its shortcomings. It *was* a place cavalry could cross slowly, unobserved by the enemy. Of course, it came with its own complications: no cavalry unit would be able to cross it armed, for they would have to leave their weapons on the far side of the marker line, lest they wanted to die or be driven insane before they even reached the river. What little use the crossing could be, Jai could not fathom, but at least he had *something* relevant to report to the general.

They had ridden back to the lands of the living and crossed the line of markers with an explosion of breath and wild eyes. They found the hidden cache where they had secreted their weapons and retrieved them, and it was not until noon the next day, some thirty miles from the markers, that the men began to speak of their journey and to make nervous jokes.

Three weeks after they had ridden south from Jalnapur, the horsemen returned to their camp, and now, on a hot, sizzling afternoon, Jai and his men crested the hill and looked down upon the fields of death. Jai was disheartened to see the movement taking place, though he'd half-expected it. On their return journey they had noted how the low ground had largely dried out and was now firm enough to traverse. Which meant a return to hostilities.

The cannon were moving from their lofty positions on the hillsides, being brought down by oxen to the low ground, where they were being distributed and positioned around the plain, where they would be within good range of the enemy, able to cause horrific damage to the imperial forces. There were no shots ringing out yet, despite the fact that several machines were already in place, having earth ramparts and emplacements built about them. Jai wondered whether the general was waiting until his entire artillery was in position, or whether he was just reluctant to start the bombardment, but a glance across the river provided a third possibility.

The western forces were also moving artillery into place. They had kept their great weapons in position during monsoon season, since they had been prepared in advance, constructing high, solid platforms for them, but now they were bringing more and more weapons into the field. Jai felt a lump rise in his throat as he boggled at the sheer scale of the imperial artillery. General Jiang had the most powerful artillery in the world, but their advantage seemed far from assured when faced with the sheer number of weapons being moved into position across the river. What use were a few paltry cannon shot each hour when the western forces could now shower rocks, burning pitch and iron bolts down upon the eastern bank in a constant rain? General Cinna had clearly been busy during monsoon season. The man was an endless source of surprises.

And yet the enemy artillery stood silent as yet too, perhaps waiting until everything was in position, or perhaps, once again, because their commander was reluctant to give the order. What a world this was when neither army cared about the bridge and no one wanted to fight, including the commanders, and yet the war went on, unfeeling and unstoppable! With a sigh, Jai kicked his horse's flanks.

Riding down the slope, he dismissed his men, sending them off to dismount and rest, granting them three days of furlough for their efforts and bravery, and then made for General Jiang's headquarters.

He felt an odd sense of anticipation among the men as he passed through the huge camp. He was not sure precisely what it was he was picking up on, but there was definitely something in the air, and it only increased as he closed on the headquarters and nodded to the Crimson Guard who stood at attention around the place. He was admitted swiftly and made his way to the general's office.

Xeng Shu Jiang was sitting behind his desk, surrounded by documents and maps as usual, and looked up sharply as Jai entered.

'At last,' the general said, breaking into a weary smile. 'I had begun to think you lost.'

Jai rolled his shoulders and saluted with a tired grin of his own.

'I have had an interesting but tiring journey, General, with a few items of interest to report.'

'And I shall be fascinated to hear all about it, Jai, but I have tidings of my own that must override your report.'

Jai's skin prickled once more at that feeling of anticipation prevalent in the camp. 'General?'

'My opposite number seeks a parley.'

Jai frowned. 'I cannot imagine what for, sir, since neither of us is likely to agree to pull out, but a parley should not be difficult to arrange.'

'Interestingly, though, General Cinna seeks a parley somewhere neutral and away from our forces.'

'Sounds dubious,' Jai murmured, musing on the inventiveness of the enemy commander.

'Agreed, and I would have smelled a trap but for one thing. When we first spoke to the enemy commander, the parley was a formal affair and he invoked his rank and position and the authority of the mad emperor for whom he spoke. On this occasion, the request was delivered by his adjutant somewhat quietly, without pomp, and rather tellingly without the invocation of imperial authority.'

'Sir?' Jai prompted, a little befuddled by the meaning of all this.

'Their bureaucracy and rigid form is second only to ours, Jai. It is a simple requirement of all diplomacy to cite the authority one claims. That Cinna has requested a parley on no authority other than his own is paramount. Unless I miss my guess by a wide margin, it means that this parley is Cinna's idea, and the emperor and his administration are not party to it. Cinna wishes to talk to me personally, not as a representative of his emperor.'

Jai nodded slowly. 'It could still be a trap.'

'It could,' agreed the general, 'but we are running out of options, Jai. Both our armies have moved their killing machines forward, ready to turn Jalnapur into a sea of blood and severed limbs, and those men who would rather see me fail are on their way. Unless you bring me a solution to the war neatly bundled courtesy of your expedition, I believe is it at least worth *speaking* to General Cinna.'

Jai paused, an image of that ferry slipping into his mind's eye. But it was no true solution, for a cavalry force would not be able to take their weapons. It was a false hope at best.

'No sir. Tantalising near-possibilities, but nothing more.'

'Then I shall arrange to meet Cinna and speak to him, man to man.'

A thought occurred to Jai. 'General, if you do this, and you hope to meet Cinna as an equal, that means you will have to do the same. You cannot do so on the authority of the Jade Emperor.'

'Quite so.'

Jai pictured the endless reports and missives that were dispatched to the imperial capital with repetitive regularity. Everything was reported. *Everything.* It was the way the Jade Empire worked.

'How will the emperor react when he learns that you have spoken to the enemy *off the record*, so to speak?'

'You answer your own question, Jai. This will be entirely off the record.'

Jai's pulse quickened. 'Sir, that is foolhardy and dangerous. The emperor will find out. Someone will submit a report. There will be court spies among the men. You know that nothing escapes the Jade Emperor's attention.'

'It is worth the risk, Jai. My opponents are coming with their armies to take part in this war, and they will be here sooner than you think. If we are to avert total disaster, we need to do whatever we can to resolve this before they arrive. If that means standing alone and in defiance of the emperor, then that is what I must do. It is said that the Jade Emperor and his empire are one. They are not, Jai. No matter what is drilled into us, we need to understand that the emperor is *not* the empire, and vice versa. And sometimes we must place the needs of the empire above those of the man who rules it. Right now I intend to serve the empire in attempting to avert total ruin, regardless of the wishes of the emperor.'

Jai felt a chill run through him. It was utterly logical, but the very idea of defying the Jade Emperor... Heads would roll for such offence, and it would not be the general's fate alone. Yet it was hard to deny the sense of it.

'You speak sense, General. It is not foolhardy. But it *is* dangerous. Where will you meet?'

'I am not sure, Jai. The general's emissary desired some place other than the bridge, and I can see the value in that. If he is intending to treaty with me against the will of his master, which seems the most likely explanation, then doing so in the midst of both armies would be foolish. Yet we cannot meet on either bank for similar reasons. Perhaps we can arrange to meet a few days' north, where there are other smaller crossings.'

'The dead lands, sir,' Jai said suddenly, surprising himself.

'What?'

'The land of the ghosts in the south, sir. It was to be part of my report. We forayed a few miles beyond the line of markers and discovered a small ferry crossing. There you could meet on neutral ground, far from the armies. Moreover, no man can carry a weapon beyond the markers without signing his own death warrant at the hands of the spirits, so no one will take a weapon to the meeting, and if they do, then they will not make it to the meeting. If it *is* a trap, then we can circumvent the worst danger that way.'

The general frowned. 'I thought you disapproved of people entering these lands. Sacred and deadly was the impression you gave me.'

'Quite so, sir. And it is not a place I would go to lightly or even willingly under normal circumstances. But these are not normal circumstances. If you are to meet with any element of safety and secrecy, it is there that such a meeting should be held. It is a nerve-racking place, but we spent a day there and survived. Moreover, if the western general is willing to meet you in such a place, you will know he is serious, since the enemy are as respectful of the southern lands as we are.'

Jiang nodded. 'You speak a lot of sense. It will take some time, though, will it not? You have been gone three weeks.'

'We travelled in a rather meandering route, sir. On good horses and riding direct at speed, you could make the ghost lands in seven days at most. Six, probably.'

General Jiang leaned back in his chair and exhaled noisily. 'Then I shall send an emissary across the bridge with this proposition. Cinna and his escort can travel along the far bank and we can travel along this one. We shall meet in these ghost lands of yours. I shall take just a unit of the Crimson Guard and you. You are content to act as guide?'

No, thought Jai. *The very* last *thing I want to do is walk into the dead lands with a unit of the Crimson Guard to meet an enemy deputation.*

192

'Yes, sir,' he said, swallowing the fear once more.

CHAPTER 15

My grandfather, who predicted this entire slide into universal oblivion, was a man who never failed to face up to his responsibilities and to accept the realities of the world. While my father was much the same, it is to my rather visionary grandfather that I owe my own personality and system of values.

One of the things my grandfather held as an article of faith was that there is no such thing as coincidence. Just the unfolding of what was meant to be. Another was that no man can run away from the world. From what he told me, when the Jade Empire's forage parties started to come, my father expressed his intention to simply move the people of Initpur out of their reach. In retrospect, now that I think on it, perhaps there is more of my father in me than I realised.

Regardless, my grandfather made my father promise to do no such thing, but to stay and face his fate, which of course he did. A man cannot run from fate, the old man had said. Fate simply follows him. You can attempt to shut yourself away from the world as much as you wish, but the world will find you.

I had thought that of all places, the dead lands were the one place that the world would not find me. But my grandfather was, as always, correct. Even here, the world would not leave me alone, and though what was to happen brought me fear and apprehension, it brought me joy from the most unexpected sources.

'The river crossing… is in use.'

The watchman was breathing in gasps, having ridden from his post at breakneck pace. Some – the ever-negative Parmesh preeminent among them – had seen no need in this place to set guards, given the fact that no one came here willingly and that any who might would be unarmed or dead before they reached the monastery. Aram had disagreed and selfishly used the persuasive power of Mani and Bajaan to override the dissenters. Even in these dead lands, he would have pickets. Aram was not a

194

military man, but in his new role as not ruler but leader, he was beginning to see the value of thinking like one. The watchmen had thus been set on every path that led from the monastery at a distance of three miles, and they changed shift every three hours to remain fresh and alert.

Over the weeks they had been here, no one had reported an enemy presence. Oh, there had been plenty of panicked warnings, but they had, each and every one, been born of nerves and the constant feeling of being watched and threatened in these lands. Each time they had been more nervous of men jumping at shadows or perceived phantoms. That feeling was absent at the monastery, of course, but a few miles out, where the pickets sat alone in the wilds, it was strong and preyed on the mind of even the strongest-willed man.

They had been good weeks at the monastery, though. The whole complex had been, and still was, a mass of construction and change. New bunkhouses continued to go up to accommodate those who had spent the intervening time living on the floors of the temple or the workshops or barns. The whole place was rapidly coming to order. The surfaces had been cleaned, oil applied to machinery, grass trimmed, beds weeded and so on. Gradually the place was beginning to resemble a proper community. One of the first tasks had been the overdue harvest, and now the granaries and storehouses were crammed full of grain, vegetables and fruit, and the beasts in the fields had once more reached an acceptable stage of domestication.

Aram had been content for the first time since they had left Initpur. They were not just surviving as a community, they were beginning to thrive. And for whatever reason – perhaps that, because of the monks, this place was favoured by protective gods – there was no threat hovering in the air. The place felt peaceful. Moreover, in the weeks they had been here there had been no sign of other trespassers. The only other souls who had passed through the gates of the monastery had been those strays and displaced by the war who had been found by men sent by Aram. They came and marvelled at what they saw, unexpected in this haunted land.

So new people came and added their muscle to the work and their enthusiasm to the community.

It had all been perfect. Too perfect. Given his grandfather's teachings, Aram should have been expecting the worst.

He frowned at the watchman. 'This is not some trick of the mind?'

'No. Men. A few of them too.'

'Could they be refugees who have heard of our settlement?'

The picket shook his head. No, Aram agreed. The only people who had heard of this place were those who had been brought here deliberately by his guides.

'No. They are Jade Empire men.'

Aram felt his blood chill. 'You are sure?'

'Yes. And they seem to be important ones too. Not just some stray scout party. They wear impressive red uniforms and two of them are done up like senior officers. They all had good horses too. They were starting to use the crossing already when I left.'

Aram nodded. 'It will take them some time to cross, especially with their beasts. How many?'

'Perhaps twenty or more.'

Aram hardened his heart and steeled himself. The last thing he wanted was a fight, but there were thousands of refugees here. They had no reason to fear a score of men, no matter how dangerous they might be. They would be unarmed, else they would not have got this far. And had not the monks of this place, through their deserted training hall, inadvertently shown Aram that there was still a way to fight without weapons, even here, where the spirits were ascendant?

'Sound the assembly bell and have the gates closed once everyone is inside,' he shouted to the man by the gate. Moments later, the great bronze bell near the main temple entrance was clanging repeatedly.

Out across the fields, farmers, woodsmen and workers of all types abandoned their tasks and hurried back to the monastery at the urgent sound. Aram waited in tense silence as the population of the settlement returned, passing through the gate and seeking the assigned places of safety they had prepared for such an eventuality. Only those capable of throwing a punch and willing to stand and fight would remain out in the open with him, the rest hiding inside, away from potential danger.

Then, in the second heart-stopping moment in one morning, Aram spotted the rider charging towards the monastery from the north-west – the very road along which they had first come – shouting at the scurrying workers to get out of the way.

Aram closed his eyes for a moment. *You can find the most obscure and overlooked place in existence and conceal yourself, but the world will always find you, Aram…*

He waited as the rider approached the gate and slipped from the horse's back, leading it the last few paces towards him.

'Trouble?'

'Riders, sir. Still a few miles out to the north. They're moving slowly and carefully, but they'll be here soon enough.'

'How many?'

'Twenty or thirty.'

Aram nodded. Western men, almost certainly, coming from that direction. And it was hardly worth bothering to enquire as to whether they were refugees. But the odd synchronicity of weeks of peace and then an incursion from both sides simultaneously? Like his grandfather before him, Aram did not believe in coincidence. Coincidence was a fool's attempt to explain away fate.

'What do we do?'

Aram turned to find Mani behind him, and Bajaan hurrying over to join them. Blessedly, of Parmesh there was as yet no sign, though he would be here soon enough, arguing.

'Do? We do nothing. We shut the gate and talk. Even if both of the new arrivals decided to assail us, they would number fewer than fifty to our thousands. Attack is not within their capability. They could not be that foolish. Moreover, timing suggests that this is some mutual design of theirs, independent of our presence.'

Mani nodded. Behind them, several hundred muscular men with grim faces were gathering in the open space inside the gate, preparing to defend the colony should they be required.

In half an hour all was ready. Every full civilian was inside, lurking in the relative safety of the buildings. Every man assigned to defend the place was gathered in the open. Aram and his close companions – soon including Parmesh – were at the closed gate, standing on a raised platform inside the wall that they had constructed for observation rather than defence.

The better part of an hour passed before the first figures emerged from the jungle at the edge of the fields to the north-west. For some time, the refugees watched as the small column of horsemen, resplendent in blue and white tunics and gleaming, silvery armour, rode along the path through the monastery's territory, making for the gate. There were, at a quick count, twenty-seven of them including the two men in what appeared to be officer's garb, cloaks of gleaming white rippling behind them.

'Be ready,' he said to Mani. 'But no one moves unless the soldiers do so first. I will not be the man to start a fight here, when I suspect that is not the reason for their presence.'

He watched the men approach, and it was only when they were less than thirty paces from the gate and slowing down that he realised he recognised one of them. The stocky man with the neat, almost severe hair in the senior officer's uniform was the general to whom he had spoken at Jalnapur on their way south. That realisation went some way to calming his jangling nerves. He remembered the general as an urbane, even friendly character, who had seemed sympathetic to the plight of the Inda.

The horsemen reined in and the two officers – the other, surprisingly, being a young Inda-born fellow – came to the fore, their arms raised as if to demonstrate that they were not armed. As his eyes strayed across the second officer, something sang a strange song in his blood and, once again, he recalled his father's contempt for the concept of coincidence.

'You have come a long way,' the general said with a smile.

'I am surprised that you remember me,' Aram replied, genuinely so.

'These lands, Dev here tells me, are forbidden to the living, and yet a force of several hundred seem to wait at your command. You have to be the same rajah who passed by Jalnapur with his column of refugees.'

Aram did not answer. His eyes were scrutinising the other figure. He was Inda. Of about the right age. Of course, Dev was hardly an uncommon name among the people, but Aram did not believe in coincidence. Fate ruled all men and had brought the world once more to his door for a reason.

His heart hammering in his chest, unable to tear his eyes from the young officer, Aram coughed and attempted to clear a suddenly constricted throat.

'You are not here for us, General, and those who you expect are, I believe, less than a mile away.'

'You are well informed.'

'I keep my eyes open, as does anyone who hopes to see a new dawn these days. But fate is a curious thing,' Aram said, his skin prickling. 'Your aide, there. What would you say were I to mention Initpur?'

The adjutant, who had been perusing the walls of the monastery with a practised military eye, suddenly snapped his head round to the gate, brow furrowed.

'I...' the young man's eyes widened. 'Father?'

Now it was General Cinna's turn to look surprised. 'Dev?'

'That...' the young man's eyes were drinking in every detail of the figure at the gate and Aram felt his spirit soar. It *was* his son. He had changed in over a decade, but then so had Aram, and wondered how he must look to his estranged son. He had grown older and greyer, naturally, but it was more than that. Gone were the trappings of a rajah, even a poor one. Gone was the veneer of civilisation. Here was a man of the people. A labourer, but still one used to command, given how the others inside the wall looked to him. Dev of Initpur had quit his home long ago, but Dev's expression left Aram in no doubt that it was he who stood in front of him.

'He is my father,' Dev said in a hoarse tone. 'The rajah of Initpur, far to the north, in the lower mountains east of the great river. Father, this is General Cinna.'

'We've met,' Cinna cut in. 'I couldn't recall the name, but your father was leading his people south some months back. Many thousands of them. I hope you have not suffered losses, Rajah?'

Aram shook his head. 'Our people are inside. They do not trust outsiders – especially invaders. And I am no longer a rajah.'

'Evidence suggests otherwise,' Cinna replied with an odd smile. 'You can relinquish any crown you like, Aram of Initpur, but you have simply exchanged your beleaguered northern kingdom for a haunted southern one.'

'Father, how did you come to be here?' Dev asked. His voice cracked with suppressed emotion, and Aram suspected that he himself sounded remarkably similar.

'Seeking the only place the Inda could be saved from the war, my son. I left the north with our people when Initpur fell to the Jade Empire, but the population here is formed of peoples from all over the western Inda Diamond. I am pleased to see that your sojourn in the west has not been wasted. I...'

Aram's voice faltered. Emotion was beginning to overcome him.

'We are not here to impact upon your presence, Aram of Initpur,' the general said loudly. 'I give my oath that no harm will befall you or yours at the hands of my men. We are here in this place to seek a parley with the commander of the Jade Empire's forces. It will be he who you have seen less than a mile from here.'

'The Jade Empire's general,' Bajaan said quietly, close by. He leaned towards Aram and spoke in low, whispered tones, inaudible to those outside the gate. 'You realise that we have both the senior commanders of our enemies meeting outside this very gate. We could end the invasion in a heartbeat with just two deaths.'

Aram's head snapped round to his friend, eyes wide. 'No. You cannot suggest such a thing. Besides, that is not how the great empires work. These two men would simply be replaced, and I have an odd suspicion that that would not go well for anyone. Keep the men calm and under control. This, I think, could be the beginning of something important.'

'You seek a treaty with your opponent?' Aram said, framed as a question, though he was in no doubt.

'We hover on the edge of a pit whose maw waits to consume the world,' General Cinna replied with unexpected candour. 'Only a fool would not seek to avoid such a thing.'

'Then you are welcome into our monastery,' Aram said suddenly, earning himself a worried glare from Bajaan, a concerned look from Mani, and downright hostility from Parmesh.

'That is not a good idea,' Bajaan said.

'These men are seeking a peaceful solution. Is that not precisely what we have searched for? Should we not all foster such a notion?' The questions were hammered home like nails of truth into the refugees behind him. He turned to the man on the far side of the platform. 'Open the gate and let them in. Have the refectory cleared and have food and fruit juice brought in. It is time to do what we can to influence the world for a change, instead of the other way around.'

The waiting men in the open space began to pull back as the gate ponderously crawled open, making way for the new arrivals to enter. The general was first in, his manner friendly yet aloof. Dev came second, and his eyes never for a moment left the face of his father. The horsemen with them looked nervous and distinctly uncomfortable.

General Cinna turned to his men. 'Dismount, find somewhere to rest and be calm and courteous to all. I will personally tear the tongue out of the first man to cause offence among these people.' His threat delivered, the general himself slid from his horse and left his helmet hanging on a saddle horn, removing his gloves and walking in small circles to ease his muscles after the ride.

Aram approached slowly, tentatively.

'Thank you for your invitation,' Cinna said as he neared. 'It is most welcome after a long ride. I hope to repay your hospitality well, though we have little with us at this time.'

But Aram was paying precious little attention to the general and gave him a passing nod of acknowledgement. His eyes were locked in reunion with those of his son, who had dismounted and removed his own gloves.

'I...' Aram faltered. 'It would be unseemly to embrace an officer in front of his men.'

Cinna snorted with laughter. 'However important Dev might be, they're my men, not his.'

Dev shot the general an odd look, half-offended, half-grateful, then turned back to his father. 'I always intended to come back. To visit. But that's not how the empire works. Once you have a role to play you are always busy – always assigned. I have been all over the western world, but never once back home. I had...' his voice cracked again. 'I assumed you dead, Father. I mourned you quietly.'

'The Inda do not die that easily,' Aram replied. 'And while it broke my heart when you left, fate has brought us together once more. It proves that I was right to do what I did, and that perhaps I was guided by the gods.'

Close by, General Cinna, who had been listening to the exchange, nodded seriously. 'In the west we have similar notions of fate. My own father, who was a priest, urged me into the military. He believed I was destined to do something important, and saw the martial service as my path to that. Personally I am beginning to rethink the matter, since my career seems to have led me into a position where I am helping to destroy the world.'

'Hence your meeting,' Aram replied shrewdly.

Cinna nodded. 'A meeting that will almost certainly see the emperor baying for my head, but men of conscience must do what they can, eh, Aram of Initpur? Dev?' The general tapped his adjutant on the upper arm, and the young man turned in surprise. 'I need your help, now more than ever, but what you have found here is more important than anything I can ever say to you. If you wish to remain with your father, I will have the records completed to give you a legitimate dismissal.'

Dev frowned at him, and turned that creased brow back and forth between father and commander. 'No. I cannot. Perhaps when we have stopped the madness, General, but not until then.' Turning back to his father apologetically, his voice trembled. 'I am sorry, Father.'

Aram smiled. 'Do not be. My son is a powerful man who is trying to save the world. What father could ask for more?'

They had reached the doorway now, and as they began to step inside, there was a call from the gate. More riders. Aram gestured for the man at the temple door to escort the general and Dev to the refectory and turned, hurrying back to the gate. His heart was pounding, and a strange sense of anticipation had settled upon him. Fate was at work here in spades. Fate had brought Dev to him and had reintroduced him to an imperial commander who had the good of the world at heart. There was so *much* fate at work here, in fact, that Aram could not fathom how to wrap his mind around it. It therefore came as little surprise when he ascended the gate platform and spied Jai closing on him. His eldest son, who had changed surprisingly little, was dressed in the uniform of a Jade Empire officer and riding beside another commander, followed by a small unit of impressive men in red and black with demonic face masks. The man beside Jai was tall and elegant – an impressive specimen.

And he was here to make peace. That much was clear. It was the whole reason for this meeting, and fate had decreed that such a meeting be held in this place, where Aram was privy to the matter. A frisson of energy ran across his skin. Fate was clearly all-encompassing.

'General,' he said loudly from his platform.

The small party of impressive soldiers and the two officers at their head reined in their horses before the open gate. The general turned a quizzical expression on Aram. 'We are expected?'

'General Cinna awaits you in the refectory,' Aram replied without a trace of smugness. 'As does your brother, Jai.'

The second man's head shot round to face him, and his face underwent a variety of expressions before settling rather tentatively on disbelief.

'Yes, Jai. Fate works in fascinating ways. It finds my sons coming back to me at a time of momentous change. Come. Your parley awaits, and I would speak with you once your duty is done.'

Aram motioned to the gate. It was odd, as though his mind had been programmed. As though he were simply speaking words that had been planted in his head. As he had looked down at Jai, impressive and resplendent in his uniform, he had not known what to say, and had expected to bluff and croak his way through. And yet he had dealt with the matter with impressive formality and detachment, as though fate could not risk letting him interfere and was speaking through him.

He watched the general and his eldest son pass through the gate as though the whole day were somehow happening to someone else and he just an observer.

'I must apologise,' the general said as he passed through the gate and dismounted. 'I do not wish to impose upon your hospitality. You seem to have found a safe niche far from the war, and I can only express regret for bringing reminders of it to you. Rest assured that I will keep this location from the strategists in our camp.'

Aram nodded. He had no doubt at all that the man was speaking the absolute truth. This was fate at work. They were truly in the hands of the gods now.

'Father...'

Aram turned to his son. His heart felt as though it might burst. If only his beloved wife had lived to see what their boys had made of themselves.

'Jai, it seems that the gods have gathered us together for a purpose. There will be time for us to talk, but that is after your master meets with General Cinna. I have had food and drink prepared. Come, Maja over there will show you to our other guests.'

The general noted the small gathering of impressive, well-ordered imperial troops in one corner of the open space, where they were being supplied with cold drinks, and he motioned to his own guard. 'Masks off. In fact, helmets off. Dismount and find somewhere to wait. There will be no offence caused to your opposite numbers over there, nor to the inhabitants of this place, or the wall of hooks will await you upon our return.'

Aram watched them go, escorted to the refectory by one of the women who arranged the food. He stood for a long moment after his eldest son had entered the building, the young man's face craning to see his father until he was out of sight. For a time Aram waited, rooted to the spot as though moving might disturb the delicate fabric of this living tapestry. Finally, he took a deep breath and followed on, Mani, Bajaan and Parmesh at his heel, each wearing uncertain expressions.

He could hear the exchanges of formal greeting in the room before he arrived, each general introduced by a son of Aram's, each given his formal title with any honours bestowed, yet neither, Aram noted, mentioning their emperors, which seemed curious. As he entered the refectory, he noted with a wry smile the various refugees gathered close to the door, their ears cocked, listening to the future of the world being decided within. Wearing an almost paternal smile, Aram waved them away and entered with his three-man entourage, two of Mani's best pugilists taking up a position outside to prevent further curious eavesdroppers.

The two generals were seated opposite one another, with their adjutants beside them. Everyone's expression was carefully neutral, though the astonishment was still visible in the faces of both younger men. Jai and Dev had clearly become reacquainted in the time Aram had waited outside. Maja and two of her helpers were still producing food and serving it to the four men, who politely accepted what they were given, but did not overindulge.

'None of us want this war,' Cinna said, opening their discussion with a flat statement that as far as Aram was concerned seemed to make rather a strong assumption, yet Jiang nodded his agreement.

'It gains little of value for the Jade Empire, overcommits your own army, and is poison to the Inda,' the eastern general said.

'And yet daily we send many hundreds of young men to the next world in the name of a bridge neither of us wants,' Cinna said in unhappy tones.

'Though we are at something of an impasse,' Jiang commented. 'You are unable to withdraw and cede us the bridge, and I am unable to take my army back to our own borders.'

'I presume the Jade Emperor is no more a man to change his mind than the blessed lunatic Bassianus?'

'Precisely. My emperor, like yours, is divine. His word is higher than law. His decisions cannot be questioned. Were I to turn back east and lead my force across our border and out of Inda lands, the emperor would request my head upon receiving the news. And even then, the chances of me reaching said border with the army are infinitesimally small. My army was hand-picked by me, but inevitably there will be imperial spies among them, and probably assassins also. No one is entirely to be trusted in the Jade Empire – especially known renegades, and troublesome men like me. I would almost certainly be dead before I was out of sight of Jalnapur.'

'I have a similar issue,' Cinna sighed. 'I have twice attempted to turn my emperor from this path. No man has argued with him thrice and lived. We are hopelessly and irrevocably committed, like yourselves. And Bassianus will similarly have men within my command, listening carefully, reporting and prepared to take action in his name.'

'Yet something must be done,' Jiang said, pausing to take a bite of a savoury cake proffered to him by Maja.

'If I might impose?' Aram said, slipping into a seat off to one side. Both men nodded as they nibbled on the food before them, and Aram tapped his chin. 'It seems to me that the men leading the armies would rather not fight. If I know soldiers at all, then I think we can all assume that your men would rather not be fighting. The drain in resources from your homelands must be appalling, so your own people, east and west, would almost certainly rather you were not fighting. No court in the world ever speaks with one voice, so there will be men in the highest circles of power who would rather you were not fighting. And the Inda *most certainly* would rather you were not fighting. That leads to a rather stark conclusion. Your emperors are the only men who wish you to fight. No man, no matter how powerful or what authority he can claim, should be able to destroy a world against the will of his own people.'

'You do not know Bassianus,' Cinna replied darkly.

'Or the Jade Emperor,' Jiang added.

'But I know that whatever they might claim, they are but mortal men. Wicked men should not be tolerated in positions of such power.'

There was an uncomfortable silence.

'There have been attempts on the emperor's life before,' Cinna said finally. 'They never end well. He is too closely protected.'

'There are always plots against the Jade throne,' Jiang said.

Aram shook his head. 'But you are talking about the plots of power-hungry men or passionate individuals seeking to overthrow and replace a ruler. I am not talking about such a thing. I am talking about waking up the reason inside all men and gathering a whole empire against its master.'

Cinna frowned and waved a chicken leg absently at his opposite number. 'He has a point. I do not know how things stand in the east, but the imperial court all hate and fear Bassianus. Perhaps not *all*, but certainly many of them. Perhaps there could be change if it were effected correctly. Dynasties have fallen before. Kiva Caerdin once deposed a mad emperor, and they say that history repeats itself.'

Jiang sucked on his teeth. 'It is not so simple for the Jade throne. There is no court like you have in the west. Everything is hierarchical, but perhaps there is a way. I will have to think on the matter and see what I can come up with.'

'But we are running out of time,' Cinna said, frankly. This was clearly not something Dev had not been expecting his commander to say, as his worried face turned to Cinna, who waved him down. 'Dev, it matters not if Jiang knows the truth. Perhaps it might even help us. General, the empire is in trouble. Bassianus has committed a huge force to help drive you from Jalnapur. They will arrive very soon, and once they do I will command the largest field army ever seen in the west. But in their absence, our borders will be pressured and will soon crumble. While I am facing you, our other neighbours will begin the process of devouring the empire.'

As Jiang's brow rose in surprise, Cinna glanced at Dev, who nodded.

'Also, we have become aware of something that concerns you equally. There is a new king in the northern mountains with a force of fanatics, praying to the sun as the only god, determined to bring their worship to the world. The more we weaken one another, the more we play into his hands.'

The Jade Empire's general nodded slowly. 'I had heard rumours of this Sizhad,' he replied, 'though we have less intelligence on him. Thank you. And for your candour. In return I must warn you that the Jade Emperor has also sent further forces west. Our own army stands to double in size, but the men coming with that force will intend to replace me, no matter what their initial orders were. I have been careful not to do anything foolhardy thus far, to preserve as many lives as possible. These men will have no such concern. If we are seriously looking at a way to remove the driving forces of this war, then my first concern will have to be dealing with my potential replacements. Given the size and loyalty of my army, they will not find me an easy proposition, mind.'

'But you would be willing to consider the possibilities?'

Jiang nodded to his opposite number. 'This insanity has gone on long enough. And if we are to move to end this, then we cannot lurk and skulk around as we do now. We must make a stand and be seen to be doing so for the correct reason. It was sensible to come here to meet, but if we are in agreement that we need to proceed in a uniform direction, then further discussions can now take place at Jalnapur.'

'Agreed.' Cinna smiled. 'While our very presence has been a waking nightmare for the Inda, they are lucky, I suspect, that it was you and I who led these campaigns. And now we must do what we can to save them from our own. I shall return to my camp, identify those fanatically loyal to the divine lunatic and remove them before making an appeal to my officers. I shall then work up some plans with Dev here, to see what might be possible. It will take a week to travel north once more, but in a matter of days thereafter, I suggest we meet and consider the next stage.'

Jiang nodded. 'I will perform a similar surgery on my own army. Jai here will liaise with...' He smiled. 'With his *brother*, I understand, to arrange a meeting in due course.'

Aram grinned and spread his arms wide. 'No man should depart again upon the very day he arrived. Matters of such joyous import as this deserve to be marked as an occasion, and I will beg leave this evening to reacquaint myself with my boys. I shall have your soldiers brought in as well as the major representatives of our people. We shall dine upon the fruits gathered here.'

As the two general nodded, Aram once again marvelled at the power of fate.

The two most powerful generals in the world, the two long-lost sons of Aram, and their father, all in one deserted monastery in a forbidden land, where the future of the world was being decided.

Aram took a long drink of cold mango juice, and could not stop smiling.

CHAPTER 16

Father, I know that we shall meet again soon enough and hopefully under the best of circumstances, but it pains me to part again knowing how it happened the last time, and so I felt the need to leave you this note, just in case. I would have stayed. I dearly wished to stay. But we are about to change the world, and so I cannot.

Grandfather often spoke of the Inda defining their own destiny, while you have always professed to cleave to the notion of an unchangeable fate. Perhaps it is all the time I have spent in the empire, where philosophy attempts to fill the gaps between the logical and the divine, but I find myself believing in a curious combination of chance and the forging of our own path.

I am proud to be your son.

You, by your strength and your courage, have created something here that has never been seen in the history of the Inda. You have brought together men and women from different kingdoms and managed to see them work together like one people. That alone gives me hope for the future. And despite your astounding achievement and the ancient strength of the Inda, and despite the fact that it is the two great empires who have brought such misery to the Inda, it is curious that now the future of the land lies in the hands of their two great generals.

I am proud to be Cinna's adjutant.

Perhaps it is fate driving us, perhaps it is luck. Perhaps it is that we drive ourselves, but one thing is true regardless of that. As a boy, when I left Initpur, I saw only ruination ahead for the Inda. Less than a year ago, when we first espied the forces of the Jade Empire at Jalnapur, I felt certain we were witnessing the end for our people. Now, though, between two visionary generals, a tenacious rajah and the triumph of logic, I finally see hope for the Inda and for the world.

We will meet again soon, Father. And this time I will no longer run away.

*Good luck in these strange lands where you have carved out a
civilisation.*

I am proud to be Inda.
Until I return,
Dev

They had finally passed the outer markers, which meant that
they had less than a mile to go until they met the first pickets.
Dev rode with a sense of achievement and hope, as did every
man with them, even General Cinna, though the stocky commander
also bore the permanently creased brow of a man with a problem to
solve. The very idea of defying the emperor's command and
attempting to halt the madness had seemed like a wisp of smoke
initially – tantalisingly present, yet intangible and impossible to
grasp. Now, though, it felt like a real possibility. The simple
knowledge that the enemy general was of a mind with them and
sought the same goal was enough to make that ethereal notion
solidify.

It would still be far from easy and the danger was unimaginable,
since this path would bring them into conflict with their own empire,
let alone the plethora of enemies that lay in wait. But even the
possibility was something to grab and hold tight, for everything that
had happened since they had crossed the Oxus and marched into
Inda lands had gradually spiralled the world down into chaos and
destruction, and, left unchecked, the only possible conclusion to all
of this was mutual annihilation of the world's great cultures and the
imposition of an unforgiving sun god on them all.

Not *everything* had added to the chaos, Dev reminded himself, a
smile crossing his face.

'Thinking about your family?' the general asked quietly, noticing
the change in his expression.

Dev nodded. It had been a wrench to leave the next morning, and
Jai and their father had filled his thoughts most of his waking hours
on the journey north. He had left a note for his father again, as he
had when they'd last parted, but this one had been a note of love and
of hope with a promise of reunion. When Dev had first left Initpur,
angry at the world in general and the Jade Empire's forage units in

particular, he had been focused on a path, driven by hate and loathing. That hate had still been there, albeit somewhat muted by time, when they crossed the border river with the army to face the enemy. That was what Dev had sought as a boy: to lead an imperial army east to chastise the Jade Empire. That was the very reason he had fled to the empire in the first place.

Then they had met the enemy at Jalnapur. Initially Dev had been exultant, but that had soon faded. Faced with the realities, Dev had soon come to realise that the men they faced, those on whose account he had fled his home so long ago, were just soldiers and ordinary people, the same as his own. Moreover, the few encounters he had had with them had led him to the inevitable conclusion that they had no true desire to be there. They were not the ravaging monsters who had taken his brother as a youth. They were just reluctant soldiers doing their duty. If there was a man to blame for all of this, it was the Jade Emperor himself, and not these beleaguered warriors fighting a costly war in a foreign land. The war. The foraging. Even Jai's abduction – they had all been the whim of the Jade Emperor, for that was the mentality of their people. They were more rigid and hierarchical even than the western empire.

His anger had diminished blow by blow, body by body.

Meeting General Jiang and discovering that Jai lived, not even as the slave Dev had assumed, but as a successful senior military officer, had finally dispelled what little ire remained. He could no longer hate the enemy, because they *were not* the enemy. They were the victims of this stupid, costly, futile war just as much as the forces of General Cinna. The *true* enemy was the Jade Emperor whose will had begun all of this. And the enemy was the insane emperor Bassianus, who would not compromise even if it meant the death of his own empire.

And the enemy was Ravi...

During that meeting at the monastery, and the good-natured evening of re-acquaintance that had followed, Dev had made no mention of his sojourn in the mountains and what he had found there. More than once he had found Cinna looking at him questioningly, for whenever the subject turned to the nature of, and the danger posed by, the Sizhad, Dev was oddly reticent, relating direct facts, but providing no personal details, as though he did not want to think about the Sizhad. Because he *did* not want to think about him.

Father and Jai had every right to know what had become of their younger brother, of course. That he was even alive, let alone healthy and influential. And it could be an important factor in the coming days that they were aware, though Dev could not yet see how. But the Sizhad's identity was his secret yet, which he had kept even from his general. He was not sure how his father would take the news that his young, sensitive boy – for that was how Dev remembered him – had become a zealous megalomaniac plotting world conquest and the destruction of the Inda gods. Aram had always been a pious man. Dev suspected such a revelation might break the old man more than having lost the three of them in the first place. Certainly such knowledge would have soured proceedings at the monastery for the reunited family.

No, for now Ravi was his secret and his problem. And Dev still remained hopeful for a solution to that problem. Ravi had not always been this Sizhad, after all, and while he clearly believed that was he was planning was right and good, his abandonment of the gods and clinging to the worship of the sun had been driven by grief, pure and simple, and not logic. He blamed the gods for their mother's and their sister's deaths, and the spite and hatred that had grown in him then still drove him now, more than ever. Perhaps, in a way, Ravi was every bit as mad as the emperor Bassianus, driven insane by sorrow. If so then he would be lost forever as this Sizhad. But Dev could understand such a thing. He had been almost there himself after Jai was taken, when he had fled west. But his eyes had been opened over the past half year, and the ire he had carried for so long had gone. Perhaps that was still possible for Ravi too? Perhaps the Sizhad was still a shell, with their sensitive, loving brother trapped inside. Something might yet be possible.

'You will see them again,' General Cinna said, wrongly assuming Dev's expression meant he was still thinking of the older of the brothers.

'I know. I was just pondering on how things change and what might yet be possible. Will there be resistance from the army in the coming days?' he asked, changing the subject. He knew the answer. They had talked of the matter often enough on the journey north.

Cinna huffed and shifted his grip on his reins. 'I would be lying if I said I thought it would be a simple matter. There will be officers who cannot bring themselves to draw a blade against the administration and the man at its head. And the men themselves swear an oath to the emperor as part of their recruitment, as you know. What they will do remains to be seen, for military men hate breaking an oath. Bassianus is far from popular, but still his very name is enough to frighten many into submission. We will have to play all of this very carefully. Firstly, word must not get out. That can be your first task, actually, Dev. Cut all the lines of communication with the west and put an end to the courier system. Once we know that anything said at Jalnapur stays there and is not leaked back to Velutio, we will then have to deal with the imperial spies in our midst.'

'How do we go about that, sir?'

'I'm not entirely sure yet, but there are ways of identifying them. If all else fails we will have an unannounced search made of all possessions. All imperial agents carry a ring with an inscription on the inside in order to identify themselves when necessary, though they are easy to discard at short notice and so there is no guarantee we will find them all that way. But we can and will find them somehow. And once those agents are removed from circulation, we work on the officers, starting with the ones I know and can trust, like Sidonius and Evodius, then the other ones who are likely to be sympathetic or have a reason to hate the current emperor. Most units are more loyal to their own commanders than to some lunatic back in the capital no matter how powerful he is, so will fall in with their officer's choices. Bassianus, after all, does not stand with them on a battlefield like their own commanders. We clear out the troublemakers and then work down from the top. And we contain it so that we can neutralise anyone who stands against us before he can influence his men.'

'How many soldiers can we rely on, then?'

The general turned a wry smile on Dev. 'Rely? At this stage very few. What we are about to do has not happened for centuries. Not since General Caerdin burned the mad emperor Quintus in his palace and began the interregnum. And *he* had the advantage of being the emperor's personal friend and confidante and could get close enough to do it. We are restricted to insurrection on a foreign battlefield. Our only advantage is that we will have the vast majority of the imperial army under our control by the time the emperor even knows what is happening. Or at least that's the plan. But until we can sound out the officers, the only people I would rely upon are my own personal guard, each of whom owes fealty by oath to me alone, and is paid by me independently of the army. I have enough enemies in the administration and command that I have always thought it prudent to keep my own force of loyal guards and not rely upon men assigned to me by the high command.'

'Wise,' Dev noted. 'And fortunate now.'

He looked around at the blue, white and silver riders of the general's guard. There were two hundred of them in total, or at least that many on paper. In the army a man learned to knock at least a quarter off any unit's recorded strength to account for deaths, sickness, desertions and the like. But with the guard being Cinna's private company, possibly they really did number two hundred. Even then, it was not a large number upon which to rely when contemplating treason amid an army.

'With luck there will be...'

General Cinna's voice trailed off into silence as they crested the last hill above Jalnapur. He stopped his horse.

'Gods!' Dev halted beside him, as did the guards. The twenty-seven riders sat silent astride their horses on the hill, overlooking the war zone as the nearest pickets scurried over to them, bowing respectfully. There was something in their expressions that Dev did not like, but there were more important things to think about right then.

The plain of Jalnapur was a veritable sea of humanity. If Dev had thought their army large before, nothing had prepared him for the sheer scale of what he was now witnessing. The reserves had come east, and Dev felt hollow panic at the realisation of just how many men had been taken away from the defence of the empire elsewhere. The reality of what was happening was hammered home once more.

'Things have just become a great deal more difficult, if not impossible,' General Cinna said with a grave expression. 'Come on.'

They urged their mounts forward again and suddenly paused once more in shock, horses rearing, as a great booming noise echoed out across the valley. Wide-eyed, the two officers sought the source of the noise and identified the cannon on the far bank that still smoked, its missile punching through units of men on the near side. In answer there came the rumble of multiple artillery pieces launching. Great rocks and bolts, jars of pitch and more arced across the river and robbed men of their lives in various horrifying ways.

'I left orders for minimal activity and no dangerous or costly pushes,' Cinna said breathlessly.

'Someone has clearly countermanded them, then, sir.'

Wordlessly, gazes locked on the vast force arrayed across the plain and the hills behind, the two officers and twenty-five guards accompanying them rode down the slope and into the enormous camp. The new troops must have arrived several days ago, as they had been integrated into the extant force such that tired veteran units of the Inda war stood side by side with fresh gleaming soldiers from the west. It was plain to see who had been here for so many months and who had just arrived, not only from the condition of their equipment and gear, but also from the difference in their expressions and manner. Those who were new were determined and proud. The rest were tired and hopeless.

They rode through the lines of tents and made for the headquarters on its low hill with a commanding view of the entire battlefield. The noise of a camp of this size was impressive enough that it almost covered the periodic blasts of cannon and the repetitive thuds and rattles of artillery as men died in droves on both sides of the river.

'Not good,' Cinna noted as they closed on the building.

'Sir?'

'My guard is not on duty.'

Dev nodded, worried now. Even in the general's absence, his headquarters came under the protection of his guard. Arriving at the entrance Dev noted the two soldiers standing beside the door. Both regulars, fresh and fierce-looking. He suddenly felt remarkably vulnerable.

Cinna leaned towards the officer of the guards with them.

'Take these men, find the rest of your unit and bring them to the headquarters. I want the entire guard standing to as soon as possible.'

The officer saluted and turned, his men following him as they rode off to find the guard camp, leaving Cinna and Dev alone. The young man's sense of exposure increased drastically as he dismounted along with the general and, tying their reins to the hitching post, followed him in through the door. The guards did not even look at them, let alone salute, and Dev realised with a start that he had subconsciously placed his hand on the hilt of his sword.

The general's office was occupied. They entered without announcement or query to find the great desk cleared of its usual documents and spread with a map of Jalnapur, painted wooden markers identifying the location of the various types of unit on both sides. Behind the table were five men in senior officers' uniforms, and Dev felt his chest tighten with nerves at the sight. Two of the men were officers Dev knew well from the months of stalemate at Jalnapur, one of them a friend and ally of Cinna's, the other more of an unknown. But the remaining three…

One of them, wearing the uniform of a prefect, also bore a cloak that marked him out as serving in Bassianus's personal guard, while the others were two of the empire's four marshals, the highest-ranking military men in the west. Even Cinna, a powerful general with a strong reputation, would bend his knee to those two. Dev dared not look at his commander right now. He did not want to see what was on the man's face.

The five men looked up in surprise at the sudden interruption. One of the marshals' eyebrows rose, while the other frowned.

'Cinna, where have you been?'

It was a good question, of course. A dangerous question, though. Dev tensed.

'There are a number of concerns other than the Jade Empire in this land that directly affect our military position. I have been to deal with one such, sir.'

The marshal, clearly unconvinced, looked to his peer, who shrugged. 'You left your army to go gallivanting off on some personal tour, Cinna. We arrived to find a dispirited army lounging around and not even pressing any kind of attack upon the enemy. You have constructed an impressive array of artillery, yet they were silent and unused. What do you have so say for yourself?'

Cinna glanced at Dev and then back to the senior officers, his face starting to betray a deep anger at the situation. 'There is the possibility, sir, that the enemy might be considering terms. I thought it prudent, given that chance, not to pound the living shit out of them with rocks.'

Dev felt his heart start to race. He'd not expected the general to admit as much to them, but he suddenly realised what the general had actually said. He had not confessed to seeking terms himself, nor had he intimated that there was any collusion. He had spoken the absolute truth, but by omission had made it sound as though the Jade Empire's forces were considering surrender.

The marshals were now looking at him with interest, but there was nothing about their manner that gave Dev much hope.

'There will be no terms, Cinna.'

'Marshal, I was given a remit to—'

'Your remit is no longer a concern,' the senior officer said, and Dev noted a strange, gleeful cruelty in the eyes of Bassianus's guard prefect.

'Marshal—'

'No, Cinna. You have failed in your task. The emperor had hoped by now to be the ruler of an empire that included the rich Inda lands and bordered the Jade Empire far to the east. Instead you have spent months mired down here unable – or possibly even *unwilling* – to prosecute the war for which you were selected. I warned the emperor that you were unreliable and not the correct man for the task, and I have clearly been vindicated. The emperor's men in your camp repeatedly deliver reports of hesitance and dithering. His majesty has finally lost patience with you. We are here to finish the job you started, Cinna. We outnumber the enemy now by a large enough margin to achieve victory.'

Cinna was close to exploding with anger. Dev could see the tell-tale signs, right down to the hands clenched into fists so tight they were white.

'Respectfully, sir, the emperor and the court are unaware of the many difficulties faced in the field here. And even if victory *is* possible, it will buy the emperor nothing. *Rich Inda lands?* This country is now poorer than the neediest of imperial provinces, and every month of war makes it worse. If you annexe the lands of the

Inda it will cost the empire a fortune to make it viable, far from being a source of wealth. The administration is blind to the realities.'

'You seem to be under the impression that I am some imperial clerk with no knowledge of war, Cinna. I am a marshal, and I achieved that rank by racking up every bit as many victories in the field as you. I will not be spoken to in such a manner by a lesser officer, who I also consider a lesser *man*. There has even been a suggestion of potential treachery, which carries the harshest of conceivable sentences, Cinna.'

'You do not understand,' growled Cinna.

'And you do not listen, General,' the imperial guard prefect put in with a nasty tone. 'You are no longer in a position to make policy here. You are hereby stripped of command on the authority of the emperor himself. At this time there will be no further action taken against you, though following a thorough investigation of the situation here, what follows remains to be seen.'

He left the threat hanging. Cinna and Dev both read the future in the prefect's eyes, and it was not auspicious.

'In the meantime,' the other marshal added, 'we shall need to debrief you and learn everything you know of the situation here so that we can avoid making the same mistakes. Return to your quarters, wash, shave and wait for further orders. You are confined to quarters at this time. Do as you are told, Cinna, and you might just survive this with everything but your honour intact.'

The prefect's glittering eyes suggested how unlikely that would be.

'And have your personal guard sent to me. There is no room in this war for a potential traitor's private army swanning about the camp. You shall dismiss them from service herewith and they shall be shuffled into a deserving regiment.'

Cinna, face pale with rage, saluted stiffly. Dev realised with a start that no one had yet mentioned him, and as the general turned and marched out of the room, Dev hurriedly followed before anyone could question him. In addition to being the general's adjutant, Dev was clearly of Inda blood, and he could quite easily imagine what these haughty, uncaring new officers would make of him.

As soon as the two men were out of earshot of the room, Dev turned to the general.

'What now?'

Cinna looked back at him. 'What?'

'Well surely you're not going to do as they say, sir?'

'I don't have a lot of choice, Dev.'

'Yes, you do. You were about to defy them anyway. Now you have more reason than ever. The need for subtlety is gone. Find the sympathetic officers and rouse them.'

Cinna shook his head. 'That chance has passed, Dev.'

'Sir?'

'They have been here for days and have already taken control of the army. On the way in I could see how my own good loyal units were now broken up and mixed with new soldiers of theirs, and that is to be my guards' fate. There is no force upon which we can rely. Any officer who might stand against them will already be confined to quarters the same as me. They will take no chances. Did you see Sidonius in there? A close friend of many years and the first officer I would turn to for support, and not only did he not speak up for me, he wouldn't even look at me. The marshals have complete control. Almost certainly the emperor's spies have already given them any names they needed to weed out trouble.'

'But you can't do *nothing*, sir. I saw the look on that prefect's face. The others just want you out of the way and to take over, but that prefect? He wants you disgraced, or possibly even dead. You'll be hauled into a trial and it will go badly for you.'

'Dev, listen to me. Our plans have all been undermined. There is now no way to defy the emperor. There is no way to take the army from the marshals. It can no longer be done. They've seen to that in our absence.'

'Then we need to get away, sir. You'll die if you stay here, and with my skin and my record of service to you I'll be dead a few heartbeats later.'

They emerged from the headquarters building and untied their mounts from the rail, hauling themselves wearily into the saddle. Dev caught a momentary glimpse of his commander's face and frowned. There was something different now in the man's expression. Then the general kicked his horse into movement and Dev was startled as he began to ride purposefully away, though not in the direction of his quarters.

'General?'

'You're right, Dev. It took a moment for me to stop simmering and see it, but you're right. I cannot do what I planned, but I must still do what I can. The empire is threatened by so many forces, and these fools strip it of men to fight this stupid, pointless war. If no one stops this, then the west will fall. I cannot accept that. I *will* not accept that.'

'Where are we going, then, General?'

'To my guard. They will be on their way here to muster, but I will not dismiss them and hand them over to be thrown into the mouth of a cannon. They are still loyal to me and they will have no desire to join this attack against my will. I said there was no one we can count on, but I was wrong. There are several groups we can count on. The guard will support us, as will your father, and there is another group I feel I can count on to do exactly as I anticipate. We will join with the guard, Dev, and leave the camp before the marshals realise we are gone.'

Dev, an odd nervous excitement thrilling through him, narrowed his eyes. 'Where, though, sir? To General Jiang? To my father?'

'No, Dev. Orders will have gone out now. There will be no safe way to approach the Jade Empire, and if we are tracked and we go to your father we will simply lead the marshals' men to the monastery, which could have no good ending. No. We go to that third group I can trust to be predictable. To your dangerous friend, the Sizhad, instead.'

The young officer's eyes widened in shock and alarm. 'That is not a good idea, sir.'

'I agree. But it is the only one I have. The Sizhad is now the only one who can change things.'

Dev shook his head fervently. 'Sir, the Sizhad will not help you. He will not help *anyone*. He has his own agenda, and it is simply the destruction of us all and the affirmation of his sun god as the *only* god.'

And yet had not Dev only that very morning contemplated the possibility that his younger brother might still be brought back from the brink? But how could he suggest that to the general without revealing their fraternal connection? And that would then cast Dev's own trustworthiness into doubt.

220

Cinna was shaking his head again. 'I have no doubt that the Sizhad sees me as the enemy. In fact I am counting on this.'

'Sir?'

'These idiots have come here in the expectation of an easy victory and will crush any hope of peace in the process. The only chance now is to open their eyes to the real danger and bring them down to size – make them realise I was right. They need to know it's not just the easterners across the river, but that the world is full of vicious bastards who will tear down the emperor. And since they are clearly blind to that fact, I will introduce the marshals to one of them personally. We go to find the Sizhad and his army, and we bring them south. I think we can count on the Sizhad to respond to provocation, and we will draw him to the marshals. We pit them against the imperial army here.'

'Bringing a third army to Jalnapur might make things worse,' Dev noted.

'But it might make things better, and we've run out of options.'

Ahead, a force of riders in gleaming steel, and blue and white tunics was moving towards them in ordered ranks. The general's bodyguard. The only unit in the whole of Jalnapur that Cinna could now rely upon.

'We need to move quickly,' Cinna said, 'before it's reported that I did not return to my quarters. I wish I had the chance to collect a few things, but every moment counts now.'

Dev nodded as they met with the guard and the general explained that they were going to ride out of the great camp to the north, past the now all but deserted city of Jalnapur.

The Sizhad. Ravi. The very idea of going back to that valley from which he had so narrowly escaped sent shivers through him. Would they have to face him? Would they even get as far as the valley? The last time Dev had ridden north with twice as many men and that had ended in disaster.

Dev, heart in throat, rode north.

CHAPTER 17

The wind whispers through the dead grass
Echoes of a world forgot
The wraiths of past troubles heed not
The perils of our day

Old World, by Ang Xi

'How things change in so short a time, Jai,' the general said, drawing his blade and examining the edge as the Crimson Guard around him followed suit.

The young officer nodded, his expression grim. He had not smiled since that moment they had emerged from the snaking valley and spied the field of Jalnapur. It had been a spirit-crushing sight. They had left for their illicit conference with the two forces at a safe standoff, not quite equal, but close enough to ensure that no senior officer on either side would do anything stupid. The two armies had sat glowering wearily at one another across that dreadful river, but nothing had been moving.

The view on their return had been vastly different.

Where the Jade Empire had had the numerical edge over their opponents, now the armies of the western empire filled the world with their men, animals and artillery. Things suddenly looked bleak for Jai and his general. And as they had returned to the scene of battle, the fight was already underway once more with fresh vigour and strength. Granted the bonus of new men from home, the west was pressing the attack with a vicious will, and the forces of General Jiang were fighting a defensive battle now.

Jai had wondered in that moment of shock whether the entire sojourn in the dead lands had been a cunning ruse to pull the senior commanders away from the army long enough to allow a huge reserve to be brought in and committed by the enemy. After all, the westerners could break through at any time the way they were pushing, and it was seemingly pure chance that the command party had managed to return in time to find the battle ongoing. They might well have arrived to find their forces broken and retreating.

Jiang had been the one to stamp on that notion. He knew himself to be a good reader of people and believed General Cinna to be genuine in his desire for a peaceful solution. Moreover, they had all seen the sudden and heart-warming resurrection of the fraternal bond between Jai and Dev, and neither of them could imagine Jai's brother having lied to him with such brazen ease.

No. Cinna and Dev were not behind this. It was simply unfortunate timing. And it put everything now into jeopardy. What hope there was that Cinna could remove potential enemies among his command and defy his own emperor now seemed to be infinitesimally small. That huge number of men arriving from the west would require senior officers at high level and, like Jiang's force, the new commanders would not be hand-picked for sense and loyalty as were the original army.

Jiang and his men had rushed down to their command post to find nervous officers, unable to find an adequate solution to the sudden shift in power. The westerners were adaptable, had initiative. The officers of the Jade Empire – even the best of them – had trouble with sudden changes in their rigid thinking. The enemy had pushed to take the bridge twice already in the past two days and had almost succeeded both times, denial of the bridgehead costing both sides dreadful numbers. The bulk of the eastern officers now believed this fight to be over. Jiang had realised that his own chances of defying an emperor and changing the world were now diminished to almost naught too. He would have to fight a desperate defence instead, and the only thing that would now save them was the arrival of their own reinforcements. But that in itself would end all hope of peace, for then they might win the war, but Jiang would lose control of it all. It was a dreadful situation. Hundreds of years ago a famous monk had asked the question 'What does a man choose when faced with a lake of fire before him and a precipice behind?' It had never seemed more apt to Jai and the general now.

Jiang had done the only thing he could. He had prepared to defend their position against superior odds until the new army arrived, and hoped that there was something he could do once that happened. He had, in effect, stepped back from the lake of fire and thrown himself over the precipice, hoping to find a handhold part way down.

The other officers had been disapproving of the new direction of their general's plan, though none had been able to suggest an alternative when asked. And so Jiang had taken a leaf from the military sketchbook of his opposite number. Where Cinna's forces had fortified and trapped their end of the bridge, while Jiang's had kept theirs clear for the movement and access of troops, now the westerners were infilling their pits and clearing the obstacles, while Jiang had men desperately digging pits and moving barriers into the way. A complete reversal.

And now, eleven days after they had returned to Jalnapur, it seemed the enemy were about to make the next true attempt to break the Jade Empire's forces – probably on a scale that would make the previous attempts look like mere exercises. Jiang had watched them from the observation point, eyes hawk-like as he took in every nuance of what was happening across the river. It was all done rather subtly, with just the gentle shifting of units, but Jiang was not fooled. There might be only a slow shuffling and swapping of units, but a keen eye could see that the result of the general rearrangement was that the fresh, new heavy infantry were now close to the bridge, heavy horse behind them. Jiang had distributed the orders he'd had prepared for days in anticipation of this moment and had beckoned to Jai and his Crimson Guard. The young man had frowned in surprise.

'Our world is threatened, Jai, and our men quake with fresh fear. Whatever heart we can give them, it is our duty to do so. We will join the defence of the bridge.'

And so they had ridden forth from the command post as the orders the general had disseminated were effected, walking their beasts down the slope and onto the causeway with the full unit of the Crimson Guard, frightening and impressive, at their shoulder, face masks immobile but with red-painted teeth bared for battle.

As they had moved across the plain towards the bridge the reality of what was happening had impressed itself upon Jai. The cannon placed sporadically across the eastern bank thundered their smooth-chiselled death at the enemy, belching fire and black smoke with the blasts, the artillerists instinctively recoiling with each shot, aware that no matter how skilled they were, there was always at least a small chance of a misfire. But it was happening remarkably rarely these days. The men at the machines were now experienced enough to fire the missiles in their sleep and could spot an imperfection in the great stone balls at a single glance. Moreover, the cannon with any potential faults had long since fallen apart. Now only terrible luck resulted in a misfire.

With a sound like a giant stamping angry boots, the cannon pounded the enemy again and again, jettisoning their deadly loads over the heads of the nervous soldiers.

The enemy were far from idle either. Their weapons didn't have the range of the Jade Emperor's cannon, and could only reach a certain distance across the battlefield, but wherever they could reach had become a field of twisted and mangled bodies.

Carnage. Just like their first few weeks here.

Jai felt his spirits sink that little bit further as the near end of the bridge came within sight. For months now it had been clear, the road solid if pitted with divots caused by enemy artillery, the once-beautiful white stonework of the bridge itself now greyed and brown and with barely a pace of it undamaged in some way. But it was what had been done by their own men in the past few days that brought a lump to the throat. As long as that access to the bridge had remained clear, the statement had been made: 'We still intend to cross that bridge and win.'

Now there was no access. The statement had changed. Now it was: 'We intend to stop the enemy crossing that bridge.'

A trench had been cut across the near end. Unlike the one the westerners had made, full of spikes and death, this one had been cut in a 'U' shape around the bridge, ten feet wide and as deep as the men could make it. Now the river ran around the end of the bridge, effectively sealing it off. And, given the speed of the current, it would be a dangerous torrent even for a man in underwear, let alone a man in armour.

The eastern bank of that moat-like trench had been given additional defences, with sharpened stakes jutting from the lip out towards the water, preventing anyone from climbing out of the torrent. A small fence of sharpened stakes had been constructed behind it, and archers and infantry positioned appropriately. And there, among the crowds of men gathered ready to repel any attack, standing amid smeared mud, blood and bone where men had fallen to enemy artillery over the past few days, were the rocket troop. Jiang's last throw of the dice.

Jai shuddered. Rockets were unpredictable and perilous at the best of times, and he had no idea what the general had planned, but whatever it was it would be desperate and horribly dangerous.

'Here they come,' the general said, dragging Jai's attention back to the bridge itself.

He and the Crimson Guard, and Jai too, had dismounted five hundred paces back, leaving their mounts in a guarded corral. Horses were just an inconvenience in this sort of situation.

'They're moving slowly,' Jai noted, watching the gleaming steel wall of imperial might stomping towards them, swords clattering against the bronze edges of their shields in a threatening rhythm.

'They don't want to endanger their own,' the general said. 'Shields up!' he bellowed. All across the bridgehead, men raised their shields. Carefully placed burly soldiers lifted the supports of specially constructed roofs and angled them into position, slotting the great timber legs into the sockets prepared in the ruined ground. Jiang was no fool and had prepared.

A sensible commander pounded the enemy with artillery before committing his men.

The first blow struck one of the timber roofs and the thing paid for all the hard work in that one moment as a dozen men owed it their lives, the great stone ball of the imperial onager bouncing off the heavy slats and careening away into the dirt. Men off to the side scurried out of the way.

But it was not the only blow to come, and not all of them would be so easily dodged. Jai could not help but wince each time a missile struck. Sometimes they came down between the heavy temporary roofs, and when they did the sounds were indescribable. The ninth shot to strike the central area where the two officers waited was the first to destroy a wooden roof. The enemy shot had been angled differently, and instead of glancing off the timbers and shooting away into the periphery to become the problem of other men, it struck hard, shattering timbers and slats and punching through to cause mayhem beneath. The heavy stone ball crushed two men on impact, one dead instantly, the other gasping out his last few moments from a ruined chest. Further men suffered the agony of flying splinters from the ruined roof, which were almost as bad as the missile itself.

The one reprieve during the barrage was that the enemy had forgone the use of burning pitch in those dreadful earthenware jars that exploded on impact. They could not afford to engulf in flames the world into which they sent their men. Still, the iron bolts and heavy stones came thick and fast and killed many in dreadful ways.

Then, as suddenly as it had started, the rain of missiles stopped. There was no time, nor cause, to rejoice, though, for the screams and thuds and cracks and cries were instantly replaced with the bellowed war cry of the enemy as they picked up speed and ran towards Jai and the rest. What could they hope to achieve?

Eastern archers began to loose their deadly rain now, nocking, drawing and loosing in perfect unison in a graceful dance of violence, swarms of arrows arcing up from the bank to either side to rain down upon the charging enemy as they came into range. Men fell, but not enough of them to make a difference. Their shields studded with shafts, they still came. It was only when the howling, furious faces of the western soldiers were perhaps forty paces from the moat that their plan became clear. For a moment, Jai had thought they had produced their own roof against the Jade Empire's arrow storm, but quickly he realised that what he'd taken to be a roof was, in fact, a floor.

Bellowing men suddenly picked up extra speed, racing ahead of their compatriots, carrying those great timber boards. They neared the ditch, some of them dying to arrows and falling by the wayside, but numerous enough to proceed even with heavy losses. And as they reached the end of the bridge, they threw forward their burden.

It was a timber ramp perhaps fifteen feet long, which neatly reached across the water. Jai felt his throat constrict at the sight. More were coming behind as well. Two more wooden ramps were brought forward and hurled across the gap.

Desperate men at the front of the defensive line tried to reach through their own fence of stakes to push the timber bridges into the water with the curved sickle blades of their ji polearms, but it was too difficult, and already the infantry were beginning to cross. They paid little or no heed to the fact that they were rarely running on stone or timber, but mostly on the bodies of their compatriots who had fallen to the arrow storm from each side. More western soldiers fell with every heartbeat, but there were so many of them on the bridge now that it was like trying to use a net to hold back a wave.

Jai braced himself, though he was far from the front, a dozen men between him and immediate danger, men of the Crimson Guard to his side. The meat-grinder of battle began a moment later, and Jai was aware of it not by the sounds, which hardly changed, but by the sudden lurch backwards as the men in front were thrown against him.

Never had the difference between the two empires been so ably demonstrated. The heavy infantry of the Jade Empire lunged and swung with their ji in perfect symmetry as though demonstrating on a parade ground, their weapons forming a sweeping barrier of steel, whirling and deadly and yet with a beautiful and graceful precision. The soldiers of the western legions met the glinting thrashing machine with a wall of shields and short blades, the great rectangular boards taking the brunt of the eastern assault as chips and shards of wood and bronze were ripped away and sent through the air. Then the value of the western form showed as those short blades began to lance out like vipers between the shields, finding openings and biting into flesh. Within moments the Jade Empire's front of whirling death began to fall apart. Jai had never been so acutely aware of the dangers of such rigid formation. To the casual observer both forces must seem as disciplined and ordered as the other, but the westerners were so adaptable, so individual, despite their wall of shields.

The ji-wielding footmen – those who still lived, anyway – backed off or leapt aside to make way. The Jade Empire's heavy swordsmen moved in to take on the western shieldwall, their swords held high in readiness for the first form of all sword combat, the attack of the west-facing stork, their three-pronged parrying knives held low and ready. The two forces met with a crash and clang and the scrape of metal on metal, and the world became a mass of figures, obscuring the details for Jai, further back in the press.

Somehow, as though the soldiery instinctively knew to avoid a general, Jiang was not pushed back the same as Jai, and the general was waving his sword in the air, exhorting his men to greater heights of bravery as the Crimson Guard joined the front ranks to lend their specialised veteran killing arms to the fray. They would need all the help they could get. The tide flowing across the bridge seemed unstoppable. Whoever was in charge of this attack, Jai thought in the struggle, it was not Cinna. *This* man had no care for the men under his command. He saw them as disposable assets and was willing to throw them away in droves to achieve any kind of victory. The westerners were dying in their hundreds. In their *thousands*, probably. Dozens at a time plummeted over the sides of the bridge clutching the arrows that had pierced their chests, limbs, necks, faces. Others screamed and went down to be mercilessly trampled by men they had called brother mere hours ago.

Jai knew his own general, like Cinna, would never have thrown away such a huge number of men in the hope of a win here. But then Cinna had not had such large numbers to commit at the time. Would he have been any different now?

This was not the time for pondering what might have been. Jai grunted as a boot came down hard on his foot in the press. Ahead, he could just see the faces of western soldiers bellowing the jagged, incomprehensible names of their gods as they cut their way forward. The men of the Jade Empire were not giving their lives or ground easily, though, and were fighting hard for every pace, killing westerners in droves. The world was now constantly flecked with blood, and tiny flecks of matter that no sane man would examine closely. Muscle, bone, cartilage, teeth, fragments of iron and leather and flesh. It was not hard to see the front of the fighting through the haze of gore, for there was so little space in which to struggle that the dead were piling up underfoot and the frontline mêlée was rising to such a height as to be visible over the heads of others. Now they were struggling to fight inside the wooden shelters and the structures were removed, one way or another. One somehow made its way back among the enemy to act as strengthening timbers for their temporary bridge.

Jai found himself in the depth of battle quite suddenly as the soldier two men in front vanished with an agonised cry and a burst of crimson, and the man in between lasted mere moments, a spear thrust from some unseen source punching through his scale shirt, sending tiny bronze plates out in a shower and impaling him neatly.

The spear almost took Jai with it as it emerged from the man's back, and he dodged to the side just in time.

The world became a blur of combat. Jai had trained for years in the best academy in the Jade Empire, and he knew the forms better than most, but this was not a dance of blades with adherence to form. This was butchery and savagery with little time to think or plan. Yet it was as he parried and leapt, swung and thrust, that Jai realised the value of the Ishi masters' training. For all that he had no opportunity to plan his attacks or consider the appropriate defence, he became oddly aware of the fact that instinct was doing it for him. The forms and their many variants had become a memory within his body itself so that it anticipated without conscious thought, pirouetting through the slaughter with delicate movement.

A soldier, snarling his harsh western words through bloodied teeth and a barrage of spittle, launched at him, a sword driving straight for his heart. Before Jai had even realised he was doing it, his body had bent into the defence of the reluctant crane and the enemy blade had swept through the air beneath his armpit. His own sword came down in the attack of the mindful scorpion. His blade, angled seemingly impossibly in the press, punched down into the neck of the man's breastplate, finding the notch in the throat and carving through his organs. Any amateur would now lose his sword, buried deeply in the man's armour as he fell away, but Jai was no amateur. Almost casually, he walked up to the falling corpse, whipping the blade free and whirling in the attack of the seven-eyed demon to take the head neatly off another man and then carve into the throat of the man behind. His red-coated sword came free as the man fell and caught the advancing sword of another, lifting it and then dropping into the attack of the unexpected viper, plunging into the same armpit he had just exposed. Forms upon forms, each one making a widow and filling the air with blood. The world was blood. Life and death: blood. All was blood. Jai was in danger of finding joy in the simplicity of it – something his tutor had avidly warned him against.

Briefly, in this display of deadly prowess, he caught sight of General Jiang, who was now involved in the fighting himself, and Jai recognised a fascinating and inventive combination of two offensive and one defensive forms, allowing the senior commander to dispatch two opponents in a single move and still be in position to block a spear that sought his head. Jai had no time to truly consider it, but there could be little doubt that Jiang had the skill of an Ishi master himself, and Jai would love – or would he hate? – to face the man in a duel.

The killing went on seemingly forever, as though the world were ending around them, which in a very real way it was. Jai was aware of the sun's progress across the heavens and the gradual darkening of the sky as he spun and stabbed, fought and parried. Occasionally, he found himself hauled back out of danger by a lesser officer and realised he had fought almost to exhaustion. Each time he rested as men before him died, and then, after he had counted off enough heartbeats, he took a deep breath and joined the fray once more.

They were losing. There was no doubt about it. Over three hours of struggling at the bridge end, throwing seemingly endless numbers of men at the enemy, they had given ground to the tune of some hundred paces. It didn't sound much, but it would be enough. A hundred paces meant that the enemy were now managing to pour from the bridge onto the bank with increased ease and in greater numbers. It also meant that the front line of the fighting defence had been stretched and had given way to both sides near the river bank.

Jai heard his general's voice calling his name and, delivering an expert thrust to an exposed throat, pulled back, allowing men to pour into the gap he left and hold the line. As he pushed back through the ranks, seeking General Jiang, Jai could see the next step in their defeat taking place. The collapse of the defensive line at the riverside was allowing the enemy to slip past in increasing numbers and they were making for those units of archers who poured death down upon the men crossing the bridge. Already the torrent of the great Nadu ran pink with blood, and bodies were visible like logs in storm water, washing away into the distance, some caught in eddies at the edge. But fewer men were toppling into the water with every heartbeat as enemy infantry found units of archers and laid waste to them. Western cavalry were now coming across the bridge too, and their arrival would cause fresh hell for everyone.

Jai knew that his general had plenty of units in reserve, and some of these would even now be racing forth to head off those men ravaging the archers, but with more pouring across the bridge all the

231

time, things were looking bleak. Moreover, the enemy troops that had been committed to the push were the late arrivals, fresh and spoiling for a fight, while every man on the eastern bank was tired and soul sore.

'Jai!'

He followed the voice and found General Jiang standing in a small clearing, surrounded by men, a medic tying a tourniquet around his thigh. It was neither the wound, though, nor the press of men, nor even the sense of defeat in the air that struck Jai. What immediately grabbed his attention and held it was the rider. The man was dusty and travel-worn, and still astride his horse even while addressing a senior officer on foot, which was not appropriate etiquette. Moreover, the man's face was a picture of horror and misery, matched only by the general's.

'What has happened?'

'The reserves are not coming,' Jiang said in a hollow, quiet voice.

'What?'

The general waved away the medic and limped over to Jai, indicating the rider in passing.

'Our friend here just delivered the glad tidings at the most opportune moment imaginable. The relief force reached Yuen but there they stopped. They have rebelled against the Jade Emperor. Can you believe that? Here are we fighting a war we don't want on his behalf and the men he sends to make sure we keep doing it rise up against him. They turned around and marched on the capital. There will be civil war at home, Jai.'

A strange mix of ideas washed through Jai. He wasn't sure that he was that disappointed with the idea of a change in emperor. It might be terrible for the empire, but it could be good for the Inda. It might also...

'Does that mean we are free to negotiate with the westerners?' he asked urgently.

Jiang snorted. 'We *would have been*. A month ago it would have made all the difference. But these new commanders over there? See how rabidly they press the attack, heedless even of their own high losses? These men are not here to negotiate. All they might accept is surrender, and that with only adequate humility and executions.'

'Then what do we do?'

The general straightened. 'We deny the enemy this bank for as long as we can in order to save the army. I am not an autocrat, and I will not tell my men to commit to any action when I cannot for myself say whether I approve of it. What happens now is down to the conscience of each individual.'

Jai became aware suddenly that a number of officers were closing on them, pushing through the crowd in response to the general's call. 'Signal the rocketeers,' Jiang told his signaller. The man hauled a great red flag into the air and waved it.

Jai frowned, still wondering at the value of rockets in this situation.

There was a long, odd pause among the Jade officers, the sounds of battle somehow dulled by expectation. And then it happened. With a 'crump', the eastern end of the bridge seemed to contract oddly. Then, with a boom that made the ears of all present ring, the entire eastern end of the structure, some seventy paces long, detonated. Shards of white stone hurtled into the air in every direction, escaping a roiling, boiling cloud of red flame and black smoke. Men were vaporised by the score in the explosion.

Jai and all the other officers stared in shock as the black cloud gradually dissipated and the last of the debris – stone and flesh – came down into water and onto land like heavy, grisly rain.

The bridge was now uncrossable. Seventy paces of the structure were utterly gone, even the pylons upon which it had stood destroyed down to well below the water's surface. The surviving western troops were milling about on the truncated crossing, some falling into the water in the press, many rolling around in screaming agony, burned and maimed by the explosion and flying shards of stone. The damage was appalling.

'Sir,' one of the officers said in a breathless voice, 'what have you done?'

'I have bought you all time to live. The enemy are coming. We are beaten. And the empire needs you all. The reserve army has rebelled against the emperor and raised a usurper. He has yet to show green eyes, so the old emperor still lives. That means there will be war at home. Each of you must look to your men and to your duty. You all took an oath to the emperor, but we have also all seen the madness to which his policies have led. You alone can decide whether you cleave to your oath or whether you seek a new path. I will not decide for you. But in a matter of hours that enemy force will begin to cross in earnest, for we shall no longer hold against them. We cannot, else we all die and our land will be torn apart. Gather your men to your signals and leave the field. Go east and there decide which banner you will seek, but go there now before the westerners cross. I feat there will be no quarter given by their new commanders when they do.'

Jai watched the horror of the news sink into every man in that gathering as General Jiang limped from the circle and began to move back along the causeway. What was left of the Crimson Guard who had been fighting alongside him in the press – some two hundred, all that remained of a force once twice that size – gathered protectively around their commander. The Crimson Guard took no oath to the emperor, purely to their general. They were loyal even beyond death. Jai hurried after him, thoughts churning.

'Sir—'

'Jai, you must choose your path now,' the general said over his shoulder without turning.

'My path is with you.'

'Your service to me is done, Jai.'

'Where will you go, sir? Who will you support?'

General Jiang stopped and turned, and Jai felt shock at the look of defeat and utter hopelessness on the man's face. 'Support, Jai? No one. Who *can* I support? The emperor who started this entire mess, who will demand my head for my failure? Or the usurper raised by my enemies – men who wish nothing more than to see me fail? No. I cannot go back. The Jade Empire is closed to me no matter who wins control of it.'

Jai shook his head. It was true and clear, of course, but he'd never considered what it would be like for the man not to be able to go home.

'South, General. To my father. To safety.'

'No, Jai.' Jiang gestured back over the bridge. 'The enemy will want my head. They will seek me out above all others to take as a prize for their insane emperor. I will be hunted like a beast and they will be relentless. And no matter how much a man tries to disappear, he will always leave a trace. Your father told me something along

234

those lines that day in the monastery. No. If I go south and seek your father, all I will do is lead the enemy to his door. Always, since we came here, I have been pushed in different directions, and now is no different. I cannot go south. To both east and west men will seek my head. I must go north.'

'Then I will come with you.'

'No, Jai.' The general wagged a finger at him. 'This is my fate, not yours.'

'Now you sound like my father.' Jai sighed. 'But whatever fate has in store for you, General, I share it. I know that. I have known it since we first came here. You ride north, and I ride north with you. Perhaps we will find sanctuary with this Sizhad. Whatever the case, I have no wish to face an uncertain future on my own.'

Jiang stood for a long moment, then finally nodded. Around them, they could hear three distinct groups of sounds. On the bridge was angry, belligerent dismay as the westerners, halted in their victorious advance, struggled to pull back and put together a new plan. Close to the water was the ongoing sound of battle, where westerners who knew they were trapped there either attempted to take as many archers as possible with them or tried to flee the scene, only to be caught by those reserves who had come forward to protect the missile units. And finally horns were beginning to sound as flags waved across the battlefield, summoning units to muster, their commanders desperate to flee the field before the enemy came again.

'Very well, Jai. Then you and I and my men here will seek our future in the mountains to the north. We will have to ride hard, and I will rely heavily upon your knowledge of the land – especially as we near your home – in order to throw enemy pursuit off our scent. I have no pressing desire to see my head separated from my shoulders just yet.'

Fate, Jai pondered, as they hurried back to the small corral where their horses waited with those of the guard, was a curious thing. He had been taken from the Inda by marauding Jade Empire soldiers, brought up as one of theirs and then sent back with them to invade his own lands. And now here he was in his homeland again, no longer serving the Jade Empire. And though the westerners were ascendant on the far bank, recent experience had taught Jai not to revel in such comforts, for had not the easterners been in that very position just weeks ago? Somehow Jai felt that fate was not yet done with him, nor with the general with whom he had thrown in his lot. There were moves to play out yet in this game.

Suddenly he found himself wondering where, in all this nightmare, Dev was.

CHAPTER 18

How the world changes. Once upon a time the lands of the Inda rajahs were bright, colourful, lively places full of wonder and glory and exotic life, while beyond the line of markers was a land of death and madness and terror of such infamy that a natural no man's land came to exist between the two where no sane man would settle.

Now the world of the Inda is one of misery and blood, downtrodden people and rotting corpses, lacking in all glory and life, and invariably the colour of blood. There, the unburned, tortured souls would be creating a new land of the dead. Yet here, beyond the markers, we have carved out a life more oddly peaceful and prosperous than even that which I once knew at Initpur.

Yet there are things that nag at me in the small hours of the night. I find myself wondering what will happen when we are discovered by others, for that time must come. Even if Generals Cinna and Jiang keep secret our world, since they stumbled across us others must do so eventually. And also I wonder what the world is like south of here, for we are only a day's good journey past the markers, and there is at least a week's journey south through these lands to the Isle of the Dead itself, and I can only imagine that things become steadily more dangerous the further one trespasses. And I wonder at the bodies of the scouts we found when we first crossed the line and how they died with such horrified faces, and what criteria the spirits use to decide whether to let men pass or to kill them or drive them mad. And I wonder where the monks have gone. And I wonder why the monastery seemed so prepared for us. And I ponder the meaning of fate and just how much my path has been mapped out in advance.

All I can do is my best.

A ram watched the picket riding in from the east in the bright early autumn sunshine amid the calls of exotic birds and the hum of insects. The man's attitude and his horse's gait were brisk but did not smack of desperation. The rider closed on the monastery swiftly and Aram noted the lookout at the gate platform move close to the warning bell, ready to ring it like mad. The old man shook his head slightly.

'I don't think that will be necessary. Wait for now.'

The rider reached the gate and leaned over the sweating horse's neck, patting it as he addressed the leader of the free Inda. 'Men are coming. Quite a few, using the crossing.'

'Be specific. How many? What men?'

'Maybe a hundred. Maybe more. They're soldiers of the Jade Empire, but they're moving like refugees. Some are wounded and they all look beaten. They have discarded their weapons outside the markers and many are unarmoured too.'

Aram felt crestfallen at the news. So much hope lost so soon. 'It sounds as though the generals have failed to achieve their goal of peace. A terrible thing, when they had come so close within these very walls.'

For a soul-freezing moment he pictured Jai lying in a bloodied heap amid the muddy fields of Jalnapur, but he shook off the image, biting down on his lip. Fate had brought them all together for a reason, and if it was not to put an end to the war as the generals had planned, then there was something else still to achieve. Jai would be safe until that happened, Aram was sure, as would Dev.

'If they are coming south, does it mean they have lost?' the picket asked.

'Possibly,' Aram said. 'Whatever the case, we have nothing to fear from a hundred unarmed men. We are prepared, strong and numerous. Let them come.'

'Shall I gather the defence?' the gate lookout asked.

The monastery's leader shook his head. 'If these men are wounded and beaten, they are not seeking trouble. If we meet them with a force of gathered muscle we cannot be certain how they will react. Let us treat this as a meeting of minds, not of muscle. Summon the medics. They have wounded.'

As the medics were sought and the picket dismounted and took his horse to the stables, those workers outside began to drift in, and some of the population moved inside to safety. No matter that the alarm bell had not been rung, the arrival of one of the pickets suggested that someone was coming, and many of the Inda were still not willing to risk even the slightest chance of encountering an enemy.

Aram adjusted his garments and stepped out of the gates into the dusty, well-trodden space before them. People scurried past him on their way to perceived safety, though some remained at their tasks in the fields and orchards, trusting that there was no danger since the bell had not tolled. There Aram waited as the sun baked the ground beneath him. After a while, half a dozen men and women gathered by the gate with their baskets of equipment. The medical staff of the monastery numbered two midwives, a horse doctor, two village healers, and a surgeon who had served one of the more important western rajahs upon a time. Together they were capable of dealing with any medical situation that arose among the complex's populace, but how they would deal with war wounds remained to be seen.

It was almost an hour before the first men emerged from the jungle along the eastern path, making their way between the fields and the few men and women still working them, and closed on the monastery. The group moved together, as though for mutual protection, and as they came closer, Aram could see not only the defeated faces of a losing army, but also wide-eyed fear born of something entirely different. He was no expert in military matters, but he had long known the Jade Empire – all his life, in fact – and he knew their adherence to rules and order was paramount. That was what made this group so unusual for their people. They did not march in unison, but shuffled close together. They were not clad in the same garb either, but bore at least three different uniforms, which meant these were the survivors of several different units. The group seemed to be led by three officers, though their ranks were a mystery to Aram. One was clearly senior, since he stepped forward as the party came to a halt a score of paces from the Inda leader and the others looked to him to act.

'Do you speak my tongue?' the man asked in a strange, nervous voice. Aram almost laughed. It was the first time in his life he had heard anyone of the Jade Empire display nerves when faced with the Inda. How things had changed within a year.

'With reasonable proficiency,' Aram said. 'Your people have been coming to our lands for a long time.'

The officer had the good sense to look apologetic at that, but it was still almost lost beneath a wave of fear and despair. Aram took pity on him.

'Have your wounded move over to the bales by the wall, the most urgent cases to the fore. Our medics will tend to them.'

'Thank you,' the officer said with genuine feeling. 'I am surprised, and of course relieved, to find you here. I was led to believe there was no one beyond the statues. Only...'

'Only ghosts,' Aram finished for him. 'Almost true. I believe we are the only ones, though I suppose it is possible that similar colonies have sprung up. We were forced to flee the war and seek a place of refuge. We found it here, but there will be only spirits south of this place, all the way to the isle.'

'The spirits...' one of the other officers said, shuddering, his eyes wide. 'I saw... things. *Heard* things. Others fled south when we lost the bridge but did not heed the warnings. They would not leave their weapons outside. We are taught never to disarm in war. But they... We found some of them in the jungle. They...'

Aram nodded. 'I know. I have seen it. You did well to listen to the tales. They are *not* just myth.'

'We will not be the last to come here,' the senior officer interrupted.

'The war is over?'

'Not yet, but it *is lost*. The Jade Empire crumbles from within. There is civil war. And the westerners' mad emperor sent so many men to Jalnapur that we could not hold them. They ravage now across the heart of this land, seeking to control and enslave, while our forces scatter before them. Many have gone east to fight for a flag in the hope of serving the next emperor, whoever he might be, and some went north into uncertainty. Others are coming south. But it will not just be us – not just men of the Jade Empire. When the westerners learn we have come into these forbidden lands, they will be sure to follow in their hunger for total victory. I saw them after the bridge. They were merciless. Wanton. Nightmarish.'

Aram nodded. 'We are far from defenceless, even lacking weapons. And the gods and the spirits surround us. We do not fear them.'

240

'You should,' the officer said, darkly. 'They are animals, and they will come. I wish you no harm, spirit-rajah, but others will. I will lead my men further south, away from the danger.'

'Further south is *into* danger,' Aram countered. 'If you have heeded the warnings thus far, then you know that. The south is the island of the dead. A world of ghosts.'

The officer sighed. 'Why worry about an *island* of the dead when north of here is a whole *world* of the dead? I have no fear left in me to feel. We go south. And before the westerners decide to cross into these lands, I recommend that you go too.'

Aram shook his head. Whatever the case, whether they were in danger here or not, there was something yet coming, he was sure, and he could not flee into the unknown when his sons were still out there and would come back.

'No. We have a haven of civilisation here and we will protect and nurture it as long as we can.'

'Then I wish you luck, but we shall not stay,' the soldier said. 'With your permission, though, I would leave our wounded to your care? I am not sure they will make it through the jungle.'

'I am not sure *you* will,' Aram said darkly, but nodded. 'Of course we will take your wounded.'

'*I* would stay with you,' said the other officer, the one with the wide eyes. The senior man cast a surprised look at him and the second officer shrugged. 'The westerners are dangerous, sir, but the things we saw on the way... I... I feel safe here. If it is like that all the way south, full of spirits and fear and death, then I have no wish to go there.'

The senior officer peered at him for some time, then gave a dissatisfied nod. 'Very well. If this rajah will take you, then anyone who wishes to stay may do so.'

Aram nodded. Briefly, in his head, he calculated the space in the monastery. They had acquired several hundred more souls in the past few weeks as refugees drifted south, close to the border, and were brought in by Aram's scouts, but he estimated there would still be room and supplies for seven or eight hundred more. Beyond that, they would be stretching their capabilities. There were perhaps forty here stepping out to join them, plus a dozen wounded. But if other such defeated men were still to come, how long could they manage?

No matter how hard you might try, you simply cannot hide from the world, Aram...

AUTUMN, THE NORTHERN MOUNTAINS

The Sizhad watched the soldiers in the valley below, his fingers picking at the crumbling mortar of the ruined watchtower. A couple of hundred figures in blue and white moving slowly and carefully, as though expecting an ambush at any moment. Had this been back in the valley of the sun, he would have had them cut down by archers instantly, but there was something nagging at the back of his mind, and he had instead sent the advance missile unit off to the side, where they now lurked in the shade with the cavalry vanguard, waiting for the bulk of the force to catch up.

'They are definitely imperial troops,' one of his Faithful said. 'A senior officer and his bodyguard. Curious to see them here in the valleys so far from Jalnapur.'

The Sizhad squinted into the shade of the deep valley that wound across the landscape below this high pass of which no foreigner would be aware as he addressed his man.

'With the Jade Empire collapsing in on itself and their army scattering, likely the western heretics are pressing their advantage, seeking to expand their control over the Inda. They must be in these mountains ascertaining what they face in the coming days. They *cannot* be expecting us yet.'

Although his brother had escaped. Had he survived? Had he told them about the Faithful?

The Sizhad turned and looked back. The mountain pass was dotted with his scouts and outriders in white and beige, hard to spot among the brown earth and light-grey rocks. Beyond them, as yet out of sight, the army of the Faithful marched, full of the glorious light of the sun, ready to fall upon the legions of demon worshippers. They had been moving for four days now and were closing on the edge of the highlands, ready to descend into the lower lands and bring the true faith to the godless.

'We should fall upon these dogs and kill them,' the rider beside him said fervently.

Perhaps they *should*, at that. But then there was that little something nagging at him, stopping him. The Sizhad looked up at the great ball of light in the sky, giver of life, preserver of the world, and stared as long as he could, then looked back down into the valley, the purple and green blotches filling his vision. They neatly obscured the riders. The sun had spoken, and it was a relief that his instincts had not been wrong.

'No. They are important. But they are also in the way. If we wish to crush their army, which we must if we are to proceed, then we need to go south. Perhaps...' He smiled at a notion. 'Perhaps the lord of light is telling us not to ambush and attempt to surprise the heretics. Such subterfuge is, after all, a thing of shadow and gloom. Perhaps the time has come to announce our presence to the world.'

The eagerness in the Faithful riders around him was tangible at the sentiment.

'We shall destroy their army, which is now somewhat dispersed, chasing away their beaten foe and pressing down their occupying footprint. It will not be a hard fight. The sun is with us. Then we shall turn west and fall upon their unprotected empire. All of their military might is here and their lands are ripe for conquest. Their heathen temples and images of demons shall be cast down and the sun shall rise in their place, bringing with it a new empire of prosperity and piety.'

The riders were positively buzzing with readiness. The Sizhad smiled. The world needed to change, and it took *belief* to do such a thing. His Faithful had belief to spare.

'Signal the army to pick up the pace. Tell them to cross the pass like sunlight chasing away the darkness. Let the riders down there see the Faithful in all their power and glory and flee before our might, carrying word of the glory to come.'

PART FOUR

A WORLD OF GHOSTS

CHAPTER 19

The rose and the snow lotus grow proud
Garden and mountain-doting parents
Separate and lone
Yet together in glory

Ong Dynasty, author unknown

Jai watched the scout coming back across the hillside as he bit the side of his tongue in anticipation. They had travelled through the low moorlands and up into the foothills of that range of mountains imperial geographers knew as the Spine of the World, all the time staying ahead of trouble, if only just. In their rabid thirst for violent victory, the enemy had pursued and harried the shattered eastern army with the tenacity of terriers, the scent of blood in their nostrils.

Inevitably, news reached the small party as they moved, despite their urgent pace, for rumour travels faster than any animal in the world. According to word from the south, already the central plains and hills of the Inda Diamond were becoming subjugated, and the victorious imperial force had been split into smaller armies to control, conquer and chastise. If rumour was to be believed, no quarter was being offered to the fleeing eastern soldiers. When they were found they were executed publicly, the result of western soldiers taking out their frustration over such a long and corrosive campaign. Whatever the reason for such savagery, the news boded badly for the defeated men of the Jade Empire, and already word of the missing commanders had spread. A bounty had been offered for the head of the former general Xeng Shu Jiang and his Inda adjutant, as well as a number of other senior officers. Jai had been simply staggered by the sum offered for the general, or even for tidings of him, and had been oddly pleased at the impressive figure attached to his own name. It seemed he was worth hunting.

They had lived with that danger all the way from Jalnapur, and it was a clear and ever-present peril, for a tall, impressive easterner in the company of an Inda male, both well dressed and well-armoured and riding with a guard of two hundred men in red demon masks, were hardly inconspicuous. Even if Jai and the general had disguised themselves, the guard would give them away, and there was no way in this climate any of them were going to surrender their weapons and armour for the sake of anonymity.

Yet despite the potential reward, no one had sold them out. No one had made an attempt on them during the night and, seemingly, no one had even passed on information as to their whereabouts, or at least not soon enough to lead to their capture. If Jiang's policy of being as fair and reasonable with the Inda as was possible had not won him the land, it had at least gained him a level of respect. With word that the westerners were imposing harsh rule upon the lands they took, as the small party passed, the natives treated them with care and deference, feeding and aiding them where they could, almost as though Jiang and his men were Inda themselves. Certainly the eastern invaders that had seemed so unpalatable earlier in the year were being cast in a new light by these westerners.

And so they had reached the north without a run-in with imperial troops. Jai travelled with the constant worry of pursuit, as was natural, though their objective also plagued him with sleeplessness and concern. It had become clear as they travelled that there could be only one destination for them. Unless they planned to hide in a mountain village for the rest of their life, they would have to seek a place with the one strong force that did not yet want them dead. And Dev had made his feelings about this Sizhad quite clear: the man was a lunatic and his army a frenzied force of zealots. Jai could not see sanctuary with such a group being any more palatable than being on the run. Still, there was not a great deal of choice. Neither empire would welcome them while they breathed, the horse clans of the north would simply enslave them, and the Inda were all but gone.

Jai peered ahead at their route. They were past Initpur now, and they had blessedly skirted the lands of his father without treading old ground. He was not sure how he would feel about returning home after so long, especially to a home devoid of all that he remembered and held dear. But they had passed by and moved onto one of the

247

less-travelled routes – they had stuck to minor trails and hidden ways as often as possible throughout their journey to throw off potential pursuers. From Initpur, three old trade roads ran along the wide valley into the forest, one through the once important great market site. All such roads would be used by the enemy and would therefore be highly dangerous. But *this* trail, which ran across the top of dusty and craggy ridges, was used only by local farmers and villagers and was unlikely to be patrolled by anything more dangerous than goats.

The track ran along the side of an escarpment and descended ahead to cross a seasonal river, before climbing once more onto another hog's back of a hill. To the left – south – the hills rolled on into the distance, full of crags, rocks and woods impassable in many places by horse. To the right, some two hundred paces away, the steep, scree-covered escarpment led down to a lush valley. The men of Jai's party were bound to the trail here, unable to deviate until they passed down into one of the dips, but no one had worried about the possibility of ambush on the ridge, whether it be from bandits or rogue soldiers. The terrain to each side was just too troublesome.

Which is why Jai was startled when the general reached out and tapped him on the arm, his other finger pressed to his lips in silent warning. Jiang stopped his horse and motioned for Jai to do the same. The Crimson Guard behind came to an instant halt at a gesture and sat silent and expectant. As the general slid from his saddle as quietly as he could, Jai followed suit, frowning and cocking his head to one side, trying to discern what it was that had alerted the general.

Then he heard it.

Steel on steel, albeit distant and faint.

A fight.

Jai followed his commander as the tall easterner hurried with cat-like grace to the top of the escarpment, where he made for a row of three boulders shaped oddly like fat bovines of some kind. There they crouched and peered over the edge.

Below was a farm, long abandoned, probably due to the depredations of the war. A farmhouse stood surrounded by overgrown gardens, its roof partially fallen in, an orchard behind and other ramshackle outbuildings scattered about, the whole circled with fields of overripe, ruined wheat. Figures were slipping through the area around the farm, creeping forward, moving against some unseen defender. Even as Jai's gaze picked out the various besieging figures, one of them released an arrow at the ruined house, the missile disappearing into the interior with unknowable results.

'Who are they?' whispered Jai as loudly as he dared, which was little more than an exhaled breath.

Using standard scouting gestures, the general indicated another group visible further out in the valley, and Jai's eyes narrowed as he took in the details. Six men, one of them an officer of the western empire, a banner flying behind him. They were imperial troops.

'What do we do?' Jai mouthed at the general.

Jiang gestured back to the horses and the two men left the precipice and scurried out of sight once more. As they reached the beasts and mounted, the general beckoned the guard officer. With him and Jai close, the commander pointed to the slope and the rocks.

'Imperial soldiers,' he said in a quiet voice. 'Thirty or so, by my estimate. They are besieging someone in a farmhouse. We will move slightly south, further out of audible range, then ride at speed for the descent ahead. Once we reach the ground, I want thirty men to make straight for the officer with his banner. Kill without mercy and leave no survivors. The rest of us will deal with the men attacking the house.'

'But why?' Jai asked. 'It's dangerous. Why put ourselves in such danger? We have been trying to avoid such groups all the way.'

'Whoever is in that house is worth hunting. Anyone the western empire goes to such lengths to kill could be a valuable ally for men like us, Jai.'

It still seemed foolish and dangerous to Jai, but he nodded his compliance anyway, and the small force of easterners – tiny compared to the army the general had commanded at Jalnapur, yet large enough and resolute enough to deal readily with such a small group – rode for the slope ahead and to battle for the first time in many days.

The descent along the trail was easy and the easterners moved down swiftly, all too aware of the time-sensitive nature of their attack. Every moment they delayed increased the chance that whoever defended the farm would fall to the aggressors. Soon enough, though, they had reached the dry riverbed and the flat ground, veering to the north and towards that green valley where the enemy were fighting. At a signal from the general one unit of the guard broke off and made for the enemy commander. They could not currently see his small group, but the sounds of shouted commands in the distance made his location plain.

The rest moved onto a wider, more regularly used road and made for the farm. At further signals, the guard spread out, those at the periphery urging an extra turn of speed from their horses so that the near-two-hundred-strong force of riders became a crescent, the tips closing with every pounding of hooves.

Jai realised with that familiar thrill of battle that he and the general were at the centre of the crescent, in the forefront of the fight to come. He drew his sword and tested its weight. He had not drawn it for days. Swinging it carefully and experimentally around his wrist, he saw the rest of the riders who had not already done so drawing their own weapons. There was something terrifying about those immobile, savage demon masks, and he could only imagine what the riders must look like to the enemy.

They came across the farm faster than he had expected, and Jai spotted one of the attackers stepping out from behind a tree, circling the house, just as a sudden scream was cut off sharply some distance behind them. The enemy commander had fallen.

Jai concentrated on the man before him, who somehow hadn't heard the scream. He had been confidently padding towards the farmhouse until an arrow whispered out of the run-down structure and almost struck him. Startled, he ran for the nearest tree, slightly closer to the house, and dived behind it.

It was then that he and his fellow attackers heard the hoof beats and turned. Shouts of alarm went up at the sight of more than a hundred red-faced demons descending upon them on horseback. A few of the imperial soldiers turned to face this new threat. More ran for their lives, though with precious little hope of escape. The general's tactics were sound. The crescent of horsemen would envelop the enemy and encircle them. With the open farmland around the house there was nowhere for them to find immediate shelter, and they were too close to the building itself to escape the circle of riders. As long as the thirty men dispatched earlier managed to deal with the small command group, there would be no one fleeing the scene with news of the struggle.

The man who had moved from tree to tree and dodged the arrow had a waisted steel blade in hand and armour of segmented plates on his torso, heavily encased in steel. With no shield his only clear weak spot was his legs, which would be an impossible blow for a man on horseback, and with a tree at his back, he was well-protected. The man was readying to maim Jai's horse and unseat the rider – the usual anti-cavalry tactic once again. Recognising the danger and the minimal options available to him, Jai suddenly recalled the time he had been disciplined for ignoring all the forms and sinking to base, thug-like tactics to achieve a winning blow in an important academy competition. It was not gentlemanly combat, and he had suffered for his presumption, but this was true battle, not some duel in a courtyard, and rules could go hang.

Ripping his pouch from his belt with his left hand he slung it as he closed on the man. In that academy duel it had been a handful of gravel and he had temporarily blinded his opponent. This would not do the same, but it was the distraction that was important.

Sure enough, the man flinched. It was a natural human reaction that overrode all martial training. Few men can stand steady and calm when something unexpectedly hurtles at them. The soldier's sword was momentarily forgotten as he ducked to the side to avoid the unidentified missile. By the time he had recovered and straightened and the pouch had thudded harmlessly into the dust behind him, it was too late for the man. He tried to recover and strike his intended blow, but Jai's sword came down and caught him between helmet and metal collar, carving deep into the flesh of the neck and delivering a death blow.

As Jai rode on into the grass beyond, it occurred to him that the unseen archer in the house might be just as ready to put an arrow in him as in the man he'd just killed, and he began to shout 'Friends!' in the western tongue as he hauled on his reins and looked about for any further danger. The general was trotting towards him, his sword unbloodied, while other soldiers were being dispatched with relative ease by the red demon guards.

The fight, such as it had been, was over swiftly. Sickened, Jai watched two of the imperial soldiers surrender, casting their swords to the ground and approaching the demons with their hands raised only to be dispatched regardless in a brutal and offhand manner. The general had given the order to give no quarter with good reason. The westerners had put a huge price on their heads, and they could hardly afford word of their passage through this area to get out.

Once it was clear that no enemy had escaped, the guard began delivering mercy blows to the howling wounded, and the thirty men Jiang had dispatched earlier hove into view leading six horses by the reins, a body across the back of each. The Jai and the general dismounted and tethered their horses to a fence rail nearby. The general sheathed his sword and Jai collected his fallen pouch, then produced his cleaning rag, wiped the gore from his own blade until it gleamed once more, then he too sheathed it.

They moved into a wide, overgrown lawn before the house's main door and came to a halt, trying not to stand too close to the bodies lying in the undergrowth, arrows rising from bloody puckered wounds in their flesh, sightless eyes staring. There was no sign of movement from inside the building, but no arrows whipped out of the shadows, which was encouraging. Jai looked across at the general, who nodded.

'I am Jai,' the younger man announced in a loud voice and in the western tongue, 'adjutant to General Xeng Shu Jiang of the Jade Empire. We mean you no harm.'

As if taking that as a cue, the men of the Crimson Guard sheathed their weapons, cleaning them first where necessary, and falling in to stand at attention in neat blocks as if on parade. There was a long silence, and finally, just as Jai was about to speak again, the farmhouse door was shoved aside on its one remaining hinge with a shriek of tortured wood, and a figure emerged.

Jai was surprised to see that it was a man dressed in an imperial uniform not dissimilar to those very men they had just killed. The soldier, a gash on his forehead lending the left side of his face a bloody sheen, stepped out onto the grass and a second figure, sword at the ready, emerged blinking behind him.

'Strange,' Jai murmured to the general, indicating the uniforms on the two men. A third and fourth appeared through the door, both carrying bows.

'You do not hold tight to the notion of fate in the same manner as your father and I, Jai, but here in this ruined farmhouse I find some of the strongest evidence for its influence I have ever seen. How can a man deny that we are driven to a goal when faced with this?'

Jai frowned as he peered at the four dirty, weary imperial soldiers. What was so special about them, he could not imagine. The general gave him an irritating, knowing smile.

'These men accompanied your brother when we met at the monastery, Jai.'

The younger man blinked in surprise and disbelief, and Jiang chuckled. 'They are General Cinna's men, and I would wager that if they are here, then the general and your brother are not far away.'

'How do you know?'

'Tsk, Jai,' smiled the general. 'I was led to believe you were the best scout in the western provinces, with a keen eye. Observant. Can you not tell the differences in uniform? These men bear an eagle above a crown and spear on their chest armour. In all the months we have fought across Inda lands I have only seen that symbol once, upon the men of Cinna's own guard.'

Jai shook his head in wonder as the general spread his arms and addressed the four soldiers in blue directly.

'I am General Jiang. I am acquainted with your commander. He and I, I suspect, remain friends despite all that has passed between our peoples. Will you take us to him?'

It was something of a gamble, of course. It was very possible that Cinna was now basking in the glow of his achievements in the destruction of the Jade Empire, and walking into his camp could be a disastrous move. Or, more likely, the men they'd just saved would refuse to lead them to the general. But somehow – whether or not this was the fate that his father and Jiang so readily accepted – he felt certain that not only would Cinna and Dev be there and welcome them, but that Cinna and Jiang were still two allies in a world of aggressors, despite everything.

There was a strange pause while the four men looked at one another, seeking consensus. There were nods, and the one with the sword who had emerged first sheathed it. His companions did the same, lowering bows and returning their arrows to the quivers at their hips.

'I am Decurion Vulso of the general's cavalry guard. I recognise you, General Jiang. From the monastery.'

Jiang gave Jai another infuriatingly smug smile.

'The general is a little over four miles from here,' the man went on. 'But we have lost our horses.'

Jiang gestured to the riders who had defeated the enemy officers. Four of the bodies were unceremoniously tipped from the beasts, freeing them for new riders.

'Problem solved,' General Jiang smiled.

'Come, then, sir,' the man said as he and his men crossed to the horses and pulled themselves up into the saddle. They hauled on the reins to turn the animals and, waving to the easterners to follow, began to walk the beasts back between the red-masked soldiers. Jai and the general rode forward to fall in beside the decurion.

'What happened to you?' the general asked.

'It's rather a long story, sir,' the blue-clad guardsman replied. 'The general will no doubt fill you in on most of it. Suffice it to say that we're in a bit of a pickle. The general is a hunted man and we are surrounded by enemies on all sides. Everywhere we go now, a small scout party of guards is sent ahead to make sure the way is clear. There were eight of us and we were unfortunate enough to get ourselves trapped by an imperial patrol. I tried to talk my way out of it, but our insignia is too much of a giveaway as you yourself noticed. Thank you for your timely interruption, by the way, General.'

The decurion sucked on his teeth pensively. 'It is imperial policy to assign such scout units on a roving basis, covering the land within a certain distance of any installation. These men must have been based at the Chara Gorge station, which means there will be little chance of bumping into another patrol until after we've passed Chara. Fortunate, as the... *enemy*... are gaining on us.'

Jiang nodded, though he glanced at Jai with one raised eyebrow at this oddly coy comment.

They rode for just less than an hour, the imperial soldiers conversing lightly, though circumspectly, and avoiding answering the subtle probes and questions of General Jiang. Finally, as the sun reached its zenith and baked the land and the riders passing through it, they emerged from a low side valley to the south-east into a wide bowl with a small lake at the centre. A gathering of men and horses was visible at the southern edge of the lake, and it was for this group that the riders made.

The general allowed his mount to fall back a little, letting the four blue-clad soldiers take the lead. Jai also dropped behind, and as they approached three figures detached themselves from the gathering and strode forward to meet the new arrivals. Jai felt that odd lurch that he was beginning to suspect heralded fate intervening in his life as he saw that Dev was one of the three, General Cinna and his guard commander being the others. The blue and white guardsmen were all armed and armoured, though dismounted, and there were no tents in evidence, so they were clearly not encamped here.

General Cinna wore an odd expression as he waved in greeting to the Jade Empire officers, something between a frown of uncertainty and a smile of relief. The general was clearly in two minds as to the benefit of what was happening.

'General,' the injured decurion greeted his commander, wiping his bloody brow.

'Vulso. You have found a friend or two hundred.'

'Sir, we ran into a spot of trouble. General Jiang and his men arrived just in time to save us.'

'How many escaped?'

'None,' replied Jiang, cutting in on the conversation.

'Good. We do not want the marshals to be aware of my involvement. It would distract them from more important matters.'

'It is odd to see you here, Cinna, in such a place, and heading south if I am not mistaken, towards your main force. Yet you withhold information from your marshals?'

Cinna sighed. 'I suspect we are in similar straits, Jiang. The marshals have stripped me of my command and taken control of my army. I was to be investigated for possible insurrection – rightly so, as you know – and tried. Of course, I would have died accidentally long before I could argue my case. It would be too inconvenient for them if I managed to make them look bad. Dev and I took the opportunity to leave before matters came to a head. I am, however, surprised to see *you* coming west, given the dangers. You have decided not to return home with the rest of the army? I know that my countrymen appear to be on a rampage of conquest right now, but whatever they would *like* to do, they simply cannot attempt the conquest of the Jade Empire. They are too weak, and intend to consolidate here for the time being.'

'The Jade Empire is no longer a safe place for me, Cinna.'

The western general's eyes narrowed. 'The Jade Emperor is not particularly forgiving of failure, I would suspect.'

'Precisely. There is civil war in the east, but neither side favours me, and I would lose my head there whoever comes out on top.'

'I am not certain that is adequate reason to ride into the lands of your more direct enemy.'

'We were a little stuck for choices, Cinna. Given that our empire is riven at its heart, the horse clans would skin us on sight and the Inda territories are full of rampaging imperial troops, north to the mountains seemed the obvious choice.'

'We could not risk leading your countrymen to the monastery,' added Jai, eyes locked on his brother, 'so the south was clearly not an option.'

'Quite,' Cinna replied. 'We had similar thoughts. However, the monastery must be your destination now.'

Jiang's eyebrow shot up. 'We thought to seek out this Sizhad and determine whether he might be negotiated with.'

Now Dev shook his head. 'The Sizhad will not negotiate. Nor will he compromise. All that will satisfy him is conquest in the name of his living sun god.'

'You have spoken to him?'

Dev nodded. 'Some time ago.' He glanced at the western general for permission. Cinna nodded, and so he continued. 'We thought to save further depredations here and preserve what we could of the empire. We rode north to the Sizhad and his men to goad them into coming south. The sight of the fanatic's army would likely send the marshals running back across the Oxus with their armies. It would be a winning move in a number of ways. The empire gets its absent military strength back before being entirely overrun with barbarians, the Inda get the oppressor's heel removed. The only unknown is what the Sizhad will do then.'

'You succeeded in persuading the Sizhad, then?' General Jiang asked, and Jai remembered now the decurion's odd phrasing. *The enemy are gaining on us.*

'Persuasion was not exactly required,' Cinna replied. 'We moved north and almost walked straight into them. They were coming south already on a warpath. I believe they are aware of our presence slightly ahead of them, but we are far enough in front that it is too much trouble for them to press hard to deal with us. Besides, I suspect they are hoping we will spread the word of their coming. You know what sort of panic that could create.'

'If they are already coming south,' Jiang frowned, 'why bother goading them further? Why not just head to safety and let them get on with it?'

Cinna rubbed his neck wearily. He looked travel-worn and tired. 'Because once they are down from the hills and onto the plains on the Nadu's west bank, there is a very good chance that they will ignore the army here entirely and simply head west to ravage and conquer the poorly protected empire. We must do all we can to draw them into the sight of the marshals. What happens then is up to those lunatics running my army and the madman leading his fanatical one. Who can say how *that* will turn out, but it is the only way I could see that granted all of us even a chance of survival.'

'How do the lands stand to the west of the Nadu?' Jiang asked.

'I have only second-hand reports and rumour,' Cinna replied. 'If they are to be believed, then the west is relatively calm and empty at the moment. The bulk of the imperial forces are in the east pursuing your countrymen and imposing the imperial peace upon new Inda territories. We already largely control the west, so there are just a few garrisons in place. You're not thinking of travelling on the west bank?'

Jiang laughed an empty laugh. 'Where else *shall* I go, Cinna? Back to the east bank where your former army is hunting me for profit? These marshals of yours will not look for me in their own lands. We can, with a little luck and the favour of the gods, slip through imperial-controlled lands and to the south, seeking out the monastery.'

Cinna pondered this with a furrowed brow. Finally, he straightened. 'It sounds utterly insane, but I cannot fault your logic, Jiang. Would that we could join you, but I must walk meekly into the lion's mouth to guide the Sizhad there.' The stocky westerner turned to Dev. 'But there is no need for *you* to risk your neck with me. I do not mean to denigrate your value, Dev, but the Sizhad's forces will pursue me whether you are with me or not. And I needed your knowledge and skills in the north, but I know the lands back towards the south and have to do little but lead the enemy across them.'

Dev shook his head, though his eyes were on his brother. 'Respectfully, General, I intend to see to it that you get out of Jalnapur alive again. We have come too far now for you to fall so late in the game. I am coming with you, and we will *both* survive it.' *Besides*, thought Dev in the privacy of his head, *I suspect it is more my presence that is drawing my insane brother than yours...*

Cinna looked at his adjutant in silence for some time, allowing plenty of opportunity for a change of mind. Once it became clear that Dev was resolute, he nodded to Jiang. 'You are seeking sanctuary with the old man in the dead lands, then. It is an eminently sensible move. My colleagues will not violate the sanctity of that. We are a pious and superstitious people, and Dev tells me he believes the Sizhad will be even more so. It seems that these mysterious lands are the only ones that will be safe for any of us.' He chuckled. 'How strange. I am sought by my own peers, considered an enemy by yours, and will face trial and death if I return to my home. It seems that we are oddly tied to a path, Jiang. Dev and I, and our guard, will seek you out at the monastery when we have finished at Jalnapur.'

Jai looked deep into his brother's eyes. It seemed incredible that after all these years the two of them should find one another again, face to face across a battlefield, and yet be destined to seek a place of peace together. Fate. Their father had always been wise.

But could fate overcome even the gravest dangers? For the journey south would be perilous for the men of the Jade Empire, and no easier for Dev and his general.

It would have to.

258

CHAPTER 20

They made an incongruous group as they travelled south – a true meeting of cultures. Two great generals and two elite bodyguard units, each drawn from one of the world's oldest and most powerful cultures, and with them two Inda brothers. Strange to think that if the world had managed to achieve what these four hundred men had done, there would be peace and harmony everywhere. But it had not. And there was not. And as long as there were men like the lunatic Bassianus, the frenzied Sizhad and the disputed rigid overlordship of the Jade Emperor, there never could be.

Dev had marvelled at the strange glory of fellowship between such intransigent parties – an odd bond forged by necessity and mutual peril. It struck him as odd and yet entirely appropriate how much at ease the two generals seemed in one another's presence, and he remembered how respectfully Cinna had talked of Jiang even in the early days of Jalnapur, after their initial parley. While Jiang's Inda was strongly accented and a little shaky, his command of the western tongue was impressive, and as they rode and discussed the differences and similarities of their armies and their worlds, Dev caught a sense of sharing, even hearing his own general using occasional Jade Empire terminology. More interesting still was how often he heard both of them using Inda terms and phrases. A year of cultural clashes had taught everyone a great deal. It was sometimes easier to learn from an enemy than from a friend.

It had been a nervous journey, though, despite the fascinating ease between former enemies. While the vast majority of the imperial army were on the far side of the Nadu now, laying claim to Inda territory and chasing the last remnants of the beaten Jade army back across their borders, the western Inda lands were still staunchly under imperial control. Food was scarce after half a year of constant war and depredation, many regions were largely depopulated, once carefully tended towns and villages were now empty, broken and overgrown. Everywhere were signs of imperial ravages, despite Cinna's policy of clemency and care. It seemed that a month or so under careless men had undone any good the general had achieved in his time in command.

As they journeyed, the travellers suffered more with each passing day. What rations the men carried had long since been exhausted, and though hunting and foraging was fine for a party of half a dozen men, half a thousand were significantly harder to feed. They had become used to eating bread hurriedly made from rat-infested grain stores, augmented with rotting, overripe vegetation and a few chunks of meat from the poor pickings in the countryside.

And if constant slogging south and increasing hunger were not enough to dishearten a man, there was the need for subtlety and a measured pace. The western empire had left garrisons in each former Inda kingdom, at major crossings and junctions, in cities and fortresses, and there was the constant danger of falling foul of one of them. For the most part Cinna and Dev were aware of the likely locations, and after months of studying the maps could pick out the safest route with relative ease, but once or twice they still failed, for things were beginning to change under the new commanders.

On those few occasions, they had been exceedingly lucky. The vast majority of imperial cavalry had been deployed to the east, where they could be used to speedily hunt down the enemy, while the land west of the great river was largely garrisoned with infantry. The result was that whenever the strange multinational party stumbled across a garrison for which they were unprepared, they were able to race away at a gallop and outdistance the soldiers before their insignia could be recognised.

That was paramount, lest the Sizhad's army lose interest in them and turn west.

They had maintained a uniform distance ahead of the zealot force and had on occasion been forced to slow and essentially taunt them into pressing on south. Parts of the great white army had split off at times and moved west, and that had made Cinna and Dev wince, but there was nothing they could do about it. They just had to draw the bulk of the zealot army south against the main force of the marshals and hope that the empire could raise the strength to deal with the smaller group moving to take control of its border. Thus Cinna and his men had been forced to maintain their identity, despite the inherent danger that carried, what with half the imperial army on the lookout for them. It was, Cinna believed, their identity that drew the Sizhad and his army on. Not so the men of the Jade Empire. Before they had even left the northern hills, the officers and the Crimson Guard had packed away their uniforms and armour on the back of their horses, adopting stolen or traded native clothes and binding their heads with turbans to help conceal their nationality.

From a distance they appeared to be a unit of imperial cavalry with a native levy contingent, and it was only closer examination that would give them away. If anyone got close enough to tell the difference they were in trouble anyway. It was sufficient, or it had been thus far anyway, for the tense journey south.

The greatest benefit of that long, hungry, nervous trek was the chance for Dev to speak to his brother. While the former generals passed the time on their ride pondering best-case scenarios, the chances of any of them coming to fruition infinitesimally small, Dev and Jai spent day after day discussing the years of their separation, comparing their experiences and laughing or commiserating appropriately. It was oddly cathartic for both, despite their current desperate situation. When they had last met for the night at the monastery, they had talked and even reconnected in many ways, but there had been a tense, underlying strain that had prevented a relaxing openness. Now the pressure to maintain the position of their empires had lifted. As fellow fugitives, there was nothing to lose, and the pair were rapidly becoming brothers again in more than just name.

They had talked of their years of separation, of their growth and changes as they became men of empire rather than sons of the Inda. Of how Dev's natural talents in administration and control had led him to find a place in the military of the west that capitalised on his abilities and had made him something of a strategist, while Jai's physical skills had been honed by the killing academies of the east, turning him into a formidable warrior. They talked of their changed tastes, of the friends and lovers they had both found and lost along the way, of how they had both dreamed of finding their family one day, when the chance arose. Neither of them had ever truly believed it might happen, and if anything hinted at the existence of fate, this was it.

And the more they shared and opened up, the more they realised that despite the differences between the east and the west that had influenced them over the years and those between them and the Inda, there had always been a common thread. Humanity. That, it seemed, was the true division in the world. Not a matter of east and west or of noble and poor. But of good and ill. Men who sought the best in the world and men who revelled in the worst. And nothing had brought that to the fore better than this awful war.

Thoughts of good and ill repeatedly dragged Dev back to his time in the north among the Faithful. Dev had still not revealed the true nature of the dreadful Sizhad who followed them doggedly. It was not that he was precious about the secret, or that he felt he needed to protect Jai in the way he had his father. In fact, when he thought about it there was no good reason not to tell Jai about Ravi, yet still something made him hold his tongue.

Now Jai was momentarily distracted, fishing in his bags for some dry, hard morsel he had been saving, and Dev's reverie was shattered by the sound of General Cinna's voice.

'Stop!'

Dev reined in along with the other officers, Jai abandoning the search of his bag for a moment. They looked to the stocky general in anticipation as the column sat astride their mounts on the road through the rolling green with birds chirruping in the background and the gentle sizzle and hum of an Inda autumn afternoon. Flies buzzed around the horses the moment they became stationary, tails flicking and riders swatting away the pests.

'When we cross the next hill, we will be within view of the Jalnapur plain,' Cinna said. 'We will begin to encounter trouble there. From here on in, it will become increasingly dangerous for all of us, but while among the imperial army there may still be officers and men sympathetic to our plight, and others unaware of the importance of our insignia, not one man down there will be under the impression that Jiang and his men are anything but soldiers of the Jade Emperor.'

'*Which* Jade Emperor?' snorted Jai irritably, earning himself a disparaging look from his general.

'All our lives will be more difficult with you alongside us,' Cinna said flatly. 'This is the place we must part company for now. Jiang?

Jai? Take the road just over there by the burned tree. It is one of the lesser routes south, not part of the supply chain or the garrison system we set in place. I cannot guarantee that my successors have not put new forces in place, but with what information we have, that is the most likely safe route south. Once you reach the line of markers, travel east until you find the one that has my eagle, crown and spear insignia scratched into the moss on the base. That is the one that will lead you to the monastery from this direction.'

General Jiang walked his horse across and grasped his peer's hand. 'Thank you, Cinna. We will maintain the same approach we have used by your side thus far, avoiding all contact and outrunning anyone we cannot avoid. I have no intention of finding myself embroiled in some insane mini-war in your hinterland. We will make our way to the monastery and there await you, or word of your exploits. With luck and the gods at your back, you will be with us within a day or so. And if luck and the gods fail, there is always fate, which seems to be ever more active in these lands.'

Cinna smiled. 'We each have our troubles, eh, Jiang? Be careful and try to reach the markers without a trail of hunting soldiers following close.'

'And you, Cinna. Be very, very careful. I fear the men by that river would rather have your head than mine. You are playing a dangerous game. In my land, the artillerists call it "lighting the taper blind".'

Cinna frowned in incomprehension.

'A blind man with a flame trying to fire a cannon,' explained the tall, elegant easterner. 'There is as much chance of him being gathered up in a bucket as his enemy.'

'Thank you for your words of encouragement.'

'He's right, General,' Jai added. 'To attempt to draw one foe against another and escape from the middle unharmed is truly a madman's quest. Be careful.'

'I have not reached this age navigating the court of the mad emperor without care,' smiled Cinna.

'May the Nine Spirits of Righteous Truths guide your hand and your tongue,' Jiang said, straightening in his saddle.

'And Pardus, God of Journeys and Beginnings, watch over your travels.'

The two generals issued commands to their officers, and the blue-clad imperial riders began to separate from the drab, incognito Crimson Guard. It was strange to feel the palpable air of regret at the units' parting, not all of which was born of the old adage 'safety in numbers'. Over the many days of travel the two groups had managed to shed their initial wariness, gradually becoming better acquainted until they began to treat one another more as allies than opponents. They then began to intermingle, though there was still a significant language barrier. Perhaps one in ten of the easterners spoke the western tongue, and not one of the imperial soldiers spoke the language of the Jade Empire. Still, they were learning a few words of each other's language gradually. It had been fascinating to watch and, as the two units made to go their separate ways, Dev smiled to hear them departing with words of encouragement in each other's tongue.

Dev watched Jai go with a sense of regret, oddly tinged with a touch of relief. He would miss his brother, but it gave him a little comfort to think that Jai was moving to a place of relative safety – while he would ride into further danger with the general.

They remained still and waited until General Jiang and his men had disappeared from sight into the trees, then Dev turned to his commander. 'Do you have a plan?'

Cinna nodded. 'A rather fluid one, but yes. We need to cross the rise and determine precisely what lies ahead and how close the pickets are likely to be. Then we turn north and move carefully until we are in sight of the Sizhad's forces again. Once they take the bait and follow us, we ride like the wind for the imperial camp.'

'Then?'

'Then we trust to luck. If we are fortunate, our specific insignia will escape the notice of the marshals' force. Either way we need to warn them what is following just over the horizon. If they make any attempt to stop us, we ride for the nearest path away from Jalnapur and attempt to outrun them.'

'With respect, General, that's not much of a plan.'

'It's all we have, Dev. At this stage it is almost certain that the zealots will simply continue on straight into the face of the marshals' force, and we could simply sit to one side and wait. But we cannot afford to take chances. This is a major crossroads. All it takes is for the Sizhad to decide to turn west for the easy pickings that lie there, and there is every possibility that his force might miss the imperial army altogether. I cannot risk having led the Sizhad this far only to fail now.'

Dev nodded, and the general gestured to his guard captain. 'Stay here. We are just going to scout ahead.'

The guard nodded, though he looked less than happy with his commander moving forward without adequate protection, glancing back to the next ripple in this undulating countryside, picturing the great force of fanatics that lay beyond it. Dev chewed the inside of his lip nervously as they set off up the gentle rise, not quite sure what to expect. The beat of their horses' hooves on the packed surface of the road sounded like the tense heartbeat of the world.

They climbed for a short time, cresting the rise, and at the top they slowed and Dev stared at Jalnapur. He wasn't sure whether to be thrilled or panicked. The last time he had been here, many weeks ago now, it had been the site of a fierce battle, stuck in the quagmire of a season of monsoons, resounding to the continual thud and boom of artillery, hospital tents treating a continuous grisly cavalcade of wounded, piles of limbs here and there, units on the move, officers hurtling this way and that, signallers and musicians constantly on the go.

Everything had changed.

The army is gone!

The bridge had been repaired with a flimsy-looking timber extension filling the gap that had been left by Jiang's explosives. The bridge was still guarded by a unit of several hundred men, and a number of artillery pieces were still in evidence. The marshals and their senior officers had moved their command centre into the city and palace of Jalnapur itself, as evidenced by their flags displayed there. The bulk of the forces had moved on, though, across the river.

Dev had to correct himself as his eyes strayed across the ruined landscape. There was actually still a sizeable force here. Between the units spread out close to the city and the bridge and those on the far bank of the river where they seemed to have captured several cannon, it was an army most officers would find more than acceptable to hold a position as important as this. But after seeing the seething masses of the giant imperial force that had broken the Jade

Empire here, it seemed a pitiful band of defenders. Certainly they would be little more than fodder for the zealot army following them. There was also scant evidence of pickets closer than the edge of the city itself. The new commanders were clearly complacent, believing themselves masters of the Inda Diamond and unassailable. They were about to learn a very painful lesson.

'Shit,' said Cinna, with feeling.

'What now?' Dev breathed, his eyes dancing across the scene.

The general turned to him, his face bleak. 'We follow the plan. What else can we do?'

'The Sizhad will obliterate this entire force in a matter of hours – if that, sir.'

'Yes. And both marshals are here, along with most of their staff. The chances of them escaping are small. And without a senior commander guiding the campaign as a whole, the army on the other side of the Nadu will be easy pickings.'

Dev shivered. 'It was never your intention to let the Sizhad destroy our army. There were supposed to be enough men here to stop him.'

'Plans can go awry, Dev. All is in the hands of the gods now. These men are doomed. All we can hope is that the Sizhad is lured across the bridge to the east by the presence there of the rest of the army. Because that's where they are. If they had gone back west, the marshals would have gone with them for a triumphant return home. The bulk of imperial forces are trapped east of the Nadu now, separated from their own empire by the Sizhad. If he decides to hold the bridge of Jalnapur, there will be a repeat of what happened this summer, but this time between our army and the zealots. And while that happens, the empire is defenceless and enemies will pour across other borders, just as I'd worried all along.'

Dev squeezed his eyes shut, trying to think of any potential solution, but such a possibility hovered out of reach.

'If the marshals are dead, couldn't you take control again?' Cinna was shaking his head, but Dev was desperate. 'You could gather those men in the east to your banner and defeat the Sizhad. He...'

Dev stopped, suddenly horribly aware that he was trying to explain to the general how to defeat his brother. Could he do that?

But it was a moot question anyway, as Cinna was still shaking his head.

'It would take many weeks – months even – to gather all those scattered forces. We don't know where they are, and their commanders will almost certainly still see me as a rebel. If I wasn't speared on sight, the Sizhad's men would be on us before we could do anything about it. No, I will never command them again now.'

The younger man sighed and the general rolled his shoulders.

'It seems the empire has only two options now, Dev. Either the Sizhad invades and brings his new faith to them, destroying everything we cling to of our heritage, or he engages in a long-term war against our army here, while the empire crumbles and falls to other enemies. The Gota have been itching to take the northern territories for years and the Pelasians are only a step from annexing the south again as they did a century ago. Either way, I fear for the future of my people.'

My people, thought Dev. Were they *his* people too? They had sheltered him and trained him, but was he not still truly Inda? The thought struck him powerfully. He had thought of himself at least partially as a son of the empire for a decade now. But had that always just been a shell he had worn, that he could cast off at will?

'We can do nothing, General,' he said at last. 'It is out of our hands. We must look to our own safety now.'

There was a long pause, but finally Cinna nodded. 'When did it all start to fall apart, Dev?'

'When the mad emperor had you and me summoned to his court, sir. Or when the Jade Emperor decided that the Inda lands looked promising, perhaps.'

A commotion attracted their surprised attention, since it came not from the small forces ahead at the bridge, but from behind. The blue and white figures of horsemen were cresting the saddle behind them, their captain shouting urgently.

'Zealots!'

Dev and Cinna turned their horses and trotted over towards the guardsmen. They had not even closed on their men before their elevated position granted them an excellent view of what had sent the horsemen racing towards them.

The Sizhad's army was coming, and they were coming at pace. No longer were they moving at a steady march, following the small blue party south, but now they were racing forward, howling and whooping, an odd melody lilting beneath the cries as the more pious among the Faithful sang their hymns to the glorious golden sun above. Their cavalry streamed ahead, but they were just the vanguard. The whole army was moving to attack.

'I think that is our cue to leave,' Cinna said quietly.

Dev nodded. The Sizhad's men would fall upon the imperial army in moments and the slaughter would commence. The end of imperial control among the Inda was in motion, and if Dev and the others did not move fast they would simply number among the unsung casualties.

'The Belayari path,' Dev said breathlessly.

The general frowned again. 'That leads directly to one of the stronger garrisons. I wasn't planning to walk into their open arms, Dev.'

'But the path Jiang is following crosses it after a few miles. We can pick up the same path and catch up with him on the way to the marker line.'

Cinna nodded. 'A good thought. Come on, then, before we're surrounded by white-clad howling lunatics.'

The two men, along with their escort of cavalry, rode on across the saddle ahead of that baying army of zealots. A total of nine roads led from the field of Jalnapur's western edge. Two main routes travelled north and west, to the highlands and towards the empire and the Oxus River, the other seven to the more important towns and kingdoms among the western Inda. The one Dev sought lay towards the southern edge of the site, close to where the huge corrals lay, designed to cater to the cavalry's huge reserve of horses. Those riders were now gone from here, hunting survivors far to the east, and the great fenced areas of green sat empty and desolate, barns and timber storehouses scattered around, unused and slowly becoming derelict. Dev angled to his right, ready to race around the periphery of the Jalnapur camp towards that route which offered safe haven.

'We might have trouble,' he said, suddenly.

As the others pounded along beside and behind him, the general followed Dev's pointing finger. A small unit of imperial soldiers had emerged from one of the many buildings on that side of the camp and were preparing for a fight. They wore chain shirts and were jamming on helmets and grabbing spears as their signaller blew the warning call on his horn. They wore the black uniform of the southern army, largely drawn from desert dwellers, used to dealing with raiding horse nomads. Already, even as the general and his guard bore down on them, the enemy call was being picked up by the other units near the bridge.

A warning. They thought they were dealing with a couple of hundred rogue cavalry, but at least the warning would serve to help them prepare for the huge army of which they were not yet aware.

As the units near the bridge and the town began to fall in, Dev and Cinna and their riders angled for that small unit who were moving to intercept them, blocking access to the one road they needed to catch up with Jiang.

'Can we skirt round them?' he shouted, the very idea of fighting imperial troops settling sickeningly in the pit of his stomach. General Cinna pointed to their left. More soldiers were pouring from another building a short distance away, arming as they appeared in response to the alarm call. Further away, a mile across the plain, riders were emerging from the gates of Jalnapur's palace. The bulk of the cavalry may have been committed to the east, but at the least the two marshals' personal mounted units were still present. They would be fast, and they would be well-trained veterans.

The sight of the additional soldiers coming into play answered Dev's question. If he swung out far enough to avoid the unit that stood between them and the path into the jungle ahead, he would be in danger of becoming mired down in a proper fight with other units, possibly trapped between two groups, and chased down by strong cavalry even if they escaped.

Determination fought with dismay at the realisation that conflict was inevitable, and Dev drew his sword to face imperial soldiers for the first time in his life. The general did the same, and the hiss of two hundred blades being drawn behind them sounded like the whisper of torrential rain beneath the pounding of a thousand hooves.

Dev did not argue as the guardsmen pushed ahead to engage, forging on past the general and his adjutant. It was for this very situation that they existed as a unit – to protect their general.

Moments later Dev and his commander found themselves at the centre of a ring of riders, and as they ploughed along the edge of the Jalnapur plain towards that group of black-clad spear men, Dev realised that he was quite grateful. Not that he would not be required to fight, as such, though the notion of plunging a blade into a man who had so recently fought for him gave him no pleasure. He was simply grateful that, protected by his men, he would not even be required to see it.

They hit the imperial unit at pace and Dev was only aware that it had happened from the noise ahead. The screams of men and horses rang out, the scrape of metal on metal and the cries of fury and desperation. The captain of Cinna's guard, a little ahead in the throng, turned in his saddle and waved for the two officers to peel off to the right, his arm stiffening suddenly as a spear point emerged from his torso with a burst of shattered chain links and a shower of crimson.

Following the dying man's instruction with a grim face, Cinna wheeled his horse to the right and skirted the main fight. Dev followed him, and the guardsmen flowed around once more, trying to protect them from any potential danger and leaving them in a small pocket of safety at the centre of the blue-clad force. Dev caught horrifying glimpses of the fight as they rushed on past. The black-clad swarthy southerners knew how to stop a horse, and numerous beasts were on the floor, thrashing out their life with shattered spears jutting from their chests and necks. Riders in blue struggled on foot, wounded as they fought hard to beat down the resistant men in black.

One of the southerners had escaped the combat with a length of splintered ash spear in his grip, blood sheeting down his face from a head wound. He was staggering, half-blind and wounded, into the approaching horsemen. Suddenly realising where he was, the wounded soldier raised his broken staff in desperation and defiance, but to little avail. Dev hardened his heart as the man disappeared beneath a hundred churning hooves with a brief cry of panicked agony.

He could not afford to feel for these men. They might have been his men once, but now they stood between Dev and survival, pure and simple.

270

Another moment and they were past the soldiers. A few cavalrymen remained to put down the last of them, then rode hard to catch up. Dev glanced back as the unit reformed and he momentarily had a good view. They had lost perhaps twenty or thirty horsemen to the soldiers, and several of those riders still with them were clutching at wounds and hissing in pain as they rode. It had been a costly encounter, but a necessary one. Even now that second unit with their gleaming spear points jutting forth were running to intercept, and the riders from the city were angling towards them too. If they had skirted out to avoid the fight, they would almost certainly have ended the day fighting for their lives against most of those men. As it was there was now nothing between them and the path to sanctuary.

The first guardsmen to reach the great corrals leapt the fence with ease and pounded across the lush turf, the rest of the unit and its two commanding officers following like a human and equine wave as they rose in the saddle and jumped the fence in unison. Pounding across the turf, they were now ascending a gentle slope away from the plain of bones and destruction and closing on the jungle and the path to safety.

The first Dev knew of the arrival of the enemy was a curse from one of the guardsmen behind them. Turning in the saddle as they rose towards the treeline and safety, he could see a blanket of white on that same northern rise from which they had so recently descended. The Sizhad's cavalry had arrived.

At this sudden threat, those soldiers and cavalry desperately racing to catch Cinna and his guardsmen immediately changed course, their musicians putting out desperate, strangled warnings. The imperial army's main base in Inda lands was under attack by an unknown force, and suddenly the existence of the rebel general, Cinna, was a forgotten and unimportant thing.

They jumped another fence and climbed the last of the slope towards that path into the jungle, and as they reached the treeline Cinna reined in and gave the order for his men to do the same. Dev pulled alongside the general, his head still craned to the north as they watched wave after wave of white-clad zealots crest that pass and pour down towards the pitiful defenders of imperial Jalnapur.

'We are witnessing the end of the world, Dev.'

Something odd touched Dev's soul at the bleak statement and, though he had no desire to argue with Cinna right now, he found something rising in himself that he hadn't realised was there, which only facing imperial troops had brought to the surface.

'*Your* world is ending, General. For the Inda, the world has been ending for generations. This is only the closing chorus of the play for us.'

The look the general cast back at him was not one of irritation or denial, as Dev had half-expected, but one loaded with contrition and genuine remorse. Dev immediately regretted his harsh words, yet there *was* a truth to them. Jai and Dev, their father too, had been simply pieces in the game of empires, moved about the board in a match that *everyone* would lose in the end. Ravi too, in fact. Even the great and terrible Sizhad himself was but a victim, a product of the same violent contest that had ruined them all.

Something hardened in Cinna's face as he cleared his throat. 'And yet, my friend, your people might strangely and unexpectedly have navigated this nightmare better than any of us. The empire is on the precipice, its entire military about to be torn apart by the Sizhad and his men, while its borders crumble under barbarian pressure. I may not have had word from home, but I am under no illusions about what is happening there. And the Jade Empire is at war with itself, which rarely ends well. Yet your father had the foresight to gather what he could of the Inda and take them to the one place where total destruction cannot yet reach them. And it is to your father's banner we ride, Dev. We and those few remaining honourable men of the east. In a world without hope, your father fosters a last glimmer. Let us pray it is enough to rekindle the flame.'

Dev felt an odd smile breach his mask of sourness. This was the general he had seen in Velutio, who had stood up to the insane emperor. This was the man who could save and build empires. And Dev would follow General Cinna to the end of the world. Or in this case, *away* from it.

The riders cast one last glance at the doomed plain of Jalnapur as the paltry imperial forces gathered in an attempt to fight to the last while an endless torrent of ululating white riders poured over the hill and down upon them. Then the general and his men turned their mounts and rode away from the war for the last time.

272

But perhaps not all the gods were watching over them, for as the last blue-clad rider disappeared into the jungle, none of them saw a force of white-clad warriors split off from the huge army and race along the edge of the plain towards the scene of the recent skirmish and the departing guardsmen. And among that smaller white-clad torrent, the Sizhad himself rode, silent and grim.

With a purpose.

CHAPTER 21

I had been waiting for them. Somehow I knew the generals would come. In some way, I think I was hoping that my time of decision-making and command was coming to an end. With such illustrious leaders as they, I would surely be superfluous.

A ram digested the news from his pickets with a grim face. It was far from good news. Riders were coming to the monastery, but not just the ones he'd been hoping for. Yes, the lead group was a mix of imperial soldiers in blue and strange men in Inda clothing who could only be Jiang and his riders, but the other group...

Fortunately, Aram and his people had time to decide what to do, thanks to the new system of communication the pickets were using. It had been thought an unnecessary precaution, but with what seemed to be happening in the living world beyond the markers, Aram was happy to take every precaution that came up.

It was a number of miles from the monastery to the line of markers, and the paths that led between the two were ancient, winding this way and that according to terrain and vegetation. Aram's men, though, included foresters and engineers, carpenters and masons. In the past weeks a new path had been driven through the jungle – a secret way that led in a straight line from the pickets' position near the markers to the monastery gate. Rivulets and dips had been bridged with good timber, marshy areas lined with wooden boards or gravel, vegetation cut back to create a safe and open ride.

They had tested the results and even Aram had been impressed. A man riding a horse as fast as he dared along the winding jungle way from the ancient markers to the monastery could do so in six hours if he really pushed. A rider along the new secret line could do it in less than three. Sometimes even two.

Thus is was that the force of the two generals was still some distance from the monastery, unaware of their pursuers, while Aram, who waited for them tensely and nervously, knew already of the white-clad warriors following them.

'What do we do?' Mani asked quietly. The picket was still standing close by, wild-eyed and worried, but Aram had not yet made any of this public.

'Keep his mouth shut. I don't want word of this getting out to everyone until Cinna and Jiang get here. They are men used to dealing with military tactics and, while unarmed, they bring hundreds of trained soldiers with them. If the people here learn of enemies in the spirit lands, there could be panic.'

Especially armed ones.

How had *that* happened?

The worried-looking picket had been adamant about that. Aram had pressed him. 'Are you sure? Absolutely certain?' But the man had insisted. General Cinna and his small cavalry force had discarded their weapons at the markers, but the white-clad men came on armed. Aram could only hope that the ghosts were simply biding their time. But the knowledge that the monks all seemed to have gone offered a worrying possibility.

And Aram knew who the white-clad men were. Who they had to be. He had seen the strange mendicant priests and hermits who had shunned the Inda gods and followed the bright sun occasionally in his life and they uniformly wore white. Given what Dev and Cinna had said about the Sizhad, this had to be them.

Was it possible that a man's faith could protect him from ghosts? The monks who had built the monastery certainly seemed to have believed that.

'Mani, you've fought in battles plenty of times. Is it possible for an unarmed force to overcome an armed one?'

The soldier shrugged. 'If they are strong enough and determined enough. Mostly it would come down to numbers. We would stop them but the death toll for our people would be horrifying. I suspect you would think it unacceptable, if that helps you make a decision.'

Aram simply grunted. What decision was there to make? That was why he needed Cinna and Jiang here to take control. The generals' force had been estimated as somewhere between four and five hundred. The white-clad riders behind them numbered significantly more. Perhaps seven hundred. Perhaps more. Pickets generally did not stay around to count too closely.

Aram stood at the gate platform and fretted, his thoughts repeatedly circling through problems without ever reaching a conclusion, while Mani stood impassively, silent and strong. Bajaan was close by, drilling a dozen of the chosen defenders in the art of the open-handed punch, while Parmesh hovered by one of the granaries, ostensibly overseeing an inventory, though clearly also keeping a close eye on Aram and the men at the gate. In fact, Aram's air of tense impatience was drawing the gaze of many of the population as they passed through the open ground.

He was grateful when the first horsemen emerged from the treeline. Wearing blue and white uniforms and gleaming silvered armour, the column thundered out into the open, between the fields and directly towards the monastery gate. Behind them came another group of riders in drab brown peasant clothing. As the horsemen closed on the gate, the faces of Jiang and Jai became clear, confirming Aram's assumptions.

'Aram of Initpur,' Cinna greeted him with a face that displayed a mix of relief and sadness.

'Generals. Dev. Jai.'

His sons nodded at him, smiling, though each upturned mouth was weighted down with the same sadness as the general's. Clearly beyond having failed to stop the cataclysm at Jalnapur, something else had gone dreadfully awry, though now was probably not the time to pry.

'We have come to beg your hospitality once more, Aram,' the stocky westerner said with a touch of formality. 'This time on a permanent basis.'

Aram nodded, though his brow was furrowed.

'Trouble follows you, General.'

'Trouble always follows us, but you have a place of safety here. We would join you if you will have us.'

Aram shook his head. 'You don't understand. Our safety is compromised. You bring peril with you. White riders follow you in the spirit lands.'

Jiang and Cinna and their two adjutants shared disbelieving looks.

'We outran the Sizhad's army and left them dealing with the survivors at Jalnapur.'

'No, General Cinna. There are more than six hundred riders in white an hour behind you at most, and they are armed. Do not ask me how they managed it without being taken by the spirits, but they have. They are coming with gleaming blades.'

'How do you know this?' Jiang muttered.

'We have good communication now. I have swift routes, and most approaches are monitored. Only the ones to the south are not, and they are prepared in case we have to seal them and keep the dead out.'

Cinna and Jiang looked at one another, thinking deeply.

'Six hundred or more. Armed fanatics.'

Jiang nodded. 'I would not feel confident standing our men against them unarmed, despite their experience, let alone farmers and artisans.'

Aram felt a weight lift from him despite the words being spoken. The military decision makers were here.

'What do we do?' he asked.

The two generals turned to him in surprise. '*You* are the leader here, Aram.'

'No. I cannot command a battle. I am not a general.'

The two men paused for a moment, still deep in thought.

'The spirits have not taken them,' Dev said suddenly.

'That is true.'

'Then that means the spirits are either powerless or they have gone. And you believe the monks have gone too.'

'It has certainly appeared that way for some time,' his father replied.

'Then they have gone south. The line of markers both sides of the Nadu are neglected, the paths rarely trodden. You found this place empty. They clearly have not gone north. To east and west it appears to be the same story, and eventually there is the sea. So that leaves the south.'

'The south?' Parmesh suddenly snorted, drawing their attention. None of them had been aware of the old man's approach. 'The south is a killing land. Even the monks would never leave the borderlands and go south.'

'That's not strictly true,' Aram pointed out. 'The map in the monastery was created by people who have walked the paths of the south. But they were the monks. The chosen.' He turned back to the generals. 'He is right, though. The further south you go, the more dangerous the land becomes. That has always been known. The spirits become more jealous and harsh until finally you reach the Isle of the Dead, and no man in his right mind goes there on purpose. No one has ever been and returned. In fact, barring a few legends and ghost stories, no one has ever crossed the water at all.'

Cinna drummed the fingers of his left hand on his saddle horn, straightening in his saddle. 'I will command any battle for you, Aram, but you are still the leader here. I can present you with only two choices: run or fight.'

Aram shivered at the thought of either. To abandon the safety and comfort of the monastery...

'If you run, the only choice is south. To the north lies the end of the world by sword and fire. The sea bounds us to east and west. South holds only the unknown and legends of terror. But mark this: half a thousand armed fanatics will cut their way through us like a warmed knife in a block of butter. Even armed, my soldiers or Jiang's Crimson Guard would be unable to stop them. Bare-handed? No. We have lost men on the journey. We have just over three hundred altogether. We could defeat them by sheer weight of numbers, but that would require committing the people of the monastery, and you would lose many men. If you are to create a hope for a future you *need* those men.'

'But the spirits...' Parmesh argued.

'If the spirits have gone south...' Aram said, noting that Cinna claimed a good hundred men fewer than his picket had estimated. Had the man been as wide of the mark with enemy numbers? 'If the spirits have gone south and are not here to deal with these interlopers, then perhaps the south is the only place they can be defeated.'

'This talk is madness.'

General Jiang shook his head. 'Cinna and Aram are right, my friend. You are in awe and fear of the unknown. That is only natural. But when the known involves the death of thousands by the swords

278

of howling fanatics, the unknown starts to look surprisingly palatable.'

Dev threw his arm out and pointed back along the path. 'I have seen these men up close, seen what they can do. What they *will* do. No one will be safe. In the name of the living sun, they will burn and blind, kill and destroy. You cannot allow that to happen to our people. Father, we talked last time we were here. You told us how you had abandoned everything you ever knew and set off into the unknown to save the people of Initpur. All the generals are saying is that you need to do the same again. The danger is come upon us again, and we cannot hope to fight it without endless slaughter. You need to lead our people into the unknown again. You've done it once.'

Aram breathed slowly, eyeing his son with a tinge of pride. Dev had grown strong and sharp. And he was right. Damn him, but he was right. And so was Cinna. The unknown could be better than the known.

'Mani? Parmesh? Bajaan? Sound the muster. We are leaving.'

'No,' Parmesh snapped. 'You cannot be so stupid. To walk deeper into the dead lands? It is folly.'

'We have no *choice*,' shouted Aram, wheeling angrily on the ever-dissenting Parmesh. 'We are going. Anyone who wants to stay with you will have that choice, but they will stay only to feed the blades of the sun-worshipping fanatics. Anyone who strives to live is leaving. Mani, sound the muster.'

Though his face was troubled, Mani stepped over to the bell and rang it wildly, the sound ringing out across the monastery, before pausing and then giving three short rings, pausing again, then three more, and continuing the rhythm for some time as men and women, children and even dogs came running out of buildings to the open square. As the people of the monastery began to assemble, General Jiang leaned forward. 'How long do we have before the white riders get here?'

'I cannot say for certain. It depends how recklessly they ride. Men who travel these paths do so carefully, as you know, General.'

'These men will travel with less care,' Dev replied. 'They will come fast.'

'Less than an hour, then, I would say.'

'I have seen villages flee before,' Jiang said. 'It is not a speedy undertaking, even if people are desperate. They will need time to hook up beasts, load wagons and the like.'

'We will never outrun them if we're slowed by carts,' Dev argued, and this brought a chorus of nods.

'But without supplies the people might as well lie down here and await their fate, for starvation on the run is an unpleasant way to go,' said Cinna. 'We had supplies on our journey south, and we still felt the pangs of hunger as we hunted every last rabbit to supplement our meals. Now there will be thousands of us. They need to eat.'

'And we have good supplies,' Aram added. 'Plenty for weeks of travel.'

'All of which is precious use if they slow us down so much that the blades of the Faithful reach us first,' Dev sighed.

'Then the answer is simple,' Jiang said. 'We need to delay them to get a head start. How do we slow them, Aram? You know this land.'

Aram shook his head. He was no tactician. They had set up pickets and a few precautions, of course, but the latter were south of the monastery, to protect against whatever might come from there.

'There is no easy way to slow anyone approaching from the north.'

Cinna gestured at Mani and Bajaan. Parmesh had gone, presumably to spread his poisonous ideas. 'You two. You seem to be Aram's most trusted men. Get everyone organised as fast as you can. Get the carts loaded now and ready to move.'

The two Inda looked to Aram for a moment, but at his nod they ran off and began to prepare.

'You say "from the north",' Jiang noted. 'You can slow an approach from the south? You said you could seal the route to keep the dead out.'

Aram nodded. Early in their time at the monastery, they had checked each approach to the place. The main southern route crossed a river – not wide or deep, but boggy-banked and difficult. Parmesh had been all for demolishing the crossing there and then, for fear of what lay beyond. Aram had decided against it, though he had prepared things should its sabotage be required at some point.

'The southern route crosses a low trestle bridge. The river is not like the Nadu, but it will stop even horsemen for a while. The bridge has been prepared. Two horses and a dozen heartbeats and it will be little more than kindling in the water.'

'*There* is our advantage,' Jiang said with an air of satisfaction. 'Once we cross that river, we can buy ourselves a good lead. I remember you showing me the map in the monastery last time we were here, Aram. The roads to the south cross and wind. With enough of a head start we can lose ourselves in it and leave the Sizhad's men guessing where we are. Jai here is a master scout. He and his men could cover our tracks in mere moments, I am sure.'

Jai nodded and Aram scratched his head. 'I have had copies made of the map. It seemed prudent. We can navigate the south, barring... unforeseen problems.'

'Then we are in a strong position once we are across that bridge. But that will take time.'

Already carts and animals were being brought out behind them. Cinna and Jiang exchanged a glance. 'They need time.'

'They do. We can buy them that time.'

Aram felt his blood chill at the realisation of what they were suggesting. 'There has to be another way.'

'There is not, Aram, and you know that,' Cinna said. 'Remember, I told you you were still the leader, but that I would command any battle for you. I shall do just that, along with Jiang here.'

'Perhaps we could find weapons?' Jai put in.

'You are not coming with us,' Jiang said flatly.

'General—'

'No. I will not allow you or your brother to throw your lives away buying time for your father.'

Dev straightened. 'Neither of you can claim to command any longer. You are not generals any more. I serve you only because I wish to. You cannot command me to stay behind, and I will not.' He looked at Jai, who nodded his agreement.

Aram again felt that chill. 'You know we cannot wield weapons here,' he said quietly.

'Evidence suggests otherwise, Aram,' Cinna replied, pointing at the line of jungle to the north. 'Things have changed.' He turned to the large crowd of riders. 'The Crimson Guard need to remove this disguise and armour up. While you're doing that, my men will search the monastery and find every axe, sickle, knife and sharp stick. We might not have swords, but we can at least give them a fight.'

The eastern guardsmen looked to their general, who translated the westerner's words into his native tongue. As his men began to remove their turbans and dismount, fishing in their packs, Jiang turned to Aram. 'We will hold them only as long as we have to. Once the last cart crosses the bridge, ring the bell loud and we will come. And be fast. We can't hold them long.'

'You realise we'll probably all be dead long before the last cart crosses,' Cinna said to his peer in low tones that obviously Aram hadn't been meant to hear. Jiang simply threw the westerner a bleak expression.

'Dev, Jai, go and supervise the search for weapons,' Jiang said.

'But—'

'Go,' agreed Cinna. They waited and watched until the two young Inda disappeared sullenly into the monastery proper.

'Their pride is strong,' General Jiang noted, nodding to Aram. 'They are a credit to your blood. I will not let them fall now. Be confident. If the worst happens and we are overrun I shall make sure they are the first men back to you.'

Aram nodded. He was less than convinced, in truth, but had no doubt that the general meant exactly what he said.

'And we,' Cinna said to Jiang, 'need to decide on how best to try and hold them.'

'I believe I know just the place,' the easterner replied, as behind him men affixed their red demon masks.

CHAPTER 22

The wall crumbles.
The man stands.
The world turns.

Unnamed poem by Ji Huong

Jai was far from sure of the defensive value of his general's chosen site, though Cinna had seemed satisfied. Just under two hundred paces into the jungle, close enough to still see the monastery in the distance, they prepared, some working feverishly while others waited, tense. They had been in position for less than a quarter of an hour and still the men were busy setting everything up as per the generals' instructions.

While the makeshift weapons were being found at the monastery and distributed, the men arming themselves and swapping items according to preference, the generals had sat together, hashing out their plans. Any time Dev or Jai had come close enough to join the conversation, they had been sent off into the monastery to source something the commanders thought they might need. In half an hour the men were as armed as they were going to be and the generals had given the order to move out.

As they had left the monastery and moved back along the northern path towards the jungle and the approaching Faithful, already loaded carts were trundling south from the complex as fast as their drivers could move them. With luck they would manage to shift everything speedily and reduce the danger for the soldiers fighting to delay. It would be a close-run thing getting to the bridge ahead of the enemy, even at their best speed.

The bridge. Damn it, but did not every evil in this world seem to revolve around a bridge?

They had reached the general's favoured location with precious little time to spare, if his father's estimate of the enemy's speed was correct, anyway.

Here, the jungle path opened up. A tree to each side of the track had fallen sometime in the recent past, their trunks cut up and logged by the monastery's people. In doing so they had been forced to clear much of the undergrowth, and so the path had been widened. Yet despite the disappearance of two trees there still remained a good canopy of green above, even if it was slightly lighter and higher here than elsewhere, and creepers and vines hung from the greenery, adding to the dappled effect of the light beneath.

A hundred men drawn from both units were busy at work in the wide area, turning the two generals' various curious plans into reality. It was truly fascinating to watch the red-clad demons of Jiang's Crimson Guard working alongside Cinna's blue and white elite bodyguard. The two units were so different in every way, and yet somehow, perhaps due to constant proximity to such flexible and accommodating generals, they seemed able to work together perfectly. Jai was impressed in particular with the Crimson Guard, who displayed considerably greater ability to think for themselves than the ordinary rank and file of the east. Every man had a place and a task, thanks to the organising abilities of the officers. The second rank of soldiers were the ones currently busy with those plans. The first rank remained at ease since they would be the front line of the fight and needed to be as rested as possible. The third rank were busy sharpening weapons in preparation.

Three ranks of sixty men each, split into three further lines of twenty each. And they were all on foot. That decision had surprised Jai, but both generals had agreed that dismounted was the way to meet the fanatics. The soldiers worked among the trees ahead or waited nervously on the path, cleaning or sharpening, yet their eyes continually strayed from the repurposed tools in their hands to the deep, dark depths of the jungle to each side and back again. Logic said that the ghosts would not take them, else the enemy would not be coming for the same reason, but each man had heard the tales, and nerves are rarely quelled by logic.

Three ranks of men were set to block the track where it narrowed after the wider section, totalling nine lines in all. The front two ranks were armed with makeshift spears of various kinds, for everyone knew the value of such a weapon against horses. Many were simple wooden staves that had been sharpened to a wicked point. Others were rakes and hoes that had had the heads removed or bent and sharpened. The third rank was armed with axes, long kitchen knives, batons and sickles. And each rank was formed of a mix of blue-and-white and red-masked warriors. Somehow, the need to rely upon makeshift weapons and native supplies in unfamiliar terrain had largely removed the differences between the two units. They were all learning a new way to fight together now. It was lucky that their masters were as shrewd and adaptable as they were. There was no reserve. If the enemy got past the ninth line – the third rank – they had lost, so there was no need for a reserve.

One unit did remain behind them, though. Between there and the open land of the monastery fields, every man's horse stood at the side of the path, gathered in groups of four. Each group held one rider, who kept the reins of the other three. As soon as that bell rang in the distance – and there were men positioned for hundreds of paces back along the road to make sure it did not go unheard – every man knew the score. Turn and run. Get to the nearest horse, mount up and race for the southern bridge. It was not an elegant retreat plan, but Cinna had learned from many years of war that a simple plan was more valuable any day than a clever one, when men were required to follow it in a panic.

Other units waited too. But they were hidden. Prepared. The Sizhad's men might be rabid and cocksure, but they were in for a few nasty surprises.

Jai prepared himself and glanced across at Dev, who nodded. They had both been positioned with the third rank, in the ninth row and relatively safe from immediate danger. Dev held a hammer with a pointed hook, and Jai gripped a hatchet. Neither was expected to fight, and they knew it, which relieved Jai immensely. His brother had always been a thinker, not a fighter, and time had probably not changed that too much. The generals, who were currently busy out of sight, had made it perfectly clear that whatever happened, the brothers were to end the fight in the saddle and riding to join their father. Both had agreed. Given their oath, even. Yet just as Jai prepared himself, he could tell from Dev's stance that his brother was ready to do exactly the same thing as him.

Damn it, Dev, be careful...

They were all expecting the warning, yet it still came as a shock to hear the whistle calling, shrilly, three times from the trees ahead.

The Faithful were here.

Jai and Dev began to push forward. The generals were out of sight, and even if they reappeared suddenly they would be far too busy right now to argue with the brothers over their position in the wall of men. Jai kept moving forward, pushing between soldiers who objected and argued in two different tongues until they realised who it was jostling them out of the way. There was value to senior rank, after all. He stopped somewhere in the middle and was relieved to see that Dev had done the same. There was no point in being at the front, when the best, largest men were there, prepared. But here in the third line of nine Jai passed his axe to a man, taking his sharpened staff, and sent him back. Jai might not be the man for the front line, but he was damn well going to lend his arm to the fight and not dither at the back, protected by his rank.

Forward, he could see the open space. The wide area closed up again some sixty feet away, but the path ran on for that same distance again before curving to the right. The men ahead of the lines had now abandoned whatever preparations remained unfinished and were running back to grab their spears and fall in as the middle file. Jai let them pass as they lined up, ready, panting from their exertions.

Once the last man had taken his position, the world went silent. Well, *battle-silent*, anyway. Battle silence is something unique, for it is actually full of noise. The snorting of horses and the jingle and clang and clonk of armour. The groans of men stretching. A cough and an occasional fart. No words, though. Every man was clinging to his innermost thoughts. Some men's lips moved as they sent silent prayers to their favoured gods. Jai wondered idly whether their gods could hear, since they ruled far to the east and west and his own Inda gods might not let the prayers pass through. He smiled at his philosophical curiosity, but then the battle silence was broken as a new sound joined the symphony.

The thunder of hooves.

The Sizhad's men rounded the corner at a good speed, but at the sight of the forces arrayed across the path ahead in clumps of blue and white or of red, they charged, ululating and whooping.

Even over that thunder Jai could hear the distinctive sound of bladders and bowels giving way. It was something he had learned about war this past year. It mattered not how brave a man was, his digestive system would react to the terror of facing charging cavalry whether he willed it or not.

Men tensed. Officers called out in both languages for their men to stay steady.

'Watch 'em suffer,' said the western captain.

And they did.

The riders had broken into a gallop at the sight of the defenders, and they had been so focused on their quarry that they had failed to spot the horrors awaiting them. In the strange, sun-dappled light it was hard to see them, of course, until it was too late.

The front riders hit the first rope twenty paces before the widened area. It had been strung at the height of a horse's upper legs and fastened to trees at either side with great care for tightness and security. The rope snapped with the enormous pressure anyway, but it was accompanied by the sound of numerous shearing bones, and horses, screaming, fell across the path, shattered legs thrashing, mouths foaming, eyes rolling. The riders behind the stricken front line fared no better. Half of them hit the thrashing mounds of men and beasts and added to the collection, falling and bellowing in shock. A number of them reacted swiftly and attempted to jump the havoc.

It was these men who hit the second rope, which had been strung at neck height for a rider. Those men who were low enough to catch the rope themselves were thrown from their beasts. Where men had jumped higher in desperation, their horses caught the higher rope and were brought down to earth immediately, crashing to the ground on their sides and backs, legs breaking, men crushed under their weight.

Still the wave of cavalry came. It was all happening so quickly that there was no chance for the riders behind to learn the fate of those in front before they too were in the thick of it. The third rope caught fewer men before it broke, but still ruined men and steeds alike, adding to the carnage on the ground.

The charge had been broken. The imperial forces would still have to face the riders in vicious combat, but now they stood a chance. It was often the charge that made or broke a battle in its opening moves.

The enemy riders came on, slowing now, moving with more care and alertness, looking for ropes across the path, watching where their horses trod, skirting the worst piles of writhing, shrieking flesh. It would be hard to see with the flickering, dancing patches of light and the creepers dangling from the canopy above, high enough not to disturb riders, but constantly distracting the attention, yet now the horsemen knew the ropes were there, they were watching.

Of course, Cinna was brighter than that and, remembering his bridge-end ambush in those first days at Jalnapur, Jiang had deferred to him. The ropes the enemy were watching out for now were not there. Three was the maximum Cinna could imagine the riders falling for, and he had been exactly right.

The riders came on into the open space, snarling and yipping, relieved that they had passed the ropes. Somewhere beyond the treeline, an unseen hand undid a knot and a cord slithered free.

The fishing lines came down in a single jerking motion. Jai had thought the concept laughable when those sent to gather weapons had come back sheepishly with a huge bundle of fishing rods among them, but Cinna had immediately told them to find a length of cord and remove the trellises from the bean garden.

The lines were virtually invisible in the flickering light beneath the canopy and the first thing the riders knew of their presence was when the wicked metal hooks caught in their faces, necks, hands and arms, tearing flesh with sharp, searing pains, only to swing free, coated with torn skin and blood, and circle to catch another rider. The horsemen howled in pain as they rode through a hundred hooks, swinging and scraping, ripping and gouging.

It was far from a fatal trick, but it certainly slowed, distracted and maimed the riders. And unlike the ropes that broke on contact, these simply swung away, the damage done, and whirled to catch another rider. The advancing horsemen slowed again as they held up weapons and shields desperately trying to keep the swinging barbs away from their flesh, often failing in the process. Riders were now aware of the series of dreadful tricks and had begun to move out to the soft, grassy edge of that widened clearing in an attempt to skirt the swinging hooks.

Desperation is, as Jai's grandfather had once said, the greatest source of invention. Ropes and fishhooks, staves and tools were all the defenders had been able to gather from the monastery. Those, and the one last thing Cinna had told them to gather. The general had spotted a man carrying a large basket of crockery from one of the store sheds to load it into a cart, and had waved to the man and called him to stop. Dev and Jai, having just returned from locating ropes, had been sent to collect that basket and all other earthenware bowls, platters and cups in the monastery. Jai had snorted, at first thinking it a joke. Even after, he had assumed it a ploy of the generals to keep the brothers busy and out of the way.

Now, though, he understood the method behind Cinna's madness.

As those men rode around the periphery of the open area, the crockery began to fly from hidden throwers within the vegetation to either side. A heavy earthenware bowl hit a rider full in the side of the face, sending him hurtling from his horse – the Inda did not use the good, stable four-horned saddle of the westerners or the stirrups of the easterners, but rode with just a blanket and reins for control. The man disappeared with a squawk and fell beneath the hooves of the other horses.

It was the most peculiar missile barrage Jai had ever seen in battle, more reminiscent of an angry wife and a husband late home, but he had to give the general his due, for here and there riders were unhorsed or knocked senseless, their weapons battered from numb fingers with the hard missiles. And between the two beleaguered groups, slowing under the rain of heavy pots, the centre of the track was still filled with men howling as hooks tore at them.

It was all ingenious, of course, and was having a noticeable effect, yet it was little more than a distraction and a method of slowing them down. The force was still coming. With the ropes now gone, they were jumping the fallen with relative ease. Fishing lines were being torn down and cast to the ground, and the barrage from the wings was changing direction, which meant that the generals' men were running out of missiles. They were hurling the last few as they moved back, ready to retreat behind the wall of weapons on the path.

And beyond the clearing, Jai could see still more men pouring around the bend in the track. He began to harbour the suspicion that his father's scout had rather seriously underestimated enemy numbers.

The Sizhad's men hit the front line of the defenders at last, having navigated the various blows and hazards in the way. The missiles had stopped, the hooks were almost all gone and the ropes had snapped, but the men now riding into the line of blue, white and red spear men were no longer howling their spirited war cries. They looked wary and beleaguered, and many bore cuts and gouges in their flesh, their pristine white clothes and turbans dotted and lined with crimson.

Jai felt their whole force push back as the horsemen engaged, but it was a simple matter of pressure and weight, rather than the punching destruction of a full cavalry charge, from which the generals' little tricks had saved them. The third line was slightly out of reach of the initial fighting, but Jai did his best, hefting his sharpened staff and attempting to jab it into the nearest white figure he could see between the bobbing heads of the first two lines. Then the killing began in earnest. The defenders might be armed with only sharpened staves, but these were the hardiest and best-trained veterans of two armies, and every blow was made to count, points slamming into men and horses repeatedly, ripped back out carefully and then slammed forth once more, dripping gore, to seek a new target. Horses reared and screamed, and men cried out and tumbled back into the press.

But it was far from one-sided. The zealots had neither the training nor the discipline of the two bodyguard units, but what they lacked in those departments they more than made up for in determination and desire, and unlike the makeshift spears, their weapons were keen and dangerous, designed for killing. Here and there Jai heard a curse that surprised him coming from a supposed force of religious fanatics, and he had to remind himself that many of these white-clad lunatics had been drawn from the bandit forces of the northern mountains and would be of rough and uncultured stock. Men and horses fell repeatedly, the cries of both intermingled in the symphony of war.

Jai realised suddenly how quickly they were being destroyed as his makeshift spear was knocked aside by a sword and he fought to bring it back to bear. The front line of spear men was almost gone already and the second line was already in trouble. Risking his life, Jai turned his head for a moment, attempting to locate Dev in the press at the far side, but his brother was lost in the sea of heads and bodies and wavering spear tips. Then, momentarily, he caught a glimpse of his brother, fighting like a maniac. No glorious elegant forms from an academy, but the simple, mechanical butchery he had seen so well practised by Cinna's army at Jalnapur. It seemed that Dev had closed the martial gap between them somewhat over the years. Feeling a little more confidence in his brother's chances, he tore his attention back to the task at hand just in time as a sword lashed out and he was forced to duck to one side. He jabbed lower with the spear and felt it sink into flesh at the horse's shoulder. The beast reared but the rider controlled it, and as it came down again, the hooves caught the man in front of Jai. The man's head shattered under the powerful hooves and Jai was caught in a fine spray that made his gorge rise. He was now the front line. For a moment he wondered why he had been so foolhardy as to disobey orders and move forward. It now seemed such folly. What had appeared to be a relatively secure third-line place had become the front in a matter of heartbeats. The number of white-garbed men and beasts that had fallen to the spears was scant consolation.

The zealot brought his curved blade down in an overhand chop, designed to cleave Jai's head in two. The Inda-born swordsman reacted instinctively. This was more or less the attack of the falling star. His body responded with the defence of the uncoiling snake before he'd had time to consider the options. His torso twisted left and turned his spear, the weapon coming up at an uncomfortable angle. The defence was designed for a sword, and he almost didn't make it with the unwieldy polearm. The butt of the staff scraped on the ground, and Jai realised he had inadvertently created a new form variant as the blow slid home, though he doubted it would be one taught in any class.

The times he had practised it in the academy, the blade had come up to meet the falling arm and should plunge into the limb, between the bones of the forearm, allowing him to then twist the sword back or forth and snap both bones. The sharpened staff met the falling arm as intended, but the base was now jammed against the dusty earth and the falling arm simply drove itself down onto the spear, which slid through the limb, bursting from the top with a shower of blood and rising like some horrid victory monument from the zealot's arm.

His new form variant was a failure. As the man shrieked and fell from his horse, his sword falling from blood-soaked fingers, Jai's spear was ripped from his grasp. He was only saved from a gory death at the hands of the next froth-mouthed lunatic behind his victim by the suddenly riderless horse which buffeted this way and that, wounded, out of control and desperate to be free from the fray. As soon as that man or any of his compatriots could get to Jai, he would be a dead man, disarmed and unable to defend himself.

Taking a nervous breath, he dropped beneath the titanic struggle, into a crouch. Here the world was a mess of stamping and braced legs, wavering spear butts and staring, blood-soaked bodies. But here also were the weapons that had been dropped by the wounded and dead. His questing hand found the curved blade dropped only moments earlier by his victim. He briefly cried out in pain as a boot came down on the other hand, but it shifted a moment later and his fingers flexed, confirming no breaks as he located a second sword and retrieved it.

Jai rose once more into the fray like Shikaya, Lord of Righteous Battle. A sword in each hand, he appeared whirling and slashing, stabbing and chopping. Free of the unfamiliar and unwieldy makeshift spear, his training once more came to the fore and Jai danced the dance of war, steel cutting into foe after foe.

But the forms would not win this battle. Tactics and discipline would not win it. Determination and right would not win it. *Nothing* could win this battle. As Jai's mind slowly began to take in more than his immediate opponents, he realised the terrible peril they were in. There were still far too many white horsemen ahead and the defenders on the path were being systematically wiped out, line after line. The front rank, of which he had been one, had gone entirely, and now the middle rank of spear men were fighting with desperate thrusts, but they too had lost one line and most of the second. Jai realised with a shock that he had been forced back, unnoticed, during the fight and was now among the last few spear men. Then the enemy would be into the lines of men with axes and shovels, sticks and sickles. And if the spear men, who were armed to defend against cavalry, had fallen so quickly, the others would be gone in the blink of an eye.

His seeking sword found an opening and jabbed up into the unprotected belly of a rider while the other hand cut across the thigh of a second zealot, but Jai almost fell as someone knocked into him from behind. He risked a glance over his shoulder and felt his heart shatter at the sight of the Crimson Guard and Cinna's blue and white warriors breaking and fleeing the scene.

He shouted something in the noise and violence about cowardice and honour, but only the zealots were paying him attention.

Turning back, he danced his death, feet leaping and twisting, arms swinging, rising, falling, sword whipping and lancing, curving and slashing. Men screamed. Men died. Jai felt the first two blows land, though fortunately they were both flesh wounds, one in the left thigh and one in the left shoulder. He compensated, pressing his right towards the enemy.

'Jai!'

His surprised gaze shot this way and that across the path, seeking the source of the call even as he lunged and parried.

'For the God's sake Jai, run!' called that same voice, and Jai's eyes widened as the machine broke clear of the trees to the side. He almost fell beneath it, which would certainly have meant his death, and he took another sharp, glancing blow across the shoulder as he leapt away.

The huge timber and iron plough that had been standing on its end just off the path, tethered to the tree, fell free and smashed a horse and rider out of the way, pulverising both. Jai didn't see the matching trap at the other side for he was running now, but he heard the second plough smash down. Cinna's last ploy. The two ploughs had been rotting and rusting close to the end of the monastery lands, and it had not taken a great deal of work to drag them fifty paces into the treeline, push them upright and tie them to the tree.

But with them now smashed and tangled together, forming a barricade on the road, it would take much longer to move them out of the way, especially with the huge piles of dead in the forest path.

Cinna burst out of the undergrowth at speed along with a dozen men, running with the agility and pace of a man half his age. Jai caught sight of Jiang emerging from the other verge a short way ahead, a dozen red-armoured men with him.

'Did you not hear the bells?' Cinna shouted as they ran, making for the nearest of the tethered horses.

'No. Didn't hear anything except my own blood pumping.'

Cinna snorted. 'You're a dangerous man, Jai.'

As they ran, the younger warrior glanced back to see the Faithful at the obstacle. They were howling and cursing impotently as some of their number slid from the horses and began to try and move the ploughs to the side of the path. Others were arguing and gesticulating. Jai, though, ignored them, concentrating on the one figure. A single rider in a yellow turban sat amid the argument, silent and upright, peering on down the track, clearly watching the general and his men escaping, though oddly without becoming visibly enraged. Was this the Sizhad of whom Dev was so worried? There was certainly something deathly calm about him. And something oddly familiar too.

'Mind if I have one of those?'

He tore his gaze from the halted riders and saw Cinna pointing at the swords in his hands. Smiling grimly, he passed the straighter of the two to the general, who took it gratefully. 'That feels better.'

Moments later, they reached the nearest knot of horses and climbed up. A quick glance confirmed that, apart from a score of men with minor wounds who were almost to safety, he and the general were the last. They kicked their horses into life and rode out of the jungle into the fields, where Jai could now finally hear the bell clanging, telling them that the refugees were across the bridge.

Jai felt a wave of relief. They had done it. And there would be time for them to cross and destroy the bridge before the white-clad lunatics could catch up. They had escaped the Sizhad, and should be able to get themselves safely lost once they were across that river.

If riding into the lands of the dead could ever be considered safe...

But then, had they not taken up blades now without the guardian spirits coming for them?

With a jolt, he realised he had not seen Dev during the fight, or the retreat. Dev might be military trained, but he was no expert swordsman like Jai. He was a tactician. A thinker.

'Did you see my brother, General?' he asked Cinna, who shook his head.

'Hopefully he had more sense than you.'

They rode forward until they caught up with the next group of riders, among whom General Jiang was congratulating his men.

'Jai.'

'Sir, did you see my brother?'

Jiang nodded, and for a moment Jai's heart faltered. 'He is up ahead. He heard the bells, unlike *some*, apparently.'

Jai laughed amid an explosive release of tension.

Jiang and Cinna, Dev and his father. Against all odds, they were all still alive and well.

THE MONASTERY BRIDGE

The Sizhad sat astride his white charger and peered at the quagmire and the narrow stream.

'It will take hours to cross, Lord,' said one of his lieutenants.

'We will cross. They underestimate us. They underestimated our numbers, our willingness to follow them into the dead lands, our strength and conviction. They continue to underestimate us. We will follow. Pursue and take them.'

The lieutenant was a man he would have to keep an eye on. The man had shown distinct nervousness since passing the great marker. In Ravi's eyes these symbols of a bygone age were nothing more than signs of demon worship and held no fear for him. The sun would protect him with its rays. Even in the dark, he knew the sun would be there, in his heart. Sadly, some of his Faithful were failing to live up to their name. Their fear of this place was palpable. Ravi would show them. He would teach them they had nothing to fear from this place. It was all superstition.

Mother...

It always came back to her when he closed his eyes.

'Lord, they are just peasants and a few officers stripped of command. They are of such little value when the prize of the west lies open before us. We should turn around. Strike west.'

'No!'

The Sizhad rose, eyes flashing dangerously. 'It was enough that we followed the west's only truly able general, but now we find the Jade Empire's greatest son alongside him? They carry a legacy of success. They must not be allowed to live to regroup and rebuild.'

And they are nothing. It was Dev he sought. Dev, who had been in his hands once, but had slipped away. Dev who he should rightly have executed back in the mountains, for the good of the Faithful. But he could not. He had lost Father, and Mother, and their baby sister. But he knew the truth now, and he needed Dev to know it too. To be part of the new world.

296

But he could not tell his Faithful that he led them into the place they most feared for love of a brother. For them it would have to be the pursuit of an enemy.

'Jiang and Cinna. They will join us, or they will die. Cross this river. I care not how, but I want it done now, before their trail is cold.'

CHAPTER 23

The journey south was quite the most nerve-racking in Dev's life. He had been unaware of just how accepting and comfortable he had become with the idea of the monastery and of moving in the lands beyond the boundary markers. He had overcome those dreadful nerves he had felt the first time they had crossed into the forbidden lands with unexpected speed and ease.

But now it had all come back, and worse than ever. The *first* day he'd not felt it, and nor had the rest of the huge force of refugees, as far as he could see. The sheer arduous work involved in clearing out the monastery and moving out had occupied much of their attention. It had been busy work despite the fact that Aram had kept things organised so perfectly that departure was relatively painless, for he knew the value of being able to move out swiftly. And above and beyond the all-consuming exertion, the arrival of the Sizhad's white-clad men had taken up much of the thoughts of everyone in that huge group.

There had been neither sight nor sound of pursuit as Cinna and the last of the soldiers crossed the small bridge, and Aram's men had attached two heavy beasts of burden to the prepared ropes and turned it into so much smashed kindling that washed away downstream. They had paused there for a short while as the column moved on to make sure that the bridge was sufficiently destroyed to prevent easy pursuit. Sure enough very little remained once the dust had settled, and though initially Dev had been concerned that such a small torrent would be little obstacle for the white riders, his opinions had been changed by two discoveries. One was of the sucking, swampy murk on both sides, which covered an area much larger than the river itself and into which, in demonstration, his father pushed an eight-foot makeshift spear until it vanished right down to the tip. The other was the crocodiles that started to congregate with the presence of potential food. Dev had rarely encountered the dangerous beasts, for they were not native to his northern mountains, but there was little doubt that these animals would make anyone think twice about crossing. Most were double the length of a man, and unlike the ones

Dev had seen in captivity in the north, there was something eerie and dead about these ones. These were neither green nor brown, but a curious ash-grey. Their eyes were slightly sunken, and the overall impression was of dead animals. Dev shivered at even the memory of the beasts long after they had passed the bridge and moved on.

With Aram and his helpers leading the way, consulting his map, they meandered south for more than a week, moving gradually west as they travelled, presuming that the Sizhad's men would be more likely to assume they went another way. Jai and his chosen men had done an admirable job of erasing signs of their passage ever since the first junction they had come across, and the likelihood was that the white riders were now lost, wandering in the jungle somewhere to the east.

But being free of the worry of pursuit and the dangerous fanaticism of the Faithful had not made the journey any easier. Here and there men in the column had borne weapons as they travelled through the jungle, a thing that had long been absolutely forbidden under any circumstances, and which carried an automatic sentence of gruesome death or lunatic madness in every tale of the Inda from the last few centuries. And though no spirit had emerged from the hanging vines in the close, sweaty environment, set on tearing out Dev's eyeballs and ripping open his heart, the oppressive feeling of not being welcome grew with every mile they travelled. They never once saw a ghost, but Dev was willing to swear he could feel them all around him, all of the time. It was like being in a cloud of midges, if the insects were ice-cold and some of them carried the threat of a painful death. Dev almost began to wish he were back facing the Faithful, for at least they were a human enemy, and one you could see.

This was like living in perpetual fear of a fog.

Also, while the more northerly Inda lands had been full of ruin, with the war having wrecked many regions, and the monastery was a solitary haven of civilisation in the lands beyond the markers, the journey south brought back how long this land had been dead. The monks had not maintained the paths south of their monasteries, and had done nothing with the structures to be found there. Dev rode slowly past whole villages that had been dead and deserted for ten generations or more, now little more than overgrown, moss-covered broken walls, open to the sky. And the further they went the more dead those places seemed.

Moreover, once they had passed the crocodiles at that first small river the whole world seemed to have been stripped of wildlife. They saw no animals in the jungle, no birds in the trees. When they paused by a river, the fishermen had been able to catch nothing. The refugees became thoroughly grateful that they had brought adequate supplies from the monastery, given the complete dearth of forage. The zealots, if they were still alive, would be starving, which was something of a consolation. But the very absence of life was horrible. Dev had not spent a vast amount of time in the jungle over the years, being a man of the northern hills, but what time he had had shown him that the Inda jungle was the very epitome of life. Every root and branch, creeper and rivulet was full of it. Most of it could either eat, crush or poison a man, admittedly, but at least it was life. An empty, dead jungle was an eerie, ominous thing, and the silence seemed to have infected the travellers, stilling their tongues and crushing the urge to make noise.

It became more oppressive, quieter, eerier and generally more unpleasant with every passing mile. Likely their pursuers had given up long ago and fled back into the open, what with the hunger, the lack of a trail to follow and the sheer peril of travelling in this place. Again, that seemed little comfort. Dev had never slept so little in his life. The first few nights it had been adrenalin and concern over their safety that had kept him awake. Then, as they moved south, it was the utter silence of the jungle and the constant sense of presence. Finally, a couple of days ago, he had become so exhausted and so inured to the silence that he had begun to wake with a start when there was a noise, so rare had it become.

For a long time, Dev had ridden or walked at the rear of the column, ever watchful for pursuit, but as that had become ever more unlikely, he had moved to the front with the other leaders and officers. His father's right-hand man, a fellow called Mani who seemed thoroughly capable, and another trustworthy soldier called Bajaan, now took turns commanding a rearguard formed of the stronger Inda with intermixed units of westerners and easterners.

Five days ago they had crossed the great Nadu. Dev's breath had been stolen by the sight as they emerged from the jungle to the banks of a river that dwarfed even the one they had fought so long to cross. Here, the Nadu more resembled a sea more than a river, the far bank so distant its features could barely be made out. And the bridge...

If Dev had thought that great delicate white bridge at Jalnapur impressive, it was nothing to this incredible structure. Twice as long and twice as beautiful, this bridge was so ancient Dev could barely wrap his mind around it. The images of the gods carved into the parapets were in a style only visible in the oldest of temples, and the delicate script along the sides was the old tongue spoken only by priests. Truly the people who had lived here and become the dead of the eponymous land had once been great. Then finally they were across that immense river and moving south-east once again into the sweaty green of the jungle. The column's leaders had momentarily given thought to destroying the bridge to prevent the possibility of pursuit, but it had eventually been universally agreed that even if they no longer felt the presence of the guardian spirits, and even if they had the resources to demolish something of that size, it would be foolish to do such a thing.

Dev was only half-listening as Cinna and Jiang compared the structures of their imperial courts and administrations, identifying the strengths and weaknesses in each with the practised if jaded eye of a career soldier. Occasionally they laughed about what they would do differently, when they realised that they were falling into the same old traps and almost advocating the systems that had already failed them. Despite the constant nervous tension surrounding them, Dev smiled on those occasions, when the two generals had talked themselves in circles and Aram had stepped in and calmly, easily explained how to step out of the trap into which they had fallen. It gave him a sense of pride to realise that the men he and his brother had faithfully served this past year both deferred to his father on all non-military matters. Jai, on the other hand, seemed to be feeling the strangeness of this land every bit as much as Dev. While he was not unapproachable or unfriendly in any way, Dev's brother was as quiet and subdued as all of them.

'Gods and monsters,' he breathed in exclamation as they rounded a bend in the wide road they followed and suddenly – *quite suddenly* – the jungle ended. His eyes wide, Jai rode with the other leaders and officers out of the canopy of green and onto a wide sandy beach.

They moved out a hundred paces into the open, warm, salty air and stopped their mounts, looking about in awe and, spotting the unexpected, in some confusion.

The Isle of the Dead lay before them in all its glory. It sat baiting them across more than a mile of channel, the sea's surface rolling and rising and falling with a noise that sounded like the world breathing, and which spoke of the presence of deep water and dangerous currents. The island itself was huge, clearly. Dev realised he'd never given any real thought to the place. He'd never thought to go there for obvious reasons, and even on their journey south had assumed that would never be their destination. He had for some reason expected an island perhaps a few miles across with tombs and crumbling walls rising like a city of the dead. In fact, the isle had to be more than thirty or forty miles across, and who knew how far it stretched out of sight to the south. And it was green. Not the green of the jungle where they were now, but the green of rolling hills and meadows more like the land north of Initpur. Forest was visible here and there. It looked more inviting than Dev would ever have expected from a place bearing such a name.

But the thing that made them all pause, from innocent tired farmer to former king or foreign general, was the boats. The wide beach would be big enough to accommodate the entire mob of humanity that had travelled south, so long as they spread out well, for the tell-tale mark of the tide line was a long way from the jungle itself. And just above that line were boats. Not one or two boats as might belong to fishermen who had been blown off course, got lost and ended up here by chance. Nor the sort of boats that might have been here for eons, gradually rotting and falling apart. There were perhaps sixty boats, each no more than a decade old, all of good timber and lying empty with the oars inside.

Dev shivered.

'Explain that,' he said in a frail voice.

'I cannot,' his father answered, as the leaders congregated to examine the vessels.

'They're recent.'

'And in good condition.'

'They must have landed here and the occupants wandered off into the jungle.'

'That seems exceedingly unlikely.'

'So then where are they?'

'And perhaps as important: where did they come from?'

'It's an invitation,' Aram said, holding his arms out, palms flat in an attempt to calm things down. Ripples of excited, nervous conversation were making their way through the Inda as they arrived gradually on the sand.

'One we must not accept,' Parmesh replied vehemently, and for once everyone nodded their agreement with the serial dissenter.

'Can I draw your attention to another curiosity?' Bajaan put in, wandering across the sand and pointing down at the ground. The others hurried over and stared. A stick stood in the sand, rising perhaps three feet into the air, with a tip that had been painted white.

'Shall I pull it out?'

Aram shook his head. 'Given that we do not know what is on the other end, I would say not. Remember that no one has lived here in many centuries. Not even the monks.'

'Then who is leaving us boats and marking places with sticks?' Cinna murmured.

'There is another,' General Jiang said, pointing to a second white-tipped stick a few hundred paces away. 'If I were to say what I think, would it spread panic?'

'Go on,' Cinna said.

'They look to me like range markers.'

The stocky western general nodded. 'That same thought had occurred to me.'

'What now, then?' Jiang asked Aram. 'Thus far we have only discussed plans to set up a temporary colony by the sea. That was, I presume, based upon there being grassland or some such. I cannot imagine a successful colony growing here on the sand, pinned between dead jungle and dangerous sea.'

'And there is no running water here,' added Cinna helpfully.

'We passed a small river only half a mile back,' Aram reminded them. 'Some of our people will still be crossing it now. There will be fruit within the treeline even if there is no meat. And likely fish in this sea. I am not proposing that we stay here forever, but every man, woman and child in this assembly is tired and dispirited, and everyone could do with a rest and a little recovery time. I suggest that we begin to construct temporary shelters and send scouts out east and west along the beach to see what they can find.'

Jiang nodded. 'An eminently sensible suggestion. I would suggest, though, moving down across the sand and a little to the east. Being too close to what look like artillery range markers makes me nervous. Do we start organising the work now or wait for the entire group to be present on the beach so that you can address them?'

Again Dev smiled at the fact that the Jade Empire's most successful general was deferring to his father.

'Let us assign work parties straight away,' Aram replied. 'It is mid-afternoon, and soon the sun will begin its true descent. I think we would all feel a lot more comfortable if we had water, firewood, food and as much shelter as possible by then.'

Dev, seemingly forgotten as the two generals began to discuss arrangements with his father, caught Jai's eye, who nodded towards the edge of the jungle. He turned to the three leaders.

'Jai and I will go and look at the river we passed, see if we can work out where it comes to the sea, as it might be nearby.'

The three men nodded almost absently at him and, beckoning to his brother, Dev began to ride slowly back along the column of Inda that was still pouring from the jungle onto the beach, mouths open in wonder.

'Thank you,' Jai said as they moved towards the rear of the flow of humanity, 'I was starting to become twitchy sitting there doing nothing.'

'And if we kept doing it we'd end up chopping logs,' smiled Dev.

'You seem surprisingly at ease for a man sitting across the water from the most dangerous place in the world.'

Dev laughed. 'The world's geography has changed, brother. That label belongs in the north now. It may be that the Sizhad is busy enslaving the whole world with his heresy and that here is the only place where we can still live as Inda. Every passing day this year has made me appreciate Father's belief in fate a little more. I can hardly deny it is at work. Can you?'

Jai shrugged. 'Fate. Or luck. Or the sheer will of men. All different, but all as likely. I am undecided, though General Jiang is a firm believer in fate, I think.'

'Me too. We have been thousands of miles apart all our adult life, and not only were we thrown back together, but with Father too. And three great armies have been rampaging in the lands, all of whom would now gleefully take our heads, yet here we are on the beach in the dead lands, safe from them all.'

'But not safe from the dead lands,' Jai muttered.

Time rolled on as the brothers rode along the line of stragglers, and soon the column had moved past, making for the beach, Mani and a small group of riders following on as rearguard. The soldier was concerned at the two brothers riding back into the jungle alone, but Jai pointed out that they were only going as far as the river, perhaps half a mile beyond, and they had all travelled the path safely once that day. Reluctantly, Mani continued on, and soon the brothers were alone.

Finally they reached the small river they had crossed earlier. The water was clean and sparkling, and Dev dismounted to taste it, declaring it eminently drinkable. The flow was not fast and the bed not deep, the path here crossing it in a shallow ford. The channel ran on into the jungle to their left and if Dev's estimate of direction was anywhere near accurate and it did not deviate too much in direction, it would probably strike the beach some two miles from the place the camp was being established. That would make water retrieval much easier and less worrisome than having to delve deep into the eerie jungle for it.

'Do we follow it, then?'

Jai nodded, trusting his brother's judgement. Dev had always been good with geography. Better than Jai, anyway. 'Let's be sure.'

The going would be tougher in the vegetation, so the pair dismounted and began to walk along the river's course, sometimes on the bank where the plants and trees receded, and sometimes simply along the flow of water, relishing the chill of the river soaking their boots. They walked in relative silence – though they were still far from stuck for conversational topics, the creepiness of the still, silent jungle made speech seem intrusive.

The watercourse began to veer slightly west, adding distance to Dev's initial estimate, and Jai nudged him. 'Is it worth going on?'

'It might not change too much, and at this point we might as well find out.'

At his brother's nod, Dev pressed on. The light was starting to change now as the sun began to sink in the west. 'If we don't get to the beach soon, this is going to turn out to have been a terrible idea,' Jai noted. 'Father will be concerned.'

'It cannot be far now,' insisted Dev, sloshing along the water. The pair lapsed into silence again and gratefully stepped up onto a border of low, springy grass alongside the river, following it south.

A further quarter of an hour passed, and Dev, starting to query his own wisdom, opened his mouth to seek his brother's reassurance when he heard the voices. Instantly, he snapped his mouth shut and stopped dead, gesturing for Jai to keep quiet. They shared a concerned look. There was no way the river had come close enough to their father and his people so, unless some of those Inda had strayed far along the beach in search of wood, the voices were most likely enemies.

They tethered their horses to a low branch and stepped carefully and quietly forward. A few dozen paces away, the river split into two channels, one heading off tangentially east, back towards their camp. The other ran on ahead, and a faint lightening of the gloom there suggested they were close to the beach. The brothers motioned to each other and stepped back into the water to better disguise their footsteps. They would leave no trail, and the splashing and gurgling of the water would hide their footfalls from prying ears, whereas on the verge there was every chance they might break a twig and attract unwanted attention.

Gradually the world brightened until they finally spotted sand between the green leaves. They paused again there, listening. The voices were clearer, more distinct. The words were not precisely audible since they were issued in low tones, but they were Inda voices, with a dialect familiar from the brothers' youth. The pair crept forward and ducked sharply to one side as they spotted movement between the trees. Moving ever more carefully to a good observation point, the pair peered through the foliage towards the beach.

Their spines chilled. The voices belonged to four men in white who sat close to the river on the beach, spears jammed into the sand, chatting amiably together. Beyond them, the brothers could see numerous fires surrounded by white-garbed men. Low shelters had been erected using simple white sheets and two posts, and the distant but unmistakable sound of horses was now audible in the background. Dev waved urgently at his brother as Jai moved forward, coming dangerously close to the enemy's line of sight. Fortunately, the four white-clad men seemed oblivious, their attention more on each other and the beach than the greenery nearby. Finally, after what seemed an age, Jai reappeared and gestured back towards their horses.

They moved back along the river, and Dev barely dared breathe until they reached the fork in the river. Retrieving their horses, they hurried towards the other channel and began to follow it back towards the camp. Perhaps a mile further on, the second stream emerged onto the beach, where it flowed down to the sea. They had mercifully rounded a corner and could see nothing of the Faithful's camp. Finally, Dev broke the silence.

'There should not be a road there, and there were no marks of passage on the beach. The enemy came along the sand from the west. That means they are heading east. Towards the camp. Thank all the gods that they decided to stop there for the night, else they would have found us unprepared.'

'I don't know where that picket of Father's learned to count,' Jai replied, 'but he did a woeful job estimating their numbers. They were supposed to have six or seven hundred. We killed maybe two hundred back at the monastery, but there were still far too many on that beach.'

'How many?'

'I reckon near a thousand. I counted up and they had about forty men around each fire. I saw more than twenty fires.'

'That's too many for us.'

Jai nodded. 'We have to leave, and now, before they begin to move again.'

The two brothers raced along the beach, back to the camp, angling quickly down to the softer sand near the water where their tracks would be erased by the tide. It was just less than three miles by Dev's estimate, and they found the Inda in a state of nervous stability. All eyes repeatedly shifted to either the eerie jungle north of them or the terrifying island to the south, but they had campfires and makeshift shelters and food was now being distributed. The brothers passed a line of pickets without speaking to them and rode straight towards the camp's centre where Aram was still in conference with Jiang, Cinna, Bajaan, Mani and Parmesh.

'Father!'

'Thank the gods,' Aram shouted back. 'You have been gone far longer than I expected.'

'The Faithful are coming, Father.'

Aram's face cracked and fell. The others scrabbled to their feet and hurried over. 'What?'

'Three miles to the west or a little more. They are camped by the end of that river on the beach, and they are heading this way. They will be here by mid-morning at the latest.'

'How many?' Jiang asked.

'I don't know whether we underestimated the numbers at first or more have joined them, but I counted something approaching a thousand on the beach.'

'Too many for us to fight off,' Cinna said angrily. 'We've one hundred and eighty-five fit and ready riders. Even with Aram's trained fist-fighters we won't number more than half their force, and they are better equipped. Fighting is not an option.'

Jiang concurred with a nod.

'But where can we run?' Parmesh argued. 'If you cannot defend us then we must run, but *where*? West is into their arms. North is back where we came from, which we know is no use. We must press on east, then.'

Jiang shook his head. 'Many of your people are on foot. The enemy are mounted. They will catch up with you in no time, especially on open ground like the beach. Besides, following the coast east will eventually just bring you back out past the markers and into the war zone, towards the border with the Jade Empire where everything is currently in turmoil.'

'Then what do you suggest?' spat Parmesh angrily. They all watched Jiang expectantly, though he said nothing. It took only moments for them to realise that the tall easterner was looking over their heads across the water. They turned as one.

'No,' Parmesh whispered.

'Then give me a feasible alternative to consider.'

'The island is the home of the dead. No living man can survive there.'

'So say your tales,' put in Cinna. 'The ones that claimed we would be dead or driven mad when we passed the markers and that no man can carry a weapon beyond them.'

Parmesh was shaking his head, and even Aram looked horrified.

'There has to be an alternative,' the old man breathed.

Cinna shrugged. 'I said I would lead for you in war. Well I tell you this straight: if we fight a thousand angry, well-rested and well-armed cavalry with less than five hundred men armed with sticks, we will all die. And so will hundreds or even thousands of your civilians before the enemy are overcome. Fighting is simply not an option. We cannot go east, west or north, for reasons we have already clearly stated. Someone – don't ask me who – has conveniently left us boats. If we do not use them, we will all die. You are the leader, Aram, and you purport to believe strongly in fate. Give me your appraisal of our options.'

Aram stood silent, his mouth open but unable to find adequate words. He peered at the faces around him and then at the looming dark shape of the island in the evening gloom, and finally at the boats.

'The people will not like it.'

'Then they are welcome to stay and discuss the matter with the Sizhad's men,' Cinna said harshly.

The two generals caught one another's eye. Cinna tilted his head towards the island and Jiang nodded. 'I will go across with the first boat,' the stocky man said. 'I will take half the good fighting men in as many boats as it takes. Then each boat will return, rowed by two men. I can make sure all is safe and then signal with a torch if we are secure, before the civilians begin to cross.'

'You will have to be sure the torch is hidden from the west,' Jiang noted.

'Of course.'

'And even if things are safe there and the population agree, the journey will be slow. It will take all night to cross that many times, possibly half the morning as well. It will be a tight race.'

'We'd best get started now, then. I will gather up the first trip. The rest of you need to inform the people of our plan. At least when it's done all the boats will be across the channel and the Sizhad's men will not be able to reach us.'

All eyes rose once more to the island across the sparkling water and Dev shivered.

That was it. Once they crossed that channel, the island was a dead end.

Literally.

CHAPTER 24

Jai had watched, tension twanging like torsion artillery, as the first boats crossed. It was almost dark by the time they were halfway across that wide stretch, their location visible only as black shapes that blotted out the silvery ripples of moonlight on the waves. Eight boats had gone – just enough to ferry a small force and create a bridgehead. The watchers on the beach had lost track of the boats somewhere in that last stretch and had waited nervously, barely daring to draw breath until a tiny pinprick of light sprang up close to the far shore, waving from side to side – the signal that nothing untoward had happened to Cinna and his men.

The crossings had begun in earnest then. The revelation that Cinna and his men had not been stripped to the bone by the vengeful dead as they disembarked had given everyone a little hope. Before even those first boats had returned to the beach, the rest were filled and launched out into the water on their own crossing.

Despite seeing the crowds on the beach and the length of the column as they had travelled south, Jai had not previously truly comprehended just how many Inda there were in this band of refugees until he watched them pass across the channel. Large groups were moved at a time, yet the multitude on the beach barely seemed to shrink.

He could not sleep, despite the lateness of the hour. The knowledge that the Faithful were less than four miles away and that their arrival would herald certain death for anyone left on the mainland kept him awake. Dev was the same – they all were – and so he spent most of his time either watching the endless chain of boats streaming back and forth or peering nervously west along the beach, half-expecting the enemy to heave into view at any moment. The night wore on. No one seemed to speak, beyond those words required for the task at hand. Gradually the moon slid away and the inky night began to acquire a cerulean tint in the east.

Jai had looked around then, as the change heralded the approaching morning, and begun to truly worry. Too many people remained on the beach. They had lost precious hours when they should have been ferrying people away while he and Dev had followed a river and found an enemy. Now they would pay for the delay. He could not say how many trips remained to be made, but it seemed clear that there would be people trapped there when the Faithful came.

His tension continued to mount until the sun put in its first appearance over the water. Dev had explained the timings of the Faithful's devotions, and the enemy should be engaged in their first litany at that moment. His father had carried out a headcount on the beach, concluding that there were still more than eight hundred people. That meant at least three more journeys once the boats returned. They were moving faster than Jai had thought, but it would still be a close-run thing.

The sun climbed and Jai worked through it all in his head – the Faithful finishing their devotions, swiftly dismantling their camp and mounting up and heading east – and from that moment on, he began to watch the western beach constantly, forgetting the boats.

He jumped as a hand squeezed his shoulder, and looked round to see his father and Dev.

'I want you both on the next boat,' the old man said.

'No.' As simple as that.

'Jai—'

'No.' He glanced across at Dev and could see the same defiance in his brother's eyes. 'No. There are few men here who can truly fight. The Faithful are coming and we can make a difference.'

'I cannot let you sacrifice yourself.'

Jai squared up to his father. 'Are these not the values you and Grandfather espoused back in Initpur in our youth? That a rajah is beholden to his people. He rules, but he is a *servant* of the realm, not a despot. It is the duty of those who can save lives to do so.'

He drew his sword and ran a thumb carefully along the edge, testing it.

Their father marshalled a dozen arguments over the next quarter of an hour, each of which was dismantled or swept aside by the brothers. It was understandable that their father wished them to be safe, yet when they turned the same arguments on him and suggested that he leave the beach, he had simply refused.

The sun continued to climb. The boats arrived and took another two hundred.

The western beach remained empty.

Jai's nerves were twanging constantly now. Had the Faithful gone inland? Had they decided on a day of rest? Had they turned around? Where *were* they?

The boats reached the isle across the water and began to disembark.

Jai suddenly felt a shiver run through him for no clear reason and turned, instinctively, to the west. A single horseman had rounded the treeline and stopped.

'Father, General – look.'

Aram and Jiang hurried over, Dev beside them.

'A scout. The others will be close behind. We are out of time.'

They turned to see the boats coming back slowly across the water. A mile was a long distance to row, and it took some time. General Jiang was the first to move.

'The Faithful are here,' he shouted in all three languages. 'All civilians down to the water line. Prepare to move with the next flotilla. All armed men to me.' He turned to Aram. 'Go.'

'No,' Aram said defiantly.

'I am not saying this out of deference or sentimentality, Aram,' Jiang hissed forcefully. 'When those boats are beached there will be panic, chaos and violence. There is not enough space for everyone, and all will want a place, even those who argued and told you they would not go. Only someone with authority and a calm head will prevent disaster. I will hold the beach as long as I can. Go.'

Aram dithered desperately, but the sound of an argument broke out at the water's edge behind him, and somehow the rajah in his soul took over. He nodded grimly and turned, hurrying along the beach. Almost two hundred men were converging on them from the west, and Jai felt fear grip him. Five-to-one odds were insane, but then the general knew they could not win. All they could do was hope to buy time with their deaths so that as many of the Inda as possible could escape.

'What can we do, General?' Jai asked.

'Our priority is to slow them down and stop them getting to the boats. Roughly a third of the men here are armed with some sort of polearm. We retreat towards the boats a little so that we have a shorter perimeter, then set up four feet apart so there is not enough room for a horse to ride between us. Every four feet a man with a spear will brace to defend against cavalry, each accompanied by two men with other weapons to defend him from attacks. Remember, we cannot fight to win – only to delay. Make no mistake. None of us are leaving this beach, but every heartbeat we endure saves lives. Stay up as long as you can and let none past.'

The grimness of that appraisal sank into every heart and Jai could see what it meant to the men of Inda blood. There would be no one to burn the bodies or say the rites. They were condemning themselves not only to death, but to an eternity of unrest, haunting this beach.

It came as no surprise then when a third of the men threw down their weapons and ran, making for the crowd awaiting the boats. Jiang said nothing, just watched them go. Those left were mainly of the Crimson Guard, with a few of Cinna's soldiers among them. They were stone-faced and steady.

The Faithful rounded the edge of the trees and started to pound towards them, perhaps half a mile away, whooping and ululating as they came. Jai once more felt his heart leap into his throat at the sight. Death was coming for them... death in a white turban with a gleaming sword point. Jai cast a prayer up to the gods, hoping that one day, when this was over, someone would find his body and free his spirit from it with the sacred fire.

Now he was moving into position. He was denied even the close presence of a friend at the end, for the general had placed Dev at the water's edge, Jai at the far end and himself in the centre, spaced out among the men to give them heart and encouragement. The blue and white and the red now worked together almost instinctively – a brotherhood born of necessity in the jungle. The enemy came like a wave of whitecaps rolling across the beach. There was no organisation to this attack; it was not intended as a cavalry charge to knock them aside or drive a wedge through the line. This was every white-clad bastard aiming on taking a head for his sun god, unfettered and insane.

Jai tensed as the riders bore down on them. A man never appreciates how swift a horse can be until he is braced with a spear

314

and waiting for one. The heartbeats ticked away, each one bringing that nearest horseman a little closer, making the shape of looming death a tiny bit larger.

The man holding the spear beside Jai braced tighter and tighter, wide, staring eyes on the bay gelding racing straight for him, the man on its back whirling a curved sword above his head and howling like an enraged beast. The rider would die. That, Jai vowed. They might all fall to the next horseman who came along, but that first rider at least would pay for everything.

Jai prepared. The other man by his side hefted a cleaver, grunting through his red demon face plate as the spear man began to pray to his western gods.

There was a sound like a mountain shattering under the hammer of the gods, and the world erupted into utter annihilation. One moment the white-clad horseman was racing towards them, whooping and snarling, whirling a sword in the thunder of hooves. The next moment he was gone in an eruption of gold and red. Jai felt himself thrown back bodily into the sand, the spear man landing on top of him before rolling off to one side. Jai's face felt as though it were on fire. His whole body in fact felt like it was burning, but as he struggled in the sand, the feeling in his face faded to be replaced by a stinging salty sea breeze.

He pulled himself up to his elbows, wondering oddly where his sword had gone. All he could hear was an oddly muffled roaring noise as though he were underwater, listening to the rough waves of the channel above. His skin felt raw.

Ahead, where moments before there had been an army of white horsemen bearing down on them, was now a conflagration of epic proportions. The beach was on fire from the water's edge almost to the treeline. Even the sand was ablaze, which suggested something like pitch at the heart of the fire. Black roiling smoke poured up into the air, stinking of tar and burned meat. As Jai's dancing eyes began to right themselves, he started to pick out shapes in the dreadful blaze. Men and horses alike existed only as living torches, burning on the black beach amid the huge explosion of billowing orange and black. The roar in his ears gradually resolved into the rumble of blazing fire and a mass chorus of agonised screams.

The Faithful were gone.

And there was another sound on the edge of hearing, almost suppressed beneath the roaring. A song. A dirge. The rites being sung for the burning bodies – *a parody of the Inda funeral?*

Slowly, baffled and stunned, Jai rose to his feet. Wild-eyed, he scanned the sand for his sword and quickly retrieved it. Then, grabbed by a thought, he spun. The returning boats had begun to reach the sand now, but the crowd at the landing had broken off their struggles and were all staring in shock along the beach.

'To the boats,' a voice bellowed over the din, and Jai recognised the tones of his general. In response, perhaps half the braced warriors turned and ran for the water, while the others, perhaps too stunned to react, perhaps too deafened to hear, simply stood and stared at the blazing army.

Jai only became aware of the general's proximity when Jiang spoke beside him.

'They *were* range markers. And well-placed too, for whoever did this, they utterly destroyed the Faithful.'

Jai nodded, still stunned, unable to adequately form words, trying to pick out the threads of the rites being sung somewhere above the blaze. The two men stood side by side for a while watching the forms of the burning Faithful writhing, then lying still and finally finding release from their agony.

'That,' Jai noted, 'is a terrible way to die.' *But at least they would not haunt the beach.*

'There is no *good* way to die in combat,' the general replied. 'A lifetime of war teaches that lesson harshly.'

'We are not alone,' Dev said, staggering through the sand towards them and rubbing an ear. They looked across at him and at the twenty or so Crimson Guard gathering on their position. Dev was pointing up the beach. They turned again towards the treeline to see a score of figures making their way from the jungle out onto the sand, their mouths moving, forming the sacred chants that would free the souls of the blazing Inda, regardless of the path they had chosen. They wore billowing trousers of yellow and jackets of red, with long decorative orange robes, their heads shaved and turban-free. Jai became aware of the general looking at him, a question in his glance.

'Monks,' explained Jai. 'Possibly even those very monks from our monastery.'

'Monks,' the general nodded, 'who can aim and discharge artillery too, I would wager.'

Jai blinked, but the statement made sense. Who else could have done it? No one on the beach, and the island was a mile away.

'Sir,' one of the Crimson Guard shouted, drawing their attention back. Figures were approaching from another direction, along the beach, a dozen paces out in the water, skirting the still-burning mass. Perhaps a dozen figures in white, though their pristine clothes were now smoke-blackened and ruined. Similarly, black faces and singed skin were evident. Some were limping. Jai suddenly realised that he probably looked similar. The blast had been enough to sear his face and throw him backwards, after all.

'Go,' Jiang said, waving at Jai and Dev.

'No.'

'Go to your father. We are no longer in danger. I will finish this.'

'No, you won't,' Dev replied, grabbing a discarded curved knife from the sand by his feet.

'Dev—'

'No. I *know* this man. *I* will finish it.'

Jai threw an odd, questioning glance at Dev.

'It's him,' Dev noted, pointing at the crowd. Jai squinted into the group of charred figures, unhorsed and staggering through the water with blades bared. One of them, and only one, bore a yellow turban rather than white.

'He came for us himself? Why?'

'He came for *me*,' replied Dev, as he turned and started stamping off through the soft sand towards that small group of survivors. Jai looked around at the general, who nodded, and a moment later the two of them, accompanied by the Crimson Guard, were hurrying after Dev.

The Faithful, such as they were, passed onto the sand and stopped there, waves crashing mere feet behind them. Their weapons were still brandished, but their approach bore more resemblance to a parley than a fight as Jai and the others closed with them.

'You should have let us flee,' Dev shouted at the Sizhad as he staggered towards them.

The yellow-turbaned figure, his face and arms flensed and charred by fire, his white robes soot-grey, stepped forward from the others.

'No,' the Sizhad said. 'It was important that you understood. There is still time for you. Still hope.'

'Hope is *gone*,' Dev shouted angrily. 'Men like Bassianus and the Jade Emperor have taken hope from the world and torn it apart. And you. You took what was left and burned that in the glare of your precious sun.'

Jai frowned at the exchange. Dev had *met* the Sizhad, he suddenly realised. His brother had been curiously evasive about the fanatic every time the subject was raised, releasing what detail was required but always holding something back. And though he had never once admitted to having been face to face with the man, clearly that was the case. There was such familiarity between the two – more like old friends than new enemies.

'But coming into these lands has proved me right, Dev.'

Dev? Jai frowned. *Too much* familiarity.

'How so?'

'Your ghosts and spirits and superstitions – the devils we all worshipped so long ago – they are false and powerless in the face of the true faith. I defied them. Many of my people would not come past the markers, their old fears still driving them. But a true believer can see the falseness of it all. Tricks and ghost stories. Such will fade in the new world. But that new world will need men of vision. Men like you. Come with us.'

Dev was shaking his head. 'Never. Your new world will put the Inda in chains again, but this time to a god, not a man. But you made a mistake coming here, Sizhad. You should have stayed at Jalnapur and left us to our peace. Because now you will never return from these lands. And those men you left behind? Their superstition and reluctance will only grow. Their beloved Sizhad went past the markers and never came back. Think on it. Even their beloved, invincible Sizhad fell to the spirits. They will never turn south again. By coming here you have guaranteed our safety for generations. And your cult has lost its great leader.'

The yellow-turbaned man stepped forward again, closer. 'There will be a new Sizhad. You don't understand, Dev. I was not the *first*, just the first to make the Faithful into an army. Others will come after me. We will grow ever stronger. Empires will quake and fall and the past will be forgotten. The demons we all worshipped as gods will fade. The sun will shine upon a new world.'

'Not here,' Dev said emphatically.

'You *have* to come. I travelled so far to bring you back. To teach you.'

'Your new world is not for us,' Dev shouted at him and stepped forward. The two men were mere paces apart now and Jai, the general and their men moved up a little closer just as the soot-blackened Faithful did the same.

'Will you kill me, Dev?'

Jai frowned, nodding urgently, willing his brother to do just that.

'I have to. No one else can, and I cannot let you go.'

'Then you will have to do it in cold blood, Dev.'

The Sizhad cast his sword out into the water and stood before Dev, and Jai found himself stepping forward urgently. The white-clad zealot sank to his knees before Dev, hands opened like a flower to welcome the sunshine into his palms.

'Do it,' bellowed Jai.

'Do it and you forever open your heart to the demons driving you,' the Sizhad said calmly.

Dev bent, placing a hand on the Sizhad's shoulder and leaning in to whisper. He said something inaudible into the Sizhad's left ear and then straightened again. Jai felt a moment of panic lurch through him at the contact, but then stared in shock. As Dev stepped back, the Sizhad remained kneeling on the sand, the hilt of Dev's knife jutting from his throat. He coughed, once, and a gobbet of blood burst forth. Then, slowly, exhaling pink bubbles, he toppled backwards into the sand.

The Faithful stared in shock for a long moment and then suddenly burst into life with a furious roar, running at Dev. But Jai and the others had been edging closer and closer throughout, and as the white-garbed lunatics ran at Dev, the Crimson Guard intercepted and began to butcher them as neatly and swiftly as possible. Several of the red-masked men fell into the sand, but it was a quick job. Jai and the general stood next to Dev as he looked down at the dead zealot in the sand, blood pooling out around the neck and head.

'Burn him,' Dev said quietly.

'What?'

'Burn them all. And have those monks say the rites.'

Jai shook his head. 'He is a heretic who denies the gods. He does not deserve...'

His voice trailed off as Dev turned, tears carving a clean track through the muck on his face. 'He was misguided and driven by grief. It could have happened to any one of us. And he is dead. He will never harm another. I will not deny him another attempt at life, and I will pray that his next one is happier.'

Jai nodded, his defiance shattered by the odd sense of loss in his brother's face.

He looked down at the Sizhad. The man was younger than Jai had expected. And even charred and in death there was something forlorn about his face. In the presence of that expression, somehow even Jai could not hate him.

'The guard will do it,' Jiang said. 'Come. To the boats. There are many things to learn, I suspect.'

EPILOGUE

*D*eep *in the Isle of the Dead, in a temple abandoned for many centuries, they learned their answers. The paintings on the wall of the circular vault were crude and faded, but still clear enough to follow without even the need for the ancient words scrawled beneath and which the monks faithfully repeated for them. Moreover, some of the paintings were clearly newer than others, the story having been continued long after the temple fell into disuse.*

Here, on this isle, once known as Elam, the first Inda had lived. Here they had walked with the gods and prospered. To the north, the lands now known as the Inda Diamond had been a world of primitive tribes and barbarians. The Inda, encouraged by their gods, had set forth across the water and begun to change the world, bringing art and religion, engineering and writing to the mainland. But in the eastern realms they had encountered a jealous enemy. For the first time, the Inda had learned of true war. And they were not strong enough for it. Gradually their power was pushed further back until they were once more trapped on Elam. And then the enemy came on ships.

The ancient Inda were destroyed utterly.

Here the painting began to change as new hands took up the brush on the Isle of the Dead following the harrowing of the ship-borne invaders.

The enemy left, and the island became a world of the dead. Indeed the southern lands, where the true Inda had been strongest, were systematically annihilated and depopulated as the enemy withdrew, and only those more northern lands where the people were still tribal and had their little kings were they left in peace. Even they should have fallen, but the easterners suddenly returned home, facing a new threat there. And so the modern Inda were born, an offshoot of their tribe, with a different tongue and a meld of cultural influences.

The gods did not desert the people. Those same gods who guided the true Inda began to nurture their children. The gods sent teachers to instruct them, in the form of gurus, and all the while they began to prepare the Inda for another cataclysm. Because like this circular vault, the Inda who had lived here knew that all things are circles. The world itself. The heavens. The life cycle of a man. Even time itself. And as those early empires had destroyed the Inda and then themselves fallen to outside aggressors, so too would time come full circle, such that the Inda faced the same fate once more.

Here, now, the paintings stopped. But they had come full circle, for the Inda had risen again. The rest of the great tale had been simple to fill in, especially with the aid of the monks. The last great guru had imparted to the monks their purpose: to create a haven so that the Inda could see out another end and pass on to the next circle. They had spent centuries fostering the myth of the haunted dead lands, living in them as monks to further the legends. They had learned to fight with fist and foot and to move silently through the jungle like panthers, bringing death and madness to those who sought to break the sanctity of the place, for the dead lands needed to remain sacrosanct and feared against the day sanctuary was sought there.

Then, when the empires had begun to move a year or so ago, the monks had put their longstanding divine plan into action. They had prepared the place of haven in their monastery as preordained, dealing with a few last incursions before moving south, paving the way for the refugees, preparing the island for its new inhabitants, setting what traps and tricks they needed to prevent the brutal empires of the world reaching the isle and opening up this secret place to the world.

And so secret it remained. The monks returned to their monasteries to perpetuate the myth, while the Isle of the Dead finally came back to life, another circle beginning.

Aram leaned on his stick as he hauled himself up the last few steps to the balcony where his sons sat with glasses of cold water, hiding in the shade of the awning from the glare of the midsummer sun. It was becoming more of a struggle to climb to the high places every day now, but Aram was far from ready to complain about his lot. He had it good. Better than most of the world.

322

The once-great imperial fortress of Vengen, home to the marshal of the northern armies for centuries, was ravaged by fire and destruction as northern warriors, fresh from their mountain fastnesses, tore through the buildings, looting and ravaging for lack of defenders, blissfully unaware that the white-clad forces of the new Sizhad approached along the next valley, bringing glorious golden fire to this far-flung world.

Ten years had passed since the refugees' boats had landed on this shore and the monks had revealed the truth to the wide-eyed Inda. Ten years of growth and toil, but ten years of freedom and safety. Ten years that showed in every square foot of the island that the inhabitants once more knew as Elam.

Pausing at the top step under the beatific smiles of Dev and Jai, he took a deep breath and scanned the land below. The town lay lively and thriving. An Isle of the Dead no more, the ancient settlement had been reborn, the stone bones of the buildings proving still solid after all these centuries – solid enough to take new roofs and doors and floors, albeit in some cases requiring considerable repair or strengthening. What had been a monument to a lost people was now a bustling town, with smoke from cook fires rising into the hazy summer air, the noises of children and animals, smiths and carpenters ringing out across the valley and down to the port.

A ringing echoed out across Velutio also, calling the people to prayer, for it was midday and the sun was at his apex. Across the city, the Faithful flooded the streets. The former priest of Balor, god of smiths and workers, cowered in his cellar, listening to his world being swept away by the Sizhad's new order. It was disheartening how quickly the people had adapted. And those who hadn't... The old man shuddered, remembering the sight of the city's high priest hanging on his cross, eyes burned out, body red-raw from the scourging and the sun. Still, even he had fared better than the mad

323

emperor Bassianus, curse his soul for eternity. Flaying had been too good for the man who had ended the empire.

The Inda town was alive. The fields had been sown for years now and were yielding excellent crops. Animals had been re-domesticated after so long being feral. Orchards were recovered from the wilderness and gardens planted. The Inda had become 'the people' once more. They were a civilisation, and they were content.

But it was not all peace and comfort they created. The symphony of construction was not restricted to civic structures. Far from it. Masons worked constantly at the walls. Carpenters raised scaffolding. Smiths worked at the forges. Because never again would the Inda be a scattered people, easy prey to any booted foot that took a liking to their land. Because now everyone knew what waited in the outside world and because Aram had instilled in them all one fact he had come to believe above all. You cannot hide from the world. Eventually the world will find you.

In Germalla, the new capital of the Empire of the Golden Sun, the new Sizhad observed his council with a curled lip. Squabbling. Which land of demons was more deserving of 'conversion' now? The Pelasians and their old monsters, the northern Gota with their fur-clad shamans? The strange island they called Alba, which claimed independence and yet worshipped those same gods the Faithful had so soundly stamped out this past decade. Perhaps the Jade Empire, which was said to be in decline now? The Sizhad had the answer, though: all of them. The cleansing fire would be like a tide flowing across the world.

The town of Elam was now enclosed in strong walls, and every month saw them becoming stronger. Extra ramparts ran down from there to the port, which was already partially defended. Fishing boats had been built those first two years by carpenters who had only ever constructed boats for the rivers of the northern lands, but who were learning with every season. And once they had come to understand

and conquer some of the difficulties with ocean-going vessels, they had begun to build other ships. Stronger ships. Ships that could carry weapons and soldiers. Because the world outside was not limited to land, and one day, perhaps, a ship would wander to their shores by chance.

And the Inda would be ready. They had brought with them to the island every skill a nation needed to expand and thrive, but more: they had brought knowledge. Dev and Cinna had spent their first year with charts and maps, plans and lists, plotting the walls and the defences of the island. As Jai and Mani had explored the length and breadth of the great island, the western general and his adjutant had planned how to defend it when the time came. Every high point and peninsula had its watchtowers, beacons and fortresses. Every cove had its sea wall and scout vessel.

Carpenters who had spent their entire lives making nothing more threatening than a chair were now producing the bolt throwers and catapults that sat silent and vigilant on artillery platforms along the walls. Better yet, Jiang had brought with him the secret of cannon. It had taken two years to locate the minerals they needed for the black powder and begin mining them, and a further year to form the great iron barrels themselves, but one thing had impressed the ageing eastern general. The Inda, a people who never did things by halves, had taken the Jade Empire's designs and somehow smoothed out the problems. Not one of the cannon produced by their smiths had misfired. Now the black, deadly muzzles of those cannon poked out menacingly from walls around the island.

And while the artisans built a civilisation, the farmers, hunters and fishermen built a life; the craftsmen built a defence for them all; and the military among them had built an army. Dev had taught all who would serve how to defend the walls and use the artillery. Jai had trained men to fight with sword and spear. Bajaan had instructed men with bows. Mani had forged them into units. And Cinna and Jiang had assigned them all and planned the grand defence of Elam.

Because one day the world would find them and the cycle would begin again.

The monks, who had returned to their monasteries by the markers, continuing to spread the myth of the dead lands, brought news every month, and it was always bleak. The Faithful, who now had an unshakable hold on what had once been the free lands of the Inda, despised the monks, who they saw as demon-worshippers, but there were still those who remembered the old gods and risked the wrath of their overlords to travel and speak with the monks.

How the world had changed in that first year. The western empire had all but collapsed; with the swift overwhelming of its army in the Inda lands it had been defenceless against numerous enemies. The new Sizhad, who had proved to be far more the warmonger than poor Ravi, had turned west with a vengeance and carved out the new world of which his predecessor had dreamed, imposing control as far as Velutio and the Nymphaean Sea. Bassianus, the mad emperor, had died a dreadful death as the white-clad fanatics rampaged through his city, and now a former governor had claimed the imperial title, though he ruled in absentia on the island of Alba. The Gota and their barbarian neighbours had reclaimed the north and the mountains, and Pelasia had taken the opportunity to annexe several hundred miles of terrain that had long been the subject of dispute, but already they were being pressured by the Faithful.

In the east, the civil war had lasted a full year, with several claimants dead before a young man rose from the ashes and imposed control once more. The chaos of the war, though, had ruined the Jade Empire. The clans of the north had raided and conquered, while the southern lands had seceded with no military there to stop them. The Jade Empire still stood independent, able to defy the growing cult of the Faithful sun worshippers, though how long that situation would last was anyone's guess.

The new Jade Emperor, green eyes fearful, probing the adult teeth that were just coming in as the regents, who ruled both him and the Jade Empire with an iron hand, shifted unit markers on the map of their shrunken, diminished empire in an attempt to halt the advance of the nomads from the north who had breached the wall in many places and the new steel-clad, masked demons from the islands of the east. Many said the Jade Empire would not last another generation. Only the current emperor knew how the vicious regents who treated him like a puppet had fed him a two-month strict diet of juza-xi fish and sharp onions to cause the green of his irises to come about, for the jade eyes had stopped appearing naturally.

On occasion, Jiang and Cinna, finally withdrawing from active life and sitting back to enjoy their golden years, would wax lyrical about what had been lost in their great empires, though neither shed too many tears for a world ruled by a madman or a green-eyed martinet. Life here was too good.

Elam. A world risen from the dead, forged in fire and drawn from the very best the west, the Inda and the Jade Empire had to offer.

'Afternoon, Father,' Dev nodded at Aram as he wandered over and dropped into a seat.

Jai poured a cup of chilled water and passed it over. Aram took it gratefully and sipped the liquid, smacking his lips. 'How goes the temple?' the older brother asked.

Aram smiled. The great temple that told the history of the Inda had been repaired and restored. Images of the gods had been touched up, and those of both eastern and western deities added, forming a great pantheon for all. The last scenes of the cycle had been added, telling the tale of the survivors of the great war and how they had come to Elam to rebuild their civilisation. And, because Aram was ever a man prepared, a new storey had been added with a plastered wall, awaiting the next cycle of the Inda.

The irony of the fact that the temple was domed, with an oculus at the centre that allowed the sun to shine down benignly on all the gods, was not lost on anyone. But for now irony was all it was. The sun worshippers would come one day, when Aram and even his sons and grandsons were long gone, but that fact no longer worried them. Somehow the knowledge that time came in cycles and that the Inda would live on had become the heart of everything they did here.

The west had fallen, as it had fallen before. It would rise again as it had risen before. The east had withdrawn into itself, but it would expand again. The Sizhad and his new world would one day be the old world.

But the Inda would go on.

Aram sipped his water happily and smiled at his sons.

AUTHOR'S NOTE

Though there is something cyclical in the very nature of this series and the saga I have told within it, this volume in particular is intended to be something of an end point. That being said, six years ago, *Dark Empress* was intended to be the last volume in the Tales of the Empire, and the involvement of Canelo in the series revitalised the whole thing and led to a further three novels.

I have, for now at least, explored every angle of this fantasy world that has leapt to mind, and there are no more stories based in this land rattling around in my head and waiting to be told. Perhaps in a few years there will be, and the series will return.

There is, after all, the *possibility* of future volumes. Though the rise of the sun worshippers and the fading of the old empires seems fairly final, the survival of an enclave of the old civilisation on the southern isle and the very idea that we have reached a period of interregnum like the one where the series began allows fertile ground for future growth when the stories are there.

Because, as I said, there is something cyclical here in the series as well as in the world of the Inda within. At the beginning, with book one, the empire had changed utterly following the demise of a mad emperor, and the lord Avitus had risen to power with his vicious megalomania. Something very similar has now happened. One could almost go from this book back into *Interregnum*. And perhaps there is room to expand one day on the next stage of civilisation, which would be the empire under its new faith, something like moving from writing about pagan Rome to early medieval Christian Byzantium.

But for now the series is finished, though I am far from done with *other* tales.

I am hoping not to have offended any group with this story. It is in the very nature of writing historical fiction to risk giving offence to someone, and this plot I know has run rather close to the edge in some respects. I have created a very stylised view of medieval China in my Jade Empire, and my western empire is based upon ancient

Rome, so will offend only those long in their grave. The Inda are clearly based loosely upon later medieval India, though drawing on elements from the entire spectrum of the history of that subcontinent. I hope that I have done them justice in style, and with hints of a very ancient and civilised culture. And then there are the Faithful. The followers of the sun. I suspect there will be a number of people who automatically assume this to be an analogy of the rise of Islam, perhaps identifying the Sizhad with Mohammed. I acknowledge that there are elements of that here. But there are also elements of the rise of Christianity, of the blossoming of the worship of Elagabalus, Sol Invictus, Mithras and Helios in the ancient world, and even of the rise of a number of pre-Abrahamic Persian cultures. The Faithful are something of a composite and, though in this tale they are the villains of the piece, I hope that in the brief flashes I have portrayed him, the whole reason for the Sizhad's zealotry is rather sad and sympathetic.

There is, of course, no correlation between the events of this book and any historic campaign. Where with *Insurgency* I extrapolated on the potential of the Huns or Mongols against the west, and in *Invasion* I built upon the Roman invasion of Britain, this one is a story born of pure imagination. If it has any root it is in the question that often floats into my head of 'what would have happened if Rome had come into conflict with China?', they being two of the world's greatest ancient powers.

The geography of this book is fairly clearly based upon the Indian subcontinent, with the Isle of the Dead being Sri Lanka (former Ceylon) at the southern tip. There is something indefinably different about that island compared to the rest of India, and that is part of what led me to placing my necessary place of refuge there. The idea of a people who disappeared is not new. Even ignoring the probably fictional Atlantis, the colony of Roanoke, the Kingdom of Aksum and perhaps the Pueblo peoples like the Anasazi were all thriving centres that disappeared under either mysterious, or more likely violent, circumstances.

My land of ghosts is also something of a nod to the haunted land of Maragor in the late, great David Eddings's *Belgariad*.

I hope you've enjoyed the book. I shall be moving onto fresh and exciting ground next, with a whole new historical series in a whole new era.

For now, though, adios. Until the next cycle…

Simon Turney, July 2017

If you enjoyed Jade Empire why not also try:

The Thief's Tale

(First book of the Ottoman Cycle)

by S.J.A. Turney

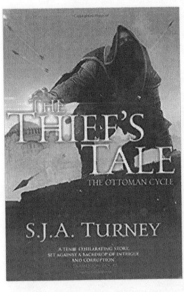

Istanbul, 1481. The once great city of Constantine that now forms the heart of the Ottoman empire is a strange mix of Christian, Turk and Jew. Despite the benevolent reign of the Sultan Bayezid II, the conquest is still a recent memory, and emotions run high among the inhabitants, with danger never far beneath the surface.

Skiouros and Lykaion, the sons of a Greek country farmer, are conscripted into the ranks of the famous Janissary guards and taken to Istanbul where they will play a pivotal, if unsung, role in the history of the new regime. As Skiouros escapes into the Greek quarter and vanishes among its streets to survive on his wits alone, Lykaion remains with the slave chain to fulfill his destiny and become an Islamic convert and a guard of the Imperial palace. Brothers they remain, though standing to either side of an unimaginable divide.

On a fateful day in late autumn 1490, Skiouros picks the wrong pocket and begins to unravel a plot that reaches to the very highest peaks of Imperial power. He and his brother are about to be left with the most difficult decision faced by a conquered Greek: whether the rule of the Ottoman Sultan is worth saving.

Marius' Mules: The Invasion of Gaul

(First book of the Marius' Mules Series)

by S.J.A. Turney

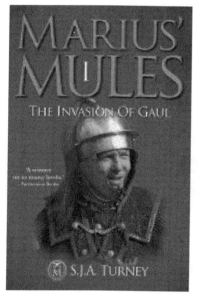

It is 58 BC and the mighty Tenth Legion, camped in Northern Italy, prepare for the arrival of the most notorious general in Roman history: Julius Caesar.

Marcus Falerius Fronto, commander of the Tenth is a career soldier and long-time companion of Caesar's. Despite his desire for the simplicity of the military life, he cannot help but be drawn into intrigue and politics as Caesar engineers a motive to invade the lands of Gaul.

Fronto is about to discover that politics can be as dangerous as battle, that old enemies can be trusted more than new friends, and that standing close to such a shining figure as Caesar, even the most ethical of men risk being burned.

Praetorian: The Great Game

(First book of the Praetorian Series)

by S.J.A. Turney

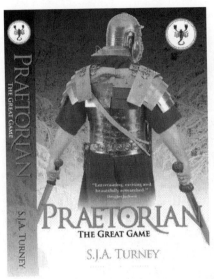

Promoted to the elite Praetorian Guard in the thick of battle, a young legionary is thrust into a seedy world of imperial politics and corruption. Tasked with uncovering a plot against the newly-crowned emperor Commodus, his mission takes him from the cold Danubian border all the way to the heart of Rome, the villa of the emperor's scheming sister, and the great Colosseum.

What seems a straightforward, if terrifying, assignment soon descends into Machiavellian treachery and peril as everything in which young Rufinus trusts and believes is called into question and he faces warring commanders, Sarmatian cannibals, vicious dogs, mercenary killers and even a clandestine Imperial agent. In a race against time to save the Emperor, Rufinus will be introduced, willing or not, to the great game.

"Entertaining, exciting and beautifully researched" - Douglas Jackson

"From the Legion to the Guard, from battles to the deep intrigue of court, Praetorian: The Great Game is packed with great characters, wonderfully researched locations and a powerful plot." - Robin Carter

Made in the USA
Middletown, DE
03 December 2022

16940031R00205